Heaven, Texas

Susan Elizabeth Phillips

Heaven, Texas

WHEELER
PUBLISHING, INC.
ROCKLAND, MA

★ AN AMERICAN COMPANY ★

Published in Large Print by arrangement with Avon Books, Inc., a division of the Hearst Corp., Inc.
in the United States and Canada.

Wheeler Large Print Book Series.

Set in 16 pt Plantin.

Library of Congress Cataloging-in-Publication Data

Phillips, Susan Elizabeth.
    Heaven, Texas / Susan Elizabeth Phillips.
        p. (large print) cm.(Wheeler large print book series)
    ISBN 1-56895-699-1 (hardcover)
    1. Large type books. I. Title. II. Series
[PS3566.H522H43 1998]
813'.54—dc21 ✓ ∫ ∫   98-47825
                                                            CIP

To all my old friends in La Leche League.
Thanks for being the first ones to tell me
that you liked what I wrote.

Acknowledgments

I would like to express my appreciation to the following people who shared their expertise with me as I wrote Heaven, Texas: Mary Lynn Baxter (and Len, too, for letting me steal a few of his lines), Katherine Johnson, Pamela Litton, John Roscich, Glenda Sanders, and Ron Struxness. I am also grateful to the National Collegiate Athletic Association for answering my questions. Thanks to my guys, Bill, Ty, and Zach; you always help me out when I need it. Special appreciation to both my editor Carrie Feron and agent Steven Axelrod. My biggest thanks go to my readers who share my books with their friends and write me such wonderful letters. To all of you. God bless.

1

"A *bodyguard!* I don't need any damn bodyguard!"

The silver toes of Bobby Tom Denton's purple lizardskin cowboy boots flashed in the sunlight as the ex-football player stalked across the carpet and planted the heels of his hands on his attorney's desk.

Jack Aikens regarded him cautiously. "Windmill Studios thinks you do."

"I don't happen to care what they think. Everybody knows there isn't a single person living in all of Southern California who's got a lick of sense." Bobby Tom straightened. "Well, maybe some of the ranchers do, but not other than that." He folded his lanky frame into a leather chair, propped his boots on the desktop, and crossed his ankles.

Jack Aikens observed the man who was his most important client. Today Bobby Tom was dressed almost conservatively in white linen trousers, a lavender silk shirt, his purple lizardskin boots, and a light gray Stetson. The former wide receiver didn't go anywhere without a Stetson. Some of his girlfriends swore he even made love wearing it, although Jack didn't quite believe that. Still, Bobby Tom was proud of being a Texan, although his

1

professional football career had forced him to spend most of the last decade living in Chicago.

With his magazine cover good looks, woman-eating grin, and imposing pair of diamond-studded Super Bowl rings, Bobby Tom Denton was pro football's most visible glamour boy. From the beginning of his career, television audiences had loved his country boy manner, but those who'd played against him weren't fooled by good ol' boy charm. They knew that Bobby Tom was smart, driven, and as tough as they came. He'd not only been the most colorful wide receiver in the NFL, he'd also been the best, and when a disabling knee injury five months earlier in last January's Super Bowl had forced him to retire at the age of thirty-three, it was only natural for Hollywood to be interested in making him the newest hero of their action adventure movies.

"Bobby Tom, the people at Windmill have a right to be worried. They're paying you several million dollars to make your first movie with them."

"I'm a football player, not a damn movie star!"

"As of last January, you became a retired foot-ball player," Jack pointed out. "And it was your decision to sign a movie contract."

Bobby Tom whipped off his Stetson, plowed one hand through his thick blond hair, and shoved the hat back on. "I was drunk and looking for new direction in my life. You know better than to let me make important decisions when I'm drunk."

"We've been friends for a long time, and I have yet to see you drunk, so that's not going to work as an excuse. You also happen to be one of the smartest businessmen I know, and you sure as hell don't need the money. If you didn't want to sign that contract with Windmill, you wouldn't have done it."

"Yeah, well, I've changed my mind."

"You've been involved in more business deals than I can count, and I've never known you to break a contract. Are you sure you want to start now?"

"I didn't say I was going to break the damn contract."

Jack rearranged two file folders and a roll of Tums. They'd been friends for a decade, but he suspected he didn't really know Bobby Tom much better than the barber who cut his hair. Despite his affability, the former football player was a deeply private person. Not that Jack blamed him. Everybody in the world wanted a piece of Bobby Tom, and the athlete had learned to protect himself. In Jack's opinion, he didn't always do a good job of it. Every ex-jock, shapely female, or hometown buddy with a hard luck story had come to regard Bobby Tom as an easy mark.

Jack peeled the silver foil coin off the end of the Tums roll. "Just out of curiosity, you know anything about acting?"

"Hell, no."

"That's what I figured."

"I don't see what difference it makes. Movies like this, all anybody has to do is kick ass and undress women. Hell, I've been doing that since I was eight years old."

That sort of comment was vintage Bobby Tom Denton, and Jack smiled. Regardless of what his client said, he had to believe Bobby Tom planned to make a success out of his movie career. He'd never known the ex-football player to take on anything he didn't plan to do well, from acquiring land to buying into new businesses. On the other hand, he certainly was taking his time about it.

Jack settled back in his chair. "I talked with Willow Craig from Windmill a couple of hours ago. She's a mighty unhappy lady, especially since you're the one who insisted that all the location shooting be done in Telarosa."

"They needed a small town in Texas. You know how bad the economy's been down there, and this'll help out."

"I thought you were doing your best to stay away from your hometown for a while, especially with all this craziness over that big festival they're planning to rejuvenate the town."

Bobby Tom winced. "Don't remind me."

"The fact is, you have to get down there. Windmill has already moved in their equipment and personnel, but they don't have you there so they can start shooting."

"I told them I'd show up."

"Just like you told them you'd show up for all those meetings and wardrobe fittings they had scheduled for you in L.A. two weeks ago."

"That was chicken shit stuff. Hell, I've already got the best wardrobe of any player in the NFL. What do I need fittings for?"

Jack gave up. As usual, Bobby Tom was going to do things his own way. For all his surface amiability, the Texan was stubborn as a mule, and he didn't like being pushed.

Bobby Tom lowered his boots from the desk and slowly rose. Although he hid it well, Jack knew that he'd been devastated by his forced retirement. Ever since the doctors had told him he'd never play again, Bobby Tom had been wheeling and dealing with the ferocity of a man poised on the brink of financial ruin instead of a sports legend whose multimillion-dollar salary with the Chicago Stars provided only a fraction of his net worth. Jack wondered if this movie deal wasn't just Bobby Tom's way of passing time while he tried to figure out what to do with the rest of his life.

Bobby Tom paused at the door and gave his agent that level, blue-eyed gaze defensive players all over the league had learned to dread. "How 'bout you get hold of those people at Windmill right now and tell them to call off their bodyguard."

Although the request was mildly uttered, Jack wasn't fooled. Bobby Tom always knew exactly what he wanted, and he generally got it. "I'm afraid somebody's already on the way. And they're sending an escort, not a bodyguard."

"I told them I'd get myself to Telarosa, and I will. If any damn bodyguard shows up and thinks he's gonna order me around, he'd better be one tough hombre because, otherwise, he's gonna end up with my initials carved in his backside."

Jack glanced down at the yellow legal pad in front of him and decided this wasn't the best time to tell Bobby Tom that the "tough hombre" Windmill Studios was sending went by the name of Gracie Snow. As he slipped the pad under a file folder, he hoped to hell Miss Snow had a gorgeous ass, a mankiller set of tits, and the instincts of a piranha. Otherwise, she wasn't going to stand a chance against Bobby Tom Denton.

Gracie Snow was having a bad hair month. As the humid night breeze of early July sent a kinky coppery brown lock flying in front of her eyes, she decided she should have known better than to trust a hairdresser named Mister Ed. She didn't believe it was productive to dwell on the negative, however, so instead of dwelling on her bad permanent, she locked the door on her rental car and made her way up the sidewalk to the house of Bobby Tom Denton.

Half a dozen cars were parked in the curving drive, and as she approached the sleek cedar and glass structure that overlooked Lake Michigan, she heard music blaring. It was nearly nine-thirty, and she wished she could postpone this encounter until morning, when she'd be better rested and less nervous, but she simply didn't have the luxury of time. She needed to prove to Willow Craig that she could efficiently discharge her first real responsibility.

6

It was an unusual house, low and sprawling, with a sharply angular roof. The lacquered front doors held elongated aluminum handles that looked like thigh bones. She couldn't say the structure was to her personal taste, but that made it all the more interesting. Trying to ignore the butterflies in her stomach, she determinedly pressed the bell and tugged on the jacket of her best navy suit, a shapeless affair with a hemline that was neither long nor short, simply unfashionable. She wished the skirt hadn't gotten so wrinkled on her flight from Los Angeles into Chicago's O'Hare Airport, but she'd never been good with clothes. She sometimes thought her sense of fashion had become warped from having grown up around so many elderly people because she always seemed to be at least two decades out of date.

As she pressed the bell again, she thought she detected the reverberation of a gong from within, but the music was so loud, it was difficult to tell. A small flicker of anticipation tingled at her nerve endings. The party sounded wild.

Although Gracie was thirty years old, she had never attended a wild party. She wondered if there would be pornographic movies and bowls of cocaine set out for the guests. She was almost certain she disapproved of both, but since she had no actual experience with either one, she thought it only fair to reserve judgment. After all, what was the point of making a new life for herself if she didn't stay open to new experiences? Not that she would ever experiment with drugs, but, as for pornographic movies...Perhaps just a short peek.

She pressed the bell twice in a row and pushed another wayward lock of hair back into her lumpy french twist. She had hoped her new perm would eliminate the need for the unfashionable, but convenient, hairstyle she'd worn for the past decade. She'd envisioned something soft and wavy that would make her feel like a new woman, and the tight permanent Mister Ed had given her wasn't at all what she'd had in mind.

Why hadn't she remembered from her teenage years that her efforts at self-improvement always resulted in catastrophe? There had been months of green hair from a miscalculation with a bottle of peroxide and raw, inflamed skin from an allergic reaction to a freckle cream. She could still hear the howls of laughter from her high school classmates when the wadded tissues in her bra had shifted while she was giving an oral book report. That incident had been the final blow, and right then she had promised to accept the words her plainspoken mother had been dispensing since Gracie was six years old.

You come from a long line of homely women, Gracie Snow. Accept the fact that you'll never be pretty and you'll be a lot happier.

She was of medium height, neither short enough to be cute, nor tall enough to be willowy. Although she wasn't exactly flat chested, she was the next closest thing. Her eyes were neither a warm brown nor a sparkling blue, but a nondescript gray. Her mouth was too wide, her chin too stubborn. She no longer bothered to feel grateful for the clear skin that lurked between the freckles scattered across the bridge of her nose, or the fact that the nose itself was small and straight. Instead, she concentrated on being grateful for the more important gifts God had given her: intelligence, a quirky sense of humor, and an insatiable interest in all aspects of the human condition. She told herself that strength of character was more important than beauty anyway, and only when she was at her most dispirited did she wish she could trade in a speck of integrity, a dab of virtue, a morsel of organizational ability for a larger bra size.

The door finally opened, cutting into her thoughts, and she found herself facing one of the ugliest men she had ever seen—a hulking bruiser with a thick neck, bald head, and bulging shoulders. She regarded him with interest as his eyes swept down over her navy suit, neat white polyester blouse, and no-nonsense black pumps.

"Yeah?"

She straightened her shoulders and lifted her chin a notch. "I'm here to see Mr. Denton."

"It's about time." Without warning, he grabbed her arm and pulled her inside. "Did you bring your own music?"

She was so startled by his question, she received only the vaguest impression of the foyer: limestone floors, a massive aluminum wall sculpture, and a granite boulder holding a samurai helmet. "Music?"

"Jeez, I told Stella to make sure you brought your own. Never mind. I've got the tape the last girl left here."

"The tape?"

"Bobby Tom's in the hot tub. The boys and me want to surprise him, so wait here while I get everything ready. Then we'll go in together."

With that, he disappeared through a sliding shoji screen off to her right. She stared after him, her emotions catapulting between alarm and curiosity. He had obviously mistaken her for someone else, but since Bobby Tom Denton wouldn't accept any phone calls from Windmill Studios, she wondered if she shouldn't take advantage of the misunderstanding.

The old Gracie Snow would have patiently waited for him to return so she could have explained her mission, but the new Gracie Snow craved adventure, and she found herself following the sound of raucous music along a curving hallway.

The rooms she passed were like none she had ever seen. She had always been a secret sensualist, and sight alone didn't satisfy her. Her hands itched to stroke the rough pieces of sculpture sitting on oxidized iron pedestals and the granite blocks that held irregularly shaped tabletops that looked like cross sections cut from prehistoric trees. She wanted to trail the pads of her fingers over the walls, some of which were lacquered a pale gray, while others were covered with long swatches of distressed leather bleached to the color of human ashes. The deep-seated, low-slung furniture upholstered in canvas and zebra-print beckoned to her, and the scent of eucalyptus trailing from ancient urns tantalized her nostrils.

Mingling with the eucalyptus, she caught the scent of chlorine. As she rounded a massive set of boulders tumbling artistically from the wall, her eyes widened. The hallway opened out into a luxurious grotto, whose walls were constructed of sweeping sheets of sandblasted glass rising to the roof. Mature palms, stands of bamboo, and other exotic foliage grew from free-form beds cut into the black marble floor, making the grotto look both tropical and prehistoric. The black tiled, asymmetrical-shaped swimming pool gave the appearance of a hidden pond where dinosaurs might have gone for a midday sip. Even the starkly designed chaises and chunky tables made of flattop boulders blended with the natural ambience.

The surroundings might be prehistoric, but the guests were thoroughly modern. There were perhaps thirty people in the mixed group. All of the women were young and beautiful, while the men, both black and white, had bulging muscles and thick necks. She knew nothing about football players except for their unsavory reputations, and as she observed the scanty bikinis worn by most of the women, she couldn't suppress a small spark of hope

11

that some sort of orgy might be about to take place. Not that she would ever participate in such a thing—even supposing anyone should ask her to—but it would be interesting to observe.

Shrill female squeals drew her attention to the foaming hot tub that sat inside a cluster of boulders on a raised platform near the windows. Four women frolicked in the bubbles, and Gracie experienced both envy and admiration as she observed their glistening, suntanned breasts bouncing in brief bikini tops. And then her gaze moved beyond the women to the lone man occupying the platform, and everything inside her went still.

She recognized him at once from his photographs. He stood next to the hot tub like a sultan surveying his harem, and as she watched him, all her deepest and most secret sexual fantasies came to life. This was Bobby Tom Denton. *Dear Lord.*

He was the embodiment of every man she'd ever dreamed about; all the high school boys who'd ignored her, all the young men who never remembered her name, all the handsome professional men who complimented her on her clear thinking, but never thought to ask her out for a date. He was a glittering superhuman creature who must have been put on earth by a perverse God to remind homely women like herself that some things were unobtainable.

She knew from the photographs she had seen that his Stetson concealed a head of thick blond hair, while the brim shadowed a pair of midnight blue eyes. Unlike her own, his cheekbones could have been chiseled by a Renaissance sculptor. He had a strong, straight nose, a determined jaw, and a mouth that should have come with a warning label. He was utterly and supremely masculine, and as she gazed at him, she felt the same piercing longing she experienced on warm summer evenings when she lay in the grass and stared at the stars. He shone as brightly, and he was just as unreachable.

He wore a black Stetson accompanied by snakeskin cowboy boots and a velour bathrobe patterned in red and green lightning bolts. He held an amber beer bottle in one hand, and smoke curled from the cigar clamped in the corner of his mouth. The skin between the tops of his cowboy boots and the bottom of his robe was bare, revealing powerfully muscled calves, and her mouth went dry as she wondered if he was naked underneath that robe.

"Hey! I told you to wait by the door for me."

She jumped as the burly man who had let her in the house came up behind her, a small boom box in his hand.

"Stella said you were hot, but I told her I wanted a blonde." He regarded her doubtfully. "Bobby Tom likes blondes. Are you blond under that wig?"

Her hand flew to her french twist. "Actually—"

"I like that librarian's get-up you're wearing, but you need a lot more makeup. Bobby Tom likes his women with makeup."

And breasts, she thought, as her eyes wandered back toward the platform. Bobby Tom also liked his women with very large breasts.

She returned her gaze to the boom box, trying to grasp the specifics of the misunderstanding between them. As she began to frame a proper explanation, the man scratched his chest.

"Did Stella tell you we want something a little special, on account of how depressed he's been lately because of his retirement? He's even talking about leaving Chicago to live in Texas year round. The boys and me thought this might give him a couple of laughs. Bobby Tom loves strippers."

Strippers! Gracie's fingers convulsed around her fake pearls. "Oh, dear! I should explain—"

"There was one stripper I thought he might even marry, but she couldn't pass his football quiz." He shook his head. "I still can't believe that the greatest wideout in the game has hung up his helmet for Hollywood. Goddamn knee."

Since he seemed to be talking to himself rather than her, Gracie didn't respond. Instead, she tried to absorb the incredible fact that this man had mistaken her—the last thirty-year-old virgin left on Planet Earth—for a stripper!

It was embarrassing.

It was terrifying.

It was *thrilling!*

Once again, he regarded her critically. "Last one Stella sent over came in dressed like a nun. Bobby Tom like to bust a gut laughing.

But she wore a lot more makeup. Bobby Tom likes makeup on his women. You'd better go fix yourself up."

It was long past time to put an end to this misunderstanding, and she cleared her throat. "Unfortunately, Mr.—"

"Bruno. Bruno Metucci. I played for the Stars back in the old days when Bert Somerville owned the team. 'Course I was never a starter like Bobby Tom."

"I see. Well, the fact is—"

An outburst of shrill, female squeals erupting from the hot tub distracted her. She lifted her eyes to see Bobby Tom gazing indulgently at the women frolicking at his feet, while in the distance the lights of Lake Michigan glimmered through the glass behind him. For a moment she had the illusion that he was floating in space, a cosmic cowboy in his Stetson, boots, and bathrobe, a man not governed by the same rules of gravity that kept ordinary mortals earth-bound. He seemed to wear invisible spurs on those boots, spurs that spun at supersonic speed, shooting off giant pinwheels of glittering sparks that illuminated everything he did and made it larger than life.

A woman rose from the bubbles in the hot tub. "Bobby Tom, you said I could take the quiz again."

She had spoken loudly, and several rowdy cheers went up from the guests. As if one body, everyone in the group turned toward the platform, awaiting his response.

Bobby Tom, with cigar and beer bottle in

one hand, stuck his other hand in the pocket of his robe and regarded her with concern. "Are you sure you're ready, Julie, honey? You know you only get two chances, and you missed Eric Dickerson's career rushing record by a hundred yards last time."

"I'm sure. I've been studying real hard."

Julie looked as if she belonged on the cover of *Sports Illustrated*'s swimsuit issue. As she hoisted herself out of the water, wet blond hair streamed in pale ribbons over her shoulders. She sat on the edge of the hot tub, revealing a swimsuit made up of three tiny turquoise triangles banded in bright yellow. Gracie knew that many of her acquaintances would disapprove of such a revealing swimsuit, but as a devout believer that every woman should capitalize on her assets, Gracie thought she looked wonderful.

Someone in the crowd turned down the music. Bobby Tom sat on one of the boulders and crossed a snakeskin cowboy boot over his bare knee. "Come here and give me a kiss for good luck, then. And don't you disappoint me this time. I've just about got my heart set on makin' you Mrs. Bobby Tom."

While Julie complied with his request, Gracie gazed inquisitively at Bruno. "He gives them quizzes about football?"

"'Course he does. Football's Bobby Tom's life. He doesn't believe in divorce, and he knows he couldn't ever be happy with a woman who didn't understand the game."

While Gracie tried to absorb this piece of

information, Bobby Tom kissed Julie, then patted her wet bottom and sent her back to her perch on the edge of the hot tub. The guests had congregated near the platform to observe the action. Gracie took advantage of the fact that Bruno was also watching the interchange to back up onto one of the steps behind her so she didn't miss a thing.

Bobby Tom put out his cigar in a chunky onyx ashtray. "All right, honey. Let's start with quarterbacks. Choosin' between Terry Bradshaw, Len Dawson, and Bob Griese, which one had the highest percentage of completions? Notice I'm trying to keep this easy. I'm not asking you for the actual percentage, just who ranks highest."

Julie flipped her sleek wet hair over her shoulder and gave him a confident smile. "Len Dawson."

"Real good." The hot tub lights reflected up, so that his face was visible, even under the brim of his Stetson. Although Gracie stood a little too far away to be certain, she thought she detected amusement glinting in those deep blue eyes. As a devout student of human nature, she grew even more interested in observing what he was up to.

"Now let's see if you've got your problems from the last quiz straightened out. Slip your mind back to 1985 and name the NFC's leading rusher."

"Easy. Marcus Allen."

"The AFC?"

"Curt—No! Gerald Riggs."

Bobby Tom pressed his hand to his chest. "Whew, you about stopped my heart with that one. Okay, now, longest field goal in a Super Bowl game?"

"1970. Jan Stenerud. Super Bowl IV."

He looked around at the crowd and grinned. "Am I the only one hearin' wedding bells?"

Gracie was smiling herself at his chicanery as she leaned forward to whisper in Bruno's ear. "Isn't this a little demeaning?"

"Not if she wins. You got any idea how much Bobby Tom's worth?"

Quite a lot, she imagined. She listened as he fired off two more questions, both of which Julie answered. In addition to being beautiful, the blonde was quite knowledgeable, but Gracie had the distinct feeling she wasn't nearly smart enough to stay ahead of Bobby Tom Denton.

Once again, she whispered to Bruno. "Do those young women really believe he's serious about this?"

"Of course he's serious. Why else do you think a man who loves women as much as he does hasn't ever gotten married?"

"Maybe he's gay," she suggested, purely as a point of discussion.

Bruno's shaggy eyebrows shot up into his forehead and he began to sputter. "Gay! Bobby Tom Denton? Shit, he's nailed more tail than a frontier trapper. Cheezus, don't let him hear you say that. He'd probably—Well, I don't even want to imagine what he'd do."

Gracie had never believed that any man

18

who was securely heterosexual should be threatened by homosexuality, but since she was hardly an expert on male behavior, she could quite possibly be missing something.

Julie answered a question about a person named Walter Payton and another about the Pittsburgh Steelers. Bobby Tom rose from his chair and began to pace along the back edge of the platform, as if he were in deep thought, which Gracie didn't believe for a minute.

"All right, honey, now concentrate. You're only one question away from that long walk down the center aisle, and I'm already thinkin' about what good-looking babies we're gonna have. I haven't felt this much pressure since my first Super Bowl. Are you concentrating?"

Creases had formed in Julie's perfect forehead. "I'm concentrating."

"Okay, sweetheart, now don't disappoint me." He tilted the beer to his lips, drained it, and set the bottle down. "Everybody knows the goalposts have to be eighteen feet, six inches wide. The top face of the crossbar—"

"Ten feet above the ground!" Julie shrieked.

"Aw, honey, I respect you too much to insult your intelligence with a question that easy. Wait till I finish, or you're gonna end up with a two-question penalty."

She looked so stricken that Gracie's heart went out to her.

Bobby Tom crossed his arms over his chest. "The top face of the crossbar is ten feet above the ground. The vertical posts have to extend at least thirty feet above the crossbar. Now here's your question, sweetheart, and before you answer, remember that you're holding my heart in your hands." Gracie waited expectantly. "For the chance to be Mrs. Bobby Tom Denton, give me the exact dimensions of the ribbon attached to the top of each upright."

Julie shot up from the edge of the hot tub. "I know this, Bobby Tom! I know it!"

Bobby Tom went very still. "You do?"

A soft giggle slipped through Gracie's lips. It would serve him right if Julie answered the question.

"Four inches by sixty inches!"

Bobby Tom punched his chest. "Aw, baby! You just ripped out my heart and stomped the sucker flat."

Julie's face crumpled.

"It's four inches by *forty-eight*. Forty-eight inches, sweetheart. We were only twelve inches away from eternal marital bliss. I can't remember the last time I was so depressed."

Gracie watched him take Julie in his arms and kiss her quite thoroughly. This man might be the most blatant male chauvinist left in North America, but she had to admire his audacity. She watched with fascination as his hand, which was suntanned and exceptionally strong looking, curled over the bare globe of Julie's glistening bottom. The muscles in her own bottom tightened unconsciously in response.

The guests began to mill and a few of the men stepped up on the platform to offer condolences to the beautiful loser.

"Let's go." Bruno took Gracie's arm, and

before she could stop him, he had pushed her forward.

She caught her breath in alarm. What had started as a simple misunderstanding had begun to get out of hand, and she hastily turned back to him. "Bruno, there's something we need to talk about. It's quite funny, really, and—"

"Hey, Bruno!" Another bruiser, this one with red hair, came up next to them. He ran his eyes over Gracie and regarded Bruno critically.

"She's not wearing enough makeup. You know Bobby Tom likes his women with makeup. And I hope she's got blond hair underneath that wig. Boobs, too. That jacket's so loose it's hard to tell. You got boobs, doll?"

Gracie didn't know which was the more astonishing, being asked if she had boobs or being called "doll." She was momentarily at a loss for words.

"Bruno, who you got there?"

Her stomach plummeted as she heard Bobby Tom's voice. He had stepped to the edge of the hot tub platform and was regarding her with great interest and something that seemed almost like speculation.

Bruno patted the boom box. "Me and the boys thought we'd surprise you with a little entertainment."

Gracie watched with growing dread as a wide grin stretched over Bobby Tom's face, revealing a set of straight white teeth. His eyes met hers, and she felt as if she were walking too fast on a moving sidewalk.

"Come on over here, honey, so ol' Bobby Tom can take a look at you before you get started." His soft Texas drawl licked her body and scrambled her customary good sense, which might have been why she said the first thing that came into her mind.

"I—uh—have to put on more makeup first."

"Now don't you worry about that."

She let out a small gasp of dismay as Bruno pushed her the rest of the way forward. Before she could draw back, Bobby Tom's big hand closed around her wrist. Numbly, she looked down at the long, tapered fingers that only moments before had been molded to Julie's behind but were now pulling her up next to him on the platform.

"Let's give the lady some room, girls."

Alarmed, she watched the women leaving the hot tub so they could watch her. She tried to explain. "Mr. Denton, I need to tell you who—"

Bruno hit the button on the boom box, and her voice was drowned out by the raucous music of "The Stripper." The men began to cheer and whistle. Bobby Tom gave her an encouraging wink, released her, and walked away to sit on a boulder and watch the show.

Hot color flamed in her cheeks. She stood all alone in the center of the hot tub platform, and everyone in the room was staring at her. All of these perfect physical specimens were waiting for her, imperfect Gracie Snow, to strip!

"Come on, baby!"

"Don't be shy!"

"Shake it, honey!"

As some of the men made animal noises, one of the women put her fingers between her lips and whistled. Gracie gazed at them helplessly. They began to laugh, just as her sophomore English class had laughed when the tissues padding her bra had shifted. They were adult party animals behaving in accordance with their species, and they apparently thought her reluctance was part of the act.

As she stood frozen before them, the idea of being mistaken for a stripper suddenly became less embarrassing than the thought of shouting out an explanation over the music to all these worldly people who would instantly realize what a country bumpkin she was.

Perhaps fifteen feet separated her from Bobby Tom Denton, and she realized all she had to do was work herself close enough to him so she could whisper her identity. Once he realized that Windmill Studios had sent her, he would be so embarrassed by the mistake that he would help her make a discreet exit and give her his full cooperation.

A fresh burst of animal noises rose over the music blasting from the boom box. Gingerly, she extended her right leg several inches and pointed the toe of her sensible navy pump. Once again there was laughter.

"That's the way!"

"Show us what you got!"

The distance between herself and Bobby Tom now seemed to stretch a hundred miles. Tugging on the skirt of her navy suit, she inched toward him. More whistles joined the laughter as the bottom of her hem reached the top of her knee.

"You're hot, baby! We love it!"

"Take off that wig!"

Bruno had pushed himself to the front of the crowd and was making a giant circle with his index finger. At first she didn't understand what he wanted, and then she realized he was ordering her to face Bobby Tom while she undressed. With a gulp, she turned toward those deep blue eyes.

He tilted his Stetson back on his head and spoke just loudly enough for her to hear. "Leave the pearls for last, sweetheart. I do like a lady in pearls."

"We're getting bored!" one of the men bellowed. "Take something off!"

She nearly lost her nerve. Only the thought of what her employer would say if she fled from the house without having accomplished her mission stiffened her backbone. Gracie Snow didn't run! This job was the opportunity she'd been waiting for all her life, and she wasn't going to turn cowardly at the first sign of adversity.

She gingerly removed her suit jacket. Bobby Tom gave her an approving smile, as if she'd just done something amazing. The ten feet that still separated them seemed like a million miles. He hooked the ankle of his cowboy boot over his opposite knee, and his bathrobe fell open to reveal a very naked, powerfully muscled thigh. Her jacket dropped from her fingers.

"That's the way, honey. You're doin' real good." His eyes sparkled with admiration, as if she were the most talented dancer he'd ever seen instead of the most inept.

With a series of clumsy bumps, she wiggled closer, trying to ignore the exaggerated boos that were beginning to come from the audience.

"Real nice," he said. "I don't think I've ever seen an act quite like this."

With a final thrust of her hips, she arrived at his side, minus only a jacket, and forced her stiff lips into a smile. Unfortunately, as she leaned forward to whisper her predicament into his ear, her cheek hit the brim of his Stetson, knocking it askew. With one hand, he righted it while, with the other, he swept her into his lap.

The loud music covered her startled exclamation. She was temporarily stunned into speechlessness by the feel of his hard body beneath her own and the solid wall of his chest pressed against her side.

"You need some help, honey?" His hand went to the top button of her blouse.

"Oh, no!" She clutched his arm.

"You've got an interesting act, sweetheart. A little slow getting going, but you're probably still a trainee." He gave her a grin that held more mirth than lechery. "What's your name?"

She gulped. "Gracie—That is, Grace. Grace Snow. *Miss* Snow," she amended, in a belated attempt to put some psychological distance between them. "And I'm not—"

"*Miz* Snow." He rolled the words around in his mouth, savoring them as if they were a particularly fine wine. The heat from his body was muddling her brain, and she tried to get out of his lap.

"Mr. Denton—"

"Just the top one, sweetie. The boys are getting restless." Before she could stop him, he had opened the button at the collar of her white polyester blouse. "You must be new at this." The tip of his index finger explored the hollow at the base of her throat, making her shiver. "I thought I'd met all of Stella's girls."

"Yes, I—I mean, no, I'm—"

"Now don't be nervous. You're doin' just fine. And you've got very nice legs, if you don't mind my sayin' so." His nimble fingers opened the next button.

"Mr. Denton!"

"Miz Snow?"

She saw the same amusement in his eyes she'd noted earlier when he was giving Julie the football quiz, and she realized he had slipped another button open, exposing her pale peach demibra with its plunging center and scalloped edging. Her naughty underwear, a foolish indulgence for a homely woman, was her most closely guarded secret, and she gave a small gasp of dismay.

A raucous cheer went up from the crowd, but it wasn't in response to her pale peach demibra. Instead, one of the women standing by the pool had whipped off the top of her bikini and was twirling it around her head. Gracie saw right away that this woman needed something with more support than a demibra.

The men clapped and hooted. She reached for her blouse to clutch it together, but Bobby Tom caught her fingers, trapping them gently in his palm.

"Candi, there, seems to be gettin' ahead of you, Miz Snow."

"I thought—Perhaps—" She swallowed hard. "There's something I need to talk to you about. In private."

"You want to dance for me in private? That's real sweet of you, but my guests would be disappointed if I got to see more of you than they did."

She realized he had unfastened the button at the waistband of her skirt and was lowering the zipper.

"Mr. Denton!" Her voice was louder than she had intended, and the guests standing nearby laughed.

"Call me Bobby Tom, honey. Everybody does." The corners of his eyes crinkled as if he were laughing at some great private joke. "Now this is interesting. I don't think I've ever known a stripper who wore panty hose."

"I'm not a stripper!"

"'Course you are. Why else would you be taking off your clothes in front of a bunch of drunken football players?"

"I'm not taking off my—Oh!" His nimble ball handler's fingers were divesting her of her garments as effortlessly as if they were made of tissue paper, and her blouse fell open.

Summoning all her strength, she pushed herself from his lap only to feel her skirt slide over her half slip to her ankles.

Mortified, she reached down to snatch it up. Her face was crimson as she yanked it back into place. How could a woman who prided herself on organization and efficiency have let something so appalling happen? Clutching her blouse together, she forced herself to face him. "I'm not a stripper!"

"Is that so?" He pulled a cigar out of the breast pocket of his robe and rolled it between his fingers. She noticed he didn't seem at all surprised by her announcement.

Her words had caught the attention of the guests nearest her, and she saw that her plans for a private conversation were rapidly dissolving. She lowered her voice until it was barely more than a whisper.

"There's been a terrible misunderstanding. Can't you see that I don't look like a stripper?"

He slipped the unlit cigar between his teeth and, letting his eyes slide over her in a leisurely fashion, spoke in a normal voice. "As to that, sometimes it's hard to tell. Last one came in here dressed like a nun, and the one before that was pretty much a dead ringer for Mick Jagger."

Someone had shut off the music, and an unnatural silence had fallen over the crowd. Despite her determination to hold onto her self-control, she could no longer keep her voice steady. She snatched up the suit jacket she had discarded earlier. "Please, Mr. Denton. Could we go somewhere private?"

He sighed and uncoiled from the boulder. "I s'pose we'd better. But you've got to give me your word you'll keep your clothes on. It wouldn't be fair for me to see you naked when my guests can't."

"I promise, Mr. Denton, that you will never see me naked!"

He looked doubtful. "I don't mean to question your good intentions, honey, but judging from my past history, it might not be that easy for you to resist."

The size of his ego flabbergasted her. As she stared at him, he gave a slight shrug. "I suppose we'd better go in my study, then, and have that private conversation you're so set on." Taking her arm, he led her down off the platform.

As they crossed the floor of the grotto, she remembered that he hadn't seemed the slightest bit surprised by her announcement that she wasn't a stripper. He was too cool, too calm, too openly amused with the whole situation. Before she had time to carry this thought to its logical conclusion, the red-haired football player who'd spoken with her earlier stepped out of the crowd and gave Bobby Tom a playful punch in the arm.

"Damn, Bobby Tom. I hope this one isn't pregnant, too."

2

"**Y**ou knew all along I wasn't a stripper, didn't you?"

Bobby Tom closed the study door after them. "Not for certain."

Gracie Snow was nobody's fool. "I believe you did," she said firmly.

He gestured toward her blouse, and once again she saw the laugh lines crinkling at the corners of his lady-killer eyes. "You've got your buttons mixed up there a little bit. You want me to help—? No, I guess you don't."

Nothing was going the way she'd planned. What had Bobby Tom's friend meant when he'd said he hoped this one wasn't pregnant, too? She recalled a remark she'd overheard Willow make about one of their actors who'd been involved in several paternity suits a few years ago. They must have been talking about Bobby Tom. Apparently he was one of those loathsome men who preyed on vulnerable women and then abandoned them. It grated her to admit someone so immoral had fascinated her even momentarily.

She turned away to straighten her buttons and gather her composure. While she put herself together, she took in her surroundings and found herself facing the most colossal display of ego she had ever witnessed.

Bobby Tom Denton's study was a shrine to the football career of Bobby Tom Denton. Blown-up action photographs hung on every surface of the marbleized gray walls. Some of them showed him in the uniform of the University of Texas, but in most of them, he wore the sky blue and gold of the Chicago Stars. In several of the photographs, he was off the ground, toes pointed, his lean body curved in a graceful *C* as he snatched a ball out of the air. There were close-ups of him in a sky blue helmet emblazoned with three gold stars, shots of him diving for the goal line or maneuvering down the sidelines, one foot positioned in front of the other as gracefully as a ballet dancer's. Shelves displayed trophies, commendations, and framed certificates.

She watched him settle with lazy grace into a sling-shaped leather chair behind a granite-topped desk that looked as if it belonged in a Flintstones cartoon. A sleek gray computer sat on top, along with a high-tech telephone. She chose a tub chair resting beneath a group of framed magazines covers, several of which depicted him standing on the sidelines kissing a glamorous blonde. Gracie recognized her from an article she'd seen in *People* magazine, as Phoebe Somerville Calebow, the beautiful owner of the Chicago Stars.

His eyes drifted over her and the corner of his mouth curled. "I don't want to hurt your feelings, honey, but speaking as something of an expert, it seems only right to tell you that, if you're looking for a night job, you might think more on the lines of clerking at a 7-Eleven than taking off your clothes professionally."

She'd never been very good at icy glares, but she did her best. "You deliberately set out to embarrass me."

He worked equally hard at looking crestfallen. "I wouldn't do that to a lady."

"Mr. Denton, as I suspect you know very well, I'm here on behalf of Windmill Studios. Willow Craig, the producer, sent me to—"

"Uh-huh. You want a glass of champagne or a Coke or something?" The phone began to ring, but he ignored it.

"No, thank you. You were supposed to be in Texas four days ago to begin shooting *Blood Moon*, and—"

"How about a beer? I've noticed a lot more women are drinking beer than used to."

"I don't drink."

"Is that so?"

She sounded priggish instead of businesslike, perhaps not the best posture for dealing with a wild man, and she tried to recover. "I don't drink myself, Mr. Denton, but I have nothing against those who use alcohol."

"I'm Bobby Tom, sweetheart. I don't hardly recognize any other name."

He sounded like a cowboy just coming in off a trail drive, but from watching him give that football quiz, she suspected he was smarter than he pretended to be. "Very well. Bobby Tom, then. The contract you signed with Windmill Studios—"

"You don't look much like the Hollywood

type, Miz Snow. How long have you been working for Windmill?"

She busied herself straightening her pearls. Once again the phone began to ring, and once again he ignored it. "I've been a production assistant for some time."

"Exactly how long?"

She surrendered to the inevitable, but she did it with dignity. Lifting her chin half an inch higher, she said, "Not quite a month."

"That long." He was clearly amused.

"I'm very competent. I came into this job with vast experience in management as well as excellent interpersonal communication skills." She was also a whiz at making pot holders, painting ceramic pigs, and playing Golden Oldies on the piano.

He whistled. "I'm impressed. What sort of job would that have been?"

"I—uh—ran the Shady Acres Nursing Home."

"A nursing home? Isn't that something. Were you in the business for long?"

"I was raised at Shady Acres."

"You were raised in a nursing home? Now that's interesting. I knew a running back who was raised in a penitentiary—his daddy was warden—but I don't think I ever met anybody raised in a nursing home. Did your parents work there?"

"My parents owned it. My father died ten years ago, and I've helped my mother run it ever since. She sold it recently and moved to Florida."

"Where is this nursing home?"

"Ohio."

"Cleveland? Columbus?"

"New Grundy."

He smiled. "I don't believe I ever heard of New Grundy. How did you get from there to Hollywood?"

It was difficult for her to keep her concentration in the face of that killer smile, but she resolutely plowed on. "Willow Craig offered me a job because she needed someone reliable, and she was impressed with the way I ran Shady Acres. Her father was a resident there until he died last month."

When Willow, who headed Windmill Studios, had offered her a job as a production assistant, Gracie had hardly been able to believe her good fortune. Although it was only an entry level position and the pay was low, Gracie fully intended to prove herself so she could advance quickly in her glamorous new profession.

"Is there any reason, Mr. Den—uh, Bobby Tom, that you haven't shown up to start work?"

"Oh, there's a reason all right. You want some Jelly Bellys? I might have a bag here in my desk someplace." He began feeling around on the rough granite corners. "Hard to find the drawers, though. I think I might need a chisel to open them."

She smiled, only to realize he had once again avoided answering her question. Since she was accustomed to communicating with people whose minds wandered, she decided to come at it from another direction.

"You have an unusual house. Have you lived here long?"

"A couple of years. I don't much like it myself, but the architect is real proud of it. She calls it urban Stone Age with a Japanese Tahitian influence. I sort of just call it ugly. Still, the magazine people seem to like it; it's been photographed a whole bunch of times." Abandoning his search for the Jelly Bellys, he rested his hand on the computer keyboard. "Sometimes I'll come home and find a cow skull lying next to the bathtub, or a canoe in the living room, all that strange stuff they put in those magazine photos to make them look good, even though real people would never have things like that in their houses."

"It must be hard living in a house that you don't like."

"I've got a whole bunch of other ones, so it doesn't much matter."

She blinked in surprise. Most people she knew worked all their lives to pay for one house. She wanted to ask how many he owned, but she knew it wouldn't be wise to let herself get distracted from the topic at hand. The phone began to ring again, but he paid no attention.

"This is your first movie, isn't it? Have you always wanted to be an actor?"

He looked at her blankly. "An actor? Oh, yeah—A long time."

"You're probably not aware that every day shooting is delayed costs thousands of dollars.

Windmill is a small, independent studio, and it can't tolerate that sort of expense."

"They'll take it out of my paycheck."

The idea didn't seem to bother him, and she regarded him thoughtfully. He was toying with the mouse that sat on a gray foam pad next to the computer. His fingers were long and tapered, the nails clipped short. One strong, bare wrist showed beneath the cuff of his robe.

"Since you don't have any acting experience, it occurs to me that you might be a bit nervous about the whole thing. If you're afraid..."

He uncurled from the desk and spoke softly, but with a certain intensity she hadn't heard in his voice until that moment. "Bobby Tom Denton isn't afraid of anything, sweetheart. You just remember that."

"Everybody's afraid of something."

"Not me. When you've spent the best part of your life facing eleven men hell-bent on pulling your guts out through your nose hairs, things like making movies don't have much effect."

"I see. Still, you're not a football player any longer."

"Oh, I'll always be a football player, in one way or another." For a moment she thought she detected a bleakness in his eyes, an emotion almost like despair. But he'd spoken so matter-of-factly, she decided she'd imagined it. He came around the side of the desk toward her.

"Maybe you'd better get on the phone and

tell your boss I'll be there one of these days soon."

He had finally made her angry, and she drew herself up to her full five feet, four and three-quarters inches. "What I'm going to tell my boss is that both of us will be flying into San Antonio tomorrow afternoon and then driving on to Telarosa."

"We are?"

"Yes." She knew she had to be firm with him from the beginning or he'd take dreadful advantage of her. "Otherwise, you're going to be in the middle of a very nasty lawsuit."

He rubbed his chin with his thumb and index finger. "I guess you win, sweetheart. What time is our flight?"

She regarded him suspiciously. "Twelve-forty-nine."

"All right."

"I'll pick you up at eleven o'clock." She was wary of his sudden capitulation, and it sounded more like a question than a statement.

"It might be easier if I met you at the airport."

"I'll pick you up here."

"That's real nice of you."

The next thing she knew, Bobby Tom had her by the elbow and was steering her from the study.

He played the perfect host, pointing out a sixteenth century temple gong and a floor sculpture made from petrified wood, but in less than ninety seconds, she was alone on the sidewalk.

Lights blazed from the front windows and music drifted toward her on the scented night air. As she breathed it in, her eyes grew wistful. This was her first wild party and, unless she was very much mistaken, she had just been thrown out.

Gracie was back at Bobby Tom Denton's house at eight o'clock the next morning. Before she'd left the motel, she'd placed a call to Shady Acres to check on Mrs. Fenner and Mr. Marinetti. As much as she'd needed to escape her life at the nursing home, she still cared about the people she'd left behind three weeks ago, and she was relieved to hear that they were both improving. She'd also called her mother, but Fran Snow had been on the way to her water aerobics class at her Sarasota condominium, and she had no time to talk.

Gracie parked her car on the street, where it was hidden from the house by shrubbery but still afforded her a clear view of the drive. Bobby Tom's sudden agreeableness last night had made her suspicious, and she wasn't taking any chances.

She'd spent most of the night alternating between disturbingly erotic dreams and nervous wakefulness. This morning while she showered, she'd been forced to give herself a stern lecture. It wouldn't do any good to tell herself that Bobby Tom wasn't the handsomest, sexiest, and most exciting man she'd ever met, because he was. That made it even more important to remember that his blue eyes, lazy charm, and relentless affability hid a dangerous combination of a monstrous ego and a keen mind. She was going to have to stay on her toes.

Her thoughts were interrupted by the sight of an antique red Thunderbird convertible backing down the drive. Having anticipated exactly this sort of treachery, she flipped the key in the ignition, pushed hard on the accelerator, and shot forward to block the way with her rental car. After she turned off the engine, she scooped up her purse and got out.

The ignition keys jingled in the pocket of her latest fashion mistake, an oversize mustard-colored wrap dress that she had hoped would look crisp and professional, but merely looked dowdy and middle-aged. The heels of Bobby Tom's cowboy boots clicked on the drive as he came toward her, the barest hint of a limp in his walk. Nervously, she studied his outfit. His silk shirt, imprinted with purple palm trees, was tucked into a pair of perfectly faded and impeccably frayed jeans that molded to his narrow hips and lean runner's legs in a manner that made it nearly impossible for her to draw her eyes away from parts of him she'd be better off not looking at.

She braced herself as he tipped his pearl gray Stetson. "Mornin', Miz Gracie."

"Good morning," she said briskly. "I didn't expect you to be up so early after last night." Several seconds ticked by as he gazed at her. Although his eyes were half-lidded, she detected an intensity beneath that indolence that made her wary.

"You weren't supposed to be here till eleven," he said.

"Yes, well, I'm early."

"I can see that, and I sure would appreciate it if you'd back your car out of my way." His lazy drawl was at odds with the faint tightening at the corners of his lips.

"I'm sorry, but I can't do that. I'm here to escort you to Telarosa."

"I don't mean to be impolite, sweetheart, but the fact is, I don't need a bodyguard."

"I'm not a bodyguard. I'm an escort."

"Whatever you are, I'd like you to move your car."

"I understand that, but if I don't have you in Telarosa by Monday morning, I'm fairly certain I'll be fired, so I really must be firm about this."

He rested one hand on his hip. "I see your point, so I'm gonna give you a thousand dollars to drive away and not come back."

Gracie stared at him.

"Let's make that fifteen hundred for the inconvenience."

She'd always assumed people knew, just by looking at her, that she was an honorable person, and the idea that he could believe her capable of accepting a bribe offended her far more than being mistaken for a stripper.

"I don't do things like that," she said slowly.

He emitted a lengthy sigh of regret. "I'm real sorry you feel that way because, whether you take my money or not, I'm afraid I'm not going to be on that plane with you this afternoon."

"Are you telling me you're going to break your contract?"

"No. I'm just tellin' you that I'll be getting to Telarosa all by myself."

She didn't believe him. "You signed that contract of your own free will. Not only do you have a legal obligation to fulfill it, but you also have a moral obligation."

"Miz Gracie, you sound just like a Sunday School teacher."

Her eyes dropped.

He gave a bark of laughter and shook his head. "It's true. Bobby Tom Denton's bodyguard is a damn Sunday School teacher."

"I told you I'm not your bodyguard. I'm simply your escort."

"I'm afraid you're going to have to find somebody else to escort, then, because I've decided to drive to Telarosa instead of fly, and I know for a fact that a fine lady like yourself wouldn't be comfortable closed up in a T-bird with a hell-raiser like me." He walked over to her rental car and leaned down to peer inside the passenger window, looking for her keys. "I'm embarrassed to tell you that I don't have the best reputation when it comes to women, Miz Gracie."

She trotted after him, trying very hard not to stare at the way that tight, faded denim clung to his hips as he bent forward. "You don't have enough time to drive to Telarosa. Willow is expecting us there by this evening."

42

He straightened and smiled. "You be sure to give her my regards when you see her. Now are you going to move your car?"

"Absolutely not."

He dipped his head, shook it regretfully, and then, with a quick step forward, snagged the shoulder strap of Gracie's purse and slipped it off her arm.

"Give that back right this minute!" She lunged for the clunky black bag.

"I sure will be happy to. Just as soon as I find your car keys." He smiled agreeably while he held the purse out of her reach and riffled through it.

She certainly wasn't going to get into a wrestling match with him, so she used her sternest voice. "Mr. Denton, give me my purse back immediately. And of course you'll be in Telarosa by Monday. You signed a contract that—"

"Excuse me for interrupting, Miz Gracie, when I know you're just itchin' to make your point, but I'm a little pressed for time here." He handed her purse back without having found what he was looking for and walked toward the house.

Once again, Gracie rushed after him. "Mr. Denton. Uh, Bobby Tom—"

"Bruno, could you come out here for a minute?"

Bruno emerged from the garage, a grubby rag in his hand. "You need something, B.T.?"

"I sure do." He turned to Gracie. "Beg pardon, Miz Snow."

With no more warning than that, he slipped his hands under her arms and began to frisk her.

"Stop that!" She tried to jerk away, but Bobby Tom Denton hadn't become the best pass receiver in the NFL by letting go of moving objects, and she couldn't budge as he began to pat down her sides.

"Easy now and we can get this over without any bloodshed." His palms glided over her breasts.

She sucked in her breath, too stunned to move. "Mr. Denton!"

The corners of his eyes crinkled. "You have very nice taste in underwear, by the way. I couldn't help but notice last night." He moved on to her waist.

Her cheeks burned with embarrassment. "Stop this right now!"

His hands came to a halt as he felt the lump in her pocket. With a grin, he pulled out the car keys.

"Give those back!"

"You want to move that car for me, Bruno?" He pitched the keys over, then tipped his hat to Gracie. "Nice to have met you, Miz Snow."

Dumbfounded, she watched him stride down the drive to the Thunderbird and climb in. She began to rush toward him only to realize that Bruno was getting into her rental car at the end of the drive.

"Don't touch that car!" she exclaimed, immediately changing direction.

The engines of both the Thunderbird and

the rental car roared to life. As she gazed helplessly back and forth between the two automobiles—one in the drive, the other blocking the drive—she knew with an unshakable conviction that if she let Bobby Tom escape, she would never get close to him again. He had houses everywhere and an army of flunkies to protect him from people he didn't want to see. She had to stop him now, or she would have lost her chance forever.

Her rental car, with Bruno in the driver's seat, shot forward and cleared the end of the drive.

She whirled toward the Thunderbird. "Don't leave! We have to go to the airport!"

"Y'all have a good life now, y'hear." With a jaunty wave of his hand, Bobby Tom began backing out.

In a flash she saw herself returning to Shady Acres to take the job the new owners had offered her. She smelled Ben-Gay and Lysol; she tasted overcooked green beans and mashed potatoes covered with gelatinous yellow gravy. She saw the years slipping by, saw herself wearing elastic stockings and heavy cardigans while her arthritic fingers tried to pound out "Harvest Moon" on the battered upright that wouldn't hold its tune. Before she'd ever had the chance to be young, she'd be old.

"No!" The scream came from the very center of her being, the place where her dreams lived, all those glorious dreams that were slipping away forever.

She bolted toward the Thunderbird, running

as fast as she could, her purse banging awkwardly against her side. Bobby Tom had turned his head to check for traffic in the street, and he didn't see her coming. Her heart raced. Any second now he would be gone, sentencing her to a life of dreary monotony. Desperation gave her strength and she ran faster.

He pulled out and shifted. She increased her speed. Air filled her lungs in short, painful gasps. The Thunderbird began to move forward just as she drew even with it. With a wrenching sob, she threw herself headfirst over the convertible's passenger door.

"Awww, *hell.*"

The jolt of the brakes sent her upper body pitching forward off the seat. Her hands and upper arms hit the floor mats, while her feet still dangled over the door. She winced as she tried to catch herself. Cold air slithered across the backs of her thighs, and she realized her skirt had flipped over her head. Mortified, she groped for it, at the same time trying to wiggle the rest of herself into the car.

She heard a particularly offensive obscenity that was undoubtedly common among football players, but seldom heard at Shady Acres. Normally, it was uttered in one syllable, but Bobby Tom's Texas drawl extended it to two. Her skirts finally under control, she slumped breathlessly back into the seat.

Several seconds ticked by before she worked up enough nerve to look at him.

He was gazing at her thoughtfully, his elbow propped on the top of the steering wheel.

"Just out of curiosity, sweetheart; did you ever talk to your doctor about givin' you some tranquilizers?"

She turned her head and stared straight ahead.

"See, the thing of it is, Miz Gracie, I'm right now on my way to Telarosa, and I'm going by myself."

Her eyes shot back to him. "You're leaving *now*?"

"My suitcase is in the trunk."

"I don't believe you."

"It's the truth. You want to open that door and get out?"

She shook her head stubbornly, hoping he couldn't see how close she was to reaching the end of her resources. "I have to go with you. It's my responsibility to stay with you until you reach Telarosa. I have a job to do."

A muscle ticked in his jaw, and with a great deal of trepidation, she realized that she had finally managed to chip away at his phony country boy affability.

"Don't make me throw you out," he said in a low, determined voice.

She ignored the shiver of trepidation running up her spine. "I've always thought it was better to solve disputes with compromise rather than brute force."

"I've played in the NFL, sweetheart. Bloodshed's about all I understand."

With those ominous words, he reached for his door, and she knew within seconds, he would come around to her side, pick her up, and toss

47

her out on the street. Quickly, before he could push down on the handle, she grabbed his arm.

"Don't throw me out, Bobby Tom. I know I irritate you, but I promise, I'll make it worth your while if you let me go with you."

He turned slowly back to her. "Exactly what do you mean by that?"

She didn't know what she meant. She had spoken impulsively because she couldn't face the idea of calling Willow Craig and telling her that Bobby Tom had set off for Telarosa by himself. She knew all too well what Willow's response would be.

"I meant what I said," she replied, hoping she could bluff her way out without getting down to specifics.

"Generally when people say they're going to make something worth your while, they're offering money. Is that what you're doing?"

"Certainly not! I don't believe in bribery. Besides, you seem to have more money than you know what to do with."

"That's true, so what do you have in mind?"

"I—Well—" She frantically searched for some glimmer of inspiration. "Driving! That's it! You can relax while I do all the driving. I happen to be excellent behind the wheel. I've had my license since I was sixteen, and I've never once gotten a ticket."

"And you're actually proud of that?" He shook his head in amazement. "Unfortunately, sweetheart, nobody but me drives my cars. Nope, I think I'm going to have to throw you out after all."

Once again, he reached for the door handle, and once again, she clutched at his arm. "I'll navigate."

He looked annoyed. "What do I need a navigator for? I've made this trip so many times I could do it blindfolded. No, sweetheart, you'll have to come up with something better than that."

At that moment, she heard a peculiar buzzing sound. It took her a moment to realize that the Thunderbird was equipped with a car phone. "You seem to get a lot of calls. I could answer them for you."

"The last thing I want is somebody answering my phone."

Her mind raced. "I could, uh, rub your shoulders while you're driving, to work out the kinks. I'm very good at massage."

"That's a nice offer, but you have to admit, it's hardly worth taking an unwelcome passenger all the way to Texas. To Peoria, maybe, if you do a good job, but not any farther. Sorry, Miz Gracie, but so far you haven't offered a single thing that's caught my interest."

She tried to think. What did she have that a worldly man like Bobby Tom Denton would find at all interesting? She knew how to organize recreational activities, she understood special diets, drug interactions, and had listened to enough of the residents' stories to have a fairly comprehensive knowledge of World War II troop movements, but somehow she couldn't imagine any of that persuading Bobby Tom to change his mind.

"I have excellent vision. I can read road signs from incredible distances."

"You're grabbing at straws, sweetheart."

She smiled enthusiastically. "Are you aware of the fascinating history of the Seventh Army?"

He gave her a faintly pitying look.

How could she make him change his mind? From what she had seen last night, he was only interested in two things, football and sex. Her knowledge of sports was minimal, and as for sex...

A pulse leaped in her throat as a dangerous and very immoral idea popped into her brain. What if she offered her body for barter? She was immediately appalled. How could she even think of such a thing? No intelligent, modern day woman who considered herself a feminist would consider...The very idea...Of all the...This was definitely the consequence of allowing herself too many sexual fantasies.

Why not? a devil inside her whispered. *Who are you saving it for?*

He's a libertine! she reminded the lusty part of her nature that she tried so hard to suppress. *Besides, he wouldn't be interested in me.*

How will you know if you don't try? the devil replied. *You've dreamed about something like this for years. Didn't you promise yourself that having a sexual experience would be one of the top priorities in your new life?*

An image flashed through her mind of Bobby Tom Denton lowering his naked body over hers. Her blood raced through her veins and her skin prickled. She could feel his strong hands on her thighs, pushing them open, the touch of his—

"Is something wrong, Miz Gracie? You're looking a little red in the face. Like somebody just told you a dirty joke."

"Is sex the only thing you think about!" she cried.

"What?"

"I refuse to sleep with you just so you'll let me come along with you!" Appalled, she snapped her mouth shut. What had she done?

His eyes twinkled. "Shucks."

She wanted to die. How could she have embarrassed herself like this? She swallowed hard. "Forgive me if I've leaped to an incorrect conclusion. I know I'm a homely woman, and I'm certain you wouldn't be sexually interested in me anyway." Her face grew redder as she realized she was making things worse instead of better. "Not that I would be interested, either," she added hastily.

"Now, Gracie, there's no such thing as a homely woman."

"You're being polite, and I appreciate it, but that doesn't alter facts."

"See, now you've piqued my curiosity. You may be right about being homely and everything, but it's kind of hard to tell with the way you cover yourself up. For all I know, the body of a goddess might be hiding underneath that dress."

"Oh, no," she said with brutal honesty. "I assure you, my body is quite ordinary."

Once again the corner of his mouth kicked up. "Don't take this the wrong way, but I trust my judgment a little more than I trust yours. I'm sort of a connoisseur."

"I noticed."

"I believe I already commented on your legs last night."

She flushed and struggled for an appropriate response, but she had so little experience conversing on a personal level with virile males that she found it difficult to know exactly what to say. "You have very nice legs yourself."

"Why, thank you."

"And a pleasant torso, also."

He gave a crack of laughter. "Damn, Miz Gracie, I'm going to keep you around today just for the entertainment value."

"You are?"

He shrugged. "Why not? I've been acting crazy ever since my retirement."

She could hardly believe he'd changed his mind. She heard him chuckle as he retrieved her suitcase and asked Bruno to return her rental car. His amusement had faded, however, by the time he'd once again settled behind the steering wheel, and he gave her a stern gaze.

"I'm not taking you all the way to Texas, so get that out of your mind right now. I like to travel alone."

"I understand."

"A couple of hours. Maybe as far as the state line. The minute you start to aggravate me, I'm dropping you off at the nearest airport."

"I'm sure that won't be necessary."

"Don't bet on it."

3

Bobby Tom drove the freeways of the Windy City as if he owned them. He was king of the town, mayor of the world, top cat of the universe. As the radio blasted out Aerosmith, he drummed his fingers on the steering wheel, keeping time to "Janie's Got a Gun."

In his red Thunderbird convertible and pearl gray Stetson, he was highly conspicuous. To Gracie's amazement, drivers began pulling alongside the car, their horns blowing, windows lowered to call out to him. He waved and drove on.

She could feel her skin flush from the hot wind and the sheer delight of speeding down a big-city freeway in a vintage red Thunderbird with a man who wasn't respectable. Strands of hair escaped from her lumpy french twist and whipped her cheeks. She wished she had a hot pink designer scarf to wrap around her head, a pair of trendy sunglasses to slip on her nose, a tube of scarlet lipstick to slide over her lips. She wanted big, full breasts, a tight dress, a sexy pair of high heels. She wanted a gold ankle bracelet.

And, perhaps, a very discreet heart-shaped tattoo.

She played with this enticing vision of herself

as a wild woman while Bobby Tom placed and received calls on the car phone she'd noticed earlier. Sometimes he used the phone's speaker feature; other times he held the receiver to his ear and spoke privately. His outgoing calls seemed to involve various business deals and their tax effects, as well as charity functions he was involved in. Most of his incoming calls, she was interested to note, seemed to come from acquaintances hitting him up for money. Although he conducted these calls with the phone to his ear, she received the distinct impression that, in every case, he ended up offering more money than had been requested. After less than an hour in his presence, she'd already figured out that Bobby Tom Denton was an easy mark.

As they reached the outskirts of the city, he placed a call to someone named Gail and spoke to her in that lazy drawl that sent shivers up Gracie's all-too-receptive spine.

"I just wanted you to know I'm missin' you so bad I got tears in my eyes this very minute."

He raised his arm to wave at a woman in a blue Firebird who whizzed by blowing her horn. Gracie, a very safe driver herself, grabbed the door handle as she realized he was steering the car with his knee.

"Yeah, that's right...I know, sweetheart, I wish we could have made it, too. The rodeo doesn't come to Chicago nearly often enough." He draped his fingers over the top of the wheel, while he tucked the receiver farther into the crook of his neck. "You don't say. Well, now, you give her my best, y'hear? Kitty and

I had some real good times together a couple months back. She even took the quiz, but she hadn't studied up near enough on the '89 Super Bowl to pass. I'll call you as soon as I can, darlin'."

As he replaced the phone, she regarded him curiously. "Don't all your girlfriends get jealous of each other?"

"'Course not. I only date nice ladies."

And treat every one of them like a queen, she suspected. Even the pregnant ones.

"The National Organization of Women should seriously consider putting out a contract on you."

He looked genuinely surprised. "On me? I love women. More than I like a lot of men, as a matter of fact. I'm pretty much a card carryin' feminist."

"Don't let Gloria Steinem hear you say that."

"Why not? She's the one who gave me the card."

Gracie's eyes flew open.

He flashed a wicked smile. "Gloria is one nice lady, I'm tellin' you that."

She knew right then that she couldn't afford to lose her concentration around him, not even for a moment.

As the suburbs of Chicago gave way to flat, Illinois farmland, she asked if she could use his phone to call Willow Craig, assuring him that she would pay for the call with her new business credit card. That seemed to amuse him.

Windmill had set up its headquarters at the Cattleman's Hotel in Telarosa, and as soon as she was connected with her employer, she began to explain the problem. "I'm afraid Bobby Tom is insisting on driving to Telarosa instead of flying."

"Talk him out of it," Willow replied in her brisk, no-nonsense voice.

"I did my best. Unfortunately, he wasn't listening. We're on the road now, just south of Chicago."

"I was afraid of this." Several seconds slipped by, and Gracie could picture her sophisticated employer toying with one of the large earrings she always wore. "He has to be here by eight o'clock Monday morning. Do you understand?"

Gracie eyed Bobby Tom. "It may not be that easy."

"That's why I chose you to go after him. You're supposed to be able to handle difficult people. We have a fortune tied up in this film, Gracie, and we can't afford any more delays. Even people who aren't sports fans know Bobby Tom Denton, and we're getting a huge amount of publicity out of signing him for his first film."

"I understand."

"He's slippery. It took us months to negotiate this contract, and I want this picture made! I'm not going to see the studio bankrupt just because you don't know how to do your job."

Gracie had a small knot in the pit of her

stomach by the time she had finished listening to another five minutes of warnings about what would happen if she didn't have Bobby Tom in Telarosa by eight o'clock Monday morning.

He replaced the phone. "She really give you the business, huh?"

"She expects me to do the job I was hired for."

"Has it occurred to anybody at Windmill Studios that sending you after me was pretty much like sending a lamb to the slaughter?"

"I don't see it that way. I happen to be exceptionally competent."

She heard a chuckle that sounded faintly diabolic, but was quickly drowned out as he flipped the volume back up on the radio.

Listening to the raucous sounds of rock and roll instead of the innocuous music heard around Shady Acres gave her a moment of such delicious pleasure that her tension faded and she nearly shivered with delight. Her senses seemed especially acute. She felt dizzy from the woodsy scent of Bobby Tom's after-shave, while her hands unconsciously stroked the soft leather seats of what he had informed her was a restored 1957 Thunderbird. If only the car had a pair of fuzzy pink dice swinging from the rearview mirror, it would be perfect.

She'd had so little sleep the night before that her head began to nod, but even so, her eyes wouldn't stay closed for long. The fact that Bobby Tom had allowed her to come along on the first leg of his trip didn't lull her into thinking she could easily persuade him to change his mind about letting her stay with him. Unless she was very much mistaken, he planned to get rid of her as soon as he had the chance, which meant she couldn't let him out of her sight, no matter what.

The car phone buzzed. With a sigh, Bobby Tom pushed the button that activated the speaker.

"Hey, B.T., it's Luther Baines," a boisterous voice proclaimed. "Damn, boy, I just about give up runnin' you to ground."

The pained expression on Bobby Tom's face told Gracie he wished Luther hadn't succeeded. "How you doin', Mr. Mayor."

"Right as rain. I lost ten pounds since I last saw you, B.T. Lighter beer and younger women. Works every time. 'Course we don't have to tell Mrs. Baines about that."

"No, sir, we sure don't."

"Buddy's lookin' forward to seein' you."

"I'm anxious to see him, too."

"Now, B.T., the folks on the Heavenfest organizing committee are gettin' a little nervous. We were expectin' you in Telarosa last week, and we need to be sure that you're getting all your friends lined up for the Bobby Tom Denton Celebrity Golf Tournament. I know Heavenfest isn't till October, but we have to get some advance publicity going, and it sure would be nice to put a few of those big names up on the posters. You heard from Michael Jordan and Joe Montana yet?"

"I've been kinda busy. They'll probably make it, though."

"You know we picked that weekend because the Stars and the Cowboys aren't playing. What about Troy Aikman?"

"Oh, I'm pretty sure he'll be there."

"That's good. That's real good." Gracie heard a deep-pitched chortle. "Toolee told me not to say anything until you get down here, but I wanted you to know right away." Another chortle. "We took over the lease to the house just last week. We're going to kick off Heavenfest with the dedication of the Bobby Tom Denton Birthplace!"

"Awww, man...Luther, that whole idea is crazy! I don't want my birthplace dedicated. For one thing, I was born in a hospital like everybody else, so it doesn't even make sense. I just grew up in that house. I thought you were going to put a stop to this."

"I'm surprised and hurt by your attitude. People been sayin' it's only a matter of time before being famous went to your head, but I kept tellin' them they were wrong. Now I have to wonder. You know how bad the economy is down here, and with that lowlife sumbitch planning to pull out Rosatech, we're facing disaster. Our only hope is to turn Telarosa into a tourist mecca."

"Putting a plaque on that old house is not going to turn Telarosa into a tourist mecca! Luther, I wasn't the president of the United States. I was a football player!"

"I think you lived up North too long, B.T. It's ruined your perspective. You were the best wideout in the history of the game. Down here, we don't forget something like that."

Bobby Tom squeezed his eyes shut in frustration. When he opened them again, he spoke with infinite patience. "Luther, I said I'd help set up the golf tournament, and I will. But I'm warning all of you right now that I'm not going to have anything to do with this birthplace thing."

"'Course you are. Toolee's plannin' to restore your childhood bedroom exactly like it was when you were growin' up."

"Luther..."

"By the way, the auxiliary's puttin' together a Bobby Tom cookbook to sell in the gift shop, and they want to include a special celebrity section at the end. Evonne Emerly says for you to call Cher and Kevin Costner and some of those other Hollywood people you know for their meat loaf recipes and such."

Bobby Tom stared bleakly ahead at the empty stretch of highway. "I'm heading into a tunnel, Luther, and I'm gonna lose the signal. I'll have to call you later."

"Wait a minute, B.T. We haven't talked about—"

Bobby Tom disconnected the call. With a heavy sigh, he leaned back in his seat.

Gracie had been absorbing every word, and she was brimming with curiosity, but she didn't want to irritate him, so she bit her tongue.

Bobby Tom turned and looked at her. "Go ahead. Ask me how I managed to stay sane growing up around crazy people."

"He seemed quite...enthusiastic."

"He's a fool, is what he is. The mayor of Telarosa, Texas, is a certifiable fool. This whole Heavenfest thing has gotten completely out of hand."

"What exactly is Heavenfest?"

"It's a three day celebration they're planning to hold in October, part of a harebrained scheme to bring economic prosperity back to Telarosa by attracting tourists. They've spruced up the downtown, added a Western art gallery and a couple of restaurants. There's a decent golf course, a dude ranch, and a mediocre hotel, but that's about it."

"You forgot to mention the Bobby Tom Denton Birthplace."

"Don't remind me."

"It does seem rather desperate."

"It's insane. I think people in Telarosa have gotten so scared about holding on to their jobs it's scrambled their brains."

"Why are they calling it Heavenfest?"

"Heaven was the town's original name."

"Church groups seemed to have had a strong influence in founding some of the early Western towns."

Bobby Tom chuckled. "The cowboys named it Heaven because it had the best whore-houses between San Antone and Austin. It wasn't until the turn of the century that the town's more respectable citizens got the place renamed Telarosa."

"I see." Gracie had a dozen more questions, but she sensed that he wasn't in the mood for further conversation, and since she didn't want to irritate him, she fell silent. It occurred to her that being a celebrity had its drawbacks. If this morning was any indication, an awful lot of people seemed to want a piece of Bobby Tom Denton.

The phone buzzed. Bobby Tom sighed and rubbed his eyes. "Gracie, you mind answering that for me and telling whoever's calling that I'm on the golf course."

Gracie didn't believe in lying, but he looked so worn out that she did as he asked.

Seven hours later, Gracie found herself staring with dismay at the peeling red door of a seedy Memphis bar named Whoppers. "We drove hundreds of miles out of our way to come here?"

"It'll be an education for you, Miz Gracie. You ever been in a bar before?"

"Of course I've been in a bar." She saw no need to tell him that it had been attached to a respectable restaurant. This bar featured a neon beer sign with a broken *M* flickering listlessly in the dirty window, and a front sidewalk littered with trash. Since he had already kept her with him longer than she'd expected, she didn't want to antagonize him further, but neither could she abandon her responsibility.

"I'm afraid we don't have time for this."

"Gracie, sweetheart, you're gonna have a heart attack before you're forty if you don't learn to take life a little easier."

She gnawed nervously at her bottom lip. It was already Saturday evening, and with this detour, they had seven hundred miles left on the journey. She reminded herself that they didn't have to be in Telarosa until Monday morning, so, assuming Bobby Tom didn't try anything funny, there was plenty of time. Even so, she wasn't reassured.

She still couldn't believe he had decided to go to Telarosa by way of Memphis when, as she'd pointed out several times, the map in the glove compartment had shown that the most direct route stretched west through St. Louis. But he kept talking about how he couldn't let her live another day of her life without visiting the finest eating establishment east of the Mississippi. Until only moments ago, she had been envisioning something small, expensive, possibly French.

"You can't stay long," she said firmly. "We need to get several more hours of driving in before we stop for the night."

"Whatever you say, honey."

The raucous sounds of a country and western song assaulted her ears as he held the door open for her and she stepped into the smoky interior of Whoppers Bar and Grill. Square, wooden tables sat on a grubby orange and brown checkerboard floor. Beer signs, fly-specked calendar girl posters, and deer antlers provided ambience. As her eyes slid over the rough-looking crowd, she touched his arm.

"I know you want to get rid of me, but I'd appreciate it very much if you didn't do it here."

"You don't have a thing to worry about, sweetheart. As long as you don't irritate me."

While she was absorbing that worrisome piece of information, a heavily made-up brunette in a turquoise Spandex skirt and tight-fitting white tank top hurled herself into his arms.

"Bobby Tom!"

"Hey there, Trish."

He bent down to give her a kiss. The moment his lips brushed hers, she opened her mouth and sucked like a vacuum cleaner, drawing in his tongue as if it were a month's worth of carpet lint. He pulled away first and gave her that bone-melting grin he bestowed on every woman who came near him.

"I swear, Trish, you get more beautiful with every divorce. Shag here yet?"

"Over in the corner with A.J. and Wayne. I got hold of Pete, too, just like you asked me to when you called."

"Good girl. Hey there, guys."

Three men sitting around a rectangular table in the far corner of the bar shouted out noisy welcomes. Two of them were black, one white, and all three of them were built like Humvees. Gracie trailed after Bobby Tom as he went over to greet them.

The men shook hands and traded friendly insults laced with some incomprehensible sports talk before Bobby Tom remembered she was there.

"This is Gracie. She's my bodyguard."

All three men regarded her curiously. The one Bobby Tom had addressed as Shag, who seemed to have been a former teammate, pointed at her with his beer bottle.

"What do you need a bodyguard for, B.T.? Did you knock somebody else up?"

"Nothing like that. She's with the CIA."

"No kidding."

"I'm not with the CIA," Gracie protested. "And I'm not really his bodyguard. He just says that to—"

"Bobby Tom, is that you? B.T.'s here, girls!"

"Hey there, Ellie."

A blond sexpot in gold metallic jeans snaked her arms around his waist. Three more women materialized from the other side of the bar. The man called A.J. pulled another table over, and, without quite knowing how it happened, Gracie found herself occupying a chair between Bobby Tom and Ellie. She could see that Ellie resented the fact that she wasn't the one seated next to Bobby Tom, but when Gracie tried to change positions, she felt a strong hand clamping down on her thigh.

As the conversation swirled around her, Gracie tried to figure out what Bobby Tom was up to. Although every piece of evidence indicated the opposite, she had the sense that he wasn't enjoying himself nearly as much as he pretended to. Why had he driven so far out of his way to come here if he didn't want to be with these people? He must be even more reluctant than she'd imagined to return to his hometown, and he was deliberately prolonging the trip.

Someone thrust a beer bottle at her, and she was so distracted by a depressing picture of herself sitting gray-haired and stoop-shouldered on the front porch at Shady Acres that she took a sip before she remembered she didn't drink. Setting the bottle aside, she glanced at a clock advertising Jim Beam. In half an hour, she would tell Bobby Tom they had to leave.

The waitress appeared, and Bobby Tom insisted on ordering for her, telling her she hadn't lived until she'd tried Whoppers' bacon triple cheese jalapeño hamburger with a double order of jumbo deep-fried onion rings and a mountain of sour cream cole slaw. As he forced the cholesterol-laden food on her, she noticed that he ate and drank very little himself.

An hour passed. He signed autographs, paid for everything anyone ordered, and, unless she had misunderstood, loaned someone money for a jet ski. She ducked beneath the brim of his Stetson and whispered, "We have to go."

He turned to her and spoke softly, pleasantly. "One more word out of you, sweetheart, and I'm personally calling the taxi that's gonna deliver you to the airport." With that, he headed over to the pool table in the corner.

Another hour passed. If she hadn't been so worried about the time, she would have been thrilled by the novelty of being in a seedy bar with so many colorful people. Since she was too plain to be of romantic interest to Bobby Tom, the other women didn't regard her as a threat. She enjoyed a lengthy conversation with several of them including Ellie, a flight attendant, who turned out to be a fount of information on the male sex. And sex in general.

She noticed Bobby Tom giving her several covert glances, and she grew increasingly convinced that he planned to slip out when she wasn't looking. Although she very much needed to use the rest room, she was afraid to let him out of her sight, so she crossed her legs instead. By midnight, however, she knew she couldn't postpone the trip a moment longer. Waiting until he and Trish were deeply engrossed in a conversation at the bar, she made her way to the rest room.

The first flutters of panic settled in her stomach as she emerged a few minutes later and couldn't find him. Skimming her eyes over the crowd, she searched frantically for his gray Stetson, but didn't see it anywhere. She began making her way through the crowd to the bar, her stomach churning with anxiety. Just as she was about to acknowledge the fact that he'd gotten away, she spotted him standing with Trish in a shallow alcove next to the cigarette machine.

She had learned her lesson and had no intention of letting him get too far away from her again. Easing around the partition that divided the alcove from the front entryway, she wedged herself into a small space next to the wall phone. As she examined the telephone numbers and studied the graffiti written on the wall, she realized there was a slight echo effect. Although she hadn't intended to eavesdrop, she had no difficulty hearing that familiar Texas drawl.

"You're about the most understanding woman I ever met in my life, Trish."

"I'm glad you trust me enough to confide in me like this, B.T. I know how hard it is for a man like you to talk about your past."

"Some women I don't mind leading on, but you're a real sweet lady, Trish, and I couldn't do that to you, especially not when you're still vulnerable from your last divorce."

"I guess all of us have wondered why you never got married."

"Now you know, honey."

This was clearly a private conversation and Gracie knew she should find a more distant vantage point. Firmly repressing her curiosity, she began to step away only to pause as Trish spoke again.

"Nobody should have to grow up with a mother who's a—Well, a mother like that."

"You can say it, Trish. My mother was a hooker."

Gracie's eyes widened.

Trish's sultry voice was filled with sympathy. "You don't have to talk about it if you don't want to."

Bobby Tom sighed. "Sometimes it helps to talk about things. You might not understand this, but the worst wasn't having her bring men home at night or not even knowing who my father was. The worst was having her show up at my high school games all drunk with her

makeup smeared. She'd be wearing rhine-
stone earrings and pants so tight everybody
could see she didn't have anything on under
them. Nobody else wore high heels to Friday
night games, but my mother did. She was
the trashiest woman in Telarosa, Texas."

"What happened to her?"

"She's still there. Still smoking cigarettes,
drinking whiskey, and turning tricks whenever
the mood hits her. No matter how much
money I give her, it doesn't make any difference. Once a hooker, always a hooker, I guess.
But she's my mother, and I love her."

Gracie was touched by his loyalty. At the same
time, she felt a deep anger toward the woman
who had so dreadfully abused her maternal
responsibilities. Maybe his mother's unsavory lifestyle explained his reluctance to
return to Telarosa.

It had grown quiet in the alcove, and she
risked peeking around the corner only to wish
she'd stayed put. Trish had wrapped herself
around Bobby Tom like a fallen awning. As
the beautiful, dark-haired woman kissed him,
everything inside Gracie went soft and weak.
Despite the fact that she knew she was wishing
for the stars, she wanted to be the one pressed
against that strong, hard body. She wanted to
be the type of woman who felt free to soul kiss
Bobby Tom Denton.

She leaned against the wall and squeezed her
eyes shut, fighting a rush of yearning both
poignant and painful. Would a man ever kiss
her like that?

Not any man, her devil whispered. *A Texas playboy with a wicked reputation.*

She took a deep breath and told herself not to be foolish. There was no sense crying for the moon when good solid earth was the best she could ever hope for.

"Trish? Where is that bitch?"

Her reverie came to an abrupt end at the sound of a belligerent, drunken voice, and she saw a burly, dark-haired man descending on Bobby Tom and Trish from the entrance to the bar.

Trish's eyes widened with alarm. Bobby Tom quickly stepped forward, shielding her behind him. "Damn, Warren, I thought you died from rabies a long time ago."

Warren puffed up his barrel chest and swaggered forward. "If it isn't Mr. Pretty Boy. Sucked any cocks lately?"

Gracie gasped, but Bobby Tom just grinned. "I sure haven't, Warren, but if anybody asks me to, I'll send them right over to you first thing."

Warren obviously didn't appreciate Bobby Tom's sense of humor. With a menacing growl, he took a drunken lurch forward.

Trish drew her knuckles to her mouth. "Don't make him mad, B.T."

"Aw, honey, Warren won't get mad. He's too dumb to know when he's been insulted."

"I'm gonna take your head off, pretty boy."

"You're drunk, Warren!" Trish exclaimed. "Please go away."

"Shut up, you fucking whore!"

Bobby Tom sighed. "Now why'd you have to go and call your ex-wife something evil like that?" With a motion so fast that Gracie almost missed it, he drew back his fist and hit Warren in the jaw.

Trish's ex-husband sprawled to the floor with a howl of pain, and the crowd at the bar immediately circled the two men, temporarily shutting off Gracie's view. She elbowed her way between several of the women. By the time she got to the front, Warren had scrambled to his feet, one hand to his jaw.

Bobby Tom stood with his hands lightly splayed on his hips. "I sure wish you were sober, Warren, so we could make this more interesting."

"*I'm* sober, Denton." A surly Neanderthal who could have been Warren's womb mate lumbered forward. "What happened against the Raiders last year, pussy? You played like shit. Were you having your period?"

Bobby Tom looked as delighted as if someone had just given him a Christmas present. "Now this is getting interesting."

To Gracie's relief, Bobby Tom's friend Shag took a step into the center of the circle, pushing up his sleeves at the same time. "Two against one, B.T. I don't like the odds."

Bobby Tom waved him away. "No need to get your hair messed up, Shag. These boys are looking for a little exercise, and so am I."

The Neanderthal swung. Bobby Tom's reflexes didn't seem to have been affected by his bad knee. He ducked and caught his

71

opponent in the ribs with his fist. The man doubled over, just as Warren pitched forward and drove his shoulder into Bobby Tom's side.

Bobby Tom staggered, righted himself, and delivered a hard punch to the abdomen that sent Trish's ex to the floor. He showed no inclination to get back up.

The Neanderthal hadn't had as much to drink, so he lasted a little longer. He even managed to connect with a few punches, but in the end he couldn't overcome Bobby Tom's lethal quickness. Finally he'd had enough. Bleeding from the nose and muttering under his breath, he staggered toward the exit.

Bobby Tom's forehead crumpled in disappointment. He looked around at the crowd, a vaguely wistful expression on his face, but no other challengers stepped forward. He picked up a cocktail napkin, pressed it to the small cut at the side of his mouth, and leaned down to murmur something in Warren's ear. The man turned even paler, leading Gracie to conclude that Trish wouldn't be having any more trouble with her ex-husband. After he'd set Warren straight, Bobby Tom looped his arm around Trish and led her over to the jukebox.

Gracie breathed a sigh of relief. At least she wouldn't have to phone Willow with the news that she'd lost their star in a barroom brawl.

Two hours later, she and Bobby Tom stood at the desk of a luxury hotel located twenty minutes away.

"I hope you know I'm not used to turning in this early," he grumbled.

"It's two o'clock in the morning." Gracie had lived most of her life going to bed at ten so she could get up at five, and she was light-headed with weariness.

"That's what I'm telling you. It's still early." He finished registering for the suite he had requested, and, waving away the bellman, slipped the strap of his bag over his shoulder while he picked up the laptop computer he'd set on the desk. "See you in the morning, Gracie." He set off toward the elevators.

The desk clerk looked at her expectantly. "May I help you?"

Blushing to the roots of her hair, she stammered, "I'm, uh, with him."

She picked up her own suitcase and hurried after him, feeling like a cocker spaniel trailing its master. She slid inside the elevator just as the door was gliding shut.

He regarded her suspiciously. "You registered already?"

"Since you—uh—requested a suite, I thought I'd sleep on the couch."

"You thought wrong."

"I promise that you won't even notice I'm there."

"Get your own room, Miz Gracie." He spoke softly, but the veiled threat in his eyes discomposed her.

"You know I can't do that. The minute I leave you alone, you'll drive off without me."

"You don't know that for a fact." The doors

slid open and he stepped out into the carpeted hallway.

She hurried after him. "I won't bother you."

He looked at the door numbers. "Gracie, pardon me for saying this, but you're getting to be a real pain in the butt."

"I know that, and I apologize."

A smile flickered across his face and disappeared as he stopped in front of the door at the end of the hallway and slid the magnetic key into the lock. It blinked green, and he pushed on the handle. Before he stepped inside, he leaned down and brushed a swift kiss over her lips. "It's been nice knowing you."

Dazed, she watched the door shut in her face. Her lips tingled. She pressed her fingertips to them, wishing she could seal his kiss there forever.

The seconds ticked by. Her pleasure in the kiss faded, and her shoulders slumped. He was going to drive off. Tonight, tomorrow morning—She had no idea when, but she knew he intended to leave without her, just as she knew she couldn't let that happen.

Exhausted, she rested her suitcase on the carpet, sat down, and propped her back against the door. She would just have to spend the night here. Bending her knees, she folded her arms and rested her cheek on top. If only he'd given her a real kiss...Her eyes drifted shut.

With a soft exclamation, she fell backward as the door opened behind her. Scrambling to her feet, she turned to face Bobby Tom. Since he didn't seem particularly surprised to see her, she suspected he had been spying through the peephole, waiting for her to walk away.

"What do you think you're doing?" he asked with exaggerated patience.

"I'm trying to sleep."

"You are *not* spending the night outside my door."

"If anybody sees me, they'll just think I'm one of your groupies."

"They'll think you're a *crazy person* is what they'll think!"

For someone who was so amiable with everyone else, he had certainly gotten prickly with her. She knew she sometimes did that to people.

"If you give me your word of honor that you won't drive off without me tomorrow, I'll get my own room."

"Gracie, I don't even know what I'll be doing an hour from now, let alone tomorrow."

"Then I'm afraid I'll have to stay here."

He rubbed his chin with his thumb, a gesture that she'd already figured out meant he had made up his mind about something but wanted it to look as if he were still mulling things over.

"Tell you what. It's too early to turn in. You can keep me entertained until bedtime."

Even as she nodded her agreement, she wondered what constituted entertainment in his mind.

He set her suitcase inside the suite and shut the door. As she entered the suite, she took in the spacious living room, which was decorated in peach and green. "This is beautiful."

He looked around as if he were seeing it all for the first time. "I guess it is pretty nice. I hadn't noticed."

How could he not notice something so wonderful? A cluster of deep-seated couches and inviting chairs occupied the center of the room. A rectangular parquet table sat before a wall of windows, and a silk flower arrangement exploded with color on a bombé chest. She gazed at it all with delight.

"How could you not notice something like this?"

"I've spent so much of my life in hotels I guess I've gotten kind of numb."

She barely heard him as she rushed over to the windows and gazed out at the dark water and twinkling lights. "That's the Mississippi River out there."

"Uh-huh." He took off his Stetson and went into the bedroom.

Wonder filled her as she tried to absorb the fact that she was staying in a hotel room that overlooked such a marvelous sight. She moved around the living area, testing the comfort of the sofa and wing chairs, opening the desk drawers to touch the stationery, peering into the towering armoire that held the television. Her eyes automatically scanned the movie schedule for the week and stopped on something called *Red Hot Cheerleaders*.

The words leaped out at her. On the few occasions she had stayed in hotels, she had been tempted to view one of these adult movies, but the idea of having it show up on her bill where anybody could see it had always discouraged her.

"You want to watch something?"

Her head shot up as Bobby Tom appeared behind her. She dropped the movie schedule. "Oh, no. It's too late. Much too late. We should really—We need to get up early and—"

"Gracie, were you looking at the dirty movie schedule?"

"Dirty movies? Me?"

"You were. That's exactly what you were doing. I'll bet you never saw a dirty movie in your life."

"Of course I have. Lots of them."

"Name a few."

"Well, *Indecent Proposal* was quite erotic."

"*Indecent Proposal*? Is that your idea of a dirty movie?"

"It is in New Grundy."

He grinned and glanced down at the TV schedule. "*Pit Stop for Passion* just started. You want to take a look at it?"

Her sense of propriety barely won out over her curiosity. "I don't approve of that sort of thing."

"I didn't ask if you approved. I asked if you wanted to take a look."

She hesitated a moment too long. "Absolutely not."

He laughed, picked up the remote, and turned on the set. "Settle back on the sofa, Miss Gracie. I wouldn't miss this for the world."

He was already pushing the buttons that accessed the adult movie. She did her best to appear reluctant and primly crossed her hands in her lap. "Perhaps just this one time. I've always enjoyed movies about auto racing."

Bobby Tom laughed so hard he nearly dropped the remote. He continued to laugh as the screen filled with four naked, writhing bodies.

She could feel her cheeks begin to flame. "Oh, my."

Bobby Tom chuckled and sat down next to her. "Let me know if you have any trouble figuring out the plot. I'm pretty sure I saw this one before."

There wasn't any plot; she realized that in the first few minutes. Just lots of naked bodies carousing on top of a hot red sports car.

Bobby Tom pointed toward the screen. "See that brunette with the tool belt strapped around her waist. She's the head mechanic. The other woman's her assistant."

"Ah."

"And that guy with the real big—"

"Yes," Gracie said swiftly. "The one on the right."

"No, honey. Not that one. I'm talking about the one with the real big *hands*."

"Oh."

"Anyway, he owns the car. He and his buddy have brought it in for the girls to give it a valve job."

"A valve job?"

"It also has a leaky hose that needs attention."

"I see."

"They're worried about the ball joints."

"Uhm."

"And the dipstick's bent."

Gracie whirled around and saw that his chest was shaking. "You're making this up!"

He gave a hoot of laughter and wiped his eyes.

She raised her chin. "I could follow the plot very well by myself if you'd stop talking."

"Yes, ma'am."

Gracie turned back to the screen and swallowed hard as the man with the big hands dipped one of them into an open can of 10W-40 and trickled it over the head mechanic's bare breast. Her nipple puckered and beaded while droplets of oil drizzled down the side of the snowy mound. Gracie's own nipples tightened in response.

The delicious foreplay continued, and Gracie couldn't tear her eyes from the screen, even though she was painfully aware that she wasn't alone. She licked her dry lips. Her heart pounded. She had never been so embarrassed or so aroused in her life, and she wanted to do every single thing she was seeing on the screen with the man sitting next to her.

The actor with the big hands began to play with the woman's tool belt. His mouth followed the track of his fingers lower and lower. Moisture gathered between Gracie's breasts as his tongue settled into a cranny just to the left of her socket set.

She pressed her thighs together and squirmed. Bobby Tom shifted his weight. She glanced at him out of the corner of her eyes and saw to her dismay that he was watching her instead of the screen. And he was no longer laughing.

"I have some work to do," he said abruptly. "Turn it off whenever you want." Snatching up his laptop computer, he stalked into the bedroom.

Gracie stared after him in bewilderment. Why had he gotten so grouchy all of a sudden? And then her gaze shot back to the screen.

Oh, my!

Bobby Tom stood in the darkened bedroom and stared blindly out the windows. In the background he could hear breathy moans coming from the television. *Jesus.* For the past six months he hadn't been able to summon up the slightest bit of interest in making love with any of the beautiful women who dangled themselves in front of him like game trophies, but now Gracie Snow, with her skinny body, ugly clothes, the worst hairdo he'd ever seen on a female, and a bossy manner that set his teeth on edge, had given him a hard-on.

He rested his knuckles against the window frame. If it weren't so ludicrous, he'd laugh. That movie wasn't even close to hard-core pornography, but five minutes into it, she'd gotten so turned on that a bomb could have exploded in there and she wouldn't have noticed.

For a moment when he was watching her,

he'd actually considered taking advantage of what she'd been all too ready to offer, and that was the stupidest thing of all. He was Bobby Tom Denton, for chrissake. He might be retired, but that didn't mean he'd sunk so low he had to get it on with a charity case like Gracie Snow.

Turning his back to the window, he walked over to the desk, hooked the modem from his laptop computer into the telephone line, and sat down. But his hands fell still before he typed in the commands to access his electronic mail. He wasn't in the mood to work on any of his business deals tonight.

He kept seeing the expression on Gracie's face when she'd spotted the Mississippi River. How long had it been since he'd felt that kind of enthusiasm? All day, Gracie had pointed out things he'd ceased to notice years ago: a cloud formation, a truck driver who looked like Willie Nelson, a child waving at them through the rear window of the family van. When had he lost touch with ordinary pleasures?

He glanced down at his keyboard and remembered how much he used to enjoy wheeling and dealing. At first he'd played around in the stock market, but then he'd bought into a small sporting goods company. After that, he'd invested in a radio station followed by an athletic sneaker company. He'd made mistakes along the way, but he'd also made a lot of money. Now he couldn't seem to remember what the point of it all had been.

He'd thought that making a movie might be a good way to distract himself, but with shooting about to begin, he couldn't work up much enthusiasm for that idea either.

He rubbed his eyes with his thumb and forefinger. Tonight he'd promised Shag to help launch his new restaurant. He'd lent Ellie money and told A.J. he'd let his nephew interview him for his high school newspaper. To his way of thinking, a person who'd been star-kissed from the moment he was born didn't have the right to say no, but sometimes he felt as if he was slowly suffocating from all the demands people made on him.

Now he had to go to Telarosa to make another payment on the debt he owed the small town that had nurtured him, and he'd gotten cold feet. Despite the fact that he was the one who'd insisted the filming take place there, he wasn't ready to face all of them. He knew he was a has-been, but they wouldn't have figured it out yet, and they were still going to want a piece of him.

His presence would stir things up, as it always did, and not everybody would welcome him with open arms. He'd had a nasty confrontation with Way Sawyer a few months back over Sawyer's plan to move Rosatech, the electronics firm that supplied Telarosa with its economic lifeblood. The man was ruthless, and Bobby Tom didn't look forward to seeing him again. He'd also have to deal with Jimbo Thackery, the town's new chief of police and Bobby Tom's enemy from grade school days.

Worst of all, there would be a whole flock of women who had no idea that his sex drive had just about disappeared along with his football career, and, no matter what, he had to make certain they stayed ignorant.

He stared blindly down at the keyboard. What was he going to do with the rest of his life? He'd lived with glory for so long that he had no idea how to live without it. From childhood he'd always been the best: All-State, All-American, All-Pro. But he wasn't the best any longer. Successful men weren't supposed to face this kind of crisis until they retired in their sixties. But he'd retired at thirty-three, and he had no idea who he was any longer. He knew how to be a great wide receiver, he knew how to be the Most Valuable Player, but he had no idea how to be an ordinary human being.

A particularly prolonged female moan coming from the television interrupted his thoughts, and he frowned as he remembered he wasn't alone. Genuine amusement had become increasingly rare in his life, which was why he'd kept Gracie Snow around for the day, but as he recalled his body's reaction to her arousal, he no longer felt like laughing. Getting turned on by a charity case like Gracie was—in a way he didn't want to examine too closely—somehow the final indignity, a tangible symbol of how far he'd come down in the world. Not that she wasn't a real nice lady, but she definitely wasn't Bobby Tom Denton material.

Right then he made up his mind. He had

enough problems in his life, and he didn't need any more. First thing tomorrow, he was getting rid of her.

4

Church bells rang outside the window as Gracie crossed to the bedroom door and tapped gently. "Bobby Tom, breakfast is here."

Nothing.

"Bobby Tom?"

"You're real," he groaned. "I was hoping you were only a bad dream."

"I ordered breakfast from room service, and it's here."

"Go away."

"It's seven o'clock. We have a twelve-hour drive ahead of us. We really need to get on the road."

"This room has a balcony, sweetheart. If you don't leave me alone, I'm throwing you right over the top of it."

She retreated from his bedroom door and walked to the table, where she nibbled at a blueberry pancake, but she was too tired to eat. All night long, she'd awakened at the slightest noise, certain Bobby Tom would slip out while she slept.

At eight o'clock, after she'd called Willow to report on her questionable progress, she tried again to rouse him. "Bobby Tom, are you finished sleeping yet because we really must leave?"

Nothing.

She opened the door gingerly and her mouth went dry as she saw him sprawled naked on his stomach with the sheet twisted around his hips. His legs were splayed, one of them bent. Despite the angry scars behind his right knee, they were strong and beautiful. The skin looked bronzed against the stark white sheet and the golden hair on his calves shimmered in the morning light that crept through a slit in the drapes. One foot was buried in the blanket at the bottom of the bed; the other was long and narrow with a high, well-defined arch. Her eyes lingered over the ugly red puckered scars on his right knee, then rose to his thighs and the sheet that wound round his hips. If only that sheet were three inches higher....

She was shocked by the force of her desire to see that most private part of him. All the nude male bodies she had seen in her lifetime were old. Would Bobby Tom look like those men in the movie last night? She shivered.

He rolled over, taking the sheet with him. His hair was thick and rumpled, with a trace of curl at the temples. The skin on his cheek held a crease from the pillow.

"Bobby Tom," she said softly.

One eye opened a fraction of an inch, and his voice was gravelly from sleep. "Get naked or get out."

She walked determinedly over to the windows

and pulled the cord on the draperies. "Someone certainly is grouchy this morning."

He groaned as light flooded the room. "Gracie, your life is in serious jeopardy."

"Would you like me to turn on the shower for you?"

"You gonna scrub my back, too?"

"I hardly think that's necessary."

"I'm trying to be polite about this, but you don't seem to be catching on." He sat up, fumbled for his wallet on the bedside table, and withdrew several bills. "Cab fare to the airport is on me," he said as he held them out.

"Shower first, and then we'll talk about it." She hastily backed out of the room.

An hour and a half later, he was still trying to get rid of her. She hurried down the sidewalk to the Memphis health club, a white paper carry-out bag containing a large cup of freshly squeezed orange juice clenched in her hand. First she hadn't been able to get him out of bed, then he'd told her he couldn't even think about taking off until he'd had his morning workout. They'd no sooner entered the lobby of the suburban health club than he'd shoved some money in her hand and asked her to go to the restaurant around the corner and pick up some orange juice for him while he changed into his gym clothes.

As he'd disappeared into the locker room, his eyes had been guileless and his smile innocent, which made her certain he planned to ditch her while she was gone. She grew absolutely convinced of it when she saw he'd given her two hundred dollars for orange juice. As a result, she'd been forced to take drastic action.

Not surprisingly, the restaurant was several blocks farther away than he had led her to believe, and she'd hurried through the transaction as fast as she could. As she returned to the health club, she bypassed the entrance, heading instead for the parking lot in the back.

The Thunderbird sat in the shade with the hood up and Bobby Tom peering under it. She was out of breath as she rushed toward him. "Finished with your workout already?"

His head shot up so abruptly he banged it on the hood, knocking his Stetson sideways. He cursed softly and straightened his hat. "My back was a little stiff, so I decided to wait until tonight."

His back looked perfectly fine to her, but she refrained from pointing that out, just as she withheld comment on the fact that he had obviously planned to drive away while she was gone. "Is there something wrong with the car?"

"It won't start."

"Let me look. I know a little bit about engines."

He stared at her in disbelief. "You?"

Ignoring him, she set the damp sack on the fender, peered under the hood, and lifted up the distributor cap. "My goodness, you seem to have lost your rotor. Let me see. I just might—" She opened her purse. "Yes. I have one right here."

She handed over the Thunderbird's small rotor, along with the two screws that held on the distributor cap and her Swiss Army knife so he could refasten them. All of it had been neatly wrapped in the plastic bag she had taken from the hotel room for just this sort of emergency.

Bobby Tom stared down at it as if he couldn't believe what he was seeing.

"Make sure it's firmly seated," she said helpfully. "Otherwise, it could give you some problems." Without waiting for a response, she retrieved the orange juice, hurried around to the passenger side of the car, and slid into her seat, where she busied herself studying the map.

Much too soon, the car shuddered as he slammed the hood. She heard his boots make sharp, angry clicks on the asphalt. He rested his hand on the window frame next to her and she saw that his knuckles were white. When he finally spoke, his voice was very soft and very angry.

"Nobody messes with my T-bird."

She took a small nibble from her bottom lip. "I'm sorry, Bobby Tom. I know you love this car, and I don't blame you for being angry. It's a wonderful car. Really. That's why I have to be honest and tell you that I have the ability to do serious damage to it if you try any more monkey business."

His eyebrows shot up and he stared at her in disbelief. "Are you threatening my car?"

"I'm afraid I am," she said apologetically.

"Mr. Walter Karne, God rest his sweet soul, was at Shady Acres for almost eight years before he died. Until his retirement, he'd owned an auto repair shop in Columbus, and I learned quite a bit about engines from him, including how to disable them. You see, we had a problem with a particularly officious social worker who visited Shady Acres several times a month. He kept upsetting the residents."

"So you and Mr. Karne retaliated by sabotaging his car."

"Unfortunately, Mr. Karne was quite arthritic, which meant that I had to do the actual work."

"And now you plan to use your special expertise to blackmail me."

"It goes without saying the idea disturbs me a great deal. On other hand, I have a responsibility to Windmill Studios."

Bobby Tom was beginning to look wild around the eyes. "Gracie, the only reason I don't strangle you to death right this minute is because I know, as soon as the jury heard my story, they'd let me off, and then those sharks at the networks would turn the whole thing into a TV movie."

"I have a job to do," she said softly. "You really must let me do it."

"Sorry, sweetheart. The two of us have reached the end of the line."

Before she could stop him, he'd pulled the door open, scooped her up, and set her down in the parking lot. She gave a hiss of alarm. "Let's talk about this!"

Ignoring her, he made his way to the rear of the car, where he pulled her suitcase from the trunk.

She rushed to his side. "We're both reasonable people. I'm sure we can work out a compromise. I'm sure we—"

"I'm sure we can't. They'll call a cab for you inside." He dropped her suitcase on the pavement, climbed back into the Thunderbird, and started the car with a roar.

Without giving herself time to think, she threw herself to the pavement in front of the tires and squeezed her eyes shut.

Long, tension-laden seconds ticked by. The heat of the asphalt penetrated her one-size-fits-all mustard brown wrap dress. The smell of exhaust made her head spin. She felt his shadow fall over her.

"In the interest of saving your life, the two of us are going to make a deal."

She eased her eyes open. "What sort of deal?"

"I'll stop trying to ditch you—"

"That's fair."

"—if you do what I say for the rest of the trip."

She thought it over as she rose to her feet. "I don't believe that's going to work," she said carefully. "In case no one has ever pointed it out to you, you're not always reasonable."

Beneath the brim of his Stetson, his eyes had narrowed. "Take it or leave it, Gracie. If you want to be a passenger in this car, you're going to have to set your bossy ways aside and do what you're told."

When he put it like that, she didn't have much choice, and she decided to give in graciously. "Very well."

He returned her suitcase to the trunk. She resettled in the passenger seat. When he got back in, he gave the ignition key an angry twist.

She glanced at her watch and then the map she had been perusing earlier. "Just one thing before we start. You might not have realized it, but it's almost ten, and you have to be on the set by eight o'clock tomorrow morning. We have about seven hundred miles to travel, and it looks as if the shortest route—"

Bobby Tom tore the map from her hand, balled it in his fist, and threw it out of the car. Minutes later they were back on the freeway.

Unfortunately, they were heading east.

By Tuesday night, Gracie had to acknowledge the fact that she was a failure. As she stared at the wipers sweeping half-moons across the Thunderbird's windshield and listened to the rain spattering on the top above her, she mulled over the past few days. Despite making it as far as Dallas, she hadn't been able to deliver Bobby Tom to Telarosa on time.

Droplets of water glistened on the hood of the car from the passing headlights. She tried not to dwell on Willow's angry phone calls and, instead, attempted to look at the positive side of the situation. In the past few days, she'd seen more of the country than she'd ever imagined, and she'd met the most interesting people: country and western singers, aerobics instructors, lots of football players, and a very nice transvestite who'd shown her some clever ways to tie a scarf.

Best of all, Bobby Tom hadn't tried to shake her off. She still wasn't entirely certain why he hadn't ditched her in Memphis, but sometimes she had the eerie sense he didn't want to be alone. With the exception of that one unfortunate incident when he'd stopped the car on a bridge, dragged her to the side, and threatened to toss her over, they'd gotten along very well. Even so, tonight she found herself feeling decidedly awkward.

"You comfortable over there, Gracie?"

She kept her eyes on the wiper blades. "I'm fine, Bobby Tom. Thank you for asking."

"You look like you're sort of squished against the door handle. This isn't really a three passenger car. You sure you don't want me to take you back to the hotel?"

"I'm positive."

"Bobby Tom, sweetie, is she plannin' to stay with us *all* night?" Cheryl Lynn Howell, his date for the evening, sounded petulant as she snuggled into his shoulder.

"She's kind of hard to shake, honey. Why don't you just pretend she's not here?"

"That's hard to do when you keep talking to her. I swear, Bobby Tom, you talked more to her this evening than you did to me."

"I'm sure that's not true, honey. She didn't even sit with us at the restaurant."

"She sat at the next table and you kept

turning around to ask her questions. Besides, I don't know what you need a bodyguard for."

"There are a lot of dangerous people in the world."

"That may be, but you're stronger than she is."

"She's a better shot. Gracie's pure magic with an Uzi."

Gracie stifled a smile. He was shameless, but incredibly inventive. She shifted her weight a bit closer to the center of the seat. The lack of interior room in the antique Thunderbird hadn't been as much of a problem as she'd feared. Although she and Cheryl Lynn were supposed to be sharing the space, the former beauty queen was practically sitting on Bobby Tom's lap. She had somehow managed to straddle the gearbox and still look graceful.

Gracie glanced at Cheryl Lynn's softly draped off-the-shoulder coral lace dress with envy. Her own voluminous black wraparound skirt and red-and-white—striped knit top made her look like a barber's pole.

Cheryl settled her hand over Bobby Tom's thigh. "Explain to me again exactly who's after you. I thought you only had problems with paternity suits, not the CIA."

"Some of those paternity suits can get kinda nasty. In this case, the young lady in question didn't mention her father's close connection with organized crime until it was too late. Isn't that so, Gracie?"

Gracie pretended not to hear. Although

she was secretly entranced with the image of herself as an Uzi-toting CIA agent, she knew it probably wasn't good for his character to encourage him in falsehoods.

Once again Bobby Tom glanced at her over the top of Cheryl Lynn's fluffy blond curls. "How was that spaghetti you ordered?"

"It was excellent."

"I'm not much for the green stuff they poured over it."

"Are you referring to the pesto?"

"Whatever. I like a nice meat sauce."

"Of course you do. With a double rack of greasy ribs on the side, I'll bet."

"You're making my mouth water just thinking about it."

Cheryl Lynn lifted her head from his shoulder. "You're doin' it again, B.T."

"Doing what, sweetheart?"

"Talkin' to her."

"Oh, I don't think so, darlin'. Not when I've got you on my mind."

Grace gave a small cough, letting Bobby Tom know that Miss Lone Star Cowgirl Roundup Queen might buy his particular line of horse pucky, but she saw right through him.

Although the evening had been somewhat embarrassing, it had also been enlightening. It wasn't every day that a mere mortal like herself got to observe pure genius at work. She had never imagined any man could be such a skillful manipulator of women. Bobby Tom was eternally agreeable, perpetually charming, incessantly indulgent. He was so relentlessly accommodating that none of the women who orbited around him seemed to realize he only did exactly as he pleased.

They pulled to a stop in front of a row of mission style condominiums. Cheryl Lynn leaned closer and whispered something in Bobby Tom's ear.

He scratched the side of his neck. "I don't know, honey. That might be kind of embarrassing with Gracie lookin' on, but if you don't mind, I guess it's all right with me."

This was too much, even for Cheryl Lynn, and the beauty queen reluctantly agreed that they should call it a night. Gracie watched as he popped her umbrella and held it over her head while he escorted her to the door. In her opinion, Bobby Tom was showing good sense in dumping Cheryl Lynn, although she couldn't imagine why he'd agreed to go out with her in the first place. The beauty queen was opinionated, self-centered, and considerably less intelligent than the source of those crab legs she'd ordered for dinner. Even so, Bobby Tom had treated her as if she were a paragon of womanhood. He was the perfect gentleman with everybody but her.

At the doorway to the condo, she saw that Cheryl Lynn had wound herself around him like a snake around the Tree of Knowledge. Not that he seemed to mind. She pushed her hips against his as if they'd been there before. Although Gracie considered herself a mild-tempered person, quick to make allowances and slow to anger, the longer he took with his good-night kiss, the more she could feel her indignation growing. Did he have to do major oral surgery on every woman he met? He had so many female scalps hanging from his belt he could walk around without his pants and nobody would know he was naked. Instead of wasting time coming up with a new diet pill, the pharmaceutical companies in this country would better serve the female population by producing an antidote to Bobby Tom Denton.

Her anger simmered as she watched Miss Bluebonnet Rodeo Saddle Queen attempt to climb his legs, and by the time he returned to the car, she had worked herself into a stew. "We're going right to the emergency room so you can get a tetanus shot!" she snapped.

Bobby Tom lifted one eyebrow. "I take it you didn't like Cheryl Lynn."

"She spent more time looking around to make sure everybody noticed who she was with than she did looking at you. And she didn't have to order the most expensive items on the menu just because you're rich." Gracie was building up a good head of steam as she combined four days worth of frustration into one outburst. "You didn't even like her; that's what made it even more disgusting. You could not stand that woman, Bobby Tom Denton, and don't you try to deny it because I can see right through you. I've been able to see through you from the beginning. You've got more lines than a fisherman. All that malarkey about the CIA and Uzis. And I'll tell you another thing. I, for one, don't happen to believe a word about these alleged paternity suits."

He looked slightly amazed. "You don't."

"No, I do not. You're full of balderdash!"

"Balderdash?" The corner of his mouth kicked up. "You're in Texas now, honey. Down here we just call it plain old—"

"I know what you call it!"

"You sure are in a grouchy mood tonight. I'll tell you what. Just to cheer you up, how about if I let you get me out of bed at six o'clock tomorrow morning? We'll drive straight to Telarosa. We should be there for lunch."

She stared at him. "You're kidding."

"I'm not such a sorry excuse for a human being that I'd kid you about something so near and dear to your heart."

"You promise we'll go straight there? No side trips to see an ostrich ranch or visit your first grade teacher?"

"I said we would, didn't I?"

Her crankiness evaporated. "Yes. All right. Yes, that sounds wonderful."

She settled back in the seat certain of one thing. If they made it to Telarosa tomorrow, it would be because Bobby Tom had decided he wanted to be there, not because of what she wanted.

He turned back to her. "Just out of curiosity, how come you don't believe me about those paternity suits? They're pretty much a matter of public record."

She had spoken impulsively, but as she thought over what she had said, she became convinced that this was simply another example of Bobby Tom stretching the truth. "I can imagine you doing many nefarious things, especially involving women, but I can't imagine you abandoning your own child."

He glanced over at her and the corners of his mouth formed an almost imperceptible smile. It broadened as he returned his attention to the highway.

"Well?" She regarded him curiously.

"You really want to know?"

"If it's the truth instead of one of those tall tales you spin for the rest of the world."

He tipped the brim of his Stetson forward a fraction of an inch. "A long time ago a lady friend slapped me with a paternity suit. Even though I was pretty certain the baby wasn't mine, I had all the blood work done. Sure enough, her old boyfriend was the guilty party, but since he was a born-again sonovabitch, I decided to help her out a little."

"You gave her money." Gracie had watched Bobby Tom in action long enough to understand how he worked.

"Why should an innocent kid suffer just because his old man is a jerk?" He shrugged. "After that, word got out that I was an easy mark."

"And more paternity suits came along?"

He nodded.

"Let me make a guess. Instead of fighting them, you made settlements."

"Just a couple of small trust funds to take care of essentials," he replied defensively.

"Hell, I've got more money than I can spend, and they all signed papers admitting I wasn't the father. What's the harm?"

"No harm, I suppose. But it's not really fair. You shouldn't have to pick up the bill for other people's mistakes."

"Neither should little kids."

She wondered if he was thinking of the tragedy of his own childhood, but his expression was unreadable, so she couldn't tell.

He pushed the buttons of his car phone and propped the receiver to his ear. "Bruno, I didn't wake you up, did I? That's good. Say, I don't have Steve Cray's number. You mind giving him a call and telling him to fly the Baron down to Telarosa tomorrow." He pulled into the left lane. "All right. Yeah, I thought I'd do some flying when I'm not working. Thanks, Bruno."

He replaced the phone and began to hum "Luckenbach, Texas."

Gracie struggled to speak evenly. "The Baron?"

"A classy little turbo-charged twin. I keep it at an airstrip 'bout half an hour from my house in Chicago."

"You're telling me that you fly?"

"I didn't mention that to you?"

"No," she said unsteadily. "You didn't."

He scratched the side of his head. "Shoot, I must have had my pilot's license—let's see...I guess it's going on nine years now."

She clenched her teeth. "You own your own plane."

"Sweet little thing."

"And a pilot's license?"

"Sure do."

"Then why did we have to *drive* to Telarosa?"

He looked wounded. "I just had it in my mind, is all."

She dropped her head into her hands and tried to conjure up a picture of him staked out naked in the desert with vultures eating his maggoty flesh and ants crawling in his eye sockets. Unfortunately, she couldn't make the image gruesome enough. Once again, he had done exactly what he wanted without regard for anyone else.

"Those women don't know how lucky they are," she muttered.

"What women are you talking about?"

"All of them who were fortunate enough to *fail* your football quiz."

He chuckled, lit up a cigar, and launched into the chorus of "Luckenbach, Texas."

They headed southwest out of Dallas, driving through rolling pastureland dotted with grazing cattle and shady pecan orchards. As the land grew hillier and rockier, she began to see frequent signs for dude ranches as well as glimpsing some of the local wildlife: quail, jackrabbits, and wild turkey. Telarosa, Bobby Tom informed her, sat on the fringes of the Texas Hill Country, a hundred miles from nowhere. Because of its relative isolation, it had missed the prosperity of towns like Kerrville and Fredericksburg.

In her conversation with Willow that morning, her employer had ordered her to bring Bobby Tom directly to the Lanier spread, a small horse ranch located several miles east of the city limits, where they would be doing much of the shooting, so Gracie wouldn't actually see the town until that evening. Since he seemed to know the location Willow had described, Gracie refrained from reading the directions aloud.

They turned off the winding highway onto a narrow asphalt road. "Gracie, this movie we're making...Maybe you'd better tell me a little something about it."

"Like what?" She wanted to look her best when they got there, and she reached into her purse for a comb. She had put on her navy suit that morning so she'd look professional.

"Well, the plot for one thing."

Gracie's hands stilled. "Are you telling me you didn't read the script?"

"I never got around to it."

She closed her purse and studied him. Why would a seemingly intelligent man like Bobby Tom accept a part in a movie without having read the script? Was he that undisciplined? She knew he wasn't very enthusiastic about the project, but even so, she would have thought he'd take some interest. There must be a reason, but what could it possibly—

At that moment she was overcome by a horrible suspicion, one that made her feel almost ill. Impulsively, she reached out and curled her hand around his upper arm.

"You can't read, can you, Bobby Tom?"

His head shot around, eyes flashing with indignation. "Of course I can read. I did graduate from a major university, you know."

Gracie understood that colleges gave their star football players a great deal of latitude when it came to academics, and she was still suspicious. "In what field of study?"

"Playground management."

"I knew it!" Her heart filled with sympathy. "You don't have to lie to me. You know you can trust me not to tell anyone. We can work on improving your reading together. No one would ever have to know that—" She broke off as she saw the gleam in his eyes. Belatedly, she remembered his laptop computer, and she gritted her teeth. "You're teasing me."

He grinned. "Sweetheart, you've got to stop stereotyping people. Just because I was a football player doesn't mean I didn't learn the alphabet. I managed to struggle through U.T. with a respectable grade point average and earn myself a degree in economics. Although I'm usually too embarrassed to admit it, I happened to be an NCAA Top Six scholar athlete."

"Why didn't you say so in the first place?"

"You're the one who decided I couldn't read."

"What else was I supposed to think? No one in his right mind would sign a movie contract without reading the script first. Even I read the script, and I'm not even in it."

"It's an action adventure movie, right? I'm

supposed to be the good guy, which means there'll also be a bad guy, a beautiful woman, and a lot of car chases. Now that we don't have the Russians to kick around, the bad guy'll either be a terrorist or a drug runner."

"A Mexican drug lord."

He gave her an I-told-you-so nod. "There'll be a bunch of fights, all kinds of blood, gore, and cussing, most of it gratuitous, but still protected by the First Amendment. I'll be running around looking manly, and the heroine, movies being what they are, will prob'ly be running around naked and screaming. Am I pretty much on target so far?"

He was right on target, but she didn't want to encourage his slipshod study habits by saying so. "You're missing the point. You should have read the script so you could understand the character you're playing."

"Gracie, sweetheart, I'm not an actor. I wouldn't have the slightest idea how to be anybody but myself."

"Well, in this case, you're going to be a drunken ex-football player named Jed Slade."

"Nobody's named Jed Slade."

"You are, and you're living on a run down Texas horse ranch you bought from the brother of the heroine, who's a woman named Samantha Murdock. I presume you know that Natalie Brooks is playing the part of Samantha. The people at Windmill feel quite lucky to have signed her." As Bobby Tom nodded, she went on. "You don't know who Samantha is, though, when she picks you up in a bar and seduces you."

"She seduces me?"

"Just like in real life, Bobby Tom, so that part shouldn't give you any trouble."

"Sarcasm just doesn't suit you, sweetheart."

"Unbeknownst to you, Samantha drugs you when she gets you back to your house."

"Before or after we do the wild thing?"

Once again, she ignored him. "You pass out, but you have the constitution of an ox, and you wake up in time to see her tearing up the floorboards in your house. The two of you have a big fight. Normally, you could easily overpower her, but she has a gun and you're groggy from the drugs. There's a struggle. Eventually, you start strangling her so you can take the gun away and force the truth out of her."

"I am not strangling a woman!"

He looked so outraged that she laughed. "In the process, you discover that she's the sister of the man you bought the ranch from, and that he was running drugs for a wealthy Mexican kingpin."

"Let me guess. Samantha's brother decided to hold out on the kingpin, who had him iced, but not before the brother hid a wad of cash from one of his drug runs under the floorboards of the house."

"That's where the heroine thinks it's hidden, but it's not there."

"The kingpin, in the meantime, decides to kidnap the heroine because he thinks she knows where the money is stashed. Old Jake Slade—"

"Jed Slade." She corrected him.

"Old Jed, being a gentleman in addition to being a drunk, naturally has to protect her."

"He's falling in love with her," she explained.

"Which makes for lots of excuses to keep her naked."

"I believe you also have a nude scene."

"Not in a million years."

5

The Lanier ranch had known better days. A cluster of wooden buildings with peeling paint sat on a flat section of land that stretched back from the banks of the South Llano River. Chickens scratched in the dirt beneath an old oak in the front yard. Next to the barn, a windmill with a broken blade turned listlessly in the July heat. Only the well-fed horses in the corral looked prosperous.

The equipment trucks and trailers being used by the film company sat close to the highway, and Bobby Tom parked the Thunderbird next to a dusty gray van. As they both got out of the car, Gracie spotted Willow standing in a coil of cables near a portable generator, where she was talking with a thin, studious-looking man holding a clipboard. Crew members worked near the corral, adjusting large lights set on sturdy tripods.

Willow looked up as Bobby Tom, nearly two weeks late, strolled toward her. He was resplendent in black slacks, coral shirt, and diamond-patterned gray silk vest topped by a charcoal Stetson with a snakeskin band. Gracie waited with a good deal of relish for her sharp-tongued employer to light into him.

"Bobby Tom."

Willow spoke his name as if it were a sonnet. Her lips curved in a soft smile and her eyes lit up with dreamy pleasure. Her sharp edges seemed to melt away, and as she walked forward, she extended her arms to grasp his hands.

Gracie felt as if she were choking. All the verbal lambastings she had endured came rushing back to her. Bobby Tom was getting a hero's welcome when he was the one responsible for the trouble!

She couldn't stand watching Willow drool on him. As she turned away, her eyes fell on the Thunderbird. Dust streaked its shiny red finish and the windshield was splattered with bug gore, but it was still the most beautiful car she'd ever seen. As frustrating as the past four days had been, they had also been magical. Bobby Tom and his red Thunderbird had transported her into a new and exciting world. Despite the conflicts and arguments, this had been the best time of her life.

She walked over to the catering wagon to fetch a cup of coffee while she waited for Willow to finished worshiping at Bobby Tom's feet. An exotic-looking, dark-haired woman with long silver earrings stood behind the counter. She had heavily made-up eyes, olive skin, and bare tan arms with silver bangles at her wrists.

"You want a donut to go with that?"

"No, thanks. I'm not too hungry." Gracie filled a Styrofoam coffee cup at an urn.

"I'm Connie Cameron. I saw you driving in with Bobby Tom." She took in the navy blue suit in a way that made Gracie realize she had once again dressed wrong. "Have you known him for long?"

The woman's manner was less than friendly, and Gracie decided it was better to clear up any misunderstanding right at the beginning. "Only a few days. I'm one of the production assistants. I escorted him here from Chicago."

"Nice work if you can get it." Connie's gaze was carnivorous as she watched Bobby Tom in the distance. "I spent some of the best times of my life with Bobby Tom Denton. He sure does know how to make a woman feel one hundred percent female."

Gracie didn't know how to answer that, so she smiled and carried her coffee over to one of the folding tables. As she took a chair, she forced herself to put Bobby Tom out of her mind and start thinking about her new responsibilities instead. Since production assistants were at the bottom of the totem pole, she could end up working with the prop people, typing crew sheets, running errands, or performing any of a dozen other jobs. As she saw Willow approach, she hoped her boss hadn't decided to send her back to L.A. to work in the office. She wasn't nearly ready for this adventure to end, and the thought of never seeing Bobby Tom again gave her a sharp pang.

Willow Craig was in her late thirties, a woman with the lean and hungry look of an obsessive dieter. She bristled with frantic energy, chain-smoked Marlboros, and could be curt to the point of rudeness, but Gracie still admired her tremendously. She began to stand to greet her, but Willow gestured her back into her chair and sat down next to her.

"We need to talk, Gracie."

The brusqueness in her tone made Gracie uneasy. "All right. I'm anxious to hear about my new duties."

"That's one of the things I want to discuss." She pulled a pack of Marlboros from the pocket of her peach jumpsuit. "You know that I'm not happy with the way you did this job."

"I'm sorry. I did my best, but—"

"It's performance, not excuses, that count in this business. Your failure to get our star here on time has been extremely costly."

Gracie bit back all the explanations that were bubbling to her lips and said, simply, "I realize that."

"I know he can be difficult, but I hired you because I thought that you could handle difficult people." For the first time, her voice lost its edge and she regarded Gracie with a trace of sympathy. "I'm partly to blame. I knew you lacked experience in the business, but I hired you anyway. I'm sorry, Gracie, but now I'm going to have to let you go."

Gracie could feel the blood draining from her head. "Let me go?" she whispered. "No."

"I like you, Gracie, and, God knows, you saved my life when Dad was dying at Shady Acres and I was so distraught. But I didn't get where I am today by being sentimental. We're on a tight budget, and there's no room for dead weight. The fact is, you were given a job to do, and you couldn't handle it." Her voice softened as she stood up. "I'm sorry it didn't work out for you. If you'll stop by the office at the hotel, you can pick up your check."

With that, Willow walked away.

The hot sun beat down on Gracie's head. She wanted to turn her face into it and let it burn her up so that she wouldn't have to face what she feared the most. She had been fired.

In the distance Bobby Tom emerged from one of the trailers followed by a young woman with a tape measure draped around her neck. She laughed at something he said, and he gave her an answering smile so charged with intimacy that Gracie could almost see the girl falling in love. She wanted to yell at her, to warn her it was the same smile he gave tollbooth operators.

Tires squealed and a silver Lexus peeled into the compound. The driver had barely brought the vehicle to a stop before the door flew open and an elegantly dressed blond-haired woman jumped out. Once again Bobby Tom's face lit up with a lady-killer grin. He ran toward the woman and pulled her into his arms.

Sick at heart, Gracie turned away. She stumbled blindly through a quagmire of cables, not paying attention to where she was going, knowing only that she had to be alone. On the other side of the equipment trucks, she saw a shed that rested at a crazy angle next to the hull of a rusted car. Slipping behind the weather-beaten structure, she sagged down in a patch of shade and leaned against the rough wood.

As she buried her head in her hands, she felt all her dreams slip away and despair gripped her. Why had she tried to reach so far above herself? When would she learn to accept her limitations? She was a homely woman from a small town, not some wild-eyed adventuress who could take on the world. Her chest felt as if it were being squeezed by a giant fist, but she couldn't let herself cry. If she did, she would never be able to stop. The days of her life stretched in front of her like one of the endless highways they had traveled. She had hoped for so much and ended up with so little.

She had no idea how long she sat there before the squawk of a bullhorn cut through her misery. Her navy suit was much too heavy for the hot July afternoon, and her skin was sticking to her blouse. Rising, she glanced without any real interest at her watch and saw that a little over an hour had passed. She had to get into Telarosa to pick up her paycheck. Nothing could make her stay here any longer, not even her suitcase locked away in Bobby Tom's trunk. She'd make an arrangement with someone in the office to pick it up for her.

She remembered having seen a road sign indicating that Telarosa was only three miles to the west. Certainly she could walk that far and spare herself the indignity of having to beg a ride from someone at Windmill. They could have her job, she told herself, but they weren't taking the few shreds of pride she had left. Squaring her shoulders, she made her way across the field to the road and began to walk along the dusty shoulder.

Barely fifteen minutes passed before she realized that she had seriously underestimated her stamina. The strain of the last few days, the sleepless nights she'd spent worrying, the meals she'd only picked at, had left her exhausted, and her black pumps weren't designed for walking any distance. A pickup flew by, and she lifted her arm to protect her eyes against the dust. Less than three miles, she told herself. That wasn't far at all.

The sun beat down on her head, and the sky was bleached to the color of bone. Even the weeds along the side of the road looked parched and brittle. She peeled off her damp suit coat and carried it over her arm. Off to her right she caught glimpses of the river, but it was too far away to provide any relief from the heat. She stumbled, but quickly righted herself. As she glanced above her, she hoped the dark birds circling overhead weren't vultures.

Forcing herself to ignore both her growing thirst and the blister her pumps had rubbed on her heel, she tried to decide what to do. Her financial nest egg was pitifully small. Although her mother had urged her to take a larger share of the profits from the sale of the nursing home, Gracie had refused because she wanted to make certain her mother had plenty to live on. Now she regretted not setting aside a little more. She would have to return to New Grundy immediately.

She winced as her ankle turned on the uneven surface but she kept moving. Her throat felt like a tube of cotton, and she was dripping with perspiration. She heard a car coming from behind her and automatically lifted her arm to shield her eyes from the dust.

The car, a silver Lexus, pulled to a stop beside her, and the passenger window slid down. "Would you like a ride?"

Gracie recognized the driver as the blonde she'd seen throwing herself at Bobby Tom several hours earlier. The woman was older than she'd realized, probably in her early forties. She looked rich and sophisticated, as if she drank bottled water between tennis games at the country club and slept with a good looking ex—wide receiver when her husband was out of town. Gracie didn't want to face another encounter with one of Bobby Tom's women, but she was too hot and tired to refuse.

"Thank you." As she opened the door and settled into the cool gray interior, she was enveloped by the scent of expensive perfume and the lilting music of Vivaldi.

With the exception of a wide wedding band,

the woman's hands were free of jewelry, but pea-sized diamond studs glittered in her earlobes. She wore her frosted blond hair in the soft, side-parted pageboy favored by wealthy women, and a belt of hammered gold links loosely cinched the waist of a gracefully cut oyster white sheath. She was slender and lovely, and the faint web of lines fanning out from the corners of her eyes only seemed to make her look more sophisticated. Gracie had never felt dowdier.

The woman at the wheel touched her finger to the button that raised the window. "Are you going into Telarosa, Miss—?"

"Snow. Yes, I am. But, please, call me Gracie."

"All right." Her smile was friendly, but Gracie sensed a certain reserve. The wide gold cuff on her right wrist glimmered in the sunlight as she turned down the volume on the radio.

She knew the woman must be curious about why she had been walking along the highway, and she appreciated the fact that she wasn't being pressed for explanations. On the other hand, her personal unhappiness was no excuse to be rude.

"Thank you for picking me up. The walk was a bit longer than I'd thought."

"Where would you like me to drop you?" Her accent was distinctly Southern, but it carried more of a lilt than a twang. If she hadn't personally witnessed her rescuer throwing herself at Bobby Tom, Gracie would have believed this woman represented everything gracious and civilized.

"I'm going to the Cattleman's Hotel, if that's not too far out of your way."

"Not at all. I assume you're with the film company."

"I was." She swallowed hard, but she wasn't quite able to hold the words back. "I've been fired."

Several long moments passed. "I'm sorry."

Gracie didn't want pity, so she spoke briskly. "So am I. I'd hoped it would work out."

"Would you like to talk about it?"

Her rescuer managed to sound both sympathetic and respectful, and Gracie could feel herself responding. Since she was very much in need of a confidante, she decided that, if she didn't reveal too much, it would be all right to talk about it.

"I was a production assistant for Windmill Studios," she said carefully.

"That sounds interesting."

"It's not a very prestigious job, but I'd wanted to make some changes in my life, and I felt lucky to get it. I had hoped to learn the business and work my way up." Her lips tightened. "Unfortunately, I got tangled up with a self-centered, irresponsible, egotistical, womanizing *bounder*, and I lost everything."

The woman's head whipped to the side, and she regarded Gracie with dismay. "Oh, dear. What did Bobby Tom do this time?"

Gracie stared at her across the interior of

the car. She was so startled that long seconds ticked by before she found her voice.

"How did you know who I was talking about?"

The woman arched one smooth brow. "I've had lots of experience. Believe me, it wasn't hard to figure out."

Gracie regarded her curiously.

"I'm sorry. I haven't introduced myself, have I? I'm Suzy Denton."

Gracie tried to sort it out. Could this woman be his sister? Even as the notion flickered through her mind, she remembered the wedding band on her finger. A married sister wouldn't have the same last name.

Her stomach plummeted. That lying snake! And after all his talk about football quizzes.

Fighting dizziness, she said, "Bobby Tom didn't tell me he was married."

Suzy gazed at her with kind eyes. "I'm not his wife, dear. I'm his mother."

"His *mother*?" Gracie couldn't believe it. Suzy Denton looked much too young to be his mother. And much too respectable. "But you're not a—" She cut herself off in mid-sentence as she realized what she'd almost let slip out.

Suzy's wedding ring clicked against the steering wheel as she gave it a hard smack. "I'm going to kill him! He's been telling that hooker story again, hasn't he?"

"Hooker story?"

"You don't have to worry about sparing

my feelings. I've heard it before. Did he tell you the one about me showing up drunk at all his high school games or the one where I proposition his coach on the practice field in front of his teammates?"

"He—uh—didn't mention a coach."

Suzy shook her head in annoyance and then, to Gracie's surprise, the corners of her mouth began to curl. "It's my fault. I know he'd stop if I insisted, but—" A trace of wistfulness had crept into her voice. "I've just always been so very respectable."

They reached an intersection, and Suzy put on the brakes at a stop sign punctured by a bullet hole. At the base of the hills off to their right, Gracie saw several low industrial buildings marked by a black-and-bronze sign reading ROSATECH ELECTRONICS.

"For the record, I was happily married to Bobby Tom's father for thirty years until he was killed in an automobile accident four years ago. When my son was growing up, I was his Cub Scout den mother, his homeroom mother, and team mother. Contrary to the stories he puts about, Bobby Tom had an entirely conventional upbringing."

"You don't look nearly old enough to be his mother."

"I'm fifty-two. Hoyt and I were married a week after I graduated from high school, and Bobby Tom was born nine months later."

She looked nearly ten years younger. As always, being with someone so different from herself piqued Gracie's curiosity, and she couldn't resist a little gentle probing.

"Did you ever regret getting married so young?"

"Never." She gave Gracie a knowing smile. "Bobby Tom is the image of his father."

Gracie understood completely.

Although Suzy was doing her best to conceal her curiosity, Gracie could almost see her wondering how a plain mouse with dowdy clothes and bad hair had gotten tangled up with her lady-killer son. But now that Gracie knew with whom she was speaking, she could hardly complain about his behavior.

They crossed a set of railroad tracks and entered the downtown area. Gracie saw right away that Telarosa was doing its best to hide its troubles from the world. To conceal the fact that too many of its stores were empty, civic groups were using the windows for display. She saw craft projects in what had been a shoe store and posters advertising a car wash in an abandoned bookstore. The marquee over the empty movie theater announced HEAVEN-FEST, THIS OCTOBER THE WORLD COMES TO T'ROSA! On the other hand, several of the stores looked new: an art gallery with a Southwestern motif, a jeweler advertising hand-crafted silver, a Victorian house that had been turned into a Mexican restaurant, complete with wrought-iron tables on the porch.

"It's a pretty town," Gracie observed.

"The economy has hurt Telarosa, but we've

had Rosatech Electronics to keep us stable. We passed the plant coming into town. Unfortunately, the new owner seems determined to close it and move the work to another plant near San Antonio."

"What will happen then?"

"Telarosa's going to die," Suzy said simply. "The mayor and the city council are trying to promote tourism to keep that from happening, but we're so isolated that it's going to be difficult."

They passed a park with neat flower beds and an ancient live oak shadowing the statue of a war hero. Gracie felt incredibly selfish. Her problems seemed small compared with the disaster facing this pleasant town.

The road curved and Suzy pulled up to the entrance of the Cattleman's Hotel. She shifted her car into park and removed her foot from the brake. "Gracie, I don't know what happened between you and Bobby Tom, but I do know that he isn't unjust. If he's wronged you, I'm sure he'll want to make amends."

Not likely, Gracie thought. When Bobby Tom found out she'd been fired, he was going to click his heels and treat everyone in town to a steak dinner.

6

Bobby Tom pulled off his Stetson, ran his fingers through his hair, and then put it back on as he regarded Willow with cool, level eyes. "Let me make sure I understand this. You fired Gracie because *I* didn't make it here by Monday morning."

They were standing next to the production trailer. It was just past six o'clock, and they had finished shooting for the day. Bobby Tom had spent most of the time either standing around sweating in the heat or having somebody fuss with his hair. Neither activity appealed to him, and he was hoping the work would get more interesting tomorrow. So far the only acting he'd done had involved coming out of the back door of the house, dunking his head in a bucket of water, and walking over to the corral. They'd photographed him from every possible angle, and David Givens, the *Blood Moon* director, seemed happy.

"We're operating on a very tight budget," Willow replied. "She didn't do her job, so she had to go."

Bobby Tom dipped his head and rubbed his eyebrow with his thumb. "Willow, I'm afraid you don't understand something that was evident to Gracie the first time we met."

"What's that?"

"I'm completely irresponsible."

"Of course you're not."

"I sure am. I happen to be immature, undisciplined, and self-centered, pretty much a little boy stuck in a man's body, although I'd appreciate it if you didn't quote me on that."

"That's not true, Bobby Tom."

"The fact is, I never think about anybody but myself. I probably should have told you that from the beginning, but my agent wouldn't let me. I'm going to be honest with you. If somebody's not around to keep me in line, there's a good chance you're not ever going to get this picture made."

She fiddled with her earring, the way some women did when they were nervous. "I suppose I could have Ben take care of you." She gestured toward one of the grips.

"That goofy-lookin' character in the Rams' hat?" Bobby Tom gazed at him in disbelief. "Do you seriously think I'd pay attention to a Rams' fan? Sweetheart, I earned my Super Bowl rings playin' for a real team."

Willow clearly didn't know what to make of this. "You seem to have been taken with Maggie in props. I'll assign her to you."

"She's a real pretty lady, that Maggie. Unfortunately, the two of us struck passion-sparks the minute we looked at each other, and it seems once I start romancin' a woman, I can talk her into just about anything. I'm not saying this to brag, you understand, but just as a point of information. I doubt Maggie'd be able to stay in charge of me for too long."

Willow regarded him shrewdly. "If you're angling to have Gracie back, you can forget it. She's already proved she can't control you."

Bobby Tom gaped at her as if she'd lost her mind. "You're kidding, aren't you? That woman could give lessons to a prison guard. Shoot, if it'd been up to me, I prob'ly wouldn't have been here till October. Fact is, I had an uncle I wanted to visit in Houston, and I think it's un-American to go anywhere near Dallas without a visit to the rodeo in Mesquite. I also need a haircut, and the only barber I trust lives in Tallahassee. But Miss Gracie kept putting her foot down, and I couldn't get her to lift it back up. You've seen her. You tell me she doesn't put you in mind of one of those old maid English teachers you had in senior high."

"Now that you mention it..." Willow seemed to realize he had almost cornered her, and she immediately retrenched. "I understand what you're trying to do, but I'm afraid it's not going to work. I've made up my mind. Gracie has to go."

He sighed. "I apologize, Willow. I know what a busy woman you are, and here I am wasting your time by not making myself clear." His smile grew more gentle, his voice softer, but his blue eyes were as hard and cold as ice chips. "I'm going to need a personal assistant, and I want it to be Gracie."

"I see." She dropped her eyes, well aware that she'd been given an ultimatum. "I suppose I should confess that there's been a lot of belt-tightening going on around here, and we've had to streamline several jobs. If I hire her back, I'll have to fire someone else, and we're already short of staff as it is."

"There's no need to fire anybody. I'll take care of her salary, although we'd better keep that piece of information quiet. Gracie is real funny about money. How much do you pay her?"

Willow told him.

He shook his head. "She could do better delivering pizzas."

"It's an entry level position."

"I'm not even going to speculate on what kind of position she had to assume for that particular form of entry." He turned to walk toward the Thunderbird and then paused.

"One more thing, Willow. When you talk to her, I want you to make one thing absolutely clear. Tell Gracie I'm in charge. One hundred percent. Her whole purpose in life is to keep me happy. I'm the boss and whatever I say goes. You understand?"

She stared at him in bewilderment. "But that defeats the purpose of everything you've said."

He gave her a wide, bone-melting grin. "Now don't you worry about it. Gracie and I'll work it out just fine."

By nine o'clock that night, Willow still hadn't found Gracie, and even Bobby Tom's brutal workout in the exercise room he'd built next to the apartment over the garage hadn't relieved his frustration at her incompetence. Fresh from his shower, he settled down on the ruffled chaise in the bedroom of the white frame house that sat in a small pecan grove just outside Telarosa. He'd bought it three years ago so his mother could have some peace when he came home. Proving his point, the phone began to ring. He ignored it and let the answering machine pick it up. When he'd last checked, the machine had registered nineteen messages.

In the past few hours, he'd done an interview with the *Telarosa Times*; Luther had popped up at the door to ask about Heavenfest; two of his old girlfriends, along with one woman he didn't know, had shown up to invite him to dinner; and the high school football coach had asked him to make an appearance at practice that week. What he really wanted was to buy a mountaintop somewhere and sit there all by himself until he felt like being with people again. He'd do it, too, if he didn't hate being alone so much right now. Being alone made him remember that he was thirty-three years old, and he didn't know how to be anything but a football player. Being alone made him remember that he no longer knew who he was.

He still couldn't quite explain why he hadn't gotten rid of Gracie back in Memphis, except that she'd kept surprising him. She was one crazy lady, he thought, remembering the way she'd sabotaged his car and thrown herself in front of the wheels. But she was nice, too. The best thing about having Gracie along was that no matter how mad she made him, she didn't wear him out like a lot of other people. When he was with her, he didn't have to use up all his energy just trying to be himself. She also amused the hell out of him, and right now in his life, that counted for a lot.

Where the hell was she? Between her innocence and her damned curiosity, she'd probably already landed herself in a mess. According to Willow, no one knew how she had gotten into town, only that she'd picked up her paycheck at the hotel and disappeared. He still had her suitcase in his trunk. Not that there was anything in it that shouldn't be burned for the greater good of mankind. Except for her underwear. During her striptease and that vault she'd made over his car door, he hadn't failed to notice that Gracie did have herself some nice underwear.

Tossing his legs over the side of the chaise, he got up and began to dress. He didn't want people in Telarosa to think he'd gotten a big head, so he bypassed his Levi's for a pair of Wranglers, then pulled on a baby blue T-shirt, a sleeveless black denim vest, and a pair of boots. Just before he left the room, he grabbed a straw cowboy hat from his closet. So far he'd managed to avoid going into town, but with Gracie missing, he knew he couldn't put it off any longer.

With a combination of despair and resignation, he walked over to a small painting of a ballerina, opened it by pulling back on the gilded frame, and entered the combination on the wall safe behind. When the lock released, he extracted a royal blue velvet jeweler's box and flipped it open with his thumb.

Inside lay his second Super Bowl ring.

The team logo of three interlocking gold stars in a sky blue circle had been replicated on the top of the ring, with the points of the stars executed in white diamonds while three larger yellow diamonds formed the centers. More diamonds spelled out the Super Bowl roman numeral designation and the year of the game. It was big and flashy, which was pretty much a requirement for Super Bowl rings.

Bobby Tom's lips tightened as he slipped it on his right hand. Although he'd always had an aversion to gaudy masculine jewelry, his reaction wasn't based on aesthetics. Instead, wearing the ring made him feel like so many of the retired players he'd known over the years, men who were still trying to live out their glory days long after they should have put the past behind them and gotten on with their lives. As far as Bobby Tom was concerned, once he'd blown out his knee, he hadn't ever wanted to touch this ring again. Wearing it was a reminder that the best days of his life were behind him.

But he was in Telarosa now—the favorite son of a dying town—and what he wanted didn't matter all that much. In Telorosa he had to keep the ring on his finger, just as he'd worn its predecessor, because he knew how much it meant to everybody who lived here.

He walked into the living room and headed toward a round table nestled between two gilt chairs. The table's overskirt was printed with pink-and-lavender flowers and streamers of green ribbon. A small cut glass bowl filled with dry rose petals sat on top, along with a white marble statue of Cupid and a bone china pitcher bearing clusters of violets. Bobby Tom picked it up and tilted out the keys to his pickup truck.

After replacing the pitcher, he gazed around the living room and began to smile. As he took in the pastel wallpaper, the lace curtains caught back with candy-striped bows, the plump chintz sofas and overstuffed easy chairs with deep ruffles that brushed the carpet, he reminded himself never again to give a lady who was pissed off at him the job of decorating one of his houses.

Everything was either lace, pink, covered with flowers, or had a ruffle on it. Sometimes all four at once, although his former girlfriend/decorator had been careful not to overdo. Since he didn't fancy the idea of having his buddies bust a gut laughing at him, he had never permitted any of the decorating magazines to photograph the interior of this particular house. Ironically, it was the only one he really liked. Although he'd never admit it to a soul, this silly little candy box of a house relaxed him. He had spent so much of his life in exclusively masculine enclaves that entering this place always made him feel as if he were taking a short vacation from his life. Unfortunately, the minute he walked out the front door, the vacation was over.

The spacious freestanding garage that sat behind the house held his Thunderbird along with his black Chevy pickup. He'd turned the area above it into a weight room for himself as well as a small apartment where he could tuck away all the visitors who didn't think twice about dropping in on him without warning. A retired couple from town took care of everything when he wasn't here, which was most of the time, because being in this place he loved more than any other spot on earth was sometimes more than he could bear.

He maneuvered the pickup down the gravel drive to the highway. Across the road, he could see part of the landing strip he'd built on some additional acreage he owned. The Baron was tucked into a small hangar set back from the highway amidst the mesquite and prickly pear.

A truck loaded with pigs blew by. After it had passed, he turned out onto the asphalt. He remembered all those summer nights when he and his friends used to run drag races on this very road. Then they'd go down to the South Llano, where he'd drink too much and throw up. By the time he was seventeen, he'd already figured out that he didn't have the stomach for hard liquor, and he'd been a light drinker ever since.

Thoughts of the river reminded him of the nights he and Terry Jo Driscoll had spent down there. Terry Jo had been his first real girlfriend. She was married to Buddy Baines now. Buddy'd been Bobby Tom's best friend all through high school, but Bobby Tom had moved on in the world and Buddy hadn't.

He reached the city line and saw the sign that had been erected when he'd been named All American his sophomore year at U.T.

Telarosa, Texas
Population 4,290
Home of Bobby Tom Denton
and the Telarosa High School Titans

There had been some talk of taking his name off the sign when the Chicago Stars had drafted him before the Cowboys had a chance. It had been hard on the town to watch its favorite son go to Chicago instead of Dallas, and whenever his contract with the Stars had come up for renewal, he would receive a series of phone calls from the town's leading citizens urging him to remember his roots. But he'd loved playing for Chicago, especially after Dan Calebow had taken over as head coach, and the Stars had paid him millions of dollars to make up for the embarrassment of his becoming a part-time Yankee.

He passed the turnoff that led to the small enclave of executive homes where his mother lived. She'd had to attend a Board of Education meeting that evening, but they had talked earlier on the phone and would spend some time together this weekend. Until recently, he'd thought his mother had adjusted well to his father's death. She had taken on the presidency of the Board of Education and kept up with all her volunteer work. Lately, however, she'd begun to ask his opinion about things she never used to bother him with: whether to get the roof repaired or where she should take her vacation. He loved her dearly, and he would have done anything for her, but her growing dependency was uncharacteristic, and it worried him.

He crossed the railroad tracks, glancing up at the water tower decorated with the flying orange *T* of Telarosa High, and then turned onto Main Street. The sign advertising Heavenfest on the marquee of the old Palace theater reminded him he had to call some of his buddies one of these days and invite them down for the celebrity golf tournament. So far, he'd been making up the guest list off the top of his head just to keep Luther quiet.

The bakery had closed since his last visit, but Bobby Tom's Cozy Kitchen was still in business, along with BT's Qwik Car Wash and Denton's Championship Dry Cleaning. Not all of the businesses in Telarosa were named after him, but sometimes it seemed that way. As far as he knew, nobody in town had ever heard of such a thing as a licensing agreement, and if they had, they would have dismissed it as some kind of left-wing horseshit. In Chicago, local businesses had paid him nearly a million dollars over the years to use his name, but the citizens of Telarosa freely appropriated it without giving a thought to asking for permission.

He could have put a stop to it—if it had happened any other place he would have—but this was Telarosa. The people here figured they owned him, and they would only have been mystified by any arguments to the contrary.

The lights were out at Buddy's Garage, so he went around the corner to the small wooden house where his former best friend lived. As soon as his truck entered the drive, the front door burst open and Terry Jo Driscoll Baines came running out.

"Bobby Tom!" He grinned as he took in her short, plump body. After two babies and too many bake sales, she'd lost her figure, but in his eyes, she was still one of the prettiest girls in Telarosa.

He jumped out of the truck and gave her a hug. "Hey there, sweetheart. Do you ever look anything but gorgeous?"

She swatted him. "You are so full of it. I'm fat as a pig, and I don't give a damn. Come on. Let me see it."

He dutifully extended his hand so she could see his newest ring, and she let out a squeal of delight that could have been heard all the way to Fenner's IGA. "Gawd! It is just so beautiful I can't stand it. Even prettier than the last one. Look at all those diamonds. Buddy! *Bud-dee!* Bobby Tom's here, and he's wearin' his ring!"

Buddy Baines came slowly down off the porch where he'd been standing watching the two of them. For a moment their eyes locked, and decades of old memories passed between them. Then Bobby Tom saw the familiar resentment.

Although they were both thirty-three, Buddy looked older. The cocky, dark-haired quarterback who'd led the Titans to football glory had begun to thicken around the middle, but he was still a good-looking man.

"Hey, Bobby Tom."

"Buddy."

The tension between them had nothing to do with Bobby Tom having been there first with Terry Jo. Instead, their problems had begun because Buddy and Bobby Tom together had carried Telarosa High to the Texas State 3AAA Championship, but only one of them had received a full ride to U.T., and only one of them had made it to the pros. Even so, they were each other's oldest friend, and neither of them ever forgot it.

"Buddy, look at Bobby Tom's new ring."

Bobby Tom slipped it off his finger and held it out. "You want to try it on?"

With any other man, he would have been rubbing salt into an open wound, but not with this one. He knew that Buddy figured at least a couple of those diamonds rightly belonged to him, and Bobby Tom figured so, too. How many thousands of passes had Buddy thrown to him over the years? Short, deep, down the sidelines, over the middle. Buddy had been throwing footballs at him since they were six years old, and they'd lived next door to each other.

Buddy took the ring and put it on his own finger. "How much does something like this go for?"

"I don't know. Couple of thousand, I guess."

"Yeah, that's what I figured." Buddy acted as if he priced expensive rings every day when

Bobby Tom knew for a fact that he and Terry Jo never had anything left over at the end of the month. "Do you want to come on in and have a beer?"

"I can't tonight."

"Come on, B.T.," Terry said. "I need to tell you about my new girlfriend, Glenda. She just got divorced, and I know you're exactly what she needs to take her mind off her troubles."

"I'm real sorry, Terry Jo, but a friend of mine is missing, and I'm kind of worried about her. You wouldn't have happened to rent a car to a skinny white lady with funny hair, would you, Buddy?" In addition to running the garage, Buddy had the town's only rental car franchise.

"No. She with those movie people?"

Bobby Tom nodded. "If you see her, I sure would appreciate it if you'd give me a call. I'm afraid she might have gotten herself into some trouble."

He chatted with both of them a few minutes longer and promised to hear all about Glenda on his next visit. As he was getting ready to leave, Buddy pulled the Super Bowl ring off his finger and held it out to his former best friend.

Bobby Tom kept his hands at his sides. "I'm going to be real busy for the next couple of days, and I'm afraid I won't get a chance to stop in and visit your mama right away. I know she'll want to see that ring. Why don't you hold on to it and show her for me? I'll pick it up over the weekend."

Buddy nodded as if what Bobby Tom had proposed was only fitting and slipped the ring back on his finger. "I'm sure she'll appreciate that."

With the possibility that Gracie had rented a car eliminated, Bobby Tom spoke next with Ray Don Horton, who operated the Greyhound depot, then Donnell Jones, the town's only taxi driver, and, finally, with Josie Morales, who spent most of her life sitting on her front step keeping track of everybody else's business. Because he'd played ball with so many black, white, and Hispanic kids, Bobby Tom had always moved freely across the town's racial and ethnic boundaries. He'd been in most everybody's house, eaten at all their tables, felt at home everywhere, but despite his network of connections, no one he spoke to had seen Gracie. All of them, however, expressed their disappointment that he wasn't wearing his ring and everybody either had a girl they wanted him to meet or needed a loan.

By eleven o'clock, Bobby Tom was convinced that Gracie had done something stupid like hitch a ride from a stranger. Just the thought of it made him crazy. Most of the people in the state of Texas were good solid folk, but there were lots of certifiables, too, and with Gracie's overly optimistic view of human nature, she was likely to have run into one of them. He also couldn't figure out why she hadn't tried to retrieve her suitcase. Unless she hadn't been able to. What if something had happened to her before she got the chance?

His mind rebelled at the thought, and he debated stopping at the police station to talk with Jimbo Thackery, the new chief of police. He and Jimbo had hated each other's guts since elementary school. He couldn't remember what had started it, but by the time they'd reached high school and Sherri Hopper had decided she preferred Bobby Tom's kisses to Jimbo's, it had escalated into a full scale feud. Whenever Bobby Tom came back to town, Jimbo'd find some excuse to act nasty, and somehow Bobby Tom couldn't imagine the police chief going out of his way to help him find Gracie. He decided to make one last stop before he threw himself on the dubious mercy of the Telarosa Police Department.

The Dairy Queen sat on the west end of town and served as Telarosa's unofficial community center. Here, Oreo blizzards and Mr. Mistys managed to accomplish what all America's civil rights legislation had never been able to achieve. The DQ had brought the people of Telarosa together as equals.

As Bobby Tom pulled into the parking lot, he saw a pickup held together with baling wire sitting between a Ford Bronco and a BMW. There were a variety of family vehicles, a couple of motorcycles, and an Hispanic couple he didn't recognize climbing out of an old Plymouth Fury. Since it was a weeknight, the crowd had thinned out, but there were still more people inside than he wanted to face, and if he weren't so worried about Gracie, nothing would have made him come here to this cemetery of his old glories, the place where he and his high school teammates had celebrated their Friday night victories.

He parked on the farthest edge of the lot and forced himself to climb down out of his truck. He knew that, short of using a loudspeaker, this was the fastest way to get the word out that Gracie was missing, but he still wished he didn't have to go inside. The door of the DQ swung open, and a familiar figure came out. He cursed softly. If someone had asked him to make a list of the people he least wanted to see right now, Wayland Sawyer's name would have been right on top of Jimbo Thackery's.

Any hope he'd had that Sawyer wouldn't notice him disappeared as the owner of Rosatech Electronics stepped down off the curb and halted, the vanilla cone in his hand stalling in midair. "Denton."

Bobby Tom nodded.

Sawyer took a bite of ice cream while he stared at Bobby Tom with cool eyes. Anyone looking at Rosatech's owner in his plaid shirt and jeans would have figured him for a rancher instead of one of the top business minds in the electronics industry and the only man in Telarosa who was as rich as Bobby Tom. He was a large man, not as tall as Bobby Tom, but solid and tough. At fifty-four, his face was compelling, but too rough-hewn to be classically handsome. His dark, wiry hair was cut short and threaded with gray, but his hairline had barely receded. It was as if Sawyer had drawn an invisible boundary on his scalp and declared that not a single follicle dare shut down behind it.

Since the rumors had surfaced about the closing of Rosatech, Bobby Tom had made it his business to learn everything he could about its owner before he'd met with him last March. Way Sawyer had grown up poor and illegitimate on the wrong side of Telarosa's railroad tracks. As a teenage troublemaker, he'd been tossed into jail for everything from petty theft to shooting out porch lights. A stint in the marines had given him both discipline and opportunity, and when he'd come out, he'd taken advantage of the GI Bill to earn an engineering degree. After graduation, he'd gone to Boston, where, with a combination of intelligence and ruthlessness, he'd climbed to the top of the growing computer industry and made his first million by the time he was thirty-five. He'd also married, had a daughter, and divorced.

Although the people of Telarosa had followed his career, Sawyer had never returned to town. Therefore, everyone was surprised when, after announcing his retirement from corporate life, he'd shown up eighteen months ago with a controlling interest in Rosatech Electronics and announced his intention to run the company. Rosatech was small potatoes to a man with Sawyer's reputation, and no one could figure out why he'd purchased it. Then, six months ago, rumors had surfaced that he would be closing the plant and moving its equipment and contracts to an operation in San Antonio. From that point on, the townspeople had been convinced that Sawyer had only purchased Rosatech to take his revenge against the town for not treating him better when he was a kid. As far as Bobby Tom knew, Sawyer had done nothing to dispel that rumor.

Sawyer gestured with the cone toward Bobby Tom's damaged knee. "I see you got rid of the cane."

Bobby Tom set his jaw. He didn't like to think about those long months when he'd been forced to walk with a cane. Last March, during his recuperation, he'd met Sawyer in Dallas at the request of the town fathers to try to persuade him not to move the plant. It had been a fruitless meeting, and Bobby Tom had taken a strong dislike to Sawyer. Anyone ruthless enough to ruin the well-being of an entire town didn't deserve to be called a human being.

With a flick of his wrist, Way tossed his barely eaten cone into the stubbly grass. "How are you adjusting to retirement?"

"If I'd known it would be this much fun, I'd have done it a couple of years ago," Bobby Tom said, his expression stony.

Sawyer licked his thumb. "I hear you're going to be a movie star."

"One of us has to bring some money into this town."

Sawyer smiled and pulled a set of car keys from his pocket. "See you around, Denton."

"Bobby Tom, is that you?" A female shriek came from the direction of a blue Olds that had just pulled into the parking lot. Toni

Samuels, who'd played bridge with his mother for years, came rushing forward and then froze as she saw who he was talking to. Her cheerful face hardened with hostility. No one made a secret of the fact that Way Sawyer was the most hated man in Telarosa, and the town had turned him into a pariah.

Sawyer seemed impervious. Palming his keys, he gave Toni a courteous nod, then walked away toward a burgundy BMW.

Thirty minutes later, Bobby Tom parked in front of a big white colonial on a tree-shaded street and got out of his truck. Light splashed on the sidewalk from the front windows as he approached. His mom was a night owl, just like him.

The fact that nobody at the DQ had seen Gracie had escalated his worries, and he'd decided to stop and see if his mother could come up with any additional ideas about how to locate a missing person before he went to see Jimbo. She kept a spare key under the potted geraniums, but he rang the bell instead because he didn't want to scare her.

The spacious two-story house had black shutters and a cranberry red door with a brass knocker. His father, who'd built up his small insurance agency over the years until it was the most successful one in Telarosa, had bought the house when Bobby Tom went off to college. The home Bobby Tom had been raised in, the small bungalow the city foolishly planned to convert into a tourist attraction, lay on the other side of town.

Suzy smiled when she opened the door and saw him. "Hello, sweetie pie."

He laughed at the name she'd called him for as long as he could remember and, stepping inside, tucked her under his chin. She slipped her arms around his waist and gave him a hard squeeze.

"Have you had anything to eat?"

"I don't know. I guess not."

She gazed at him in gentle reprimand. "I don't know why you had to buy that house when I've got plenty of room here. You don't eat right, Bobby Tom. I know you don't. Come on into the kitchen. I've got some leftover lasagna."

"Sounds good." He tossed his hat on the brass rack in the corner of the hallway.

She turned to him, her forehead creased in an apologetic frown. "I hate to bother you, but did you get a chance to talk with the roofer? Your father always handled that sort of thing, and I wasn't sure what I should do."

Hearing this sort of uncertainty from the woman who so competently oversaw the budget for the public school system worried Bobby Tom, but he kept his feelings to himself. "I called him this afternoon. He seems to be giving you a good price, and I think you should go ahead with the job."

For the first time he noticed that the pocket doors leading into the living room had been pulled shut. He couldn't ever remember that room being closed off and he gestured toward it with a tilt of his head. "What's going on?"

"Eat first. I'll tell you later."

He began to follow her, but came to a sudden stop as he heard a strange, muffled sound. "Is somebody in there?"

No sooner had the question slipped out than he realized his mother was dressed for bed in a light blue silk robe. He felt a painful constriction. She'd never mentioned anything about seeing other men since his dad had died, but that didn't mean she wasn't.

He told himself it was her life, and he had no right to interfere. His mother was still a beautiful woman, and she deserved every bit of happiness she could find. He certainly didn't want her to be lonely. But no matter how much he tried to convince himself, he felt like howling at the idea of his mother being with any man other than his dad.

He cleared his throat. "Look, if you're seeing somebody, I understand. I didn't mean to walk in on anything."

She looked startled. "Oh, no. Really, Bobby Tom..." She began fiddling with the sash on her robe. "Gracie Snow is in there."

"Gracie?" Relief rushed through him, followed almost immediately by anger. Gracie had scared the life out of him! When he'd been imagining her dead in a ditch somewhere, she'd been cozying up with his mother.

"How did she end up here?" he asked in short, clipped tones.

"I picked her up on the highway."

"She was hitchhiking, wasn't she? I knew it! Of all the damn fool—"

"She wasn't hitchhiking. I stopped when I

140

saw her." Suzy hesitated. "As you can probably imagine, she's a bit upset with you."

"She's not the only one who's upset!" He
pivoted toward the sliding doors, but Suzy's
hand on his arm restrained him.

"Bobby Tom, she's been drinking."

He stared at her. "Gracie doesn't drink."

"Unfortunately, I didn't realize that until
she'd gone through my supply of wine coolers."

The idea of Gracie slugging down wine
coolers made him even angrier. Gritting his
teeth, he took another step toward the doors,
only to have his mother once again interrupt
him.

"Bobby Tom, you know those people who
get giddy and happy when they drink?"

"Yeah."

She lifted an eyebrow. "Gracie isn't one of
them."

7

Gracie sat curled up on the sofa with her
clothes rumpled and her hair standing out from
her head in coppery clumps. She had a blotchy
face, red eyes, and a pink nose. Some women
could cry pretty, but Bobby Tom saw right away
Gracie wasn't one of them.

She looked so miserable that his anger
faded. As he gazed down at her, he found it
hard to believe that this sorry excuse for a female
was the same spunky, bossy lady who'd done

the worst striptease in history, thrown herself over his car door like a human cannonball, sabotaged his T-bird, and given Slug McQuire a blistering lecture on sexual harassment after he'd come on a little too strong to one of the waitresses at Whoppers.

Normally, he would rather have been locked in a room with a swarm of killer bees than a crying woman, but since this particular woman was Gracie, and she'd somehow become his friend, he made an exception.

Suzy gazed at him helplessly. "I invited her to stay the night. She was fine at dinner, but when I came home from my board meeting, I found her like this."

"She sure is carryin' on."

At the sound of his voice, Gracie looked up, gazed at him with bleary eyes, and hiccupped. "Now I'm"—a drawn-out sob—"not ever going to"—another sob—"have *sex*."

Suzy made a beeline for the door. "Excuse me, but I believe I have some Christmas cards I need to address."

As she disappeared, Gracie fumbled for the box of tissues that sat on the sofa next to her, but she had trouble locating it through her tears. Bobby Tom walked over, plucked one out, and put it in her hand. She buried her face in it, her shoulders shaking, pitiful mewing sounds coming from her lips. As he sat down next to her, he decided she was, without a doubt, the most miserable drunk he'd seen in his life.

He spoke softly. "Gracie, honey, how many of those wine coolers did you drink?"

"I don't d-drink," she said between sobs. "Alcohol is a cr-crutch for the weak."

He rubbed her shoulders. "I understand."

She looked up and, tissue in hand, pointed toward the oil painting of him that hung over the fireplace. His father had given it to his mother as a Christmas present when Bobby Tom was eight years old. It showed him sitting cross-legged in the grass hugging the dog he'd grown up with, a big old golden retriever named Sparky.

She jabbed her finger toward the portrait. "It's h-hard to believe a sweet child like that could grow up into such a d-depraved, egotistical, immature, w-womanizing, job-stealing rat!"

"Life's funny that way." He handed her another tissue. "Gracie, honey, do you think you could stop crying long enough for the two of us to talk?"

She shook her head in a wobbly arc. "I'm not ever going to st-stop. And do you know why? Because I'm going to sp-spend the rest of my life eating m-mashed potatoes and smelling like disen—disen—*fectant.*" Another wail. "Do you know what happens when you're around d-death all the time? Your body dries up!" She startled him by clasping her hands over her breasts. "They're drying up. I'm drying up! Now I'm going to die without ever having s-sex!"

His hand stilled on her shoulders. "Are you telling me you're a virgin?"

"Of course I'm a virgin! Who would want

to have sex with someone as h-homely as me?"

Bobby Tom was too much of a gentleman to let that one go by. "Why just about any healthy red-blooded male, honey."

"Ha!" She withdrew her hands from her breasts and reached for another tissue.

"I'm serious."

Even drunk, Gracie wasn't taking any of his malarkey. "Prove it."

"What?"

"Have s-sex with me. Right now. Yes! R-right this very minute." Her hands flew to the buttons on the front of her white blouse, and she began pulling them open.

He stilled her arms and kept a firm rein on the smile that wanted to break loose. "I couldn't do that, sweetheart. Not with you so drunk and everything."

"I am not dr-drunk! I told you before, I do not drink." She snatched her hands from beneath his and clumsily stripped the blouse off her arms. Before he knew it, she was sitting before him, bare from the waist up except for a bra made of transparent pink nylon embossed with tiny hearts that looked like little love bites sprinkled over her breasts.

Bobby Tom swallowed hard as his groin shot from soft to hard in 0.9 seconds. He had the wild thought that he was going crazy, right along with Gracie. After secretly worrying because his sex drive seemed to have deserted him at the same time his career had ended, he was now even more worried to find himself being turned on by something so tame.

She looked at the expression on his face and promptly burst into fresh tears. "You don't want to have s-sex with me. My br-breasts are too small. You only like women with gr-great big ones."

She'd spoken the truth, so he didn't understand why it was so hard for him to drag his eyes away from those pint-size morsels curving out from her chest. Probably because he was tired and coming back to Telarosa had lowered his emotional defenses to the point where he'd react to anything. He was careful not to hurt her feelings. "That's not true, honey. It's not size that counts so much as what a woman does with what she has."

"I don't *know* w-what to do with what I've got," she wailed. "How am I supposed to know when nobody's ever sh-shown me? How am I supposed to know when the only m-man who's given me any encouragement is a p-podiatrist who kept asking me if he could k-kiss my instep?"

He didn't have a good answer for that one. One thing he did know, however, was that he wanted Gracie to put her blouse back on.

As he reached over to pick it up from the floor where she'd dropped it, she jumped unsteadily to her feet. "I'll bet if I stripped n-naked right in front of you, you still wouldn't want me."

His head shot up just in time to see her

fumbling with the button on the side of her ugly navy skirt.

He got to his feet. "Gracie, honey..."

Her skirt dropped to her ankles and he couldn't quite conceal his surprise. Who would have thought those ugly clothes could have been hiding such a sweet little figure? Sometime that evening, she'd gotten rid of both her shoes and her hose, leaving her only in bra and panties beneath her clothes. Her breasts were small, it was true, but she had a slim waist to match, round, well-proportioned hips, and straight, slender legs. He told himself the contrast she presented with those perfectly toned, hard-muscled Amazons he'd been keeping company with for half his lifetime was the only reason he found her appearance so appealing. Her hips weren't rock hard orbs sculpted by two hours of step-aerobics every day, and her biceps hadn't been molded with free weights into ropes of steel. She had a natural woman's body, soft and slim in some places, round in others.

His groin ached as he noticed that her underpants matched her bra. The panties, however, had only one heart on them, a large pink one right at the center that wasn't quite big enough to hide the wisps of curly hair peeking around the sides. He experienced a perverse desire to strip them off her right here in the living room of his mother's house, right here with Sparky looking on. He wanted to open those legs and see if she was as dried up as she claimed. And if she was, he wanted to use every trick he'd learned to make her sweet and wet and ready for him.

He actually found himself toying with the idea. Investing a couple of hours under the sheets with Miss Gracie wouldn't kill him. It would almost be a humanitarian gesture. Then reality asserted itself. The last thing he needed in his life right now was another woman. He'd been trying to get rid of them, not add a new one to the menagerie. Besides, even though he had almost twenty years of sexual experience, none of it was with an almost middle-aged old maid who'd probably have a stroke if she saw a man naked, no matter how much she might think she wanted to taste the forbidden fruit.

He wasn't heartless, however, and the misery on her face got to him. He walked over to take her in his arms. She gave a long, heartrending sigh and molded her body to his as if the two of them had been heat-fused.

Something went off inside him that felt like a Fourth of July rocket. She smelled sweet and old-fashioned, like lavender and lilacs. Her ugly hair was soft under his chin, the smooth skin of her back turned into silk beneath his fingers. He let his hands slide down along her spine to her waist and then lower still. He was surprised at how small she felt against him. Because of her bossy nature, she seemed like a much larger woman.

Her arms crept around his neck. "Are we going to have sex now?"

Despite his throbbing groin, he was amused

to note that she sounded nearly as apprehensive as she did eager. His fingertips touched the top edge of her underpants and slipped inside. He caught her bare bottom in the palms of his hands and pulled her tight against him, vaguely ashamed of the fact that he was copping a cheap feel from a maiden lady too drunk to defend herself. On the other hand, it had been a long time for him, and his reaction was understandable.

"Not yet, sweetheart."

"Oh. Could we kiss?"

"I s'pose we could do that." He looked down into her tear-smeared face. She had a nice mouth, wide and generous, with a Cupid's bow perched right in the middle of her top lip. Bending his head, he covered it with his own.

She kissed like a teenager on her first date, and the innocence of it both excited and annoyed him. It wasn't right that a thirty-year-old woman didn't have any more experience with men than this. He started using his tongue on her, just a little bit, to get her used to the idea.

She was a quick learner, and it didn't take long at all for her lips to part. With a soft sigh, she let him in.

She tasted like fruit and tears. He stroked her with his tongue, while his hands continued to enjoy the sheer pleasure of caressing female hips that weren't as muscular as his own. As he enjoyed her small, soft body, he forgot about her bossy nature and aggravating ways. She made him remember exactly how many years has passed since he'd been with a virgin.

He heard little moans against his mouth, and her tongue took off on an adventure of its own. His body reacted violently. Drawing his hands out of her panties, he lifted her by the backs of her thighs. She splayed them automatically and wrapped them around his hips. As she gripped his shoulders, he realized he'd started to sweat. If he didn't stop right now, he was going to forget who she was and take her right here on the floor of his mother's living room. A room, he reminded himself, with a set of unlocked doors and the portrait of an innocent child looking on.

"Gracie..." He eased her legs from around his hips to set her back down, then reached up to unlock her arms. "Sweetheart, we're going to have to slow down a little here."

"I don't want to. I want you to show me what happens next."

"I can see that. But the fact is, you're not ready for anything more than kisses right now." He set her firmly away from him and bent over to pick up her clothes, adjusting himself when his back was turned because he didn't want to shock her to death.

He coaxed her into her clothes not a moment too soon because he'd just fastened her skirt when the doors slid open and his mother came in.

"How's she doing?"

Before he could reply, Gracie gave a loud, offended sniff. "Your son is no gentleman. He refused to have sex with me."

Suzy patted his arm, her eyes dancing with

149

amusement. "Words to warm a mother's heart."

Bobby Tom had definitely been around females long enough for one night. He turned to Gracie. "Now listen to me, sweetheart. You're going to sleep here tonight, and I don't want you to worry about a thing. Willow will be coming around to see you first thing tomorrow morning."

Once again, Gracie peered past him to Suzy. "You don't happen to have any dirty movies in the house, do you?"

Suzy shot her son a disapproving look, then linked Gracie's arm with her own. "The two of us are going to take a little walk upstairs now."

To his relief, Gracie went along without protest.

He followed them into the hallway and retrieved his hat from the rack. As they began to mount the stairs, he looked up at his mother. "Just how many of those wine coolers did she drink?"

"She had three," Suzy replied.

Three! Bobby Tom couldn't believe it. After only three drinks, she'd stripped off her clothes and demanded that he have sex with her.

"Mom?" He shoved on his hat.

"Yes, dear."

"Whatever you do, don't let her anywhere near a six-pack."

Aspirin burned in Gracie's belly and the late-morning sun knifed her eyeballs as she let herself out the sliding door that led to Suzy Denton's patio. Bougainvillea grew along the back of the house and honeysuckle trailed over a rustic fence on one side of the yard, which was shaded by an old pecan and several magnolias. A colorful annual garden in a sunny spot held frilly pink and white petunias, geraniums, daisies, and periwinkles. A sprinkler hissed near some low shrubbery, and everything smelled clean and fresh from its morning watering.

Her hostess, wearing khaki shorts and a brightly colored T-shirt with a parrot on the front, knelt on the ground before a small herb garden. She looked up and smiled. "Did Miss Craig leave?"

Gracie nodded and immediately regretted making such a drastic movement with her head. She winced, then walked slowly to the end of the patio where Suzy was working.

"Willow wants to hire me back." She gingerly lowered herself to sit on the top step.

"Oh?"

"But not as a production assistant. As Bobby Tom's assistant."

"Oh."

"I told her I'd think about it." Gracie tucked the skirt of her sadly crumpled navy suit around her legs, all she had to wear since her suitcase was still tucked away in the trunk of the Thunderbird. She swallowed hard. "Suzy, I can't tell you how sorry I am about last night. After all you've done for me, I abused your hospitality and embarrassed you in your own home. My behavior was reprehensible, the most reprehensible thing I've ever done in my life."

Suzy smiled. "You really have been sheltered, haven't you?"

"That's no excuse."

"You had a bad shock yesterday," Suzy said kindly. "Any woman would have been upset."

"I *threw* myself at him."

"He's used to it, dear. I'm certain he's already forgotten about it."

Gracie's pride bristled at the idea that she was simply another in the long line of women who'd embarrassed themselves over Bobby Tom, but she couldn't deny the truth. "Has he always had such a strong effect on women?"

"He's had a strong effect on almost everybody." Suzy withdrew a spading fork from the green plastic garden caddy next to her knees and began to loosen the soil around the edge of her herb garden. "In a lot of ways, life has come easily to Bobby Tom. From childhood on, he was the best athlete, and he's always been an excellent student."

Gracie inwardly winced, remembering her offer to help him learn to read. Suzy crushed a sprig of lavender in her fingers and brought it to her nose to breathe in the scent. Gracie assumed she wasn't going to say any more and was surprised when she brushed off her hands and went on.

"He was popular with the other children. Boys liked him because he didn't try to bully them.

And even in elementary school, the girls made excuses to come to the house. He hated it, of course, especially in fourth grade, when they really made his life miserable. They'd send him love notes and follow him around on the playground. The other boys teased him unmercifully."

Her hands grew still on the spading fork, and she spoke in a slow, measured manner, as if she were having difficulty choosing her words. "One day Terry Jo Driscoll—she's Terry Jo Baines, now—chalked a big red heart in the driveway with 'Bobby Tom loves Terry Jo' written next to it. She was drawing flowers all around it just as he was coming up the sidewalk with three of his friends. When Bobby Tom saw what she was doing, he flew right across the front yard and tackled her."

Gracie didn't know much about nine-year-old boys, but she could imagine how embarrassing that must have been for him.

Suzy renewed her attack on a clump of weeds growing near the basil plants. "If the other boys hadn't been watching that would probably have been the end of it. But by this time they'd seen what she'd written and all of them were laughing. She started laughing, too, and telling them that Bobby Tom wanted to kiss her. He lost his temper and punched her in the arm."

"I suppose that's an understandable reaction for a nine-year-old."

"Not as far as his father was concerned. Hoyt heard the commotion and reached the front door just in time to see Bobby Tom hit her. He took off outside like a rocket, hauled Bobby Tom up by the scruff of his neck, and walloped him right there in front of all his friends. Bobby Tom was humiliated; his friends were embarrassed. It was the only time Hoyt every spanked him, but my husband didn't believe a man could sink any lower than hitting a woman, and he refused to make allowances for the fact that his son was only nine at the time."

She leaned back on her heels, looking troubled. "Bobby Tom and his father were very close, and he never forgot that lesson. This might sound foolish, but sometimes I think he learned it too well."

"What do you mean?"

"You have no idea how many women have thrown themselves at him over the years. But even so, I've never heard him be impolite to a single one of them. Not to any of the football groupies, the married women, the parasites, the gold diggers. As far as I know, he's managed to keep his distance without ever uttering an impolite word. Doesn't that seem strange to you?"

"He's developed a lot more sophisticated strategies than simple rudeness for getting around women." Gracie wondered if Suzy knew about the football quiz.

"Exactly. And it's become so automatic over the years that I'm not sure he realizes how thick the barrier he's built around himself has grown."

Gracie thought about that. "He's incredible. He smiles at women, flatters them outrageously, tells them exactly what they want to hear. He makes every one of them feel like a queen. Then he does exactly what he wants."

Suzy nodded, her expression unhappy. "Now I think Hoyt would have been smarter to have looked the other way when Bobby Tom socked Terry Jo. At least it was a straightforward statement of his feelings, and he was never a cruel child, so he wouldn't have made a habit of it. Goodness knows, Terry Jo recovered. She was his first serious girlfriend." Her mouth tightened in a grim smile. "The irony is that when I mentioned the incident to him not long ago, he said that his father did exactly the right thing. He doesn't seem to have any idea what it might have cost him."

Gracie wasn't certain it had cost him anything. Bobby Tom possessed an abundance of charm, talent, good looks, and intelligence. Was it any wonder he'd grown an ego to match? He didn't believe there was a female on the planet who was good enough for him. Certainly not a thirty-year-old from New Grundy, Ohio, with small breasts and bad hair.

Suzy slipped the spading fork back into the green plastic caddy and stood. For a moment she gazed around at the pleasant garden. The scent of basil, lavender, and freshly turned earth filled the air. "I love working out here. It's the only place where I feel peaceful." She looked embarrassed, as if she'd just made a deeply personal statement and wished she hadn't.

"I know it's not any of my business, Gracie, but I don't think you should let what happened stand in the way of taking this job." She picked up her garden caddy. "You told me you didn't want to go back to Ohio, and you don't have another offer. Bobby Tom's used to women losing their heads over him; I'm certain last night held a lot more significance for you than it did for him." With a reassuring smile, Suzy disappeared inside.

Gracie knew Suzy was trying to comfort her, but the words hurt, especially because she knew they were true. She meant nothing to Bobby Tom, while he meant everything to her. She had lost her head over him, and even more shattering, she was very much afraid she had lost her heart.

She squeezed her eyes shut against the knowledge that she didn't want to face, but it was no use. She never lied to herself, and she couldn't do it now. Wrapping her arms around her knees, she faced the fact that, in the past week, she had fallen in love with Bobby Tom Denton. She had fallen deeply and hopelessly in love with a man who was so far beyond her reach it would have been comical if it weren't so very sad. Those deadly wine coolers had merely brought out the truth of what had taken place inside her the moment she had set eyes on him.

She ached for him. He was wild and reckless, larger than life, everything she couldn't

She made promises to herself. This fierce love she felt for him wouldn't keep her from seeing him clearly, the good and the bad, his monstrous ego and too soft heart, his keen intelligence and dangerously manipulative charm. Her love wouldn't let her compromise her principles either. She only knew how to be herself, and even though that wouldn't be enough for him, it was all she had.

She closed her eyes and saw him in her mind, a cosmic cowboy with his big Stetson and killer grin, a man who scattered stardust when he walked. That stardust had fallen on her, giving new life to her parched body and waking up her shriveled heart.

She knew there would be no happily-ever-after for her with Bobby Tom Denton, and while her heart soared, her head needed to stay firmly anchored in reality. He wasn't going to love her in return. Extraordinary men were meant for extraordinary women, and she was hopelessly ordinary. The only way she could come out of this emotionally intact was by never forgetting that she had fallen in love with a man who was as much legend as human. Her sense of honor wouldn't allow her to take anything from him the way everybody else did. She would give herself to him out of the fullness of her heart, not with the hope of receiving anything in return. And when it was over, this man who had been kissed by the gods would at least be able to remember that Gracie Snow was the one person in his life who had never taken anything from him.

An hour later, still queasy from making such a shattering decision, Gracie approached the brown-and-gray motor home that had been assigned to Bobby Tom. Between the incident last night, her hangover, and her new-found self-knowledge, she was going to have a difficult time facing him, but it had to be done. Before she could mount the steps, however, the door of the neighboring motor home opened and Natalie Brooks stepped out.

Gracie observed the descent of the leggy brunette actress who was being touted as the "new Julia Roberts," and her spirits sank even lower as she remembered all the love scenes Bobby Tom would be doing with this glorious creature. Gracie took in her trademark dark brown mane of hair, tamed now into a youthful ponytail that didn't detract one bit from her beauty. Despite the fact that her face was scrubbed clean of makeup, the twenty-four-year-old actress was breathtaking. Her features were bold: heavy dark brows, tilted green eyes, a wide, generous mouth, and even white teeth. She wore her wrinkled brown shorts and an equally wrinkled pink polo shirt as if they were designer originals.

"Hi." She gave Gracie a friendly smile and extended her hand. "I'm Natalie Brooks."

"Gracie Snow." She winced slightly from the sudden movement as she returned the firm handshake. "I've enjoyed your pictures so much, Miss Brooks. I'm a real fan."

"Call me Natalie. Elvis is sleeping now, so we have some time to talk." She gestured toward a pair of folding aluminum chairs set up in the shade of the trailer.

Gracie had no idea who Elvis was, but she wasn't going to pass up the opportunity to chat with a celebrity like Natalie Brooks, especially when it gave her a good excuse to postpone her encounter with Bobby Tom. After they were settled, Natalie said, "I know from Anton that your references are impeccable, and my husband and I appreciate you flying in on such short notice. We're determined to have only the best for Elvis."

Even though Gracie couldn't imagine what she was talking about, she found the actress's desperate earnestness rather endearing.

"The first thing I need to tell you is that Anton and I don't believe in schedules. Elvis is on demand feeding, so as soon as he starts to fuss, I want you to bring him to me. He's to receive no supplements of any kind. Anton and I want him to have the immunities that only breast milk can provide. We're also worried because we have allergies in the family—Anton has a first cousin who's highly allergic—so Elvis isn't receiving anything but breast milk for his first six months. You are supportive of breast-feeding, aren't you?"

"Oh, yes." More than once Gracie had imagined herself with a baby at her breast, and the vision always filled her with a poignancy so sharp that it was almost painful. "But isn't six months a long time for a baby not to have

161

anything else? I thought they needed cereal."

Natalie looked as if Gracie had suggested she feed the baby arsenic. "Not at all! Breast milk alone is the perfect food for the first six months of a baby's life. I should have made Anton cover all this with you. It's so hard— He has a business in L.A., you see, and this is our first separation. He'll be flying in on weekends, but it's still going to be difficult."

Gracie decided it was a poor reflection on her character that she found being mistaken for a nanny less flattering than being mistaken for a stripper. "I'm sorry, Natalie. I should have interrupted right away, but I was so fascinated by what you were saying that I got distracted. I do that sometimes. As it happens, I'm not your nanny."

"You're not?"

Gracie shook her head, only to be reminded by the lingering ache in her temples of her night of drunken debauchery. Holding herself very still, she said, "I'm one of the production assistants. Well, I *was* a production assistant, but now I'm Bobby Tom Denton's assistant."

Gracie expected Natalie to become melty-eyed like everyone else did whenever Bobby Tom's name was mentioned, but the actress merely nodded. Then her head shot up and her eyes flared with alarm. "Did you hear that?"

"Hear what?"

She shot up from the chair. "Elvis. He's crying." Her long movie star legs flew up the steps. Just before she disappeared inside, she said, "Wait here and I'll show him to you."

Gracie found herself liking Natalie Brooks, despite her rather intense attitude toward mothering, and she was curious to see her baby. Even so, she knew she couldn't postpone her responsibilities much longer.

At that moment, one of the equipment trucks moved and she saw Bobby Tom by the corral talking with several attractive young women. It was obvious from their fashionable outfits that they weren't members of the crew, and she suspected that the ladies of Telarosa had already begun to line up to take the football quiz. He wore only jeans and boots. The sun sparked in his tawny hair and glowed on his bare chest. Her heart jumped at the sight of him.

One of the makeup artists approached him and began to spray his chest from a plastic bottle so that his muscles glistened with oil. He glanced down at himself. Even from a distance, she could see that he looked befuddled, and she couldn't help smiling as she observed his reaction to what he certainly saw as unnecessary adornment.

Natalie reappeared with a flannel-wrapped bundle in her arms and a beatific smile curling her famous mouth. "This is Elvis," she said as she settled back down into the chair. "He'll be four months tomorrow. Say hello, precious. Say hello to Gracie."

Gracie gazed into the face of the homeliest baby she had ever seen. He looked like a miniature sumo wrestler. His nose was squashed, his small eyes nearly hidden in wrinkles of fat from his cheeks, his chin almost nonexistent.

"What a—uh—beautiful baby," she said dutifully.

"I know." Natalie beamed.

"An unusual name."

"It's an old and honorable one," she replied with a trace of defensiveness. And then she looked worried. "I just called my husband to see what had happened to the nanny. He found out last night that she insists on cereal for babies at four months, so I'm afraid we're back to square one. Now he's making inquiries about one of the nannies who worked for the British royal family."

Gracie saw by the doubtful expression on her face that Natalie wasn't certain even that would be good enough.

She reluctantly excused herself and made her way toward Bobby Tom, only to lose her courage at the last minute and make a detour toward the catering truck. Maybe after another cup of coffee she'd be ready to face him.

8

Bobby Tom was in a foul mood. Watching grass grow would be more interesting than making a movie. All he'd done since he'd arrived here yesterday was walk around with his shirt off while he drank cold iced tea from a whiskey bottle and pretended to fix the corral fence. Before he could even start to work up a good sweat, they called "cut" and he had to stop. He didn't like wearing makeup, he didn't like being outside without his Stetson, and he especially didn't like having them spray baby oil on his chest, not even when they brushed dirt on top of it.

All the fussing made him feel like a pansy. They'd even fixed the fly on his jeans so he couldn't zip them up all the way. They fell open in a V that dipped so low he couldn't wear his briefs under them. The jeans were also a size too tight, and he hoped like hell he didn't get a hard-on because, if he did, the whole world was sure enough going to know about it.

Compounding his bad mood was the fact that half the population of Telarosa had shown up on the set this morning with matchmaking on their minds. He'd been introduced to so many Tammys, Tiffanys, and Tracys his head was swimming from the overload. Then there was the matter of Miss Gracie Snow. In the light of day, the previous night's incident no longer seemed quite so funny.

The lady was so sex starved that it was only a matter of time before she found somebody to satisfy her itch, and he doubted she'd have the presence of mind to inquire too deeply into her lover's health history before she hopped into bed with him. In New Grundy her prospects had been limited, but here, the men on the crew vastly outnumbered the women, and it probably wouldn't take much persuasion for one of them to put an end to

Gracie's virginity, especially if word got out about the sweet little body tucked away underneath those ugly clothes. He resolutely pushed away that particular memory.

It was hard to believe she'd made it to the age of thirty still intact; although between her bossy manner and her guerrilla tactics with car engines, she'd probably scared away the better part of New Grundy's male population. He'd seen her with Natalie Brooks awhile ago. When they'd finished talking, she'd started to approach him, but then she'd lost her nerve and detoured to the catering wagon, where he imagined Connie Cameron, one of his old girlfriends, had given her a hard time. Now she was lurking behind the cameras, and, unless he was mistaken, she was doing deep breathing exercises. He decided to put her out of her misery.

"Gracie, come on over here, will you?"

She almost jumped out of her skin. He supposed if he'd carried on like she had last night, he wouldn't be too anxious to face the primary eyewitness, either, and as she came toward him, she might as well have been dragging concrete blocks from her feet. Her wrinkled navy suit looked as if it had been made for an eighty-year-old nun, and he wondered how any one human being could have such dismal taste in clothing. She stopped in front of him and pushed her dark glasses on top of her head, where they sank into a lump of hair. He took in her wrinkled clothes, red-rimmed eyes, and chalky skin. *Pitiful.*

She couldn't meet his gaze, so he knew she was still embarrassed. Considering her usual dictatorial ways, he realized he had to take strong offensive action right from the start if he wanted to keep her in line while she was working for him. Although it wasn't normally in his nature to kick somebody who was already down, he knew it wouldn't bode well for the future if he didn't draw back his foot right now and remind her who was in charge.

"Sweetheart, I've got some jobs I want you to do for me today. Now that you're working for me, I've decided I'm going to have to let you drive my T-bird, even though it goes against my better judgment. The car needs gas. My wallet and keys are on the table in the motor home they gave me to use. And speaking of that motor home. It's not nearly as clean as I'd like to see it. You might try to round up a scrub brush and some Lysol while you're in town so you can take a few licks at the linoleum."

That brought her to attention real quick, just as he'd known it would. "Are you telling me you expect me to scrub the floor in your motor home?"

"Only the dirty parts. And, honey, when you're in town, stop by the drugstore, will you, and pick me up a box of condoms."

Her mouth flew open in outrage. "You want me to buy you condoms?"

"I sure do. When you've made yourself a walking target for paternity suits, you learn to be real careful."

A flush crept from her neck all the way up

167

to her hairline. "Bobby Tom, I am not buying you condoms."

"You're not?"

She shook her head.

He shoved his fingertips in the back pocket of his jeans and shook his head regretfully. "I was hoping I wasn't going to have to do this, but I can see we need to clear our communication channels right from the beginning. Do you happen to remember what your new job title is?"

"I believe I'm to be your—uh—personal assistant."

"That's exactly right. And what that means is, you're supposed to be assisting me personally."

"That doesn't mean I'm your slave."

"And here I was counting on Willow to have explained all this to you." He sighed. "When she was telling you about your new job, did she happen to mention that I'm in charge?"

"I believe she did mention that."

"And did she say anything about the fact that you're supposed to do what I tell you to?"

"She—Well, yes, she said—But I'm sure she didn't mean—"

"Oh, I'm sure she did. Starting today, I'm your new boss, and as long as you follow orders, I know the two of us are going to get along just fine. Now I'd appreciate it if you could get to that linoleum before we finish shooting today."

Her nostrils flared and he could almost see the steam coming out of her ears. She puckered her mouth as if she were getting ready to spit out bullets and hitched up her purse.

"Very well."

He waited until she'd almost gotten away from him before he called her back. "Gracie?"

She turned, her eyes wary.

"About those condoms, sweetheart. Make sure you get the jumbos. Anything smaller is too tight a fit."

Until then, Bobby Tom had never seen a woman blush on top of a blush, but Gracie managed it. She fumbled for her sunglasses, slapped them back over her eyes, and fled.

He chuckled softly. He knew he should feel bad about bullying her, but instead, he was inordinately pleased with himself. Gracie was one of those women who could drive a man crazy if he let her. All in all, it was better to establish the natural order of things right from the beginning.

An hour later, with her purchases made, she pulled out of the drugstore parking lot in Bobby Tom's Thunderbird. Her cheeks still burned as she remembered what had just happened at the pharmacy counter. After having reminded herself that modern, socially aware women purchased condoms all the time, she had finally worked up enough nerve to set her purchase next to the register only to have Suzy Denton come up to her at exactly that moment.

The box had sat in plain view like a ticking grenade. Suzy saw it, of course, and immediately busied herself studying a photograph of a two-headed dog on the front page of one of the tabloids. Gracie had wanted to die.

Now she shared her feelings with Elvis, who was tucked into an infant car seat next to her. "Just when I think I can't embarrass myself in front of Suzy any more than I already have, something else happens."

Elvis burped.

She smiled despite herself. "Easy for you to say. You weren't the one buying the condoms."

He chortled and blew a saliva bubble. As she'd been leaving the ranch, she'd run into Natalie, who was frantically dashing around trying to find someone reliable to watch over Elvis for an hour or so while she filmed her first scene of the day. When Gracie had volunteered, Natalie had showered her with gratitude and a lengthy series of instructions, relaxing only when Gracie had finally started taking notes.

Gracie's hangover had disappeared and her head no longer ached. She'd retrieved a clean dress, a sadly wrinkled black-and-brown—striped shirtwaist, from the suitcase in the trunk and changed into it in the motor home before she'd left. Now, she once again felt human.

She had just reached the edge of the town when a pungent odor prickled her nostrils, followed by the unhappy sounds of a baby who didn't like lying around in a dirty diaper. She looked over at him. "You stinker."

He puckered up his face and began to wail. There was no traffic coming so she pulled to the side of the road, where she managed to change the baby. She had just resettled behind the wheel when she was distracted by the crunch of tires in gravel.

As she turned in her seat, she watched an imposing-looking man in a beautifully tailored light gray suit climb out of a burgundy BMW parked on the shoulder of the road behind her. For an older man, he was very attractive: short dark hair barely flecked with gray, an arresting face, and a powerful body that didn't seem to have an extra ounce of fat on it.

"Do you need help?" he asked, coming to a stop next to the side of the car.

"No, but thank you." She nodded toward the baby. "I had to change a diaper."

"I see." He smiled at her, and she found herself smiling back. It was nice to know there were still people in the world who would inconvenience themselves to help out someone else.

"This is Bobby Tom Denton's car, isn't it?"

"Yes, it is. I'm his assistant, Gracie Snow."

"Hello, Gracie Snow. I'm Way Sawyer."

Her eyes widened ever so slightly as she remembered the conversations she'd overheard on the car phone between Bobby Tom and Mayor Baines. So this was the man everyone in Telarosa was talking about. She realized this was the first time she'd heard Way Sawyer's name without the words "that sonovabitch" in front of it.

"I take it you've heard of me," he said.

She sidestepped. "I've only been in town a little over a day."

"Then you've heard of me." He grinned and tilted his head toward Elvis, who had once again begun to squirm in his seat. "Is that your baby?"

"Oh, no. He belongs to Natalie Brooks, the actress. I'm baby-sitting."

"This sun's in his eyes," he said. "You'd better get back on the road. Nice meeting you, Gracie Snow." With a nod, he turned away and began walking back to his car.

"Nice meeting you, too, Mr. Sawyer," Gracie called after him. "And thanks for stopping. Not everyone would have."

He waved and, as she pulled back onto the highway, she wondered if the people of Telarosa weren't exaggerating Mr. Sawyer's villainy. He seemed like a very pleasant man to her.

Despite his dry diaper, Elvis screwed up his face and began to fret. She glanced at her watch and saw that she'd been gone well over an hour. "Time to get you back to the old chuckwagon, cowboy."

The sack containing the box of condoms bumped against her hip, and she remembered her vow not to ignore Bobby Tom's faults just because she'd fallen in love with him. With a sigh of resignation, she knew she had to take action. Even though he was officially her boss and the man who made her heart race, he needed a reminder that he couldn't run roughshod over her without accepting the consequences.

"Four clubs."

"Pass."

"Pass."

Nancy Kopek gave her bridge partner a sigh of exasperation. "That was Gerber, Suzy. I was asking you for aces. You shouldn't have passed."

Suzy Denton smiled apologetically at her partner. "I'm sorry; I lost my concentration." Instead of her bridge game, she had been thinking about what had happened in the drugstore several hours earlier. Gracie seemed to be preparing herself to make love with her son and because she liked her very much, she didn't want to see her hurt. Nancy nodded good-naturedly at the two other women sitting around the table. "Suzy's distracted because Bobby Tom's home. She hasn't been herself all afternoon."

Toni Samuels leaned forward. "I saw him at the DQ last night, but I didn't get a chance to mention my niece to him. I know he'll be crazy about her."

Toni's partner, Maureen, frowned and led the six of spades. "My Kathy is a lot more his type than your niece, don't you think so, Suzy?"

"Let me freshen everybody's drinks." Suzy laid down her hand, glad she was the dummy so she could escape for a few minutes. Normally, she enjoyed her Thursday afternoon bridge game, but today she wasn't up to it.

When she reached the kitchen, she set the glasses on the counter and walked over to the bay window instead of going to the refrigerator. As she stared out at the bird feeder that hung from a magnolia next to the patio, she unconsciously pressed her fingertips to her hip and felt the small flesh-colored patch that supplied her body with the estrogen it could no longer produce on its own. She blinked her eyes against the sudden sting of tears. How could she be old enough for menopause? It seemed as if only a few years had passed since that hot summer day she'd married Hoyt Denton.

An all-encompassing wave of despair settled over her. She missed him so much. He had been her husband, her lover, her best friend. She missed the clean soapy smell of him after he got out of the shower. She missed the solid feel of his arms wrapped around her, the love words he'd whisper when he drew her down on the bed, his laughter, his corny jokes and awful puns. As she gazed out at the empty bird feeder, she folded her arms across her chest and squeezed, trying for a moment to imagine that he was holding her.

He'd just turned fifty the day before his car had been broadsided by a semi during a terrible storm. After the funeral her desperate grief had combined with a stomach-gnawing anger at him for leaving her alone and putting an end to the marriage that had been the foundation of her life. It had been a horrible time, and she didn't know how she would have survived it without Bobby Tom.

He had taken her to Paris after the funeral, and they'd spent a month exploring the city, driving through French villages, touring châteaux and cathedrals. They'd laughed together, cried together, and, through her pain, she'd been filled with a humble gratitude that two scared youngsters had managed to produce such a son. She knew she'd begun to rely on him too much lately, but she was afraid if she stopped, he'd slip away from her, too.

She'd been so certain when he was born that he would be the first of several children she would bear, but there hadn't been any more, and sometimes she ached to have him small again. She wanted to hold him in her lap, to stroke his hair, bandage his bruises, and smell that sweaty, little boy smell. But her son had been a man for a long time now, and those days of dabbing mosquito bites with calamine lotion and healing hurts with kisses were gone forever.

If only Hoyt were still alive.

I miss you so much, my darling. Why did you have to leave me behind?

By six o'clock, shooting had finished for the day. As Bobby Tom walked away from the corral, he was hot, tired, dirty, and irritable. He'd been eating dust all afternoon, and the schedule called for more of the same tomorrow. As far as he was concerned, this Jed Slade character was about the stupidest excuse for a human being he'd ever seen. Bobby Tom didn't consider himself an expert on horses, but he knew enough about them to be absolutely certain that no self-respecting rancher, whether he was a drunk or not, would try to break a horse while he was half dressed.

Throughout the course of the day, Bobby Tom's irritation over his artifically oiled and dirt-smeared chest and his unzipped jeans had flared into righteous indignation. They were treating him like a sex object! It was damned demeaning, that's what it was, being reduced to a set of oily pecs and a tight ass. Shit. A dozen years in the NFL, and this was what it had all come down to. Pecs and ass.

He stormed toward his motor home, the heels of his boots churning up puffs of dust. He intended to take a quick shower, head for home, and lock the door for a while before he went to visit Suzy. He hoped to hell Gracie hadn't run off because he was looking forward to taking out his bad mood on her. He pulled the door of the motor home open and stepped inside only to come to an abrupt halt as he saw that the interior was filled with women.

"Bobby Tom!"

"Hey, there, Bobby Tom!"

"Hi, cowboy!"

Six of them were scampering around like cockroaches, setting out homemade casseroles, cutting pies, and pulling beer from the refrigerator. One of them was an old acquaintance, three others he remembered having met that day on the set, two of them he didn't recognize at all. And every bit of the activity was being directed by the seventh woman, an evil witch in a black-and-brown—striped dress that looked like a raccoon tail, who gave him a gloating smile as she stood in the middle of the commotion and handed out orders.

"Shelley, that casserole looks delicious; I'm sure Bobby Tom is going to enjoy every bite. Marsha, I don't remember ever seeing such a beautiful pie. How thoughtful of you to bake it. You did a wonderful job on the floor, Laurie. I know Bobby Tom appreciates it. He's very particular about his linoleum, aren't you, Bobby Tom?"

She gazed at him with the serenity of a madonna, but her clear gray eyes glittered with triumph. She knew damn well that a gaggle of matrimonially inclined females was the last thing he wanted to face right now, but instead of getting rid of them, she had encouraged them to hang around! He finally understood Gracie's function in his life. She was God's joke on him.

A woman with big hair and a stretchy top handed him a can of beer. "I'm Mary Louise Finster, Bobby Tom. Ed Randolph's nephew's wife is my first cousin. Ed told me I should stop in and say hello."

He took the beer and smiled automatically, even though his cheeks ached from the effort. "It sure is nice to meet you, Mary Louise. How's Ed doing these days?"

"Why, just fine, thank you for asking." She turned to the woman at her side. "And this is my best friend, Marsha Watts. She used to go out with Riley Carter's brother Phil."

One by one the women pressed themselves

forward. He dispensed courtesies and flattery like Pez candy, while his head ached and his skin itched from dirt and baby oil. There was enough perfume in the air to poke a brand-new hole in the ozone layer and he fought the urge to sneeze.

The door opened behind him, slapping him in the butt. He automatically stepped aside, an action that unfortunately permitted another woman to push her way in.

"You remember me, don't you, Bobby Tom? I'm Colleen Baxter, used to be Timms before I was married, but I'm divorced now from that cheatin' sonovabitch used to work at Ames Body Shop. Me and you went to high school together, but I was two years behind you."

He smiled at Colleen through the angry red haze swirling in front of his eyes. "You've gotten so beautiful, sweetheart, I hardly recognized you. Not that you weren't a pretty little thing back then."

Her high-pitched giggle set his teeth on edge, and he saw a lipstick smudge on one of her incisors. "You're too much, Bobby Tom."

She batted playfully at his arm, then turned to Gracie and passed over a plastic grocery sack from the IGA. "I got that Neapolitan ice cream you told me Bobby Tom just loves, but you'd better put it in the freezer right away. The air-conditioning in my car's broke, and it's gettin' real soft."

Bobby Tom hated Neapolitan ice cream. Like most of life's compromises, it just wasn't satisfying.

"Thank you, Colleen." As Gracie pulled the carton from the IGA sack, her Sunday-School-teacher smile was in sharp contrast to the devil-lights flashing in her gray eyes. "Wasn't that sweet of Colleen to drive all the way back into town, Bobby Tom, just so you could have some ice cream?"

"Real sweet." While he spoke evenly, the look he gave her carried such clear promise of evil intention that he was half-surprised he didn't incinerate her right there on the spot.

Colleen tried to get a grip on his arm, but her hand kept sliding around in the baby oil, rubbing the grit deeper into his skin. "I've been studying up on football, Bobby Tom. I'm hoping I get a chance to take the quiz before you leave Telarosa."

"I've been studyin', too," her friend Marsha piped in. "The library's entire collection of football books was picked clean the minute word got around that you were comin' back."

He'd reached the end of his patience, and with a sigh of pure regret, he placed a hand on each woman's shoulder. "I'm sorry to do this to you, ladies, but truth is, Gracie passed the quiz just last night and consented to be Mrs. Bobby Tom."

A deep silence fell over the trailer. Gracie froze in place, the half gallon of Neapolitan ice cream beginning to drip in her hands.

The women's eyes flew back and forth between the two of them, and Colleen's mouth flopped like a guppy's. "Gracie?"

"*That* Gracie?" Mary Louise said, her eyes

cataloging every one of Gracie's fashion and grooming mistakes.

Bobby Tom gave his intended the best fac-simile of a tender smile he could manage to bestow on someone he planned to murder in cold blood. "This sweet lady right here." He squeezed through the Reba McEntire hairdos to get to her side. "I told you we weren't going to be able to keep it a secret for long, darlin'."

Slipping his arm around her shoulders, he hauled her against his bare chest where he did his best to smear dirt and baby oil all over the side of her face. "I'm tellin' you, ladies, Gracie knows more Super Bowl history than any woman I ever met. Lordy, but she is pure magic when it comes to quoting postseason game records. The way you called out those passing percentages last night, sweetheart, just 'bout brought tears to my eyes."

She was making funny little strangling sounds against his chest, and he squeezed her tighter. Why hadn't he thought of this before? Passing Gracie off as his fiancée was the perfect way to buy himself some peace and quiet during his stay in Telarosa.

He shifted her across his body so he could smear up the other side of her face, then sucked in his breath as a frigid half gallon of Neapolitan hit him square in the stomach.

Mary Louise Finster looked as if she'd swallowed a chicken bone. "But, Bobby Tom, Gracie isn't—She's real nice and all, but she isn't exactly—"

He inhaled sharply against the cold and dug his fingers into the hair on the back of Gracie's head where nobody could see. "Shoot, are you talkin' 'bout the way Gracie looks right now? She just dresses like this sometimes 'cause I ask her to. Otherwise, she gets too much attention from men, isn't that right, sweetheart?"

Her response was lost against his chest as she tried to ram the carton into his side. He tightened his grip on her hair and jiggled her head up and down while he smiled to beat the band. "Some of those boys on the crew look sort of wild, and I'm afraid they might get too worked up around her."

Just as he'd hoped, the announcement of his engagement took away the girls' party spirit. Doing his best to ignore the leaking ice cream, he kept Gracie close to his side while he said good-bye to his visitors. When the trailer door finally shut behind the last of them, he released her and looked down.

Dirt and oil smeared her face and most of the front of her raccoon tail dress, while melting ice cream sloshed out from under the lid of the squashed container and ran in muddy chocolate, strawberry, and vanilla trickles over her fingers.

He waited for an outburst of indignation, but instead of exhibiting anger, her eyes narrowed with determination. Just as he remembered that Gracie hardly ever reacted in a predictable fashion, her hand shot out and she grabbed the *V*-shaped opening at the top of his jeans. Before he could react, she had dumped melting ice cream down the front of his pants.

He yowled and leaped straight up in the air.

She dropped the carton to the floor with a splat and crossed her arms over her chest. "*That*," she said, "is for making me buy condoms in front of your *mother*!"

It was hard to yell, hop up and down, cuss, and laugh at the same time, but Bobby Tom somehow managed it.

While he suffered, Gracie stood in a spreading pool of melting Neapolitan and watched. Fairness compelled her to admire his attitude. He had been wrong to bait her, she had retaliated, and, with the exception of an excess of vulgar language, he was being a remarkably good sport about it.

At that precise moment, Gracie saw his hand move to his zipper and knew she had allowed herself to relax too soon. She took an instinctive step away from him only to feel her heel catch on the ice cream carton. The next thing she knew, she was lying flat on her back looking up at him.

"Well, now, what do we have here?" A diabolical gleam sparkled in his eyes as he gazed down at her, one hand still on his zipper, the other on his hip. Cold slapped the bare backs of her thighs where her skirt had ridden up. She planted the heels of her hands on the linoleum so she could scramble to her feet only to have Bobby Tom drop down on his knees next to her.

"Not so fast, sweetheart."

She regarded him warily while she tried to scoot away. "I don't know what you've got on your mind, but whatever it is, forget it right now."

One corner of his mouth curled malevolently. "Oh, it'll take me a long time to forget something like that."

She gave a hiss of alarm as his gooey hands settled on her shoulders and he flipped her over onto her stomach. Her cheek squished into a mound of melting vanilla and she yelped. Before she could scramble back up, something that felt very much like his knee settled into the small of her back.

"What are you doing?" she cried as she found herself pinned to the linoleum.

He began working at the hook above her zipper. "Now, don't you worry 'bout a thing, honey. I've been undressing women longer than I can remember, and it won't take me but a few seconds to get this dress right off you."

When she'd imagined storing up memories, this wasn't what she'd had in mind. "I don't want you to take my dress off!"

"'Course you do." The hook gave. "Stripes are a funny thing. Unless you're planning to officiate at a football game, I'd suggest you avoid 'em in the future."

"I don't need a fashion lecture from—Oh! Leave that zipper alone! Stop that!" He peeled the back of her dress open, lifted his knee, and, ignoring her squeals of protest, began pulling it down over her hips.

183

"Steady now, sweetheart. Dang, you do have some nice underwear." In one motion, he removed the dress and flipped her onto her back, but he gazed at her white lace demibra and bikini underpants a moment too long.

Her hand closed around a clump of semi-solid chocolate, and she flung it at him.

He gave a startled yelp as it hit him in the jaw, then he lunged for the carton. "That's going to be a fifteen-yard penalty for unnecessary roughness."

"Bobby Tom..." She screeched as he scooped out a big messy glob, dropped it on her stomach, and began rubbing it over her skin with the palm of his hand. Gasping against the cold, she struggled to get away.

He grinned down at her. "Say 'Forgive me, Bobby Tom, sir, for causin' you all this trouble, and I promise I'll do every single thing you tell me from now on. Amen.'"

She repeated one of his favorite rude words instead, and he laughed, giving her a golden opportunity to catch him in the chest with some strawberry.

From then on, it was a free-for-all. Bobby Tom had the advantage since he still wore his jeans and had better traction on the slippery linoleum than she did. He was also a well-conditioned athlete who knew far too many dirty tricks for someone who had once been named Sportsman of the Year. On the other hand, he kept having funny lapses of attention when he was smearing various parts of her with ice cream, and she took advantage of each one of them to plaster him with everything she could grab. She was yelping, laughing, and imploring him to stop all at the same time, but he had much more endurance than she, and it wasn't long before she ran out of steam.

"Stop! No more!" She fell back to the floor. Her breasts strained against the lacy bra cups as her chest heaved from exertion.

"Say 'Pretty please.'"

"Pretty please." She gulped for air. She had ice cream everywhere, in her hair, her mouth, all over her body. Her once white underwear was streaked with muddy pink and brown. Not that he looked much better. She was especially pleased with the amount of strawberry she'd been able to work into his hair.

And then her mouth went dry as her eyes slid over his chest to the arrow-straight line of golden brown hair that traveled from above his navel down into the open *V* of his jeans. She stared at the large bulge that had grown there. Had she done that to him? Her eyes flew to his.

He regarded her with lazy amusement. For a moment neither of them moved, and then he spoke in a husky voice. "Pretty please with ice cream on top of it."

She shuddered, not from the cold but from a coil of heat spreading through her. The excitement of the struggle had camouflaged her body's violent reaction to the bombardment of sensations it was receiving. She was suddenly conscious of the contrast between the frigid ice cream and the blistering heat of her skin. She felt the rough scrape of denim against her thigh, the slipperiness of the oil between her fingers, the faint abrasion caused by the dirt that had been smeared on his chest and now covered her as well.

He dipped his index finger into the liquid strawberry puddle around her navel and painted a gentle downward path, stopping when he reached the narrow elastic band at the top of her ruined bikini panties.

"Bobby Tom..." Her heart felt as if it had stopped beating, and she spoke his name on a whisper of air so that it sounded like an entreaty.

His hands moved up to her shoulders, where he slipped his thumbs under the straps of her bra and pressed them into the small hollows there for a gentle massage.

The sharp, sweet yearning that flooded her was nearly unbearable. She wanted him so desperately.

As if he could read her mind, he dropped his hands to the center fastening of her bra and flicked it open. She went completely still, afraid he would remember that he was the man every woman wanted, and she was the girl who'd sat home alone the night of her senior prom.

But he didn't stop. Instead, he peeled the cold, wet lace away and gazed down. Her breasts had never seemed so small, but she wouldn't apologize for them. He smiled. She held her breath, afraid that he was going to make a joke about their size, but instead he spoke in a soft, drawling voice that sent tongues of flame licking through her veins.

"I'm afraid I missed a couple of spots."

She watched as he dipped his finger into the misshapen carton that lay open near her shoulder. He withdrew a dab of vanilla ice cream and carried it to her nipple. She sucked in her breath as he dropped it on the sensitive tip.

Her nipple stiffened into a tight, hard point. With the pad of his finger, he painted a tiny circle around and around the beaded flesh and up over its tiny crest. She gasped; her head thrashed to the side. He dipped his finger back into the ice-cream carton and carried another dab to the opposite nipple.

A moan slipped through her lips as she felt the exquisite pain of the cold on such a sensitive part of her. Her legs instinctively parted as the flesh between them throbbed. She wanted more. She sobbed as he toyed with both nipples, pinching them between his thumb and index finger to warm them, only to dip back into the ice cream and chill them again.

"Oh, please...Please..." She realized she was begging him, but she couldn't stop herself.

"Easy, sweetheart. Take it easy."

He continued to paint her nipples with cold, rub them warm, then paint them again. Fire and ice. She had turned to fire. Heat burned between her legs while her nipples puckered with need. Her hips began to move in an ancient rhythm and she heard herself sob.

His fingers stilled on her breasts. "Sweetheart?"

But she could no longer talk. She was on the brink of something inexplicable.

He lifted his hand from her breast and slipped it between her legs. She felt the heat of his touch through the thin fabric of her panties as he moved the heel of his hand against her.

Just like that, she shattered.

9

Bobby Tom stood in the center of the clean linoleum and gazed out the rear windows of the motor home while he waited for Gracie to finish her shower so he could take one himself. He was more shaken by what had happened than he cared to admit. For all his experience with women, he'd never seen one come like that. He'd barely touched her and she had shot right over the edge.

Afterward, they had cleaned up the kitchen in silence. Gracie had refused to look at him, and he'd been so upset with her that he hadn't wanted to talk. What in the hell had she been thinking to stay a virgin all this time? Didn't she understand she was too responsive to have denied herself one of life's most basic pleasures?

He wondered whether he was madder at her or at himself. He'd needed every bit of his self-control to keep from ripping those little bikini underpants right off her and taking advantage of what she was offering. And why hadn't he? Because she was Gracie Snow, dammit, and he'd given up mercy fucking a long time ago. It was too damned complicated.

Right then he made up his mind. His sex drive was back in full force, and he was going to fly to Dallas the minute he got a chance. When he got there, he intended to pay a call on a beautiful divorcée he knew, who liked the free and easy life as much as he did and was more interested in gettin' naked than in having candlelight dinners and long conversations. Once he stopped living like a monk, he'd stop being tempted by Gracie Snow.

He remembered he hadn't fetched her suitcase from the trunk of his T-bird as he'd promised, and he let himself out of the trailer. In the distance, he saw some of the crew members gathered over by the corral. He was glad they were far enough away that he wouldn't have to explain why he was covered with dried-up ice cream.

Just as he opened the trunk of the car, he heard a drawling voice coming from behind him. "Well, well. And here I thought it was dog shit I smelled. What's that crap you got all over you?"

He extracted the suitcase without turning. "Good to see you, too, Jimbo."

"That's Jim. *Jim*, you understand?"

Bobby Tom turned slowly to face his old nemesis. Jimbo Thackery looked as big and dumb as ever, even in uniform. His dark eyebrows grew so close together they almost met in the middle, and he had the same five o'clock shadow Bobby Tom swore he could remember

189

from kindergarten. The police chief wasn't stupid—Suzy'd said he'd been doing a good job ever since Luther had appointed him—but he sure looked that way with his burly body and big head. He also had too many teeth, and he was displaying every one of them in a smarmy grin that made Bobby Tom want to do a little creative dentistry with his fist.

"I guess if the ladies could see you now, Mr. Movie Star, they wouldn't think you're such a stud."

Bobby Tom regarded him with exasperation. "Tell me you aren't still holding a grudge about Sherri Hopper. That was fifteen years ago!"

"Hell, no." He ambled toward the front of the T-bird and put his foot up on the bumper. "Right now I'm holding a grudge because you're endangering the citizens of this town by driving around in a car with a broken headlight." He pulled out a pink pad and, grinning widely, began to write out a ticket.

"What broken head—" Bobby Tom stopped. Not only was his left front headlight broken, but pieces of glass lay on the ground beneath it, giving him a pretty good idea who'd kicked it in. "You sonova—"

"Careful, B.T. Around here, you've got to watch what you say to the law."

"You did that, you bastard!"

"Hey, B.T. Jim."

Jimbo stopped what he was doing and turned to grin at the dark-haired woman in the tinkling silver bracelets who came up behind

190

them. In a bid to catch his attention, Connie Cameron, Bobby Tom's old girlfriend and the woman who operated the catering truck, had done everything but undress in front of him since he'd arrived yesterday. Now, as he saw the love lights glimmering in Jimbo's eyes, he resigned himself to more trouble.

"Hi, sweetheart." Jimbo brushed his mouth over her lips. "I go off duty in a few minutes, and I thought I'd take you out for dinner. Hey, B.T., did you hear that me and Connie are engaged? We're tying the knot at Thanksgiving and we're expecting a real nice wedding present from you." Jimbo gave him a smirk and went back to writing out the ticket.

"Congratulations."

Connie gazed at Bobby Tom with hungry eyes. "What happened to you? You look like you've been rolling around with the pigs."

"Not even close."

She regarded him suspiciously, but before she could question him further, Jimbo slapped the ticket in his hand. "You can pay this at City Hall."

"What's that?" Connie asked.

"Had to give B.T. here a ticket. He's got a broken headlight."

Connie studied the headlight and then the broken glass lying on the ground. With a look of disgust, she pulled the ticket from Bobby Tom's fingers and tore it in two. "Forget it, Jim. You're not starting up with B.T. again."

Jimbo looked as though he was going to explode, but at the same time, Bobby Tom could see that he didn't want to do it in front of his beloved. Instead, he slipped his arm around her shoulders. "We'll talk later, Denton."

"I can't wait."

Jimbo glared at him, then led Connie away. Bobby Tom gazed at the torn ticket lying in the dirt and had the distinct feeling that Connie hadn't done him a favor.

"I don't understand why you won't tell me what happened to the headlight."

"Because it's none of your damn business, that's why." Bobby Tom slammed the door harder than necessary as he got out of the car.

Gracie was so offended by his stubbornness that she didn't even glance at his house as she stalked up the front walk after him. He was freshly showered and dressed in a blue chambray shirt that he'd rolled up at the sleeves. His perfectly faded jeans and his pearl gray Stetson made him look like a Guess? ad, while she had been forced to slip into a wrinkled olive drab skirt and blouse that she'd bought in a misguided fascination with the safari look.

After what had happened between them in the trailer, she very much needed to pick a fight. All the satisfaction had been one-sided, which wasn't what she'd wanted at all. She wanted to give, not just take, but she was very much afraid he had come to regard her as an object of pity. Between the way she'd thrown herself at him last night and what had happened this afternoon, what else could he think?

By breaking into a trot, she finally caught up with him. "I was the last person to drive it."

He glared at her from beneath the brim of his Stetson. "You didn't break the headlight."

"Then why won't you tell me how it happened?"

"I'm not talking about it anymore!"

She was just getting ready to press him when her attention was caught by his house. The simple, white frame structure looked so different from his Chicago residence that she found it difficult to believe that the same person owned both places. Four painted concrete steps led up to a porch with a white railing, a wooden swing, and a broom propped near the door. The wide floorboards of the porch were painted the same serviceable dark green as the front door. No shutters softened the double hung front windows that looked out on the grove of pecan trees in the yard. No brass lanterns or shiny door knockers dressed up the exterior. The house was small, sturdy, and utilitarian.

And then Bobby Tom opened the front door and she walked inside.

"Oh, my."

He chuckled. "It sort of takes your breath away, doesn't it?"

A sense of wonder filled her as she gazed around the candy box entryway and took three slow steps into the living room on her left. "It's beautiful."

"I figured you'd like it. Most women do."

She felt as if she'd entered an adult-sized dollhouse, a delicate pastel world of pink-and-cream accented with soft lavender and the palest of seafoam greens. The ruffles and florals and lace could have been overpowering, but everything had been executed with such exquisite taste that she wanted to cuddle up in one of the pink-and-white—striped armchairs with a cup of peppermint tea, an Angora cat, and a novel by Jane Austen.

The room smelled of roses. Her hands itched to explore the contrasting textures of lace curtains, polished chintz, cut glass, and gilt. She wanted to stroke the watered silk cushions with their fringed borders and twine her fingers through the loops of ribbon that held up a floral table skirt. Did the lush fern spilling from the white wicker basket sitting between the two front windows smell of rich, sweet earth? Would the spray of wheat and dried pink roses perched on the fireplace mantel crackle under her fingertips?

And then her heart lurched as Bobby Tom moved into the center of the room. He should have looked silly in the midst of such delicate surroundings, but instead, he had never looked more intensely masculine. The contrast between the room's frivolous delicacy and his tough uncompromising strength made her insides go weak. Only a man with no doubts about his virility could walk with such assurance through so feminine an environment.

He tossed his Stetson on a plump ottoman

and tilted his head toward an arched opening at the rear. "You want to really see something, take a gander at my bedroom back there."

Several seconds ticked by before she could force herself to look away from him. Her legs felt shaky as she walked down a narrow hallway painted the pearly pink of the inside of a seashell and entered the room at the end. She paused in the doorway, so dumbstruck she didn't even know he had come up behind her until he spoke.

"Go ahead. Say what's on your mind."

She gazed at a queen-size bed with shiny gilt posts and the most incredible canopy she had ever seen. Layer upon layer of gossamer white lace tumbled in a frothy waterfall caught up in swags with nosegays of pink-and-lavender satin ribbon.

Her eyes sparkled. "Do you have to wait for the prince to kiss you every morning before you can wake up?"

He laughed. "I keep meaning to get rid of it, but I never seem to get around to it."

The fairy-tale room with its canopy bed, gilded chests, pink-and-lavender throw pillows, and ruffled chaise lounge looked as if it belonged in Sleeping Beauty's castle. After years of living inside institutional beige walls and walking on hard tile floors, she wished she could stay here for the rest of her life.

The phone began to ring in his office, but he ignored it. "There's a little apartment over the garage where you can stay. My weight room's up there, too."

She gazed at him with astonishment. "I'm not staying here."

"Of course you are. You can't afford to stay anyplace else."

For a fraction of a moment, she didn't know what he was talking about, and then she remembered her stilted conversation with Willow that morning. Windmill Studios had been responsible for her room and board when she worked on location as a production assistant, but Willow had made a point of stating that her new position had no provision for a living allowance. Gracie had been so upset by everything else that had happened, she hadn't considered the problem that presented.

"I'll find an inexpensive motel," she said firmly.

"On your salary, it'd have to be more than inexpensive; it'd have to be free."

"How do you know what my salary is?"

"Willow told me. And it made me wonder why you don't just buy yourself a bottle of Windex, so you could stand at a traffic light and do windshields instead. I guaran-damn-tee you, you'd earn more money."

"Money isn't everything. I was willing to make a small sacrifice until I proved myself with the studio."

Once again the phone began to ring, and once again he ignored it. "In case you've forgotten, the two of us are supposed to be engaged. People around here know me too well to believe you'd be living anyplace but close by."

"Engaged?"

His lips tightened in annoyance. "I distinctly remember that you were standing right next to me when I told all of those ladies in the trailer that you'd passed the football quiz."

"Bobby Tom, those women didn't take you seriously. Or at least they won't when they start thinking about it."

"That's why we've got to be aggressive about this."

"Are you telling me that you seriously want people to believe the two of us are engaged?" Her voice caught on a high, squeaky note as her hopes blossomed, only to be firmly squelched by her instincts for self-protection. Fantasies were meant to be dreamed, not lived. It would all be a game to him, but not to her.

"That's what I said, isn't it? Contrary to what you may think, I don't talk just to hear the sound of my voice. For the rest of our stay in Telarosa, you're the future Mrs. Bobby Tom."

"I most certainly am not! And I wish you'd quit saying that. Mrs. Bobby Tom! As if the woman who marries you isn't anything more than your appendage!"

He released a long, put-upon sigh. "Gracie...Gracie...Gracie....Every time I think the two of us have our communication channels open, you do something to prove me wrong. The most important part of your job as my personal assistant is to make certain I get some peace and quiet while I'm here.

Exactly how do you expect that to happen when every Tom, Dick, and Harriet who's known me since I was born has an unattached female they want me to meet?"

As if to prove his point, the doorbell began to chime. He ignored it the same way he ignored his telephone. "Let me explain something to you. Right this very moment, there are at least a dozen women between here and San Antone who are trying to memorize the year Joe Theismann played in the Pro Bowl and figure out how many yards a team gets penalized if the captain doesn't show up for the coin toss. That's just the way things are around here. Without even looking, I can pretty much guarantee that's a female at the door now, or someone who's got one in tow. This isn't Chicago, where I've got some control over the women I see. This is Telarosa, and these people own me."

She tried to appeal to his sense of reason. "But no one in their right mind is going to believe you'd marry me." Both of them knew it was true, and it might as well be said.

The ringing stopped and pounding took its place, but he didn't move. "Once I get you fixed up a little bit, they will."

She regarded him warily. "What do you mean 'fixed up'?"

"Just what I said, is all. We're going to do one of those whadyacall—One of those makeovers, like they do on the 'Oprah' show."

"What do you know about the 'Oprah' show?"

"You spend as many days sittin' in hotel rooms as I've spent, you get to know day-time TV pretty well."

She heard the amusement in his voice. "You're not serious about this at all. You're just getting even with me for letting those women into your motor home."

"I've never been more serious. Today was only a sample of what's in store for me for the next few months unless I have a gen-u-ine fiancée standing at my side. The only person besides us who has to know the truth is my mother." The noise at the door had finally stopped, and he walked over to the telephone. "I'm gonna call her now to make sure she plays along."

"Stop! I didn't say I'd do this." But she wanted to. Oh, how she wanted to. She had so little time with him that every second was precious. And she had no delusions about his feelings toward her, so she wasn't in danger of confusing reality and illusion. She remembered the promise she'd made to herself to give and not take, and for the second time that day, she decided to spread her wings and free-fall.

He was giving her that cocky look that said he knew he'd won, and she reminded herself that she cared about him too much to contribute to his character flaws by letting him dictate all the terms. She stalked over to him and crossed her arms.

"All right," she said in a low, determined voice. "I'll go along with this. But you are not, under any circumstances, to refer to me again as 'the future Mrs. Bobby Tom,' do you understand? Because if you say that just once, just *once*, I will personally tell the entire world that our engagement is a fraud. Furthermore, I will announce that you are—are—" Her mouth opened and closed. She'd started out strong, but now she couldn't think of anything terrible enough to throw at him.

"An ax murderer?" he offered helpfully.

When she didn't reply, he tried again. "A vegetarian?"

It came to her in a flash. "Impotent!"

He looked at her as if she'd gone crazy. "You're going to tell everybody *I'm* impotent?"

"Only if you call me that obnoxious name."

"I seriously advise you to stick with that ax murderer idea. It'll be more believable."

"You talk big, Bobby Tom. But from personal observation, I'd say that's about all you do."

The words slipped out before she had time to think about them, and she couldn't believe what she'd said. She, a thirty-year-old virgin with no experience at flirtation, had issued a sexual challenge to a professional libertine. He gaped at her, and she realized she had finally rendered him speechless. Although her knees were showing an alarming tendency to tremble, she stuck her chin up in the air and marched out of the bedroom.

By the time she reached the front hallway, she had begun to smile. Surely a competitor like Bobby Tom wouldn't let a remark like that go unchallenged. Surely, even now, he was planning some appropriate form of retaliation.

10

"**M**r. Sawyer will see you now, Mrs. Denton."

Suzy rose from the leather couch and crossed the well-appointed reception area toward the office of the CEO of Rosatech Electronics. She stepped inside and heard a soft click as Wayland Sawyer's secretary shut the carved walnut door behind her.

Sawyer didn't look up from his desk. She wasn't certain whether he had made a calculated decision to put her in her place or if he simply had no more manners than he'd had in high school. Either way, it didn't bode well. The city and the county had already sent a flock of important representatives to talk with him, and he had been maddeningly noncommittal. She knew that she, as the female president of the Board of Education, was considered a rather pathetic last-ditch effort.

The office was decorated much like a gentleman's library, with richly paneled walls, comfortable furniture upholstered in deep burgundy, and hunting prints. As she walked slowly across the Oriental carpet, he continued to study a folder of papers through the lenses of a pair of half glasses that looked very much like the ones she, after a lifetime of perfect vision, had recently been forced to buy.

The cuffs of his blue dress shirt had been turned twice, revealing surprisingly muscular forearms for a man of fifty-four. Neither the dress shirt, the neatly knotted navy-and-red—striped tie, nor the half glasses could disguise the fact that he looked more like a roughneck than a captain of industry. He reminded her of a slightly older version of Tommy Lee Jones, the Texas-born actor who was a favorite of her bridge club.

She tried hard not to let his silence rattle her, but she wasn't like these talented young women who functioned better in a boardroom than a kitchen. Growing an herb garden interested her far more than competing for power with men. She was also from the old school and accustomed to common courtesy.

"Perhaps this isn't a good time," she said softly.

"I'll be with you in a minute." His voice was impatient. Without looking at her, he jerked his head toward one of the side chairs in front of his desk, just as if she were a dog he was ordering to lie down. The offensive gesture forced her to realize exactly how futile her mission was. Wayland Sawyer had been impossible in high school, and obviously nothing had changed. Without another word, she made her way back across the carpet toward the door.

"Where do you think you're going?"

She turned to him and spoke quietly. "My

visit is obviously an intrusion on your time, Mr. Sawyer."

"I'll be the judge of that." He snatched off his glasses and motioned toward the chair. "Please."

The word was barked out as a command, and Suzy couldn't remember when she'd taken such an instant dislike to someone; although, as she thought about it, she realized it wasn't all that instant. Way had been two years ahead of her, the biggest hood at Telarosa High, and the kind of boy only the fastest girls had gone out with. She still had a vague memory of seeing him standing behind the gym with a cigarette dangling from the corner of his mouth and his hard eyes slitted like a cobra's. It was difficult to reconcile the teenage hoodlum with the multimillionaire businessman, but one thing hadn't changed. He had terrified her then, and he still did.

She swallowed her trepidation and made her way to the chair. He studied her openly, and she found herself wishing she'd ignored the blistering summer heat and worn a suit instead of her chocolate silk wrap dress. The garment tied loosely at the side and fell in soft folds over her hips as she sat. She had brightened the simple neckline with a chunky matte gold necklace and small, matching earrings. Her sheer, chocolate-tinted stockings were the same shade as her designer pumps, which were embellished around the sides of the square polished heels with a parade of tiny gold panthers. The outfit had been ridiculously expensive, she was certain, a birthday gift from Bobby Tom after she'd refused to let him buy her a condo on Hilton Head.

"What can I do for you, Mrs. Denton?"

His words held the trace of a sneer. She could deal with the more aggressive male members on the board because she'd known most of them all her life, but she was clearly out of her element with him. As much as she wanted to leave, however, she had a job to do. The children of Telarosa were going to lose so much if this awful man had his way.

"I'm here representing the Telarosa Board of Education, Mr. Sawyer. I want to make certain you've considered the consequences that closing Rosatech is going to have on the children of this town."

His eyes were dark and chill in his raw-boned face. Propping his elbows on the desk, he pressed his fingers together and studied her over the tips. "In what capacity are you representing the board?"

"I'm the president."

"I see. And is this the same Board of Education that kicked me out of school a month before I could graduate?"

His question stunned her and she had no idea what to say.

"Well, Mrs. Denton?"

His eyes had darkened with hostility, and she realized that, for once, the gossip was accurate. Way Sawyer believed he had been wronged by Telarosa, and he had returned to take his revenge.

The old stories came back to her. She knew that Way had been illegitimate, a condition that had made both him and his mother Trudy outcasts. Trudy had cleaned houses for a while—she'd even cleaned for Hoyt's mother—but eventually she'd become a prostitute.

Suzy crossed her hands in her lap. "Do you intend to punish all of the children just because you might have been mistreated here forty years ago?"

"Not quite forty years. And the memory's still young." He gave her a thin smile that didn't make it past the corners of his mouth. "Is that what you think I'm doing?"

"If you move Rosatech, you'll turn Telarosa into a ghost town."

"The company isn't its only source of income. There's the tourist industry."

She saw the cynical twist to his lips and stiffened as she realized that he was baiting her. "Both of us know tourism won't ever support this town. Without Rosatech, Telarosa is going to die."

"I'm a businessman, not a philanthropist, and my responsibility rests with making the company more profitable. Right now, it looks as if consolidating with a plant in San Antone is the best way to do that."

Controlling her anger, she leaned forward slightly. "Would you let me take you on a tour of the schools next week?"

"And have all those little children run screaming in terror when they see me? I think I'll pass."

The mockery in his eyes told her that being the town's pariah didn't bother him all that much.

She looked down at her hands in her lap and then back at up him. "There's nothing I can say to change your mind, is there?"

He stared at her for a long moment. She was conscious of muffled voices in the outer reception area, the soft tick of the wall clock, the sound of her own breathing. Something she didn't understand flickered across his face, and she felt a stab of foreboding. There was an almost imperceptible tension in his posture that threatened her.

"Maybe there is." His chair squeaked as he leaned back, and the hard, unforgiving lines of his face reminded her of the rugged granite slopes found in this part of Texas. "We can discuss it over dinner at my house on Sunday evening. I'll send a car for you at eight."

No polite invitation, but a direct command, and phrased in the most insulting manner. She wanted to tell him that she'd eat dinner with the devil before she'd eat with him, but the stakes were too high, and as she stared into those grim, implacable eyes, she knew that she didn't dare refuse.

Gathering up her purse, she stood. "Very well," she said quietly.

He had already slipped his half glasses back on and returned his attention to his papers. As she left his office, he didn't bother to say good-bye.

She was still fuming when she reached her

car. What a despicable person! She had no experience dealing with someone like him. Hoyt had been open and sunny, the opposite of Way Sawyer. As she fumbled for her car keys, she wondered what he wanted from her.

She knew Luther Baines would be expecting a phone call from her as soon as she got home, and she didn't know what she would say to him. She certainly couldn't tell him that she had agreed to have dinner with Sawyer. She couldn't tell anyone that, especially Bobby Tom. If he ever found out how Sawyer had intimidated her, he'd be furious, and too much was at stake for her to risk his interference. No matter how upsetting, she would have to handle this herself.

"I'd rather not, Bobby Tom."

"Now don't let those pink flamingos and that tractor tire flower garden throw you off, Gracie. Shirley's real good with hair."

Bobby Tom held open the door of Shirley's Hollywood Hair, which was located in the garage of a small, one-story house on a dusty residential street. Since he didn't have to be on the set until noon, he had announced he was using the morning to get her started on her make-over. He gave her a determined nudge inside the salon, and goose pimples broke out on her arms. Like every other public place in Texas, the beauty shop was air-conditioned to the temperature of a deep freeze.

Three walls of the small shop were painted Pepto-Bismol pink, while one wall was covered in black-and-gold—mirrored tiles. There were two beauty operators in the salon, one a trim brunette in a light blue smock, the other a blowsy blonde sporting one of the biggest beehives Gracie had ever seen. Her pudgy thighs were encased by purple stretch pants and a tight pink T-shirt clung to a huge pair of breasts. The T-shirt read GOD, I WISH THESE WERE BRAINS.

Gracie prayed that the Shirley, who was supposed to do her hair, would prove to be the trim brunette, but Bobby Tom was already walking over to the other beauty operator. "Hey there, doll face."

The woman looked up from the mound of coal black hair she was teasing and let out a throaty gargle. "Bobby Tom, you good-looking sonovabitch, it's about time you came by to see me."

He planted a kiss on a cheek covered with a garish rouge circle. She slapped his butt with her free hand. "You still got the best one in the state."

"Coming from a connoisseur like yourself, I consider that a compliment of the highest order." He smiled at the other operator and her customer, then greeted the two women peeking out from under the helmets of their hair dryers. "Velma. Mrs. Carlson. How you ladies doin' today?"

They giggled and tittered. Bobby Tom looped his arm around Gracie's shoulders and drew her forward. "Everybody, this is Gracie Snow."

Shirley regarded her with open curiosity.

"We've heard all about you. So you're the future Mrs. Bobby Tom."

He took a hasty step forward. "Gracie's sort of a feminist, Shirley, and she doesn't like it when people call her that. To be honest, we might be dealing with a hyphen situation here."

"For real?"

Bobby Tom shrugged, palms extended, the last sane man in a crazy world.

Shirley turned on Gracie, and her painted eyebrows arched into her forehead. "Don't do it, honey. Gracie Snow-Denton sounds just plain peculiar. Like you should live in a castle in England somewhere."

"Or show up on a weather map," Bobby Tom offered.

Gracie opened her mouth to explain that she had no intention of hyphenating her last name, but then snapped it shut as she saw the trap he'd laid for her. Silvery devil-lights danced in his eyes, and she firmly repressed a smile. Was she the only person on earth who saw through him?

Shirley resumed her work on the head of hair in front of her while she studied Gracie in the mirror at the same time. "I heard you wouldn't let her fix herself up, Bobby Tom, but I never figured you'd let it get this far. Whatcha want me to do with her?"

"I'm going to leave it in your hands. Gracie's pretty much a wildcat, though, so don't get too conservative."

Gracie was appalled. Bobby Tom had just

told a beautician with a blond beehive and Ringling Brothers makeup not to be too conservative when she worked on her hair! She started to offer a sharp rebuttal, but he distracted her with a quick peck at the lips.

"I've got some errands to run, sweetheart. Mom's going to pick you up and take you clothes shopping so you can get a head start on that trousseau you're so set on. Now that I'm lettin' you get gorgeous again, don't you change your mind about marryin' me."

All the women burst into laughter at the absurdity of the idea that any woman would back away from the opportunity to marry Bobby Tom Denton. He tipped his hat at them and headed out the door. Despite her annoyance, she wondered if she was the only one who felt as if the sunlight had gone with him.

Six pairs of curious eyes locked in on her. She smiled weakly. "I'm not really a—uh—wildcat." She cleared her throat. "He sometime exaggerates and I..."

"Take a seat, Gracie. I'll be with you in a minute. There's a new *People* magazine you can look at."

Thoroughly intimidated by this person who held the future of her hair in her hands, Gracie dropped into a chair and grabbed the magazine. One of the women under the dryers peered at her through the clear plastic frames of her eyeglasses, and Gracie braced herself for the inevitable.

"How did you and Bobby Tom meet?"

"How long have you known each other?"

"When did you pass the quiz?"

The interrogation was swift and relentless, and it didn't stop when Shirley called her over to her chair and began work. Since Gracie didn't believe in telling lies, she had to concentrate so hard on circumnavigating the truth without actually uttering a falsehood that she couldn't supervise the damage being inflicted on her hair. Not that she could have seen it, anyway, since Shirley kept the chair turned away from the mirror.

"You've got a good perm here, Gracie, but you have an awful lot of hair. You need some layers. I like layers." Shirley's scissors clicked away and wet, coppery hair flew everywhere.

Gracie dodged a question about the regularity of her menstrual cycle while she worried about what was happening to her hair. If Shirley cut it too short, she'd never be able to get it into her french twist, which, even if it hadn't been exactly flattering, was at least neat and familiar.

A heavy lock, nearly three inches long, fell into her lap, and her anxiety escalated. "Shirley, I—"

"Janine's gonna do your makeup." Shirley nodded her head toward the other operator. "She just started to sell Mary Kay this week, and she's looking for customers. Bobby Tom said he wanted to buy you a fresh supply of cosmetics to replace all the stuff you lost in that South American earthquake when you were guarding the vice president."

Gracie nearly choked, and then fought against laughter. He was maddening, but entertaining.

Shirley switched on the hair dryer and spun the chair to the mirror. Gracie gave a gasp of dismay. She looked like a wet rat.

"I'll teach you how to do this yourself. It's all in the fingers." Shirley began pulling at her hair, and Gracie envisioned clumps of frizz standing straight out from her head. Maybe she could hold it down with one of those big hairbands, she thought, with a trace of desperation. Or maybe she should just buy a wig.

Then, so gradually she could barely believe it, something wonderful began to happen.

"There." Shirley finally stepped back, her fingers having worked their magic.

Gracie stared at her reflection. "Oh, my goodness."

"Cute, huh." Shirley grinned into the mirror.

Cute was hardly the word for it. Gracie's hair was thoroughly modern. Reckless. Uninhibited. Sexy. It was everything that Gracie wasn't, and her hand trembled as she touched it.

The cut was much shorter than she was accustomed to, barely jaw length and side parted with a wisp of bangs. Far from being frizzy, it fell in soft, pretty waves and curly tendrils that feathered her cheeks and earlobes. Her small features and fine gray eyes were no longer overpowered by the heavy weight of her old hair, and Gracie was entranced with her reflection. Was this really her?

She hadn't even begun to look her fill before Shirley passed her over to Janine to get Mary Kayed. For the next hour, Gracie learned about skin care and a makeup application that would enhance her naturally smooth complexion. With liner, amber shadows, and dark mascara, Janine made her eyes the focal point of her face. When she was satisfied, she had Gracie do it herself. Gracie finished by dusting her cheekbones with blush, then applying the soft coral lipstick Janine handed her. She gazed into the mirror with wonder, hardly able to believe the woman staring back was herself.

The makeup was subtle and flattering. With her sweet, reckless haircut, luminous gray eyes, and spiky lashes, she looked prettier than she'd ever imagined: feminine, desirable, and, yes, a little bit wild. Her heart began to pound. She looked so different now. Was it possible that Bobby Tom might find her attractive? Maybe he would start looking at her in a new way. Maybe he would—

She reined in her runaway thoughts. This was exactly what she'd promised herself she wouldn't do. All the make overs in the world wouldn't transform her into one of those spectacular beauties Bobby Tom kept company with, and she mustn't allow herself to build dream castles.

When Gracie took out her wallet, Shirley looked at her as if she'd lost her mind and told her Bobby Tom had taken care of it. Something unpleasant uncoiled in Gracie's stomach.

She thought of the long list of people Bobby Tom gave money to and realized he had added her to his charity list.

She should have anticipated this. He didn't see her as a competent, independent woman at all, but as one more lost cause. The realization hurt. She wanted him to regard her as his equal, and that would never happen if he was picking up all the bills.

It had been easy to promise herself she wouldn't take anything from him, but now she realized that the reality wouldn't be simple at all. He had expensive tastes and he would expect her to look as if she belonged with him, but how was she to do that on her limited income? She thought of the small financial nest egg in her savings account that was her only security. Was she prepared to jeopardize it for the sake of her principles?

She didn't have to think about it for more than a few seconds to know this was too important for her to back away, and her jaw set in a stubborn line. For the sake of her soul and everything she believed in, she needed to give herself to him with a free and loving heart. That meant she could take nothing from him. She would leave him before she became another parasite in his life.

Politely, but firmly, she wrote a check to cover the hefty bill and asked Shirley to return Bobby Tom's money. The gesture exhilarated her. She would be one person in his life who wasn't bought and paid for.

Suzy arrived moments later. She admired

Gracie from every angle and was effusive with her compliments. Only after they'd left the beauty shop and were settled in the Lexus to go clothes shopping did Gracie notice that she seemed a bit distracted, but perhaps she'd had a restless night.

Gracie hadn't slept all that well herself, despite her comfortable bed in the small apartment above Bobby Tom's garage. The bleached wood and contemporary royal blue and white color scheme of the rooms made it obvious they hadn't been decorated by the same person who'd done the house. Although the quarters were compact, they had turned out to be far more luxurious than she'd imagined. Or that she could afford, she realized with dismay, as she added a mental figure for rent that would compound her financial difficulties.

The apartment featured a combination living room/kitchenette and separate bedroom, which ran parallel to Bobby Tom's weight room. Her bedroom faced the rear of his house, and when she'd been unable to sleep last night, she'd gotten up, only to discover she wasn't the only insomniac. Below her, she'd seen the flickering silver light of the television coming from the window of his office.

The bright sunlight fell on Suzy's drawn features, making Gracie feel guilty for imposing on her. "We don't have to do this today."

"I'm looking forward to it."

Her response seemed genuine, so Gracie

didn't protest further. At the same time, she realized she needed to be honest with Suzy. "I'm embarrassed about this phony engagement. I tried to convince him that the whole idea is ridiculous."

"Not from his viewpoint. People here are always after him for one thing or another. If this gives him a little peace while he's in town, I'm all for it." She dismissed the subject as she turned toward Main Street. "We're lucky to have a wonderful boutique in town. Millie will take good care of you."

The word "boutique" rang alarm bells in Gracie's head. "Is it expensive?"

"That doesn't matter. Bobby Tom's taking care of everything."

"He's not buying my clothes," she said quietly. "I won't permit it. I'll be buying them myself, and I'm afraid I'm on a limited budget."

"Of course he's paying. This was his idea."

Gracie shook her head stubbornly.

"You're serious, aren't you?"

"Very serious."

Suzy seemed bemused. "Bobby Tom always pays."

"Not for me."

For a moment Suzy didn't say anything. Then she smiled and made a U-turn. "I love challenges. There's an outlet mall about thirty miles from here. This is going to be fun."

For the next three hours, Suzy performed like a drill sergeant, leading her from one discount store to another, where she searched out bargains like a bloodhound. She paid no attention to Gracie's own preferences and, instead, dressed her in the sort of youthful, provocative clothes Gracie would never have dared choose for herself. Suzy selected a gauzy skirt and silky jewel-toned blouse, a watermelon pink tank dress that fell open from midthigh to calf, stonewashed jeans with stretchy ribbed knit tops, scandalously short skirts, cotton sweaters that clung to her breasts. Gracie tried on belts and necklaces, sandals and flats, Keds with rhinestones and free-form silver earrings. By the time the last of the garments was packed away in the trunk of the Lexus Gracie had wiped out a huge chunk of her savings. She felt dazed and more than a little nervous.

"Are you sure?" She glanced down at the hot red romper that had been their final purchase. Its off-the-shoulder bodice clung so tightly to her skin that she couldn't wear a bra, and the knit fabric sparkled with gold-tone studs. A two-inch gold metallic belt separated the clingy bodice from the looser-fitting shorts, and her sensible espadrilles had been replaced by a pair of strappy little lipstick red sandals. The outfit made her feel as if she were pretending to be someone she wasn't.

For what seemed to be the hundredth time that afternoon, Suzy reassured her. "It's darling on you."

Gracie fought to control her panic. Homely women didn't wear "darling" clothes. She seized on what she saw as a valid excuse to explain her continued hesitation.

"These sandals don't supply very much arch support."

"Do you have trouble with your arches?"

"No. But maybe that's because I've always worn sensible shoes."

Suzy smiled and patted her arm. "Don't worry, Gracie. You look wonderful."

"I don't look like myself."

"I think you look exactly like yourself. And I say it's about time."

Who the hell was driving his T-bird? And driving it too damned fast! Bobby Tom spotted the rooster tail of dust from half a mile away and grabbed his script from the top of the corral post where he'd propped it to study the scene they were shooting that afternoon.

The T-bird turned off the road, still kicking up dust, and pulled to a squealing stop next to his trailer. As he squinted against the glare of the setting sun, he saw a hot little number dressed in red step out of the car, and his blood pressure soared. Dammit! Gracie was the only person who had permission to drive his T-bird. He'd asked her to pick it up from Buddy's Garage after she'd finished with her shopping, but she'd obviously decided to teach him another one of her lessons by cajoling some predatory female into doing the job.

He set his jaw and stalked forward, still squinting from the sun as he tried to make out who it was, but he couldn't see much more than a nice little body, short sexy hair, and a face partially hidden by small round sunglasses. He swore to himself that he was going to have Gracie's hide for this. She knew better than anyone that their phony engagement was supposed to protect him from just this sort of thing.

And then he froze in his tracks as the sun picked out familiar coppery lights in that flyaway hair. His gaze slithered down over the nicely proportioned body and slender legs to a neat pair of ankles he would have recognized anywhere, and he felt as if he'd been poleaxed. At the same time, he called himself ten kinds of a fool. He was the one who had arranged for Gracie's make-over. Why hadn't he been better prepared for the results?

Gracie watched apprehensively as he approached. She knew enough about the way Bobby Tom behaved with women by now to predict exactly what he was going to say. He would flatter her outrageously, probably tell her she was the prettiest woman he'd ever seen in his life, and under his barrage of preposterous compliments, she'd have no idea what he really thought about the changes in her appearance. If only he'd be honest with her so she could know whether or not she looked ridiculous.

He stopped in front of her. Several seconds ticked by as she waited for that lady-killer grin to take over his face and the blarney to start flowing. He rubbed his chin with the back of his knuckles.

"Looks like Buddy did a good job. Did he give you a receipt?"

Stunned, she watched him walk right past her, glance at the headlight Buddy had replaced, and crouch to examine the new tires. Her pleasure in the moment faded, and she felt deflated. "It's in the glove compartment."

He stood back up and glared at her. "Why the hell were you driving so fast?"

Because the pretty lady with the reckless hair and frivolous little sandals without any arch support is a free spirit who doesn't worry about mundane things like speed limits.

"I guess I had other things on my mind." When was he going to tell her she was the prettiest little thing he'd ever seen in his life, just like he told every other female?

His mouth tightened in annoyance. "I've been planning on letting you use the T-bird to get around while we're here, but I'm seriously thinking about changing my mind after what I just saw. You were driving this car like it's some old junker."

"I apologize." She gritted her teeth as anger overcame her hurt. She had spent a fortune today, and he didn't seem to notice.

"I'd appreciate it very much if you didn't let it happen again."

She straightened her shoulders and stuck her chin up in the air, determined not to let him bully her. She knew she looked pretty, maybe for the first time in her life, and if he didn't think so, that was just too bad. "It won't happen again. Now if you're finished yelling at me, I told Natalie I'd watch Elvis for her this afternoon."

"You're supposed to be my assistant, not a baby-sitter!"

"One and the same." She stalked away.

11

The dark maroon Lincoln stopped before the entrance of the spacious whitewashed brick country house Wayland Sawyer had built overlooking the river. As the chauffeur came around to open her door, Suzy decided that Sawyer couldn't have found a better way to let the people of Telarosa know that he'd made a success of himself than by building this magnificent estate. According to local gossip, he planned to continue using it as a weekend retreat even after he'd closed Rosatech.

As the chauffeur opened the door and helped her out, her palms were damp. Ever since her meeting with Sawyer two days ago, she'd been able to think of little else. She'd chosen to wear loosely fitted cream-colored evening trousers instead of a dress. The matching tank top and hip-length silky jacket were printed with wearable art, a fanciful Chagall village scene in jewellike tones of coral, turquoise, fuchsia, and aquamarine. Her only jewelry was her wedding band and the large diamond studs Bobby Tom had given her when he'd signed his first contract with the Stars.

A Hispanic woman Suzy didn't recognize

admitted her and escorted her across the black marble floor into a spacious living room with Palladian windows that soared two stories and looked out on a softly illuminated rose garden. Silk-shaded lamps cast warm shadows on glazed ivory walls. The sofas and chairs sitting in pleasant groups were upholstered in cool shades of blue and green touched here and there with black. Matching shell-shaped wall nooks on each side of the marble fireplace held unglazed terra-cotta urns massed with dried hydrangeas.

Way Sawyer stood next to a shiny ebony baby grand piano positioned in front of the largest window. Her uneasiness increased as she saw that he was dressed entirely in black, like a modern day gunslinger. But instead of chaps and vest, his unstructured designer suit was Italian and his shirt silk. The room's soft lights did nothing to temper the harsh lines in his face.

He held a cut glass tumbler in his hand and gazed at her with dispassionate dark eyes that seemed to miss nothing. "What would you like to drink?"

"White wine would be fine."

He walked over to a small chest that held a mirrored tray filled with an assortment of bottles and glasses. While he poured her wine, she tried to calm herself by wandering around the room and studying the art hanging on the walls. There were several large oils and a number of watercolors. She paused in front of a small pen-and-ink drawing of a mother and child.

"I bought that at auction in London a few years ago."

She hadn't heard him come up behind her. He extended a gold-rimmed wineglass, and, as she took a sip, he began telling her a bit of the history of each painting. His words were slow and measured, giving her information but not putting her at ease. She had difficulty reconciling this man who spoke calmly of a London art auction with the sullen-faced hoodlum who had smoked cigarettes by the gym and gone out with the fastest girls.

In the past few weeks, she'd done some research to fill in the holes about Sawyer's past. According to the story that she'd been able to piece together from some of the older residents, his mother, Trudy, at the age of sixteen, had claimed to have been gang-raped by three highway workers, one of whom was Way's father. This had happened several years before the end of World War II, and no one had believed her story, so she had become an outcast.

In the years that followed, Trudy had barely scraped together a living for herself and her son by cleaning the houses of the few families who would let her in the door, and apparently the hard work and social ostracism had gradually broken her down. Around the time Way had started high school, she seemed to have given up and accepted everyone's judgment of her. That was when she began selling herself to the men who passed through town. At the age of thirty-five, she had died of pneumonia, and Way had joined the marines not long after.

As Suzy studied him over the rim of her wineglass, her uneasiness grew. Trudy Sawyer had been the victim of grave injustice, and a man like Way Sawyer wouldn't have forgotten it. To what lengths would he go in order to even up the balance sheet?

To her relief, the maid appeared to announce dinner, and Way escorted her into a formal dining room decorated in pale green accented with jade. He made polite, meaningless conversation during the salad course, and by the time the main course of salmon and wild rice arrived, her nerves felt raw from the strain. Why didn't he tell her what he wanted from her? If she knew why he'd insisted she dine here with him tonight, maybe she could relax.

The silence that fell between them didn't seem to bother him, but it became unbearable to her, so she broke it. "I noticed your piano. Do you play?"

"No. The piano was my daughter Sarah's. I bought it for her when she was ten and Dee and I divorced. It was her consolation prize for losing her mother."

It was the first personal remark he'd made. "You had custody of her? That was unusual for the time, wasn't it?"

"Dee had trouble being a mother. She agreed to the arrangement."

"Do you see your daughter often?"

He broke a poppy seed roll in half, and for the first time that evening, his features softened. "Not nearly often enough. She's a commercial photographer in San Francisco, so we get together every few months. She lives in this fleabag apartment—that's why I still have the piano—but she's self-sufficient and happy."

"These days, I guess that's the most a parent can ask." As she thought of her son, she toyed with a piece of salmon on her plate. He was certainly self-sufficient, but she didn't believe he was all that happy.

"Would you like more wine?" he said brusquely.

"No, thank you. If I have more than one drink, I get a headache. Hoyt used to say I was the cheapest date in town."

He didn't even smile at her weak attempt to lighten the atmosphere. Instead, he abandoned all pretense of eating, settled back in his chair, and gazed at her with an intensity that made her conscious of how seldom people truly looked at each other. She was startled to realize that if she'd been meeting him for the first time, she would have found him attractive. Although he was the polar opposite of her sunny-natured husband, his rugged good looks and powerful presence had an appeal that was difficult to ignore.

"You still miss Hoyt?"

"Very much."

"The two of us were the same age, and we went through school together. He was Telarosa High's golden boy, just like your son." His smile didn't make it to his eyes. "He even dated the prettiest girl in the sophomore class."

"Thank you for the compliment, but I wasn't even close to being the prettiest girl. I still had braces on my teeth that year."

"I thought you were the prettiest girl." He took a sip of wine. "I'd just worked up the nerve to ask you out when I heard you and Hoyt were dating."

She couldn't have been more startled. "I had no idea."

"It's hard to believe I really thought I had a chance with Suzy Westlight. After all, I was Trudy Sawyer's son, and I lived in a different world from Dr. Westlight's daughter. You came from the right side of the railroad tracks and had pretty clothes. Your mother drove you around in a shiny red Oldsmobile, and you always smelled clean and new." His words were poetic, but he spoke them in hard, clipped tones that robbed them of any sentiment.

"That was a long time ago," she said. "I'm not new anymore." She brushed her fingers over the silky fabric of her evening trousers and felt the small bump on her hip from her estrogen patch. It was another sign that life had lost its promise.

"Aren't you going to laugh at the idea of a dead-end kid like me wanting to ask you out?"

"You always acted as if you hated me."

"I didn't hate you. I hated the fact that you were so far out of my reach. You and Hoyt came from a different world, one I couldn't come close to touching. The golden boy and the golden girl, happily-ever-after."

"Not anymore." She ducked her head as she felt her throat close.

"I'm sorry," he said brusquely. "I didn't mean to be cruel."

Her head shot back up, and her eyes were glazed with tears. "Then why are you doing this? I know you're playing some kind of game with me, but I don't know what the rules are. What do you want from me?"

"I thought you were the one who wanted something from me."

His flat response told her that he was unmoved by her obvious distress. She blinked her eyes, determined not to let tears fall, but she hadn't been sleeping well since her first meeting with him, and it was difficult to hold on to her composure. "I don't want you to destroy this town. Too many lives will be ruined."

"And exactly what are you willing to sacrifice to keep that from happening?"

Fingers of dread trailed down her spine. "I don't have anything to sacrifice."

"Yes, you do."

The hard note in his voice undid her. Crumpling her napkin on the table, she stood. "I'd like to go home now."

"You're afraid of me, aren't you?"

"I don't see any reason to prolong this evening."

He got to his feet. "I want to show you my rose garden."

"I think it would be better if I left."

He pushed his chair back and came toward her. "I'd like you to see it. Please. I think you'll enjoy it."

Although he didn't raise his voice, the note of command was unmistakable. Once again he was going to have his own way, and she didn't know how to fight the firm hand that enclosed her upper arm and led her toward the French doors at the end of the dining room. He pushed down on a wave-shaped brass handle. As she stepped outside, the night settled around her like a fragrant steam bath. She smelled the lush perfume of roses.

"It's lovely."

He led her along a cobbled path that wound through the flower beds. "I brought in a landscape architect from Dallas to design it, but he wanted everything too fussy. I ended up doing most of the work myself."

She didn't want to think about him planting a rose garden. In her experience, gardeners were benevolent people, and she could never view him that way.

They had reached a small koi pond set in a ramble of tall grasses and foliage. It was fed by a waterfall trickling over terraced stone, and recessed lighting illuminated the fat fish as they swam beneath the waxy leaves of the water lilies. She knew he wouldn't let her leave until he'd had his say, and she sat down on one of a pair of verdigris iron benches decorated with twining grape leaves that provided a resting place beside the pathway.

She crossed her hands in her lap and tried to

brace herself. "What did you mean when you asked me what I was willing to sacrifice?"

He took the bench across from her and stretched out his legs. The lights in the pond threw his cheekbones and the bony ridge above his eyes into sharp relief, adding a menacing aspect to his features that further unnerved her. His voice, however, was as soft as the night. "I wanted to know how committed you were to keeping Rosatech here."

"I've lived in this town all my life, and I'd do anything to keep it from dying. But I'm only the president of the Board of Education; I don't have any real power in the county."

"Your power in the county doesn't interest me. That's not what I want from you at all."

"Then what?"

"Maybe I want what I couldn't have all those years ago when I wasn't anything more than Trudy Sawyer's bastard kid."

She was aware of the trickle of the waterfall, the distant hum of the air-conditioning units that cooled the house, and those peaceful noises made his quiet words seem all the more ominous. "I don't know what you mean."

"Maybe I want the prettiest girl in the sophomore class."

Dread crept through her, and the night that wrapped around them was suddenly full of peril. "What are you talking about?"

He propped his elbow on the back of the bench and crossed his ankles. Despite his relaxed posture, she sensed a tightly coiled

229

watchfulness about him, and it frightened her. "I've decided I need a companion, but I'm too busy running Rosatech to spend the time looking for someone. I want that person to be you."

Her mouth was so dry that her tongue felt swollen. "A companion?"

"I need someone to attend social functions with, someone to accompany me on trips and serve as my hostess when I entertain."

"I thought you had a companion. I've heard you're seeing someone in Dallas."

"I've seen a lot of women over the years. I'm looking for something a little different. A little closer to home." He spoke as calmly as if he were discussing a business agreement, but there was something about him, a heightened sense of alertness, that made her certain he wasn't as calm as he pretended to be. "The two of us would still be able to live our own lives, but you'd be..." He paused and she felt as if his eyes were burning straight through hers into her skull. "You would be available to me, Suzy."

The way he lingered over the word chilled her. "Available? Way, you're not—It almost sounds as if—" She couldn't hide her horror. "I'm not sleeping with you!"

For a moment he said nothing. "You'd hate that, wouldn't you?"

She sprang to her feet. "You're crazy! I can't believe you're suggesting this. You're not talking about a companion; you're talking about a mistress!"

He lifted one eyebrow, and she thought she had never seen a man so cold, so completely lacking in feeling. "Am I? I don't remember using that word."

"Stop toying with me!"

"I know you have an active life, and I don't expect you to give it up, but sometimes when I need you with me, I'd like you to make concessions."

Her blood pounded in her ears, and her voice seemed to be coming from very far away. "Why are you doing this to me?"

"Doing what?"

"Blackmailing me! That's what this is about, isn't it? If I sleep with you, you'll keep Rosatech in Telarosa? If I don't, you'll move the company." He said nothing, and she couldn't quite suppress the bubble of hysteria rising inside her. "I'm fifty-two years old! If you're looking for a mistress, why don't you do what other men your age do and find someone young."

"Young women don't interest me."

She turned her back to him, her nails digging into her palms. "Do you hate me so much?"

"I don't hate you at all."

"I know what you're doing. You're living out some kind of vendetta from thirty years ago."

"My vendetta is with the town, not with you."

"But I'm the one who's being punished."

"If that's the way you see it, I won't try to change your mind."

"I'm not going to do this."

"I understand."

She spun back. "You can't force me."

"I would never force you. It's entirely your decision."

The lack of emotion in his words frightened her more than an expression of anger would. He was insane, she thought. But his dark eyes regarded her with intelligence and a terrifying lucidity.

A note of pleading crept into her voice that she couldn't repress. "Tell me you won't move Rosatech."

For the first time he hesitated, almost as if he were waging some sort of private war with himself. "I'm not making any promises until you've had time to think over our conversation."

She drew a ragged breath. "I want to go home now."

"All right."

"I left my purse inside."

"I'll get it for you."

She stood alone in the garden, trying to take in what was happening to her, but the situation was so far outside her realm of experience that she couldn't absorb it. She thought of her son, and her blood went cold with fear. If Bobby Tom ever found out about this, he'd kill Way Sawyer.

"Are you ready?"

She jumped as he touched her shoulder.

He immediately withdrew his hand and offered her the purse. "My car's in the front." He gestured toward a brick path that wound around the side of the house, and she moved toward it before he could touch her again.

When they reached the front, she saw his BMW instead of the Lincoln his chauffeur had driven and realized he planned to drive her home himself. He opened the door and she slipped inside without a word.

To her relief, he didn't attempt conversation. She closed her eyes and tried to imagine that Hoyt was beside her, but tonight he seemed impossibly far away? *Why did you leave me? How am I supposed to face this alone?*

Fifteen minutes later, he stopped his car in her driveway and, looking over at her, spoke quietly. "I'm going to be out of the country for about three weeks. When I get back—"

"Please," she whispered. "Don't force me to do this."

His voice was cool and distant. "When I get back, I'll call to hear your decision."

Suzy jumped out of the car and raced up the sidewalk to her house, running as if all the hounds of hell were nipping at her heels.

Sitting behind the wheel of his car, the most hated man in Telarosa, Texas, watched her disappear inside. As the door slammed, his face contorted with anger, pain, and the barest hint of longing.

12

For the first time all evening, nobody was shoving a cocktail napkin under Bobby Tom's nose for an autograph, or asking him to dance, or poking around for details about the golf tournament. He finally had a few minutes to himself, and he leaned back into the corner of the booth. The Wagon Wheel was Telarosa's favorite honky-tonk, and the Saturday night crowd was enjoying itself, especially since Bobby Tom had been buying all the drinks.

He set his beer bottle down on the scarred table and stubbed out one of the thin cigars he occasionally permitted himself. At the same time, he watched Gracie make a fool of herself trying to line dance to a new song from Brooks and Dunn. It had been two weeks since her make-over, so he thought people should be used to her by now, but everybody in town was still fussing over her.

Despite all the improvements in her appearance, she wasn't even close to being prime-cut gorgeous. She was cute, no denying that. Pretty, even. In the land of big hair, that little flyaway cut of hers might very well be Shirley's masterpiece, and he got a big kick out of the way it fluffed around her face and glimmered all warm and coppery in the light. But he preferred his women blond and flashy, with legs up to their armpits and porn star breasts. Real live sex trophies, that's what he liked, and he wasn't going to apologize for it either. He'd earned those sex trophy females on the bloody battlefields of the NFL. He'd earned them in bruising drills and brutal two-a-day practices; he'd earned them by taking hits so violent he couldn't remember his name afterward. They were the spoils of gridiron warfare, and giving them up would be the same as giving up his identity.

He took a deep swig of Shiner, but the beer didn't fill up the empty place inside him. He should be starting the season now, but instead, he was prancing around in front of a movie camera like a damn pussy and pretending to be engaged to a bossy lady who wouldn't ever be mistaken for a sex trophy.

Not that Gracie didn't have an alluring little figure in those jeans that were so tight Len Brown couldn't seem to keep his eyes off her butt. He remembered telling his mother to make sure Gracie had a couple pair of jeans, but he didn't recall giving her permission to buy ones that were going to give her leg cramps.

The subject of Gracie's clothes made him scowl. He couldn't believe it when his mother told him Gracie had insisted on paying for her own clothes and they had ended up shopping at the outlets. He should have bought those clothes! It was his idea, wasn't it? Besides, he was rich and she was poor, and he damn well expected any woman he was supposed to be marrying to have the best. The two of them had gotten into a big argument about it when he'd found out, an argument that had escalated after Shirley sent him back the money he'd given her for Gracie's hair and makeup because Gracie had insisted on paying for that herself, too. Damn, she was stubborn. Not only did she refuse to take anything from him, but she actually had the nerve to tell him she intended to give him rent money.

He was going to have the last word, though. Just yesterday he'd gone into Millie's Boutique and picked out a dandy black cocktail dress for Gracie. Millie had promised to tell her she had a strict no return policy if Gracie tried to bring it back. One way or another, he intended to have his way on this.

He picked at the beer bottle's label with his thumb. Maybe he'd better have a talk with Willow. It had begun to occur to him that he needed to make damned sure Gracie never figured out who was funding that pitiful little paycheck of hers.

He glowered as Gracie missed some more steps. What in the hell had his mother been thinking of, advising her to wear that vest tonight? Right after he'd told Gracie he was taking her to the Wagon Wheel, he'd overheard her telephoning Suzy and asking what she was supposed to wear to a honky-tonk on Saturday night. Now he understood why he'd heard her say, "All by itself?"

Thanks to his mother, Gracie was wearing a gold brocade vest that didn't have anything under it except skin, along with tight, black jeans and a new pair of cowboy boots. The vest wasn't exactly immodest. A row of pearl buttons held it together, and the brocade fell in twin points over the waistband of her jeans. But there was something about the idea of wearing a fancy vest without anything under it that made her look like bimbo material, which couldn't have been farther from the truth, despite Len Brown's wandering eyeballs. Poor Gracie was probably embarrassed to tears right now knowing what a display she was making of herself.

The Brooks and Dunn song came to an end, and the music shifted to a slow ballad. Resigned to being a gentleman, he rose so he could rescue her before she ended up being a wallflower. He hadn't taken more than three steps, however, when Johnny Pettibone pulled her away from Len and they began to dance. Bobby Tom came to a stop, feeling vaguely foolish, and then told himself he'd have to remember to thank Johnny for being so nice to Gracie. Everybody had been real nice to her. Not that he was surprised. The fact that she was Bobby Tom Denton's intended had guaranteed everybody'd treat her like a queen.

As he watched Johnny pull Gracie closer, he felt a stab of irritation. She was an engaged lady, and they shouldn't be dancing so intimately, but Bobby Tom couldn't see that she was putting up the slightest bit of resistance. Matter of fact, she had her face turned up like a sunflower taking in Johnny's every word. For someone who should be feeling embarrassed and out of place, she certainly seemed to be having a good time.

He remembered Gracie's problem with sexual frustration and scowled. What if she couldn't control those hormones of hers now that her make-over had given her a little bit of male attention? The idea bothered the hell out of him. He couldn't blame her for wanting to do what came naturally, but she sure as hell wasn't going to do it while she was engaged to him. There weren't any secrets in Telarosa, and he didn't care to think what he'd go through if the town found out that a woman like Gracie Snow was cheating on him.

He suppressed a groan as Connie Cameron sauntered over. "Hey, B.T., want to dance again?"

She rested her arm on the lavender silk shirt he wore with his jeans and charcoal Stetson, then brushed her breasts against him. Unfortunately, their mutual engagements hadn't discouraged her one bit.

"I'd love to, Connie, but the fact is, Gracie gets real ornery if I dance more than once with a beautiful woman, so I have to mend my ways."

She pushed away several strands of dark hair that had gotten tangled in one of her long silver earrings. "I never thought I'd see the day you let a woman pussy-whip you."

"I never did, either, but that was before I met Gracie."

"If you're worried about what Jim will

239

think, he's on duty tonight. He won't ever find out we've been dancing." She emphasized the last word with a little mouth pucker so he'd know dancing wasn't all she was offering.

Bobby Tom imagined Jimbo kept close track of Connie, but that wasn't why he backed off. He simply found it difficult anymore to conceal his impatience when he was around women like her. "I don't worry too much about Jimbo. It's Gracie I'm concerned about. She's real sensitive."

Connie glanced over at the dancers and regarded her critically. "Gracie looks better since you let her get fixed up. Even so, she doesn't seem like your type. People around here figured you'd marry a model or a movie star."

"There's just no accounting for the mysterious ways of the human heart."

"I s'pose. Would you mind doing me a favor, B.T.?"

A wave of weariness swept over him. More favors. He was on the set at least twelve hours a day, and the past few days had been grueling. Normally, he enjoyed the action scenes, but not when they involved beating up a woman. He'd dreaded the fight scene with Natalie that occurred at the beginning of the movie, and he was so unconvincing they'd had to bring in a small male stuntman to double for her.

When he wasn't on the set, there were incessant phone calls, drop-in visitors, and fund-raisers. With all that, he hadn't had more than four hours of sleep at a stretch all week.

Last night after he finished work, he'd flown his plane down to Corpus Christi to make an appearance at a charity banquet and the night before that he'd made radio spots advertising Heavenfest, but the only charity activity he'd really enjoyed was sneaking in to visit the kids in the pediatric wing at the county hospital.

"What do you need?"

"Could you stop by my house some evening and autograph a couple of footballs I bought for my nephews?"

"Be glad to." He'd stop by all right. With Gracie at his side.

The song was coming to an end, and he excused himself so he could retrieve Gracie from Johnny Pettibone. Len Brown got there first, but he didn't let that deter him.

"Hi, boys. You think I could claim a dance with my little sweetheart here?"

"Well, sure, Bobby Tom." The reluctance in Len's voice annoyed him. Gracie, in the meantime, was giving him a glare that was licensed to kill over the "little sweetheart" remark. The fact that he'd managed to irritate her helped restore his spirits.

Both of them had been so busy these past few weeks that they hadn't spent much free time together, which was why he'd insisted they show up at the Wagon Wheel tonight, since nobody was going to believe they were engaged if they weren't ever seen out socially. She was so damned efficient that he couldn't think up enough things to keep her occupied. Since she hated being idle, she was turning herself into the company's all-around errand girl and Natalie's part-time baby-sitter.

He looked down into her flushed face and couldn't help but smile. She had about the prettiest skin he'd ever seen on a woman, and he liked her eyes, too. There was something about the way they sparkled that always seemed to lift his mood.

"They've got a new line dance going, Gracie. Let's give it a try."

She looked doubtfully toward the dancers, who were performing a series of fast, intricate steps. "I never quite caught on to the last dance. Maybe we should sit this one out."

"And miss all the fun?" He drew her into place, studying the dancers in front of them at the same time. The pattern was complicated, but he'd built a career out of counting steps and making cuts at precisely the right moment, and it didn't take him more than thirty seconds to catch on. Gracie, on the other hand, was having trouble.

Halfway into the song, she still wasn't going the same direction as everybody else. He decided he'd been a real heel to bring her out here when he knew she couldn't keep up, but some immature part of him had wanted to remind her this was his turf, not hers, and she shouldn't be flirting with men she wasn't engaged to. His twinge of guilt changed to irritation as he watched her tossing her hair and laughing at her mistakes, just as if she didn't care that she was the worst dancer on the floor.

Damp, coppery tendrils clung to her cheeks and the nape of her neck. She turned to face him when she should have turned away, and he saw that the top button of her vest had popped open revealing the inner curves of those cute little cupcakes of hers, which were rosy and glowing from the heat. One more button, and the rest of her would be on display. The idea filled him with indignation. She was a Sunday School teacher, for chrissake. She should know better!

She was too busy flirting with everybody in pants to notice his irritation, which only increased as he heard people he hadn't even realized she knew calling out encouragement to her.

"The other way, Gracie. You can do it!"

"That's the way, Gracie!"

The muscular college boy on her opposite side had already earned Bobby Tom's disfavor by wearing a Baylor T-shirt. When the kid caught Gracie by the hips and turned her in the right direction, Bobby Tom's eyes narrowed.

She laughed and shook her curls. "I'll never get it!"

"Sure you will." The kid raised the beer bottle he was holding right up to her lips.

She took a drink and coughed. The boy laughed and started to give her another sip, but Bobby Tom had no intention of watching her turn into an alcoholic right before his eyes. Looping his arm around her shoulders, he glared at the kid and pulled her away.

The boy flushed. "Sorry, Mr. Denton."

Mister Denton! That did it! He grabbed Gracie's wrist and pulled her toward the fire exit at the back.

She stumbled slightly. "What's wrong? Where are we going?"

"I've got a stitch in my side. I need some fresh air."

He hit the bar on the back door with the heel of his hand and dragged her out behind the building into the gravel lot where the employees parked. A battered green Dumpster sat behind the motley collection of vehicles, along with a shed built from concrete blocks.

He didn't smell anything more exotic than french fries and dust, but Gracie gave a contented sigh as she breathed in the air. "Thank you so much for bringing me here. I don't know when I've had such a good time. Everybody's been so nice."

She sounded giddy and her eyes sparkled like Christmas lights, making her look so pretty it was hard for him to remember she wasn't prime-cut. The air-conditioning unit hummed loudly, but didn't quite drown out the music from the juke box. She pushed a strand of hair away from her cheek, then locked her hands behind her neck and leaned back against the building's rough wooden siding, thrusting her breasts forward at the same time.

Where had she learned a trick like that? He suddenly wanted his old Gracie back, with her raccoon tail dress and lumpy hair. He'd been comfortable with his old Gracie, and the fact that he was the one responsible for her transformation into a honky-tonk hellcat made him even more peeved.

"Did it occur to you that I might not like my fiancée displaying her chest to everybody in town?"

She looked down at herself and her hand flew to her undone button. "Oh, my."

"I don't know what's gotten into you, tonight, but I think you'd better settle down right now and act like an engaged woman."

Her eyes shot up to meet his. She stared at him for a long moment, clamped her teeth together, and flicked open the second button.

He was so surprised by her defiance that it took him a few seconds to find his voice. "Just what do you think you're doing?"

"There's no one around. I'm hot, and you're immune to me, so what difference does it make."

She was hot, all right, and so was he. He didn't know what had gotten into her tonight, but he was putting a stop to it. "I never said I was immune to you," he retorted belligerently. "You're female, aren't you?"

Her eyes flew open. It was a nasty crack, and he was immediately ashamed of himself. His shame grew as the stunned expression on her face changed to a look of concern.

"Your knee is bothering you, isn't it? That's why you've been so grouchy all evening."

Leave it to Gracie to find an excuse for his boorish behavior. She only wanted to see the good side of people, a fact that made everybody in the world take advantage of her. Still, he wasn't up to destroying her illusions about him by telling her that his knee was doing fine. Instead, he reached down and rubbed it through his jeans. "Some days are better than others."

She cupped his wrist. "I feel terrible. I've been having such a good time that I wasn't thinking about anybody but myself. Let's go home so we can put some ice on it."

He felt lower than a snake. "I should probably keep moving so it doesn't freeze up. Let's dance instead."

"Are you sure?"

"'Course I'm sure. They're playing George Strait, aren't they?"

"Are they?"

He caught her by the hand and gathered her against him. "You mean to tell me you don't recognize George Strait?"

"I don't know much about country singers."

"In Texas, he's more of a religious figure." Instead of taking her back inside, he tucked her close and began to move. They danced between an old Fairlane and a Toyota, and her hair smelled like peaches.

As their boots shuffled in the gravel of the parking lot, he couldn't resist slipping his hand under the hem of her vest and resting it in the small of her back. He felt the bumps of her spine, the softness of her skin. She shivered, reminding him that she needed a man so badly she was in danger of falling for the first smooth-talking bastard to come along.

The idea upset the hell out of him. He wasn't ashamed to admit that he liked Gracie, and he sure as hell didn't want her stripping down for somebody who wouldn't treat her with care. What if she gave herself to one of those sons of bitches who was too damned selfish to make sure she was protected? Or some oversexed jerk who rode her too rough and ruined her pleasure in sex forever? There were a million disasters waiting out there for a desperate woman like Gracie.

He'd been playing hide-and-seek with the truth too long, and he knew the moment of reckoning had finally come. If he wanted to keep facing himself in the mirror every morning, he had to set aside his misgivings about mercy fucking and do what needed to be done. She was his friend, dammit, and he never turned his back on his friends. That left him with no choice. The only way he could be certain the job got done right was to take charge of Gracie's initiation himself.

For the first time all evening, his black mood lifted. He felt smug, even a little self-righteous, the same way he felt when he'd written out a five-figure check to a good charity. More than sex was involved here. As a decent human being, he had a responsibility to protect this woman from the pitfalls of her own ignorance. Without giving himself any more time to consider the complications that were certain to arise, he plunged right in.

"Gracie, we've been avoiding the topic for

the past few weeks, but I think we need to clear the air. That night you were drunk you said some things."

He felt her stiffen beneath his palm. "I'd appreciate it if we could both forget about that night."

"That's hard to do. You came on kind of strong."

"As you said, I was inebriated."

He'd said she was drunk, but this wasn't the best time to correct her. "Liquor sometimes has a way of bringing out the truth, and since it's just the two of us here, we don't have to tell lies to each other." He slipped his hand an inch higher on her spine and rubbed one of the bumps with his index finger. "The way I look at it, you're pretty much a sexual powder keg waiting to blow up, which is understandable considering the fact that you've denied yourself one of life's sweetest pleasures."

"I didn't deny myself. The opportunity simply never came along."

"From what I saw inside, the opportunity could come along at any minute. Those boys are only human, and, the fact is, you were flaunting yourself."

"I wasn't!"

"All right. Let's just say you were doing some heavy-duty flirting."

"I was flirting? Really?"

Her eyes widened with delight, and he realized he'd made a tactical mistake. With her typical unpredictability, she hadn't taken his comment for the criticism he'd intended it to be. Before she got so caught up with the notion of herself as a Southern belle that she forgot to pay attention to what he was saying, he hurried on. "The point is, I think it's about time we put our heads together, so to speak, and came up with a plan that'll be mutually beneficial."

The song came to an end. He reluctantly withdrew his hand from beneath her vest and let her go. Leaning back against the side of the Fairlane, he crossed his arms over his chest.

"The way I see it, we each have a problem. You're long overdue for some tutoring in the sexual arts, but since we're supposed to be engaged, you can't get your tutoring from just anybody. I, on the other hand, am used to having a regular sex life, but since I'm officially an engaged man and this is a small town, I can't just call up my old girlfriends and make arrangements, if you get my point."

Gracie was nibbling her bottom lip to beat the band. "Yes, I, uh—Well, it's certainly a problem."

"But it doesn't have to be."

Her chest began to rise and fall as if she'd just run a long distance. "I suppose not."

"We're both consenting adults, and there's no reason we shouldn't help each other out here."

"Help each other?" she said, her voice faint.

"Sure. I could give you the tutoring you need, and you could keep me off the streets. I think it'll work out just fine."

She licked her lips nervously. "Yes, it's—uh—very logical."

"And practical."

"That, too."

He heard the barest trace of disappointment shade her response, and he knew enough about women's need for romance to understand the time had come for some fancy footwork. "Now the thing of it is, sex isn't much fun if the two partners are only looking at it as some kind of convenience."

She was nibbling again. "No, that wouldn't be fun at all."

"So if we decide we're going to go ahead with this, we'd have to put all that out of our minds from the start and do it right."

"Do it right?"

"Which doesn't mean we wouldn't have to set up some ground rules. I always think knowing the rules up front makes most things work out better in the long run."

"I know you're quite fond of keeping communication channels open."

Along with that nervous flutter in her voice, he was almost certain he heard a small thread of annoyance, and he nearly chuckled aloud. Composing himself so that he sounded as serious as a TV evangelist, he regarded her gravely. "Here's what I've been thinking...It's obvious this is going to be a stressful experience for me."

Her head shot up, and she was so clearly astonished it took all his self control not to laugh. "Why should it be stressful for *you*?"

He gave her a look of wounded innocence. "Honey, that's got to be obvious. I've been pretty much a stallion from puberty on. Since I'm the experienced partner, and you don't have any experience as far as I can tell that goes much beyond having that podiatrist kiss your foot, I'm going to be completely responsible for making sure your initiation into the sexual arts goes right. There's a possibility—farfetched, I admit, but still a possibility—that I could mess everything up and you'd be traumatized for life. That sort of responsibility weighs heavy on my mind, and the only way I can guarantee everything goes right for you is to take absolute control of our sexual relationship from the very beginning."

She regarded him cautiously. "Exactly what would that involve?"

"I'm afraid I'm going to shock you so much you'll decide to back out before we even get started."

"Tell me!"

Her voice had risen to something approaching a shriek, and he could no longer remember what his earlier bad mood had been about. Her impatience reminded him of someone who'd matched the first five numbers on her lottery ticket, and was waiting to hear the last one.

He tilted the brim of his Stetson back with his thumb. "The thing of it is, for me to make certain this is going to be a good experience for you, I'd have to pretty much take control of your body right from the beginning. I'd have to *own* it, so to speak."

She sounded vaguely hoarse. "You'd have to own my body?"

"Uh-huh."

"*Own* it?"

"Yep. Your body'd belong to me instead of to you. It'd be just like I took a big ole Magic Marker and put my initials on every little part of you."

Somewhat to his surprise, she seemed more stunned than insulted. "It sounds like slavery."

He managed to look hurt. "I didn't say I'd own your *mind*, honey. Just your *body*. There's a distinct difference, and I'm surprised you can't see that without me having to point it out."

Her throat worked as she swallowed hard. "What if you force me—or my body, depending on how we're looking at it—to do something I don't want to do?"

"Oh, I'll definitely force you. No doubt about it."

Her eyes widened in outrage. "You'll force me?"

"Sure. You've got years of catching up to do, and we only have a limited amount of time. I won't harm you, sweetheart, but I sure will have to force you, or we'll never get to the advanced stuff."

He could see that remark had just about done her in. Her eyes were big gray pools and her lips had parted. Still, he had to admire her fortitude. One thing he'd figured out about Gracie right from the beginning. She had guts.

"I—uh—I'm going to have to think about this."

"I don't see what there is to think about. It either sounds right to you, or it doesn't."

"It's not that simple."

"Sure it is. Believe me, honey, I know a lot more about this than you do. The best thing right now would be for you to say, 'I trust you with my life, Bobby Tom, and I'm gonna do whatever you tell me to.'"

Her eyes snapped. "That's taking control of my mind, not my body!"

"I was just testing to make sure you understood the difference, and you passed with flying colors. I'm proud of you, sweetheart." He went in for the kill. "What I really want you to do now is open the rest of the buttons on that vest."

"But we're outside!"

He noticed she didn't protest the action, just the location, and he pressed a little harder. "As I recall, I'm the experienced partner here, and you're the virgin. You're either going to have to trust me with this body stuff or our arrangement isn't going to work out."

He almost felt sorry for her as he watched her sense of propriety do battle with that traitorous vein of sexuality she couldn't quite control. She was thinking so hard, he could practically hear her brain cells zing, and he waited for her lips to purse up so she could tell him to go to the devil. Instead, she took an unsteady breath.

When her gaze darted around the parking

lot, he knew he had her. He felt a rush of emotions—pleasure, mirth, and a queer sort of tenderness. In that moment he made a vow to himself that he'd never do anything to violate her trust. The uneasy knowledge of who was paying her salary flicked through his mind, but he resolutely pushed it aside to lean down and kiss one cheek, while he cupped the other in his palm and whispered, "Go on, honey. Do what I tell you."

For a moment she didn't move, and then he felt the flutter of her hands between her chest and his.

Her voice was husky. "I—I feel silly."

He smiled against her cheek. "I'm the one who's going to do the feelin' here."

"This just seems so...naughty."

"Oh, it is. Now open up."

Once again her hands moved between their bodies.

"Is it open all the way?" he asked.

"Y—yes."

"That's good. Put your arms around my neck."

She did as he requested. The sides of the vest brushed over the backs of his hands as he pushed them apart and felt the warmth of her bare breasts through his lavender silk shirt. Once again, he whispered in her ear.

"Unzip your jeans."

She didn't move. Not that he was surprised. He'd already managed to push her farther than he'd expected. He'd also gotten so worked up himself by their sex play that he was in danger of forgetting this was a game.

He uttered a soft groan as her body brushed against his. She stood on her tiptoes. He felt her check graze his jaw and heard her soft murmur.

"You first."

He nearly exploded. Before he could react, however, two men came stumbling around the side of the parking lot, arguing loudly with each other.

Every muscle in her body went rigid.

"Shhh..." He pushed her gently back against the building, shielding her with his body. Opening his thighs, he caught her legs between his and pressed his lips to her ear. "We'll just make out for a little bit 'til they go away. Would you like that?"

She tilted up her face. "Oh, yes."

Despite the agonizing pressure in his jeans, he wanted to smile at her lack of artifice, but he knew she wouldn't understand, so he controlled himself. Bending his head, he touched his mouth to hers, shielding their faces with the brim of his hat. Her lips remained tightly closed, and he decided there was something infinitely exciting about kissing a woman who didn't try to shove her tongue down his throat before he'd even had a chance to figure out whether he wanted it there or not.

He definitely wanted Gracie's tongue, however, which meant he had to do his best to bring out her adventurous side. With infinite patience, he coaxed her lips open. Her arms tightened around his neck, and the very tip of her tongue quivered like a tiny bird at the threshold of his mouth. She was so wrapped up in what was happening with their tongues that he didn't want to distract her by exploring those naked little breasts nestled so enticingly against his chest, so he did his best to push away the memory of the way they'd looked with trickles of ice cream running down their slopes and the small nipples puckered in tight, hard buds.

The memory almost pushed him over the edge, and he shoved his hips hard against hers. His aggressiveness didn't scare her one bit. Instead of trying to back away, she rubbed against him like a hot little kitten waiting to be scratched.

Right then and there he knew he wasn't nearly as much in charge as he wanted to be. Her fingers dug into his shoulders and she began making sweet moaning sounds deep in her throat. Every muscle in his body had grown taut and his heart was slamming against his ribs. He was so hard he throbbed, and he wanted her with an urgency that scared the hell out of him.

He dimly realized the intruders in the parking lot had disappeared and he couldn't restrain himself a moment longer. Grasping the arms that were encircling his neck, he eased her far enough away from him so that he could look down at her breasts. They glimmered in the night shadows, and the small nipples pebbled as he gazed at her. Releasing her arms, he brushed the tips with his thumbs. She leaned back against the building, head to the side, eyes closed.

He dipped his head to suckle her. Her nipples stabbed at his tongue, hard little points aggressively demanding his attention. He drew them into his mouth, raked them with his tongue, sucked hard and long. At the same time, he clutched her hips and ground himself against her, treating her far more roughly than he'd intended, but it felt so good, so damned good, and the sounds of her throaty moans in his ears threatened to push him right over the edge. He slipped his fingers between her legs, against the denim seam, and knew he had to bury himself hard and deep inside her before he exploded.

He grabbed the waistband of her jeans in his fists. Jerked at the snap.

"Bobby Tom..." She sobbed his name and his hands froze as he realized he'd scared her.

"Hurry," she pleaded. "Please hurry."

His passion escalated as he understood she welcomed his aggressiveness. At the same time, some small glimmer of sanity reminded him where they were, and he knew that what had started out as a game had backfired. He couldn't take her like this—not against the side of a building. He must have been crazy to let it get this far. What in the hell was wrong with him?

It took all of his self-discipline to close the front of her vest. Her eyes flew open, their expression revealing a mixture of passion and bewilderment. He settled his hat back into position. She was a rookie in her first big game, and he'd never let her see how close she'd come to unseating a champion.

"I think this is going to work out pretty well, don't you?" His normally agile hands were clumsy as he began fastening her buttons, and he kept talking to camouflage his awkwardness. "We're gonna take this in stages. You seemed to have missed out on all the normal messin' around, so we have to make up for that. I don't think either of us is going to last too long, you understand, but we should at least make the effort."

"Does this mean we're done for tonight?"

She looked so woeful he wanted to hug her. "Heck, no. We're just takin' a breather. When we get back home, we'll start up all over again. Maybe we'll drive down by the river and see how long it takes us to steam up the windows in my pickup."

Gracie jumped as the door next to them banged open, and Johnny Pettibone stuck his head out. "Bobby Tom, Suzy just called. She wants you to stop by the house right away. Says she thinks she might have a mouse under the sink." Johnny disappeared back inside.

Bobby Tom sighed. So much for steaming up windows. Once Suzy got hold of him, she wouldn't let go of him for a while.

Gracie gave him a sympathetic, albeit slightly shaky, smile. "It's all right; your mother needs you. I'll get a ride home with one of the production assistants. Actually, this is probably a good thing. I could use a little time to—to adjust."

Once again she began worrying her lip. "This body-owning idea of yours...I was thinking...That is, it occurred to me..."

"Spit it out, sweetheart. Neither of us is getting any younger."

"I want a turn," she said in a rush.

"A turn at what?"

"At the same thing. Body-owning. Yours."

He wanted to burst out laughing, but instead he frowned and tried to look sullen. "I never expected an intelligent woman to be so illogical. If both of us are going around owning each other's bodies, we'll never know who's supposed to make the next move."

She regarded him earnestly. "I'm sure we can work it out."

"I don't think so."

She set her jaw. "I'm sorry, Bobby Tom, but I'm going to have to be firm about this."

He started to give her a hard time, just for the pure pleasure of it, but before he could open his mouth, she'd turned her back on him and marched to the door. Just before she disappeared inside, she tossed him a prim look over her shoulder.

"Thank you for a most pleasurable encounter. It was highly educational." The door shut behind her.

For a moment he just stood there, and then he grinned. Every time he thought he had

Gracie right where he wanted her, she managed to surprise him. But he had a few surprises of his own left, and as he made his way to his truck, he knew that initiating Gracie Snow was definitely going to be one of life's finer pleasures.

13

So much for bargains, Gracie thought as she parked the Thunderbird next to Willow's Trans Am and picked up the Navaho blanket she had been sent to fetch. As she got out of the car, she sighed. Two weeks had passed since Bobby Tom had taken her to the Wagon Wheel, but to her disappointment, the physical side of their relationship hadn't progressed any farther. It was almost as if he'd changed his mind. On the other hand, the circumstances had hardly been conducive to privacy. He'd had long work days and lots of distractions.

On Sunday, after their evening at the honkytonk, Bobby Tom and Suzy had golfed, while Gracie had spent the day helping Natalie make the small house she had rented comfortable. That evening, one of his former teammates had shown up at the door and stayed several days, demanding every minute of Bobby Tom's free time. The following weekend, Bobby Tom had flown to Houston for a scheduled meeting with the American

Express people to discuss making a television commercial for them, and afterward, they had been involved in night shooting, filming a chase sequence involving Bobby Tom and the film's villain. But even though she knew they hadn't had any real opportunity for intimacy, she still found herself dwelling on the worrisome possibility that Bobby Tom's offer had merely been another of his private jokes and he had no intention of going through with it. Since the weekend was fast approaching and he'd made no plans to leave town, she should know soon.

For the past week, they'd been shooting a sequence with Bobby Tom and Natalie in a small box canyon north of town. The equipment trucks and motor homes were parked at the mouth of the canyon, far enough away so the noise from the vehicles wouldn't interfere with the shooting.

"Gracie!"

Gracie looked up to see Connie Cameron calling her from the catering truck. Her lips formed a smug smile as she stepped out from behind the counter.

"Bobby Tom's looking for you. It's hard to tell with him, but I'm pretty sure you've upset him again."

"Oh, dear."

Connie regarded her outfit critically, and Gracie reminded herself that she had no reason to feel intimidated. That morning she'd put on a scoop neck buttercup yellow knit top with a short sarong-style skirt in a jungle print. Amber hoops swung from her ears, and slim, leather thong sandals displayed her toenails, which she had painted a dark coral the night before. She wished she could work up the nerve to buy a discreet gold ankle bracelet, but when she'd asked Bobby Tom for his opinion, he'd started laughing so hard she'd discarded the idea. It was probably just as well. She couldn't afford it anyway.

Repaying Bobby Tom, even in installments, for the brutally expensive black cocktail dress he'd purchased without her permission at Millie's Boutique was decimating her meager paycheck, but Gracie had made up her mind to do it anyway. At first, when she'd learned that Millie's wouldn't take the dress back, she decided she'd simply return it to Bobby Tom and tell him to wear it himself. Unfortunately, she'd made the mistake of trying the dress on first, and it had looked so exquisite that she hadn't been able to resist. It was foolish, she knew, to own something so extravagant, but she wanted to see the expression on his face when she finally wore it for him. And the fact that she would have paid him back for every penny by then would make the moment all the sweeter.

Today was payday, and by the time she took out the money she intended to give him for her rent and made an installment on the black dress, there would be almost nothing left for essentials. Still, for someone standing on the precipice of financial disaster, she felt remarkably unburdened. She'd promised herself that her love would be a free offering, and the fact that she was keeping her word filled her with pride and a giddy sense of freedom.

Connie's breasts strained against her tight-fitting top as she leaned forward to wipe one of the tables set up under a navy canopy near the catering truck. "It's funny the two of you don't get along better. I know Bobby Tom never gets mad at me. You're the only female I've ever heard him argue with."

"We believe in keeping our communication channels open," Gracie offered with as much sweetness as she could muster.

"There you are! What took you so long?" Mark Wurst, the propmaster, rushed toward her, his graying ponytail flying.

In the past month, everyone on the set had come to regard her as the company's errand girl. Bobby Tom said people were taking advantage of her and he intended to put a stop to it, but she had asked him not to interfere. Despite the elaborate stories he wove about how much he needed a keeper, it hadn't taken her long to discover that he was one of the most competent people she'd ever known, and with each passing day, it had become increasingly apparent to her that he didn't have enough work to keep her busy. Luckily, Windmill did, and since they were officially her employer, she had the satisfaction of knowing she was more than giving them their money's worth. Even though she would never have a career in Hollywood, she was determined to work hard for as long as she had this job.

Gracie handed the blanket over to the prop-master. "You told me there wasn't any hurry, and Willow asked me to run some papers in to the office for her." Gracie had been somewhat annoyed by how easily Willow had managed to forget the fact that she'd once fired her.

"They changed the shooting schedule," Mark explained. "They're filming the love scene in the canyon this morning instead of tomorrow, and we need the blanket."

Gracie's stomach sank. She had known she would have to face this sooner or later, but she'd hoped it would be later. Few movies were shot in sequence, and although this would be the first love scene they filmed, it was actually the final one in the movie and the most romantic. She gave herself a stern lecture about behaving like a professional. Bobby Tom and Natalie had several heated love scenes, and she couldn't let herself get worked into a jealous tizzy with each one of them.

Gracie knew that it was a sad reflection on her character to be taking so much pleasure in Bobby Tom's difficulty relating to Natalie, especially since Natalie had become her friend. But Natalie's chatter about Elvis and breast-feeding had worn on his nerves. Even so, he treated his co-star so courteously that she didn't seem to realize she was driving him crazy.

"I think some things should be private," Bobby Tom had complained to Gracie during one of his breaks yesterday. "I don't want to know about her—whadyacall—let-out reflex."

"Let-down reflex."

"Whatever it is, I don't want to know about it."

"I think it's admirable that Natalie is breast-feeding her baby. It's not an easy thing for a working woman to do."

"I think it's admirable, too. But I'm not her husband, Elvis isn't my kid, and there's no need for me to get too familiar with the details."

Gracie yawned as she made her way toward Bobby Tom's motor home. After spending the past week doing night shooting, they were back to days again, and her internal time clock was out of whack. Apparently, so was Bobby Tom's. Last night when she'd gotten up to go to the bathroom, she'd looked down on the back of the house from her rooms above the garage and seen the flicker of the television through his office window.

She passed Roger, one of the makeup artists, carrying Elvis in a backpack. Natalie still hadn't found a nanny to suit her, and the baby was getting passed around whenever she was shooting. Gracie paused for a minute to tweak Elvis's chins. He chortled with delight and began bobbing up and down in the backpack. He really was a darling baby, despite his less than Gerber-perfect looks. She gave him a quick kiss on his forehead and reminded Roger that he chewed his fist when he got sleepy.

She climbed the steps to the motor home, and as she opened the door, Bobby Tom jumped up off the couch. "Just where in the sam hill have you been?"

"I went to get the blanket you'll be using in your scene with Natalie this morning."

He walked toward her, the script in his hand. She noted with relief that he was fully dressed for once. It struck her as ironic that the love scene was one of the few they'd shot so far where he got to wear all of his clothes. For a change, his jeans were zipped and a denim shirt, rolled at the sleeves, covered his bare chest.

"You're not a production assistant any longer. You're *my* assistant, and picking up a blanket shouldn't have taken three hours."

When she didn't offer an explanation for why she'd been gone so long, he regarded her suspiciously. "Well?"

"I had to take some papers in to the office for Willow."

"And..."

She surrendered to the inevitable. "I stopped at Arbor Hills."

"Arbor Hills?"

"It's a local nursing home, Bobby Tom. Surely you've seen it. I happened to notice it one day when I was running an errand for Willow."

"Oh, yeah, I remember. But what were you doing there? I thought you wanted to get away from nursing homes."

"Professional curiosity. When I was driving by, I spotted a dangerous crack in the front step. Naturally, I had to go in to bring it to their attention, and while I was there, I discovered that their recreational facilities are appalling. I'm also not too happy with the administrator." She saw no need to tell she'd recently gotten into the habit of spending time with some of the residents whenever she got the chance, and she was hoping to talk the administrator into making a few changes.

"Well, I'm not all that happy with you. I've got lines to memorize for the next scene, and I'd like a little help here."

"Don't you just moan and groan?"

"That's not funny." He began pacing the narrow width of the motor home. "In case nobody's pointed it out to you, Gracie, everything in life isn't a big joke."

Was Bobby Tom Denton, the man who never took anything seriously, actually giving her a lecture on inappropriate levity? She stifled her amusement as an interesting thought struck her.

"Bobby Tom, are you nervous about doing this love scene?"

He halted in his tracks. "Nervous? Me? You'd better come over here right now and let me smell your breath because I seriously think you've started up on those wine coolers again." He shoved his fingers through his hair. "I'll have you know I've already played out more love scenes in my life than most men have in their dreams."

"Not on camera. And not with a whole bunch of people looking on." She paused as a worrisome thought struck her. "Or have you?"

"Of course not! Well, not exactly. *Just never*

you mind! The point is, as long as I'm making this damn fool movie, I don't have any intention of looking like an idiot." He tossed the script at her. "Here. Start with, 'Those muscles of yours ought to come with a license.'" He gave her a dark scowl. "And not one wisecrack about the dialogue, do you understand me?"

She firmly repressed a smile. He really was upset about this love scene business. As she leaned back against the small kitchen counter, she felt much better than she had only moments before.

After finding the proper place in the script, she spoke the first line in as sultry a fashion as she could manage. "Those muscles of yours ought to come with a license."

"What's wrong with your voice?"

"Nothing. I'm acting."

He rolled his eyes. "Just say the stupid line."

"It's not necessarily stupid. Some people might find it provocative."

"It's stupid, and both of us know it. Now, go on."

She cleared her throat. "Those muscles of yours ought to come with a license."

"You don't have to read it like you're in a coma."

"You don't know your next line, do you? That's why you're criticizing me."

"I'm thinking."

"Instead of attacking my performance, why couldn't you just say, 'Gracie, sweetheart, I seem to have forgotten my next line. How 'bout you givin' me a little bitty hint'?"

Her imitation of his accent made him laugh. He sprawled down on the couch. It was too short for his long legs, and he propped his feet, clad in a pair of thick white socks, against the wall. "I'm sorry, Gracie. You're right. Just give me a hint."

"You say, 'You look like—'"

"I got it. 'You look like you should be packin' a license yourself, darlin'?" Damn, that line is even stupider than hers. No wonder I can't remember it."

"It's not as bad as her next one. 'Why don't you search me and find out if I am.'" She looked up from the page with concern. "You're right, Bobby Tom. This really is stupid. I don't think the screenwriter likes love scenes any better than you do. The rest of the script is so much better."

"I told you so." He sat up on the couch. "Looks like I'm gonna have to throw one of those movie star tantrums you read about in *People* magazine. We need a rewrite."

"There's not really time for that." She looked back down at the script. "You know, this just might work if the two of you don't try to play it too cute. Just sort of toss the lines away with a little smile. Both of you know it's silly. Mild sexual banter, nothing more."

"Let me see that." He held his hand out for the script. She passed it over, and he studied it. "You might be right. I'll talk to Natalie about it. When she's not going on about that baby, she occasionally shows a few remnants of good sense."

They spent the next ten minutes working on the script. Once Bobby Tom had decided he wasn't going to embarrass himself, he proved to be an amazingly quick study, and by the time he was called to the set, he was letter-perfect.

"You're coming with me for this, Gracie."

"I'm afraid I can't. I have too many things to do." Even though Bobby Tom had no romantic feelings for Natalie, he was a healthy, virile man, and inevitably, all that physical contact was going to turn him on. She didn't want to be around to see it happen. What sane woman would deliberately watch the man she loved making love with another woman, especially one as beautiful as Natalie Brooks?

"Everything can wait. I want you right there in the canyon with me." He pulled on a pair of well-worn leather boots.

"I'll be in the way. I'd really rather not."

"It's an order, Gracie. From your boss." He snatched up his script, grabbed her arm, and headed for the door. But as he reached out for the handle, he paused in midair. Turning, he began to study her in a way that made little prickles of excitement rise up all over her skin.

"Gracie, honey, if you don't mind, I'd like you to slip off those panties of yours before we go."

"What!"

"I believe I made myself pretty clear."

Her pulses raced at the sound of that husky drawl. "I can't go outside without my underpants!"

"Why not?"

"Because—Because it's outside, and I'd be..."

"You'd be naked underneath that cute little skirt of yours, but as long as you sit like a lady, I don't see that anybody's going to know. Except for me, that is."

Once again, his gaze trailed over her, making her skin feel damp and hot. He didn't understand that she wasn't the sort of woman who went around without underwear, not even in her new, made-over version.

At her hesitation, he released that overly patient sigh he used when he was about to manipulate someone. "I can't believe we're arguing about this. Apparently the fact that there've been so many distractions these past couple of weeks has made you forget we still have an agreement. You know as well as I do that I *own* what's underneath that skirt." Another sigh. "I never thought I'd have to give you—a former Sunday School teacher—a lecture on ethics."

Fighting back the urge to giggle, which would only encourage him to be even more outrageous, she tried to sound reasonable. "Former Sunday School teachers don't go around without their underwear."

"You show me where it says that in the Bible."

This time she did laugh.

"I'm losing patience, sweetheart." The sparks in those midnight blue eyes made her feel breathless. "Take 'em off, darlin', or I'll take 'em off for you."

Oh, Lord. His smoky drawl slithered through her body like an intimate caress, and she knew a moment of pure recklessness. A lifetime stretched ahead of her where she could be plain old Gracie Snow. For now, she was a wild woman.

Skin burning, she turned her back to him, slipped her hands under her skirt, and pulled off a pair of buttercup yellow panties.

Bobby Tom chuckled and whipped them from her hands. "Thank you, darlin'. I think I'll bring these along for inspiration."

He shoved the panties deep into the pocket of his jeans, and they were so tiny they didn't even make a bump.

"Those muscles of yours ought to come with a license."

"You look like you should be packin' a license yourself, darlin'."

"Why don't you search me and find out if I am?"

Natalie and Bobby Tom smiled as they tossed away the silly lines, making them sound cute, but not cloying. They were reclined on the blanket Gracie had fetched earlier, which lay spread out in a small glade shaded by sycamore and oak.

"Why don't I just do that." Bobby Tom kept smiling as he settled Natalie deeper into his embrace and tugged open the drawstring on her peasant-style blouse.

And why shouldn't he smile? Gracie thought, looking away as the fabric slipped off Natalie's creamy shoulder. He was a master at turning sex into an amusing little game.

The warm breeze trickled up under her skirt, caressing her bare bottom. Her hyper-sensitive skin prickled. She was both aroused by her nakedness and afraid that a sudden gust of wind would flip open the skirt's sarong-style front and expose her secret to the world. This was all Bobby Tom's fault. It was bad enough that she'd let him talk her into going out in public nearly naked, but while he and Natalie had rehearsed, he'd added to his sins by looking over at her and deliberately touching the pocket of his jeans, reminding her what he had there. She'd never shared a sexual secret with a man, and his teasing made her feel both light-headed and feverish.

The trees rustled above her, and the air in the canyon carried a faint hint of cedar. The dialogue continued until it was broken off by the soft sounds of a kiss. Despite her vow to act professionally, she couldn't bring her-self to look. She wanted to be the woman in his arms on that quilt. All alone, just the two of them. Naked.

"Oh, shit!"

Natalie's exclamation interrupted her reverie.

"Cut!" the director called out. "What's wrong?"

Gracie looked over in time to see Bobby Tom

pull away from his beautiful co-star. "Did I hurt you, Natalie?"

"My milk let down. God, I'm sorry, everybody. I'm leaking. I need a new blouse."

Bobby Tom leaped to his feet as if he'd just been exposed to a deadly disease.

"Ten minutes, everybody," the director announced. "Wardrobe, take care of Miss Brooks. And you'd better get a change for Mr. Denton, too."

Bobby Tom froze.

His head dropped.

An expression of abject horror appeared on his face as he saw two damp circles on the front of his own shirt.

A bubble of laughter slipped through Gracie's lips. She didn't think she'd ever seen anyone unbutton a garment so quickly. He thrust it at the wardrobe assistant and immediately made his way to Gracie's side.

"Come on."

Eyes narrowed and jaw set, he pulled her through the trees and around a rocky outcropping, walking so fast she stumbled. He drew her closer, but didn't slow his pace. Only after they were well out of sight of the others did he stop and lean back against the trunk of a walnut tree.

"This is turning into the most terrible experience of my life. I can't do it, Gracie. I would rather eat rats than go out there and take that woman's blouse off. I cannot make love to a nursing mother."

He looked so miserable that Gracie couldn't

help feeling a certain amount of sympathy for him, even though he'd offended her feminist sensibilities. She tried to use her most reasonable tone of voice, not a simple task when she was standing so close to him. "The primary function of the female breast is to nurture the young, Bobby Tom. It doesn't speak well of you that you find that offensive."

"I don't say I found it offensive. It just makes it impossible for me to forget that I'm kissing somebody else's wife. Making love to Natalie Brooks gives me the willies. Contrary to what you might have heard, I don't mess around with married women."

"No, I don't imagine you would. In your own peculiar, male-chauvinistic way, you have a lot of honor."

Some men would have regarded that as a questionable compliment, but Bobby Tom seemed pleased. "Thank you."

They gazed at each other for a long moment. When he spoke, his voice was husky. "I'm afraid you're going to have to put me back in the mood if I have any chance of doing a decent day's work out there."

"Back in the mood?"

He pulled her against his chest and pressed his mouth to hers as if he wanted to devour her. Her response was immediate. Flames raced through her blood, and she met his passion with her own. His mouth was open, his tongue aggressive. She sank her fingers into his thick hair just as he slipped his hand under her skirt. His big hands cupped her bottom and lifted her from the ground. She wrapped her legs around him and felt the harsh abrasion of denim against the sensitive skin of her inner thighs. He turned her so that her back was pressed against the tree trunk. She felt his arousal, thick and hard, press against her and some wanton part of her wanted to tear open the front of his jeans so there was no longer a barrier between them.

Years of deprivation pushed her to the limits of her control. Famished, she moaned and clasped him tighter between her thighs.

She heard a soft curse. He gentled his grip on her bottom and lowered her until her feet touched the ground. "I'm sorry, sweetheart. I keep forgetting how susceptible you are. I shouldn't have started this."

She sagged against him. He clasped the back of her head and drew it against his bare chest. He smelled so good, like soap and sunshine. She squeezed her eyes shut, wishing she had shown more restraint.

"Give me back my underpants, please."

She was afraid he'd refuse, but apparently he realized he'd teased her long enough. He released her to reach into his pocket. She kept her eyes on his chest as he handed over the scrap of buttercup yellow nylon. When he spoke, all the laughter had faded from his voice and it was steely with determination.

"Tomorrow night nothing's going to stop the two of us from finishing what we've started."

Before she could reply, he walked away.

She took several minutes to put herself back together and reluctantly returned to the area where they were filming. Natalie had donned a fresh blouse, and Elvis lay cradled in her arms. Bobby Tom, still bare chested, stood between her and the director, who appeared to be giving them some last minute instructions. The director turned away to address a cameraman, and one of the makeup people approached Natalie with a container of hair spray.

Natalie held up her hand. "Just a minute. I don't want Elvis breathing the fumes. Hold him, will you, Bobby Tom?" Without waiting for his consent, she thrust the chubby baby into his arms and stepped away to have her hair sprayed.

Bobby Tom's eyebrows rose in alarm. At the same time, his body reacted with the instincts of an All-Pro wide-receiver, and he automatically tucked the baby into his chest.

Elvis gave a happy gurgle. Feeling the familiar brush of skin against his cheek, he instinctively turned his head toward Bobby Tom's bare, well-shaped pectoral and opened his greedy little mouth.

Bobby Tom fixed him with a stern glare. "Don't even think about it, pardner."

Elvis chuckled and sucked his fingers instead.

14

The next evening as dusk gathered, Gracie and Bobby Tom sat in the top row of the wooden bleachers behind Telarosa High, gazing out at the empty football field. "I can't believe you never went to one of your high school football games," he said.

"There was a lot to do at Shady Acres in the evenings. It was hard to get away." Even to her own ears, her voice sounded strained. Yesterday in the canyon he'd said that tonight would be the night they finished what they'd started, and she was so nervous she could barely hold herself together. At the same time, he was as cool and collected as ever. She wanted to kill him.

"It doesn't seem like you had much fun as a kid." He brushed the side of her leg, and she jumped. He gave her an innocent look, then reached farther over to pick up a drumstick from the tub of fried chicken he'd bought for them, along with french fries, containers of salad, and a basket of hot biscuits.

Maybe his touch had been accidental. On the other hand, knowing him as she did, it was quite possible he was deliberately driving her to distraction. He must know she'd been on tenterhooks ever since she'd opened the door of her small apartment and seen him standing on the other side in a pair of jeans, a straw cowboy hat, and a faded Telarosa High School Titans T-shirt that might have fitted him fifteen years earlier, before he'd developed such spectacular chest muscles, but was definitely too tight for him now. Since Bobby Tom was impeccable about his clothes, she knew the old T-shirt was deliberate, part of his attempt to recreate a high school date.

She nibbled on the end of a fry and, when he looked away, slipped it through the opening behind her legs and let it fall to the ground below the bleachers because her stomach was too agitated to hold food. "You miss it a lot, don't you?"

"High school? Not hardly. All those homework assignments put a serious dent in my social life."

"I'm not talking about the homework. I'm talking about football."

He shrugged and discarded the drumstick, rubbing against the side of her arm in the process. She felt as if a shock wave had passed through her. "Sooner or later, I had to quit. A man can't play ball forever."

"But you hadn't planned on quitting so soon."

"Maybe I'll do some coaching. Just between the two of us, I've talked to a couple of people. Coaching seems a likely next step for me."

She expected to hear some enthusiasm in his voice, but she heard none. "What about your film career?"

"Some of it's all right. I like the action

stuff." His mouth twisted in disgust. "But I sure will be glad when all this love scene business is over. Do you know they actually expected me to take off my pants today?"

She smiled through her agitation. "I was there, remember? And by the time you were finished with all your chin rubbing and head shaking and 'aw shucks'ing, I don't think Willow or the director or anybody else had the slightest idea what you were saying."

"I got to keep my pants on, didn't I?"

"Poor Natalie didn't."

"Gettin' naked is a woman's lot in life. The sooner you accept that, the happier you're gonna be." He patted her bare knee, sending a shiver of desire through her as he let his hand linger there a moment longer than necessary.

It took enormous self-control not to respond to his baiting. Not only was she too edgy to match wits, but she was feeling remarkably tolerant toward him, despite his sensual torment. She'd been touched by his behavior toward Natalie the past two days as they'd filmed their love scene. His co-star's breasts had continued to leak, most of the time on him, until Natalie was so embarrassed, she'd been fighting tears. Bobby Tom had been a perfect gentleman, teasing her until she relaxed and making her feel as if this sort of thing happened to him all the time, as if a day wouldn't be complete without it, as if he looked *forward* to being soaked with breast milk.

Sometimes his ability to hide his real feelings

frightened her. No one should have that much self control. She certainly didn't. Right now, just the thought of making love with him had turned her insides to mush.

He dabbed at her bare thigh with his napkin, although she hadn't dropped anything there. His thumb brushed over the inner slope, and she caught her breath.

"Is something wrong?"

She gritted her teeth. "No—No, uh, nothing at all." He was making her an emotional wreck with his innocent little touches, brushing her leg as he shifted position, grazing her breast with his arm as he reached for a piece of chicken, every moment of contact so brief it could have been accidental, but since Bobby Tom never did anything accidentally, he had to be playing one of his games. If only he'd bring up the subject of the night ahead so they could clear the air between them and she could stop feeling so apprehensive. She'd bring it up herself, except she didn't have the foggiest notion how to go about it.

She dusted some biscuit crumbs off the lap of her crisp white shorts to give herself something to do with her hands. He was the one who had told her to wear shorts tonight, and although she considered them a bit too casual, she'd remembered his flattering comments about her legs and acquiesced. She'd also chosen a cropped turquoise cotton poor boy sweater that bared her lower back every time she leaned forward, a fact that she didn't think had escaped his attention.

"I wish you'd start watching the dailies," she said, trying to take her mind off her overheated body. "Maybe it would make you more enthusiastic about a movie career. Everybody knew you'd be photogenic, but I don't think anybody expected you to be as good as you are."

Several times she'd had the opportunity to sit in while Willow, the director, and various other members of *Blood Moon*'s production staff gathered to watch the film they had shot the previous day. Bobby Tom had a much quieter presence on screen than he did off, underplaying everything so that he didn't seem to be acting at all. It was a solid, restrained performance that managed to overcome some of the predictability of the script.

Instead of being flattered by her praise, he frowned. "Of course I'm good. You think I would have taken on something like this if I thought I'd mess it up?"

She gazed at him suspiciously. "From the beginning, you've been surprisingly confident for someone who says he's never acted before." Her eyes narrowed as a sudden thought struck her. "I don't know why I haven't already figured this out. You're pulling another one of your scams, aren't you?"

"I don't have the faintest idea what you're talking about."

"Acting lessons, that's what."

"Acting lessons?"

"You heard me. You've taken lessons, haven't you?"

He looked sulky. "I might have talked to one of my golf buddies a few times while we were playing, but that's it. A couple of conversations walking down the fairways. One or two tips between putts. That's all."

He hadn't allayed her suspicions a bit, and she gave him her steeliest glare. "Which golf buddy would that happen to be?"

"What difference does it make?"

"Bobby Tom..."

"It might have been Clint Eastwood."

"Clint Eastwood! You've been taking acting lessons from Clint Eastwood!" She rolled her eyes.

"That doesn't mean I'm serious about this business." He pulled his hat an inch lower on his forehead. "Making love with ladies I'm not attracted to isn't my idea of how I want to spend the rest of my life."

"I like Natalie."

"She's okay, I guess. But she's not my kind of woman."

"Maybe that's because she's a woman, not a girl."

His expression grew belligerent. "Now what's that supposed to mean?"

Her rising tension was making her cranky. "The indisputable fact is, you don't have the best taste when it comes to female companionship."

"That's a lie."

"Have you ever dated a woman with an IQ larger than her bra size?"

His eyes drifted down to her breasts. "A *lot* larger."

She could feel her nipples tightening. "I don't count. We're not officially dating."

"You're forgetting about my relationship with Gloria Steinem."

"You did *not* date Gloria Steinem!"

"You don't know that for a fact. Just because we're engaged doesn't give you the right to tell me what sort of ladies I'm attracted to."

He was stonewalling. He brushed her bare calf with his leg, and her skin broke out in goose bumps. Since she knew she wouldn't get any farther with him, she abandoned that particular line of attack for another.

"You certainly seem to have a head for business. Maybe you'd be happier doing that than acting. I had no idea how many successful business ventures you were involved in. Jack Aikens told me that you were born with horse sense."

"I've always been able to make money."

She'd never heard less enthusiasm, and as she slipped another french fry under the bleachers, she tried to figure out why. Bobby Tom was intelligent, handsome, charming, and he could make a success of anything he put his mind to. Except the one thing he wanted most—to play football again. It struck her that in the time she'd known him, she'd never once heard him complain about having his career ended so brutally. He wasn't a complainer by nature, but she was certain he'd feel better if he could vent his feelings.

"You keep a lot bottled up inside you. Would it help if you talked about what happened?"

"Don't psychoanalyze me, Gracie."

"I'm not trying to, but having your life turned upside down would be difficult for anyone."

"If you expect me to start whining because I can't play ball anymore, you can forget it. I've already got more than most people walking this globe even dream about, and self-pity isn't high on my list of desirable virtues."

"I've never known anyone less prone to self-pity than you, but you've built your life around football. It's natural for you to feel a sense of loss now that it's gone. You certainly have a right to be bitter about what happened to your career."

"Tell that to somebody who doesn't have a job, or tell that to a homeless person. I'll just bet they'd trade places with me in a second."

"If you follow that logic, no one who has food and shelter should ever feel unhappy about anything. But life's more than food and shelter."

He swiped a paper napkin across his lips, touching her breast with his elbow as he did and setting off a chain reaction of sensations inside her. "Gracie, don't take offense, but you're about boring me to death with this conversation."

She shot him a sideways glance, trying to see if the caress had been deliberate or accidental, but he wasn't giving anything away.

He straightened his leg to reach inside his

286

jeans pocket, and the denim tightened over his hips. A pulse thrummed in her throat. "You've aggravated me so much I nearly forgot what I wanted to do tonight." He withdrew something and closed his fist around it. "To accurately reconstruct everything you've missed in your relationship with the opposite sex, we'd have to go all the way back to playing doctor behind the garage, but I figured we'd skip that part and jump right ahead to high school when things get more interesting. Sherri Hopper never gave me back my high school ring after we broke up, so we're going to have to make do with this." He opened his hand.

Lying in his palm was the most massive man's ring she had ever seen. Its gaudy collection of yellow and white diamonds arranged to form three stars twinkled in the fading light. The ring was threaded with a heavy gold chain that he slipped over her head.

The ring settled with a thud between her breasts. She picked it up, crossing her eyes slightly to look down at it. "Bobby Tom, this is your Super Bowl ring!"

"Buddy Baines gave it back to me a couple of days ago."

"I can't wear your Super Bowl ring!"

"I don't see why not. One of us has to."

"But—"

"People in town are going to get suspicious if you don't have a ring. Everybody'll get a real kick out of this. Although I wouldn't plan on being in too much of a hurry when you go to town. Everybody's going to want to try it on."

How many bruising hits had he taken to earn this? How many broken bones and sore muscles had he endured? At the age of thirty, she finally had a man's ring, and what a ring it was.

As she reminded herself she only had it temporarily, she remembered the pangs she'd experienced as a teenager when she'd seen the girls at her high school with a boy's ring dangling from a chain around their necks. How much she had wanted one for herself.

She fought to hide her emotion. This was only pretend, and she shouldn't let it mean so much to her. "Thank you, Bobby Tom."

"Generally at this moment a boy and girl would commemorate the event with a kiss, but, frankly speaking, you're a little too hot for me to handle in public, so we'll postpone that till we have a little more privacy."

She clutched it tighter in the palm of her hand. "Did you give out your high school ring a lot?"

"Only twice. I believe I already mentioned Sherri Hopper, but Terry Jo Driscoll was the first girl I ever loved. She's Terry Jo Baines, now. Matter of fact you're going to meet her; I said we'd try to stop by her house tonight. Her husband Buddy was my best friend all through high school, and Terry Jo's real hurt I haven't introduced you to her yet. Of course, if you'd rather do something else..." He gave her a sideways glance. "We could probably postpone the visit until tomorrow."

"Tonight's fine!" Her throat was dry and her voice sounded squeaky. Why was he prolonging her agony like this? Maybe he'd changed his mind and he didn't want to make love to her. Maybe he was trying to get rid of her.

His arm brushed the bare patch of skin just above her waist as he reached behind her toward the paper carton she'd set on the seat. She jumped.

He looked at her, his dark blue eyes as innocent as a baby's. "I'll help you do dishes."

With a wicked grin, he began gathering up the fragments of their fried chicken dinner and stuffing it all back in the paper sack, touching her here and there in the process until she had goose bumps everywhere. He knew exactly what he was doing, she decided. He was deliberately driving her to insanity.

Ten minutes later, they were being ushered into the cluttered living room of a small, one-story house by a plump, but still pretty, woman with a baby face and overprocessed blond hair, who was clad in a red print top, white leggings, and a battered pair of sandals. She looked like someone who had taken more than her share of knocks in life, but hadn't let it get her down, and her affection for Bobby Tom was so open and honest that Gracie liked her immediately.

"It's about time Bobby Tom brought you around." Terry Jo squeezed Gracie's hand. "I swear, everybody in town like to die when they heard he finally got engaged. *Jo-leen!* I can hear that paper rattlin', and you get out of those Little Debbies right this minute!" She gestured across the clean, but shabby living room, toward the kitchen that lay beyond. "That's Joleen. She's our oldest. Her brother Kenny's over at his friends for the night. *Buddy!* Bobby Tom and Gracie are here! *Budd-ee!*"

"Stop yellin', Terry Jo." Buddy ambled into the living room from the kitchen, wiping the back of his hand over his mouth in a way that made Gracie suspect he had been the one rustling around in the Little Debbies instead of his daughter.

She had met Buddy Baines briefly when she'd taken the Thunderbird to his garage for new tires. Like the house in which he lived, he had a run down quality about him. With his dark hair and swarthy complexion, he was still a good looking man, but an extra roll of flesh had begun to thicken his waistline and he had the beginnings of a double chin. Still, she could imagine him as he'd been in high school, just as good looking as Bobby Tom, but dark instead of blond. The three of them—Bobby Tom, Buddy, and Terry Jo—must have been quite a sight.

After Joleen had run in to exchange a moist, enthusiastic greeting with her Uncle Bobby Tom, Terry Jo drew Gracie into the kitchen to help her carry the beer and chips. Gracie had no desire for either, but she didn't have the heart to refuse Terry Jo's cheerful hospitality. She had tucked Bobby Tom's ring inside her sweater, and it nestled between her breasts. She touched it there as she looked around the kitchen. It was as shabby and homey as the living room, with children's artwork held to the refrigerator by Bible verse magnets and a pile of newspapers stacked on the floor next to a dog's water dish.

Terry Jo held the refrigerator door open with her hip while she began pulling out beer cans and passing them to Gracie. "You might know that Buddy's daddy is Mayor Luther Baines, and he told me to tell you they've put you on the birthplace committee. You've got a meeting Monday night at seven. If you want to stop by and pick me up, we can go together."

Gracie gazed at her in alarm as she cradled four cold beer cans against her chest. "The birthplace committee?"

"For Heavenfest." She shut the refrigerator door, grabbed a bag of chips from the counter, and poured them into two blue plastic bowls. "I know Bobby Tom's told you how the town bought the house he grew up in. We're dedicating it during the festival, but we still need a lot of help getting it ready."

Gracie remembered Bobby Tom's opinion of the bizarre scheme to turn his childhood home into a tourist attraction. "I don't know, Terry Jo. Bobby Tom's not too happy about this."

Terry Jo took two of the beers back and handed Gracie one of the potato chip bowls. "He'll come around. One thing about Bobby Tom. He knows what he owes this town."

Gracie didn't necessarily think Bobby Tom owed the town anything, but since she was an outsider, she had a different point of view from the local citizens.

As the women returned to the living room, Buddy and Bobby Tom were arguing about the Chicago Stars' chances of making it to another Super Bowl. Bobby Tom had his ankle crossed over his knee, and his straw cowboy hat rested on his calf. Gracie walked to the sofa and handed him a beer. His fingers brushed hers, and she felt a tingling that traveled all the way up her arm. He gazed at her with those midnight blue eyes of his, and her knees grew weak.

As she placed the bowl of chips on the coffee table and took a seat next to him, she realized Buddy was watching her with open interest. She felt his eyes moving over her breasts and down her bare legs. When Bobby Tom looked at her like that, she got goose bumps, but Buddy's perusal embarrassed her. If she'd known they were going to stop here, she would have ignored Bobby Tom's request and worn slacks.

Buddy took a beer from his wife and, leaning back into the vinyl recliner, regarded Bobby Tom. "So how does it feel not playing in preseason? This is the first time in how many years?"

"Thirteen."

"That's tough. You broke some records, but if you'd been able to play longer, you might of got more of the important ones."

Buddy was deliberately pouring salt into Bobby Tom's wounds, and Gracie waited for Bobby Tom to deflect the gibe with one of his wisecracks. Instead he shrugged and sipped his beer. She felt oddly protective of him.

Here, among his childhood friends, he seemed vulnerable.

Impulsively, she leaned over and patted Bobby Tom's thigh through his jeans. The muscles beneath her palm felt hard and powerful. "I'm sure most of the people in town are grateful he's making a movie instead of going off to training camp. Windmill is pouring a lot of money into the local economy. But, why am I telling you this, Buddy? Your garage is getting all kinds of business from Windmill, isn't it?"

Buddy flushed. Bobby Tom shot her an assessing look. She patted his thigh again as if she had every right to touch whatever part of his body took her fancy. Terry Jo stepped into the silence with a report on the progress the various Heavenfest committees were making and finished by announcing that Gracie had been named to the birthplace committee.

Bobby Tom's eyes narrowed. "I told Luther I wasn't having anything to do with that, and neither is Gracie. It's a damn fool idea, and whoever came up with it ought to have his head examined."

"It was Luther's idea," Buddy said belligerently.

Bobby Tom raised his beer can. "I rest my case."

Gracie expected Buddy to rise to his father's defense, but instead, he grunted and grabbed a handful of potato chips from the bowl at his side. His mouth full, he turned to Gracie.

"The town was surprised to hear about the two of you. You're not Bobby Tom's usual type."

"Thank you," Gracie replied politely.

Bobby Tom chuckled.

Buddy studied her more closely, then regarded Bobby Tom. "How's Suzy taking your engagement? Or is she too busy spending time with her new boyfriend to pay attention?"

"Hush, Buddy!" Terry Jo exclaimed. "I don't know what's got into you, actin' so mean tonight. And there's no need to bring up something that probably isn't anything more than gossip."

"Bring what up?" Bobby Tom asked. "What are you talking about?"

Buddy stuffed another handful of chips into his mouth. "You tell him, Terry Jo. He won't believe me."

Terry Jo's beer can clicked on her wedding ring as she rolled it between her palms. "It's just a story going around. There's probably nothing to it."

"If it has to do with my mother, I want to know about it."

"Well, Angie Cotter was talking to Nelly Romero, and you know how she is, couldn't keep something quiet if her life depended on it. But half of what she says isn't true. Last month she saw me runnin' into the day-old bakery in Buddy's shirt, and the next thing I know, she's telling the whole town I'm pregnant again. So it's probably like that."

Bobby Tom regarded her levelly. "Tell me what she's saying."

"Well, the rumor is that Suzy's keepin' company with Way Sawyer."

"What?" Bobby Tom laughed. "I can't believe this town. Some things never change around here."

"See, Buddy, I told you it was a big lie."

Buddy leaned forward in the recliner. "Angie says she saw Way Sawyer's chauffeur picking Suzy up at her house a few weeks ago. If that turns out to be true, your mother's not going to have a friend left in this town."

"She'll have me," Terry Jo said. "I love Suzy, and I'll stand by her, no matter what."

Gracie realized she'd forgotten to mention her encounter on the highway with Way Sawyer to Bobby Tom, but now didn't seem the time to do so. She'd liked Mr. Sawyer. Not everyone would have stopped to see if she needed help, and it made her uncomfortable to hear them talking about him this way.

Bobby Tom stretched his arm along the back of the couch, grazing Gracie's shoulders, then idly slipped his thumb inside the neck of her sweater and ran it along her collarbone. The skin on her breasts prickled, and she was very much afraid something embarrassing was happening to her nipples, something the clingy material of her sweater was almost certainly revealing to everybody. Heat flooded her cheeks.

Bobby Tom kept rubbing. "I'm sure she'd appreciate your loyalty, Terry Jo, but it's not going to be necessary. Mom loves this town, and I can guaran-damn-tee you she wouldn't even think about keeping company with that sonovabitch."

"That's what I told everybody," Terry Jo said. "Honestly, Bobby Tom, I don't know how we're gonna keep goin' after Rosatech pulls out. The town's been having a hard enough time as it is. If Heavenfest doesn't put us on the tourist map, we might as well board up Main Street."

Buddy cleaned out the last of the potato chips. "Luther says Michael Jordan's playing in the celebrity golf tournament for sure."

Bobby Tom got a vague look in his eyes that made Gracie suspect he still hadn't invited the athletes as he'd promised. Since very little slipped his attention, she knew it wasn't an accidental oversight. She tried unsuccessfully to wiggle away from the delicious stroking on her neck.

"Not for sure," he said. "Pretty sure."

"If Jordan comes, that'll bring in a lot of tourists. How many of the Cowboys did you get besides Aikman?"

"Still waiting on the final count." Bobby Tom withdrew his hand from the back of her neck and slipped his hat on. As he rose to his feet, he pulled her up with him. "Gracie and I have to be goin'. I promised her we'd pick out names for all our kids tonight. Right now she's favoring Aloysius for our first boy, and I've got to nip that one in the bud."

Gracie nearly choked on the potato chip she'd been swallowing.

Terry Jo made an unmistakable gesture of friendship by telling Bobby Tom she thought Aloysius was a perfectly good name. Good manners made it necessary for Gracie to thank her, much to Bobby Tom's amusement. He patted her bottom, and she started blushing again. His hand lingered there, and she could barely manage to say good-bye. The small amount of food she'd consumed that evening had settled into a jittery lump in her stomach.

Silence stretched between them as he backed out of the driveway and headed toward Main Street. She twisted her hands in her lap. The seconds ticked away. He began fiddling with the radio.

"Are you in the mood for country or rock? Or maybe you'd like to hear some classical?"

"I really don't care."

"You sound a little testy. Is something wrong?"

His inquiry was so innocent, so completely lacking in guile that she knew he was deliberately provoking her. She gritted her teeth. "Classical would be fine."

"Sorry. That signal doesn't come in too well at night."

Her temper snapped. Knotting her hands into fists, she screeched at him. "What are you trying to do to me? Are you deliberately trying to make me crazy? Never mind. Don't answer that. Just take me home. Right this minute!"

He gave her a satisfied smile, as if she'd done something that pleased him enormously. "Man-oh-man, Gracie, you are one bundle of nerves tonight. Sweetheart, I don't think there's going to be any pain, if that's what you're worried about. Now I'm no gynecologist, but you're thirty years old, and whatever barrier might have been there when you were a youngster has got to have evaporated from old age by now."

"*That's it!* Let me out of this truck right now! I am not putting up with you a minute longer!" Although she'd never been a yeller, it felt so good to yell at him that she yelled some more. "You might think you're funny, but you're not! And you're not sexy, either, no matter what all those women tell you. You're pitiful, that's what you are. Ugly and stupid and pitiful!"

He chuckled. "I *knew* we were going to have a good time tonight."

She propped her elbows on her bare knees and lowered her forehead onto the heels of her hands. Her shoulders slumped.

He reached up under her sweater and patted her back. "It's going to be all right, sweetheart. Part of the fun's in the anticipation." He ran the pads of his fingers over the bumps of her spine.

"I don't want to anticipate," she moaned. "I want to get started so we can get it over with."

"Honey, we got started a couple of hours ago. Haven't you figured that out yet? Just because we still have our clothes on doesn't mean that we haven't been going at it ever since you climbed into my truck tonight." He drew little circles in the small of her back.

She turned her head to look at him. He withdrew his hand from beneath her sweater and smiled at her. She imagined she saw ten-derness in his eyes, but that was probably just wishful thinking on her part. The truck began to bounce and she straightened.

"Where are we?"

"By the river. I told you that's where we were headed, just like we used to in high school. We're taking this step-by-step, sweetheart, so you don't feel cheated. Now if I was being real strict about this, we'd have stopped by the Dairy Queen first for a cone, but to tell you the truth, I don't think I can keep my hands off you a second longer."

He brought the truck to a stop, turned off the ignition and headlights, then lowered the window. The cool night breeze drifted in, and she heard the sound of rushing water. Through the windshield, moonlight sparked on the leaves of the pecan and cypress trees that lined the riverbank.

She swallowed. "Are we going to...You know. Here. In the truck?"

"You want me to give you an agenda?"

"Well, I..."

He smiled and took off his hat. "Come here, Gracie Snow. Right this minute."

15

Gracie slid into Bobby Tom's arms as easily as she'd ever done anything in her life. He tucked her under his chin and slipped his hand beneath her sweater. With her ear pressed to his chest, she could hear the strong, steady beat of his heart.

He stroked her hair while he caressed the skin on her back with his thumb. "Gracie, sweetheart, you know this isn't forever, don't you?" His voice was gentle and more serious than she'd ever heard it. "You've been a good friend to me, and I wouldn't hurt you for anything, but I'm just not a settlin' down guy. It isn't too late for you to change your mind if you don't think you can handle something temporary."

She'd known from the beginning this wasn't forever, but she didn't believe he wasn't a settlin' down guy. He simply wouldn't be settlin' down with someone ordinary like her. He was used to bombshell blondes and drop-dead redheads, to women who made a career out of aerobicizing their bodies and augmenting their breasts. To beauty queens and rodeo queens and models who posed in nothing but a smile. His future wife would be somebody like that, but Gracie very much hoped she'd have brains, too, or he'd never be happy.

She breathed in his scent and traced the outline of the faded *L* on his old high school T-shirt with the pad of her finger. "It's all right. I'm not expecting happily-ever-after." She tilted her face up at him and regarded him with great seriousness. "I don't want anything from you."

He lifted an eyebrow, clearly bewildered by her statement.

"I mean it, you know. I don't want clothes or money or your autograph for any of my relatives. I'm not going to sell your story to the tabloids or ask you to make business contacts for me. When the picture's done, I'm going to give you back your Super Bowl ring and the keys to your Thunderbird. I'm not going to take anything from you."

His eyes were shuttered, his expression inscrutable. "I don't know why you're saying all this."

"Of course, you do. People are always taking something from you, but I won't be one of them." She lifted her hand and traced the hard line of his jaw with her fingers. Then she removed his Stetson and dropped it behind the seat. "Bobby Tom, show me how to please you."

His eyes squeezed shut and, just for an instant, she thought she felt him tremble, but when they opened, she saw the familiar amusement lurking there.

"You got your fancy underwear on tonight?"

"Yes."

"That's a good start."

She licked her lips, suddenly remembering she'd forgotten something very important. Determined to sound matter-of-fact, she cleared her throat. "I'm—You probably need to know before we go any farther...I'm taking birth control pills," she said in a rush.

"Are you now?"

"Right before I left New Grundy, I decided that since this was going to be a fresh start for me, I needed to be prepared so I didn't miss any…new experiences." She made eye contact with the flying T on his shirt. "But even though I'm prepared, I know you've led an active life." Once again she cleared her throat. "Sexually speaking." She paused. "So I'll expect you to…You'll have to use a condom."

He smiled. "I know this conversation isn't easy for you, but you've done the right thing bringing it up, and you make sure you do exactly the same thing with your future lovers." A shadow passed over his face, and the muscles around his mouth tightened. Then he rubbed his knuckles across her cheek. "Now, I'm going to tell you something, and even though it's the truth, I don't want you to believe me for a second because men don't like to use condoms, and they'll say just about anything to avoid wearing them. The fact is, sweetheart, I'm clean as a whistle, and I've had the blood tests to prove it. Even before those paternity suits, I was real careful in my relationships with the opposite sex."

"I believe you."

He sighed. "What am I gonna do with you? You know I tell more lies than Pinocchio. I'm the last person on earth you should believe about something this important."

"You're the first one I'd believe. I've never known anyone who hates to hurt other people as much as you do. It's ironic, isn't it, considering the violent way you made your living?"

"Gracie?"

"Yes?"

"I don't have on any underwear."

Her eyes shot up.

He grinned and kissed the tip of her nose. Slowly his smile faded and his eyes darkened. Sliding away from the steering wheel toward her side of the seat, he cupped her jaw between his hands and lowered his mouth to cover hers.

The instant their lips touched, her body flooded with sensation, and she felt as if every part of her throbbed with new life. His mouth over hers was warm and soft, and she opened to him. The tip of his tongue slid between her lips, and she reveled in the intimacy of taking that part of him inside her body. Wrapping her arms around his strong neck, she touched his tongue with her own. Her top rode up, and he slipped his hands beneath it, just above her waist.

As their kiss deepened, she felt the damp heat of his body through his T-shirt. She sank her fingers into his shoulders and took his tongue deeper into her mouth. The rest of the world disappeared, and only sensation existed. Her lungs began to burn, and she realized she had forgotten to breathe. Drawing back, she gasped for air. He buried his lips in the *V* of her throat and nipped the delicate bone with his teeth.

"Bobby Tom!" She gasped his name.

"Yes, sweetheart?" His breathing sounded even less steady than her own.

"Can we do it now?"

"No, honey. You're not nearly ready."

"Oh, I am. I really am."

He chuckled, then groaned as his thumbs brushed up along her bare sides. "This is just our warm-up. Come here. Closer." He lifted her so that she straddled his lap.

As she settled on top of him, she felt him, hard and rigid, trying to push into her right through his jeans and her shorts. "Did I do that to you?" she whispered against his lips.

"About three hours ago," he murmured.

With a shiver of pleasure, she settled down in his lap. Rubbing her hips against him, she took his mouth.

"Stop," he moaned.

"You're the one who wanted to play games," she reminded him, speaking against his parted lips.

"Sometimes I'm too much of a smart-ass for my own good. God, don't do that!"

"Do what?" She again rocked her pelvis, wanting all the barriers between them gone.

He grabbed the hem of her top and shoved it up, taking her bra with it. Pushing her back until her shoulders rested against the dashboard, he exposed her breasts.

She let out a cry when he lifted her breast and took the nipple in his mouth. She dug her fingers into his shoulders as he suckled her. Her position, straddling him with her knees and leaning back against the dash, was awkward, but her body no longer belonged to her and the unfamiliar strain in her splayed thighs only added to her excitement. She felt the hot suction of his mouth, the throbbing between her legs, the dampness of his thin, worn T-shirt beneath her palms. He shoved his hands beneath her thighs, and his thumbs slid under the legs of her shorts.

Sitting back up, she reached for his T-shirt and pulled it from his jeans, then she fumbled between their bodies for the snap at the top of his strained zipper. It gave, and she worked at the zipper. He had already opened hers, and before she knew it, he had pushed her shorts down to the point where her spread thighs stretched the material too taut to go farther.

The rasp of their breathing filled the cab of the truck. She drew one leg back over his thighs until she was kneeling on the seat next to him and could work at his zipper with both hands. He stripped his T-shirt over his head, knocking the steering wheel with his elbow in the process so that the horn sounded. He cursed, and she dipped for one of his nipples with her mouth as she continued her struggle with the stubborn zipper.

The hard nub bumped her tongue. She abraded it, just as he had done to her, and felt his entire body go rigid.

The zipper gave.

He pushed her away from him just long enough to whip her top over her head and fling it behind the seat. Her bra followed, and she knelt next to him like a pixieish slattern, hair rumpled, a Super Bowl ring hanging between her bare breasts, her unfastened shorts low on her hips.

She gazed down at his open zipper. "It's too dark," she whispered. "I can't see you." She touched his belly with her fingertip.

"Do you want to see me?"

"Oh, yes."

"Gracie…" He sounded as if he were struggling to breathe. "This seemed like a good idea, but things are going a little faster than I'd figured, and this truck is too damn small." He gave the key a hard twist and shoved the truck into gear so abruptly she bumped against the door. The tires spit gravel as he shot backward, then reversed. The truck jolted over the hard-packed ground to the dark highway.

She reached behind the seat to grab for her top. He caught her arm before she could locate it. "Come here." Without waiting for her permission, he pulled her down until she was lying on her back, her head on his thigh. Driving much too fast, he used his free hand to torment her breast.

The truck shot through the night as his fingers caressed her. Through the windshield, she could see the sky flying by and the tops of the trees. She hovered on the brink of something inexplicable, and when she could no longer bear his sweet torture, she turned her breasts against him.

The truck shot down the dark highway, and his open zipper scratched her cheek. She pressed her lips to his hard, flat belly and felt every muscle contract. He groaned and lifted her top thigh. His palm cupped her through her shorts. He moved the heel of his hand, and she began to fly.

"No, you don't," he whispered, pulling away. "Not this time. Not till I'm inside you."

She careened to the edge of the seat as he swung into the drive that led to his house. A shower of gravel sprayed the side of the cab. He slammed on the brakes. Within seconds he'd turned off the ignition and jumped from the truck.

She was still searching behind the seat for her sweater when he opened the door. "You don't need that." He clasped her waist and pulled her out of the truck.

Even though the house was isolated and the yard deserted, she pressed her hands over her breasts as he drew her across the grass. She saw his grin in the dim reflection of the single light that burned on the porch and realized he looked very much as he had the first few days on the movie set, with his bare chest and unzipped jeans. The thud of his boots on the wooden porch steps drowned out the gentler tap of her sandals. He worked the key in the lock and, as the door opened, hauled her none-too-gently into the house.

He maneuvered her to the bedroom with an urgency that both thrilled and scared her. She loved knowing he wanted her, but she wasn't at all certain she could satisfy him. She'd always been a bit clumsy at physical activities, and surely this was the most physical of all. Her eyes fastened on the Sleeping Beauty bed that dominated the room, and she swallowed hard.

"It's too late for second thoughts, sweetheart. I'm afraid we passed the point of no return a good two weeks ago." He sat down on the side of the bed and yanked off his boots and socks. His gaze meandered down to the white lace of her panties that showed through the open zipper of her shorts.

The fussy femininity of the bedroom should have made him less intimidating, but instead he had never seemed so overpowering to her, or so completely male. Her sexual excitement gave way to anxiety. She stared at him and could only wonder how she had gotten herself in such a predicament. How had it happened that she was about to offer herself to a multimillionaire Texas playboy jock who'd been pursued by the most alluring women in the world?

And then he smiled at her, and her doubts faded as her heart filled with love. She was offering herself to him because she wanted to. She was building a memory that would keep her company for the rest of her life. He held out his hand and she walked toward him.

The fingers that clasped her own were strong and reassuring. "It's all right, honey.

"I know."

"You do?" Catching her by the hips, he brought her to stand between his splayed thighs.

"Uh-huh. You've already told me that you don't do anything you're not good at."

"That's true, sweetheart. 'Course you are a handful." He carried his lips to her breast and slipped his hands inside her shorts to pull them down, along with her panties. She set one hand on his shoulder and stepped out of the lacy scrap of fabric, glad to be rid of them, feeling very much like a butterfly finally escaping from a chrysalis that had held it captive far too long. His eyes settled on the nest of coppery curls between her legs. Curling her fingers around as much of his upper arm as she could span, she tugged on him until he stood.

When he was on his feet, she slipped her fingers over the waistband of his jeans, where they had fallen open low on his hips, and discovered he hadn't been teasing when he said he wasn't wearing any briefs. Her hands trembled, and she hesitated.

He cupped the back of her head and lightly twined his fingers in her curls. "Go ahead, sweetheart. It's all right."

Her mouth felt dry as she slowly tugged on the soft denim. Keeping her eyes on the floor, she knelt. With infinite slowness, she slid the jeans over his hips and along his strong thighs to his ankles. He kicked them aside. With a sense of anticipation, she settled back on her calves.

Lifting her gaze past the scars at his knee, she paused at his hips. "Oh, my..."

She hadn't expected it to be quite so imposing, quite so...commanding. Her lips parted, and she couldn't take her eyes away.

It was magnificent, even better than she'd imagined. Incredible to have something like that thrusting out so boldly. Her forehead creased, but she refused to let the size worry her. Somehow he'd make certain she accommodated.

"This is going to be a disaster," he murmured.

Her head shot up and she gazed at him with stricken eyes. A red flush burned her skin. Mortified, she jumped to her feet. "I'm sorry! I didn't meant to stare. I—"

"No, baby!" He dragged her into his arms and chuckled. "It's not you. You're perfect. It's me. You're driving me so crazy with the way you're looking at me that we're in imminent danger of having this whole thing over in ten seconds flat."

She was so relieved she hadn't done anything wrong that a bubble of laughter rose in her throat. "I guess we'd just have to do it again, then, wouldn't we?"

"Gracie Snow, you're turning into a trashy woman right before my eyes." He slipped the chain holding the Super Bowl ring over her head. "This is definitely my lucky night."

He started kissing her again, and his hands were all over her body, kneading her buttocks, rubbing her against him. She reveled in the feel of his bare skin pressing against her own. She wrapped her arms around his neck and tangled them in the waterfall of eyelet and ribbon cascading from the canopy. He drew her free, stripped back the spread, and laid her on Sleeping Beauty's bed. But he was no fairy-tale prince with only chaste kisses on his mind.

She locked her gaze with his and slowly separated her legs, offering herself with a sense of gladness. He smiled and settled next to her on the bed, laying the palm of his hand flat on her belly. "You are one of a kind, sweetheart."

Dipping his head, he kissed her again, while his fingers trailed down through the silky curls, then detoured to stroke her inner thighs. He began to torture her with his caress, coming closer and closer, but not quite touching.

She went wild, arching against his hand, every muscle taut. "Please!" she gasped against his lips. "Don't stop there..."

"I won't, sweetheart. Believe me, I won't."

He parted her, and her breath caught on a sob as he traced her secrets with his fingertip. Her whole body began to quiver. He eased his finger inside her, and, just like that, she came apart with a great cry.

He held her through the aftershocks. As soon as she calmed and felt him, still rigid, pressed against the side of her hip, she had to fight back tears. She had wanted to give, but all she'd done was take.

"I—I ruined everything. I'm so—so sorry. I knew I'd mess this up." She swallowed a sob. "I wanted to be—to be perfect, but I was never good at phy—physical things. Nobody ever wanted me on their team in gym, and now you know why. I'm all done, and you're—you're not, and I r—ruined it." She was so stricken by her premature orgasm that she barely felt his lips moving at her temple.

"Nobody can be good at everything, sweetheart." His voice had a queer, choked sound to it.

"But I wanted so much to be—to be good at *this*!"

"I understand." He settled on top of her and nudged her legs apart with his own. "Sometimes you just have to accept your faults. A little bit wider, honey."

It was the least she could do for him.

Once again, she felt his hand brush her thighs, and then his finger invaded. He groaned. "You're so tight."

"I'm sorry. It's because I've never—" She gasped as he began a slow, rhythmic stroking that uncoiled ribbons of sensation inside her. He touched her everywhere, his skillful, inquisitive fingers making intimate silken patterns.

"Bobby Tom?" She whispered his name as if it were a question.

"Don't apologize, sweetheart. You can't help being a failure." Through her excitement, she realized he was smiling against her damp cheek. But before she could figure out why, she felt a hard probing at the small entrance to her body. Her hands convulsed around his shoulders as tingling shocks of pleasure raced through her body. "Oh..."

He eased inside, stretching her bit by bit, giving her time to adjust to his size. She could feel his restraint in the tight coiling of his muscles beneath her hands. But she didn't want restraint. She had been waiting for this forever.

"Hurry," she gasped. "Please hurry."

"I don't want to hurt you, honey." His voice sounded tight, the way it did when he lifted weights.

"Please. Don't hold back."

"You don't know what you're asking."

"I do. I want everything."

He trembled and drove into her. Shafts of delight sped through her tissues and sang in her blood. She lifted her hips and wrapped her legs around his. He shoved his hands beneath her and tilted her higher, thrusting more deeply. She reveled in her ability to bear his weight, to accept his sex, and she gave a gasp of joy at the woman's magic that permitted her body to accommodate his.

His breathing was a rough rasp in her ear, and she moved with him as if she'd been doing it forever. The sensations that swept through her felt more powerful than anything she'd ever imagined, like wind and thunder. He carried her higher and higher into the clouds, toward a mysterious place where only ecstasy dwelt. The dampness from their bodies mingled with their cries until they were part of the clouds. For a moment they hung there, perfectly suspended. And then they tumbled together in a warm shower of silver rain.

It could have been minutes or hours before she hit the earth. The world returned in bits and pieces: the brush of cool air on her arm, the distant sound of a jet passing overhead. His body grew heavy on hers. She welcomed the weight and experienced a pang of loss when she felt a gentle suction as he pulled out of her.

He rolled to his stomach, keeping his face turned toward her and laying his upper arm across her chest, just beneath her breasts. He fell into a light doze, and, as she lay on her back, she studied him, memorizing every detail of his face: the sensuous lower lip, the way his spiky lashes rested on his cheekbone, the straight, strong nose, and the curl of damp blond hair at his temple. His skin looked golden in the soft lamplight. He was so beautiful he took her breath away.

Joy surged through her. She wanted to dance; she wanted to climb up on the roof of the house and cheer. She had never been so full of energy.

"Bobby Tom?"

"Uhmm..."

"Could you open your eyes?"

"Urgmm..."

She thought of a cartoon she'd seen long ago of dancing mice holding frilly umbrellas. That's how she felt lying naked here in bed with this man, as full of happiness as a dancing mouse with a frilly umbrella. "That was even better than I thought it would be. I knew you'd be an excellent lover—you really are, Bobby Tom—I'm sure you must be exceptional. But you shouldn't have teased me when I thought

I'd ruined everything with my premature orgasm."

He opened one eye and, with his cheek still pressed against the pillow, peered at her. "In case you haven't figured it out yet, there isn't any such thing as a premature orgasm for a woman."

"How was I supposed to know that? I mean this in a constructive way, so please don't be offended, but you have an annoying habit of making jokes that only *you* understand."

He smiled and lifted the arm draped across her chest to play in her hair with his fingers. "That was just about irresistible." He gave a bark of laughter. "Premature orgasm."

"Men can have them. I don't see why women can't."

"Damn, you modern females want everything, don't you? Well, sweetheart, us men are keeping this one just for ourselves, even if you take us all the way to the Supreme Court." He yawned and rolled to his back, taking most of the sheet with him.

She sat up against the headboard. "Are you hungry? I am. I couldn't eat too much earlier because I was so nervous, but, I swear, I could eat a horse now. I'll settle for a sandwich, though, or even a bowl of cereal, or soup. Or maybe—"

"Chatty little thing, aren't you?"

"Do you think we could do it again?"

He groaned. "I need a little recovery time. I'm not as young as I used to be a couple of hours ago."

"I thought—Well, I know there are some different positions, and, to be completely honest, I'm rather fascinated by the, uh, male organ, and I didn't get much opportunity to really study it, and—"

She broke off as the bed began to shake with his laughter. "The male organ!"

She regarded him huffily. "I don't see what's so amusing. I'm too old to be this ignorant, and I have a lot of years to make up for."

His forehead wrinkled in mock alarm. "Not in one night, I hope."

"Somehow I don't think you'd have the slightest bit of trouble keeping up with me." She hadn't failed to notice that, despite his words, he'd been regarding the exposed parts of her with unmistakable signs of interest.

The telephone intruded. Although the ringer on the phone at the side of the bed had been turned off, she'd been able to hear the one in his office ringing intermittently ever since they'd entered the house. She was accustomed to the way he let his answering machine take the majority of his calls and had paid no attention. This time he sighed and rolled over to pick it up.

"Maybe if I take this one, whoever it is will leave us alone for the rest of the night. Hello...No, Luther, it's okay, I wasn't asleep...Uh-huh. Yeah, I should have that list firmed up in another day or so....You want George Strait, too?" He rolled his eyes. "I can't talk any longer, Luther. I've got a call

316

coming in on the other line, and I'm pretty sure it's Troy Aikman. Yeah, I'll tell her."

He slammed down the phone and thrust himself up against the pillows. "He told me to remind you about the birthplace committee meeting. You're not going. Damn fools."

"I think I will go, as a matter of fact. One of us needs to know what they're up to."

"Insanity, that's what they're up to, and you'd better stay away because it might be contagious." His eyes wandered to her breasts. "Are you ready for round two, or do you want to sit here jabbering all night?"

She smiled at him. "I'm definitely ready for round two."

"Good."

"But..." She gathered her courage, determined not to let him get his way in everything, even if he did have a few decades more experience than she, and even if she wasn't all that confident of her new abilities as a sex siren. "I'm ready for round two, but this time I would very much like to be the person calling the shots."

He regarded her warily. "What exactly do you mean by that?"

"There's no reason for you to feign ignorance, Bobby Tom. I believe our communication channels are completely open."

He chuckled.

She reached out for the rumpled sheet covering his hips and pushed it away. "I was thinking that the best place to satisfy my curiosity might be in the shower."

"The shower?"

"If you don't mind."

"I don't mind one bit. But are you positive you're ready? Taking a shower with me means for sure you'll be going from beginner to intermediate in just one night."

She gazed at him and her lips curved in a smile as old as Eve. "I can't wait."

16

They went up in his plane the next day, and she was thrilled with the sensations of flying in a small aircraft. Bobby Tom had announced that morning he was taking her to Austin so he could show her some of the city, including his old college haunts. The day was clear, and as he identified the rivers and canyons they flew over, she stole sideways glances at him.

Last night he'd been everything she'd dreamed he'd be: tender and demanding, praising her passion and refusing to let her hold anything back. She had given herself to him out of the fullness of her heart, and she didn't regret anything. Years from now when she was holding a paper-thin hand through its last hours of life, she would find her own comfort in the memories of the night she had been loved so well by Bobby Tom Denton.

"It sure is nice to get away from that telephone," he said, as he banked the plane. "Luther must call me six times a day, not to mention everybody else who wants a piece of me."

"You can't really blame Mayor Baines for being nervous about the golf tournament," she pointed out. "Heavenfest is two months away and you haven't given him a list of names. Don't you think you should start calling your friends to invite them?"

"I suppose," he said, without enthusiasm.

"I know why you're stalling. You'll do favors for everybody in the world, but you don't want to ask for any in return."

"You don't understand, Gracie. Athletes have people hounding them all the time. If it isn't one thing, it's another."

"Are you telling me that none of these men has ever asked you for a favor?"

"A few."

"More than a few, I'll bet." She gave him a sympathetic smile. "Why don't you give me a list of your friends? I'll make the phone calls first thing tomorrow on your behalf."

"You just want to have Troy Aikman's home phone number. Sorry, honey, but I don't think he's your type."

"Bobby Tom..."

"Hmmm?"

"I hate to lower your opinion of me, but I don't have the slightest idea who Troy Aikman is."

He rolled his eyes. "He's a pretty well-known quarterback, sweetheart. He's taken the Cowboys to a couple of Super Bowls."

"I guess I'd have a hard time passing the football quiz."

"I just hope to hell none of the ladies around here ever decides to challenge you."

She was a bit tense during the landing at the small airstrip, but he brought the plane in so smoothly she barely felt it touch down. Was there anything he didn't do well?

Once on the ground, he procured a car from one of his acquaintances at the airstrip and took her on a tour of the city, including the state capital building and the University of Texas campus. As the sunlight faded, they walked along Town Lake, a popular spot in downtown Austin.

"Pretty soon you're going to see something you won't ever see in New Grundy."

She gazed at the imposing buildings that surrounded the lake and the bridge that ran across it. People sat in boats on the water as if they were waiting for a fireworks show to begin, and she noticed a large number of dark birds swooping in the sky. She also smelled an odor that was faintly acrid, reminding her of a zoo. "I've seen a lot of things like that today. What else is there?"

His grin seemed to hold a trace of mischief. "One of Mother Nature's better shows. You like bats, honey?"

"Bats?" She stared up at the strange, dark birds. The vaguely feral scent pricked at her nostrils. She was aware of a squeaking sound. "I don't think—*Oh, my God!*"

As if on cue, a great dark wave of bats flew

out from their roost under the bridge, thousands of them. And then thousands more. As she watched, spellbound, more and more came out until hundreds of thousands of them filled the sky like thick, dense smoke. She let out a startled shriek as several swooped a bit too close for comfort.

Bobby Tom laughed and drew her against him.

Gracie wasn't a fainthearted person, and she wouldn't have missed this sight for the world, but bats were bats, and as another came nearer than she would have liked, she automatically ducked into his chest, which only encouraged him to laugh harder.

"I knew you'd like it." He rubbed her back. "Austin has the biggest bat population of any city in the world. A whole bunch of them roost under that bridge. I don't know exactly how they figure it, but they say these bats eat something like twenty thousand pounds of bugs a night. Usually they don't come out until it's darker, which makes them harder to see, but it's been dry lately and they've been coming out a little earlier so they have enough time to feed, which reminds me that I'm getting hungry. How do you feel about some good Tex-Mex?"

"It sounds wonderful."

As usual, eating out with Bobby Tom meant that she got to meet lots of new people. They ended up at Hole in the Wall, one of Austin's traditional night spots, listening to some of the city's famed local musicians. She wanted to pay for her own meal when it was time to leave, but since he had predictably picked up the tab for a roomful of people, she waited until they were walking to the car to press the bills she'd counted out from her wallet into his pocket.

He drew them back out. "What's this?"

She braced herself, knowing he wasn't going to like this. "I'm paying for my own dinner."

His eyebrows shot up, and he looked as if he were going to explode. "You sure as hell are not!" He jammed the bills back into her purse.

She knew she'd lose a physical struggle with him, so she resolved to add the money to what she owed him. "I'm not going to forget about this, especially now that we've slept together. That makes it even more important that I pay my own way. I told you, Bobby Tom. I'm not taking anything from you."

"We're on a date!"

"Dutch treat."

"I don't do Dutch treat! I don't ever do Dutch treat, so just put it right out of your mind! And that reminds me....I found a wad of cash in my desk drawer yesterday morning. I thought I must have left it there and forgot about it, but now I'm wondering. You wouldn't happen to know anything about that, would you?"

"That's money for rent—"

"Rent! You don't owe me for any rent!"

"...and that black cocktail dress you bought me."

"That dress was a present. Don't you even think about giving me money for it."

"I'm not in a position to accept presents from you."

"We're engaged!"

"We're not engaged. I pay my own way, Bobby Tom. I realize this may be a hard thing for you to accept, but it's very important to me and I want your promise that you'll respect my wishes, especially now that we've slept together."

He gritted his teeth. "That's the most ridiculous thing I've ever heard of. If you believe I'm going to touch a cent of your money, you can think again.

"What you do with it is up to you, but I pay my debts."

"They aren't debts!"

"They are to me. I told you from the beginning. I'm not taking anything from you."

He stalked away from her, cursing under his breath. As he reached the car, he drew off his hat and smacked it against his leg. She had the distinct impression that he would rather have smacked her.

Their flight back to Telarosa took place in silence. She didn't like the fact that the good mood of the day had been spoiled, but he needed to understand that she wouldn't be swayed about this. By the time they got home, he seemed to have settled down a bit. She thanked him for showing her such a wonderful time and headed up the stairs to her apartment, where she shed her clothes and stepped into the shower.

When she came out, she caught her breath

to find him sitting on the only chair in her bedroom, naked except for his jeans.

"I locked the door," she said.

"I'm your landlord, remember? I've got a key."

Her fingers tightened on the white bath towel she'd wrapped herself in. He wasn't smiling, and she didn't know what to expect.

"Get on the bed, Gracie."

"Maybe—Maybe we should talk about this."

"Do it!"

She got on the bed.

He rose from the chair and lowered his zipper. She dug the fingers of her free hand into the mattress, feeling an uneasy combination of nervousness and excitement. He came toward her.

Her heart thudded so hard in her chest she could feel it resonate in her throat. He reached down and stripped her towel away. "Are you going to pay me back for this, too?"

Before she could answer, he'd grabbed the pillow next to her and shoved it under her hips.

"What—"

"Be quiet." Bracing his knee on the edge of the bed, he caught her thighs in his hands and pushed them apart. For a moment he gazed at her, then he sat on the age of the bed and opened her with his thumbs.

Her breath caught in her throat as he lowered his head. She felt the abrasion of his beard on her inner thigh. He took a nip of the soft skin there.

"Now I'm going to please *you*," he said.

And then, because he hadn't been able to exert his mastery over her with the strength of his will, he conquered her another way.

In the end, there had been no other decision for Suzy to make. It had been nearly a month since Way Sawyer had issued his horrible proposition, and she'd been able to think of little else. He'd finally returned to town a week ago, but he hadn't called her until yesterday. Just the sound of his voice had panicked her, and when he'd announced that he was entertaining some business associates in San Antonio and he wanted her to serve as his hostess, she'd barely been able to respond.

As soon as she'd hung up the telephone, she'd tried to reach Bobby Tom, not to tell him what had happened—she couldn't do that—but merely to hear the familiar sound of his voice. He hadn't been at his house, however, and she'd learned when she talked to Gracie this morning that the two of them had been in Austin.

As the chauffeured Lincoln drew away from her house for the trip to San Antonio, a bubble of hysteria rose inside her. She felt like a menopausal Joan of Arc about to sacrifice herself for the good of the people. But she wasn't foolish enough to expect the people to be grateful. When her relationship with Way became public, she would be universally condemned for consorting with the enemy.

Way lived on the top two floors of a beautiful old white limestone residential building that overlooked San Antonio's famous River-walk. She was admitted by a maid, who took her overnight bag from the chauffeur and informed her that Mr. Sawyer would be arriving shortly.

The duplex had an airy, tropical feel. Vanilla walls with chalk white trim set off the comfortable furniture upholstered in bright yellow and geranium red. The bottom halves of the tall, narrow windows were covered with black iron grillwork, and lush greenery filled the corners, giving the room a soothing atmosphere that was at odds with her pitching stomach. The maid directed her to a small bedroom on the same floor, where she could change into her evening clothes. The room was obviously set aside for guests, but Suzy had no idea whether the maid had put her there of her own accord, or whether Way had ordered it. She clung to the hope that she would sleep here alone tonight.

She changed for dinner into a peacock blue silk dress with a row of domed mirrored buttons running across one shoulder. As she slipped into a pair of gray pumps, she heard voices from the living room and knew that Way had returned. She took as long as she could with her makeup, trying to compose herself with the familiar female rituals of mascara and lipstick, then stared blindly at a magazine that had been left on the nightstand. When she could avoid it no longer, she forced herself to make her way to the living room.

Way stood at the windows looking down on

the Riverwalk. He wore formal evening dress and turned slowly as she walked in. "You look lovely, Suzy. But you've always been the most beautiful woman in Telarosa."

She wouldn't pretend this was a normal social encounter by thanking him for his compliment, and she remained silent.

He took a step toward her. "There are three couples dining with us tonight. Are you good with names?"

"Not really."

Ignoring the chilly tone of her response, he smiled. "I'll give you a head start, then." She found herself listening out of habit as he proceeded to list the guests and tell her something about each one. Just as he finished, the elevator delivered the first couple to the door.

By the time the gathering had moved to the dining room, Suzy realized that she was actually enjoying herself. She had been afraid that Way would publicly humiliate her by making certain everyone understood she was his mistress, but he referred to her only as a longtime friend and did not insinuate anything more.

He was a considerate host, and she noticed how skillfully he managed to draw the wives into the conversation. She thought of the number of gatherings she had attended where the women sat like mutes while their husbands went on and on about business. This was also the first social occasion she could remember attending in years where she hadn't been introduced as Bobby Tom Denton's mother. Instead, Way mentioned only her work with the Board of Education, and she found herself addressing the challenges of running a small public school system instead of answering questions about her famous son.

When the guests began to leave, however, her anxiety returned. So far, she had refused to torture herself with mental images of the two of them alone in a bedroom, but as the time approached, she found it increasingly difficult to keep those thoughts at bay. She remembered Hoyt's hearty laughter, his lusty appetites, and open display of emotion. In contrast, Way was cool and remote. She couldn't imagine anything ruffling him, anything making him laugh hard or cry or give in to the normal range of human emotions.

Way shut the door after the last of the guests and turned just in time to see her shudder. "Are you cold?"

"No. No, I'm fine." She used to dread the end of her own dinner parties when she was faced with a kitchen full of dirty dishes. Now she would have given anything for that cleanup job, but a pair of efficient servants had already taken care of it.

He clasped her arm lightly and drew her back into the living room. "How's your golf game?"

Golf was the farthest thing from her mind, and the question startled her. "The last time Bobby Tom and I played, I beat him by a stroke."

"Congratulations. What did you shoot?" Releasing her, he sat down at one end of the couch and unfastened his bow tie.

"Eighty-five."

"Not bad. I'm surprised you can beat your son. He's a fine athlete."

"He hits a long ball, but he gets himself into a lot of trouble."

"You've played all your life, haven't you?"

She walked over toward the windows and looked down on the strings of tiny white lights dangling over the Riverwalk from the cypress trees. "Yes. My father was a golfer."

"I remember. I tried to get a job caddying at his country club when I was a kid, but they told me I had to cut my hair first." He smiled. "I wasn't willing to give up my D.A., so I pumped gas instead."

She had a mental image of him leaning against a locker and running a black plastic comb through his slicked-back hair. Hoyt had worn a crew cut.

He pulled his bow tie free and undid his collar button. "I made a seven-thirty tee time for the two of us tomorrow morning at my club. We can beat some of the heat."

"I don't have my clubs or my shoes."

"I'll take care of it."

"Don't you have to work?"

"I'm my own boss, Suzy."

"I—I really need to be back by noon."

"Do you have another commitment?"

She didn't, and she realized she was being foolish. If she had to spend time with him, what better place than on a golf course? "I have some errands to run, but I can do them later. Golf will be fine."

"Good." He stood, slipped off his jacket, and tossed it down on the couch. "Would you like to see the terrace?"

"I'd enjoy that." Anything to postpone what was to come.

To her alarm, he headed for the staircase. She had assumed the terrace was off this level of the duplex, but now she realized it must lie off the master bedroom upstairs.

He had reached the bottom step before he sensed that she wasn't following him. He turned and regarded her evenly. "You don't have to take your clothes off to see the view."

"Please don't be flippant about this."

"Then stop looking at me as if I'm going to rape you. I'm not, you know." Turning his back on her, he stalked up the stairs.

She followed slowly behind.

17

Suzy approached the railing where Way was standing, with his hands in his pockets, looking out over the San Antonio skyline. Keeping a careful distance between them, she came up next to him.

"Everything dries out quickly up here," he said, without looking at her. "Irrigation is a real challenge."

She glanced around at the terra-cotta tubs that held ornamental trees and the planters that displayed colorful blooming annuals. A hibiscus bearing bright yellow flowers brushed the side of her skirt. She would rather talk about gardens than what loomed ahead.

"I have the same problem with some of my hanging baskets. They're under the eaves, so they don't get any rainwater."

"Why don't you move them?"

"I love looking at them from my bedroom window."

She immediately regretted mentioning the bedroom and looked away from him.

"For a mature woman, you're as skittish as a teenager." His voice was soft and vaguely husky. She stiffened as he turned to her and cupped her upper arms in the palms of his hands. The warmth of his body penetrated the thin silk of her dress. He dipped his head.

Her lips parted in protest as his mouth covered her own. She stood rigidly and braced herself for some terrible assault, but his kiss was surprisingly gentle. He brushed his lips over hers—she had not expected them to feel so soft and warm. Her eyes drifted closed.

He shifted his weight and lightly pressed his hips to hers. She tensed as she felt his arousal. He slowly drew away from her, and, as she regarded him, she was unable to hide her confusion. Had she actually given in to him for a few seconds? Surely not. Surely it was revulsion she was feeling. Regardless of his power and his money, this was still Way Sawyer, the biggest hoodlum at Telarosa High.

He brushed a lock of hair back from her

cheek. "You look like a kid who just got her first kiss."

His comment flustered her nearly as much as his kiss. "I don't have much experience with this."

"You were married for thirty years."

"That's not what I meant. I meant—With anybody else."

"You've never been with anybody but Hoyt, have you?"

"I guess I seem like a real country mouse to you, don't I?"

"He's been dead four years."

She ducked her head and heard the night breeze carry her whispered words. "So have I."

The silence stretched between them, and when he spoke, she heard something almost like uncertainty in his voice. "I think we need a little time to get to know each other better before this goes farther, don't you?"

Hope sprang inside her, and her eyes widened as she gazed up at him. "You're not going to— You won't press me?"

The mouth that had kissed her only moments before grew hard. "Do you want me to?"

Her hope faded, replaced by a terrible anger. "You're playing games with me again. How can you be so cruel?"

She spun away from him and rushed back through the terrace doors. He caught her by the shoulders on the landing, just outside the doors to the master bedroom, and she shrank back from the bleakness in his eyes.

"You don't know what cruelty is," he said. "You were sheltered from the moment you were born."

"That's not true!"

"Isn't it? Do you know what it's like to go to bed hungry? Do you know what it's like to watch your mother die a slow death of shame?"

She could not endure his baiting for another moment. Turning abruptly toward the bedroom doors, she twisted the knob in her hands. "Let's get this over with."

As she entered the room, she heard him curse softly beneath his breath. Feeling like a condemned prisoner, she gazed around at the deep red lacquered walls. A massive mahogany bed, covered with dark paisley throw pillows, sat in a recessed cove behind her. Trembling, she turned to him.

"I don't want the lights on."

Once again, he seemed hesitant. "Suzy—"

She cut him off. "I won't do it with the lights on."

"Do you want to pretend I'm Hoyt?" he said angrily.

"I could never confuse you with Hoyt Denton."

He spoke as coldly as she had. "I'm taking you downstairs. You can sleep in the guest room."

"No!" Her hands balled into fists at her sides. "I'm not going to let you do this to me. You're not going to play any more mind games with me! Both of us know that I'm bought and paid for. But, then, I guess you understand exactly how that works. You must have learned it from your mother." She spun away, turning toward the bathroom, and then winced as her words came back to her. Regardless of the circumstances, she should never have said such a hateful thing.

"Fill the tub while you're in there."

She shivered at the deadly calm in his voice. "I don't want to do that."

"I do." He spoke with no emotion at all. "Leave the lights off if that's your preference, but fill the tub."

With a hiss of dismay, she fled into the bathroom and shut the door. Leaning against it, she felt her heart thudding, and tears stung her eyes against the ugliness of the scene. She'd thought she could simply climb beneath the covers in his darkened bedroom, open her legs, and let him do what he had to, quickly and efficiently, while she lost herself in a blessed numbness. She didn't want to bathe with him or play sexual games. She wanted this first time done with, and she wanted to emerge as unaffected as possible.

She told herself his lovemaking would be mechanical, as cold and dispassionate as the man himself, but as she fumbled with the light switch, the image of a teenage boy with angry eyes and a hungry mouth darted into her mind. She shuddered and pushed it away.

As she undressed, she avoided her reflection in the mirrors that were set against the dark red—tiled walls. The room was opulent with its gold fixtures and black marble sunken tub, which was square in shape and spacious enough to accommodate two people. She stalled as long as she could, neatly folding her clothes, placing them on a paisley upholstered bench that sat near the tub. She set her shoes underneath, side by side like good little soldiers. After wrapping herself in a thick black towel, she ran the water in the huge tub. While it filled, she tried to calm herself by thinking about her garden and what she would plant in the fall, thinking about everything except Hoyt and the fact that she was about to commit adultery.

When the tub was full, she switched on the Jacuzzi, whipping the water into a froth of camouflaging bubbles, then she turned off the lights. There were no windows in the bathroom and it was blessedly dark, so she wouldn't have to watch his eyes exploring the body that only her husband had caressed. Why did he even want her? Her skin was no longer taut; her stomach hadn't been flat for years, and she wore an estrogen patch on her hip. Discarding the towel, she lowered herself into the bubbling water.

She didn't have long to wait before he knocked at the door. "Yes?" she inquired, polite as always, because she had been reared to be polite, because women her age had been brought up to obey the rules, defer to men, and put their own needs after everyone else's.

The door opened, admitting a dim wedge of illumination from the bedroom. He didn't turn on the light, but neither did he close the door, and despite her earlier words, she was grateful for the faint glow from the other room. Although she didn't want him to be able to see her clearly, she also dreaded being alone with him in dense darkness.

She studied the silhouette of his body as he approached the tub. If only he were unattractive, this wouldn't seem like such a betrayal. He was a powerful man, not as tall as Hoyt had been, but equally imposing in a different way. She couldn't make out either the fabric or color of the robe he wore, but as his hands went to his waist, she knew he was untying the sash, and she dropped her gaze. How many grown men had she seen naked? She'd known Hoyt's body nearly as well as her own, and as a child, she'd occasionally walked in on her father. When Bobby Tom stayed at the house, he sometimes roamed in his underwear, but that didn't count. She had very little experience to draw on.

The water level rose as he lowered himself into the tub and settled his body into the opposite corner from hers. The soft whir of the Jacuzzi masked the outside noises so that the two of them could have been alone together anyplace. He propped his elbows on the rim, and his legs brushed hers as he stretched out. She stiffened as she felt his hand clasp her ankle and draw her foot on top of his thigh.

"Relax, Suzy. You can get out of the tub anytime you want."

If his words were meant to soothe her, they had the opposite effect because she knew there was no escape. If she didn't get this over with tonight, she would surely go crazy.

He made a slow circle in the arch of her foot with his thumb and her whole body jerked in response.

"Sensitive?" The anger that had crackled from him like static seemed to be gone. He drew a figure eight in her arch.

"My feet are ticklish."

"Mmm." Instead of letting her go, he began to massage her toes, rubbing them between his thumb and forefinger while he continued to caress her arch with his other hand. Despite herself, she began to relax. If only it could end here, with a warm bath and comforting massage.

A surprisingly peaceful silence fell over them, and the exquisite movements of his hands on her foot, combined with the fact that he showed no inclination to attack, began to lull her. She sank more deeply into the water.

"We should have brought a bottle of champagne in here." He sounded as lazy as she felt. "This is nice."

As he continued his sensuous game of this-little-piggy, she knew she had to apologize for the nasty remark she had made about his mother. She had never believed that other people's boorish behavior served as an excuse for abandoning her own moral code.

"What I said about your mother was cruel and uncalled for. I apologize."

"You had provocation."

"That's never an excuse."

"You're a good woman, Suzy Denton," he said softly.

A creeping languor turned her muscles to jelly. It had been so long since anyone had really touched her. All those years she'd been married, she'd taken the power of sensual caresses for granted, but she didn't anymore.

He reached for her other foot. The ends of her hair dipped into the water as she sank lower into the tub, but she was feeling too relaxed to prop herself back up. Once again he began his slow, deep kneading. She told herself it was merely because she was tired that the sensation felt so delicious.

He drew her foot to his lips and she felt the pleasant rasp of his teeth as he nipped gently on the pad of her big toe. "I assume I don't have to worry about getting you pregnant."

His statement jarred her from her lethargy. She tried to sit up, but he kept his hold on her foot, returning it to the top of his thigh where he continued to minister to it.

"No, you don't."

"You don't have to worry about me, either," he said.

What was she supposed to worry about? she wondered. Certainly not getting him pregnant.

She heard the amusement in his voice. "Suzy, it's the nineties. You're supposed to ask your potential lovers pointed questions about their sex and drug habits."

"Lord."

"It's a new world."

"Not a very nice one."

He chuckled. "I take it I'm not going to get any pointed questions."

"If you had anything to hide, you wouldn't have brought the subject up."

"That's exactly right. Now turn around, and let me rub your shoulders."

Without waiting for her to move, he tugged gently on her wrists and turned her so that she slid between his open legs. She felt the muscles of his chest against her back. His hips shifted, and she realized he was fully aroused. A thrill of awareness shot through her, immediately followed by a rush of guilt.

"Hand me that soap," he whispered, his voice as gentle as a caress, as his thumbs worked the muscles in her shoulders. "It's on your right."

"No, I—"

To her surprise, his teeth sank into the curve of her neck. He nipped her there, not painfully, but with enough strength to remind her that he was in control. She remembered that stallions frequently nipped the mares they were covering, sometimes even bringing blood. At the same time, a dim voice told her that she only needed to rise from the water for him to let her go. But the voice was too amorphous for her to hold on to as his hands glided over her shoulders and palmed her breasts.

"Lean back," he whispered. "Let me play with you."

He must have fetched the soap himself because his palms were slick with it and the sensations he aroused so exquisite her eyes stung with tears. She didn't want to betray Hoyt. She didn't want it to feel so good, but it had been too long, and as his warm, soapy hands circled her breasts, she couldn't resist. She would permit this intimate caress for a moment, and then she would draw away.

Round and round his hand traveled, coming closer and closer to the tender centers. Her breathing quickened. He brushed her nipples, then plucked them between his fingers and began massaging them as he had her toes. The sensation was delicious and familiar, like a favorite song heard again after a very long time. She had forgotten how wonderful this felt. Her body grew heavier, more languid, until it seemed to be melting into his.

He abandoned her nipples and returned to making lazy circles around her breasts, gently teasing until he once again reached the tips, then plucking and pulling. She squirmed against him. He circled again. This time she moaned when he reached her nipples and rolled them between his fingers.

Her breathing was coming heavier now, and her body felt swollen with arousal. Kissing her ear, he lifted her up onto his thighs, her back still against his chest. She felt his lips tugging on her lobe. He began to suck there, on the flesh and the diamond stud, and she shuddered at the unfamiliar sensation. She couldn't remember Hoyt ever doing that to her, but when she tried to recall if he had, her thoughts kept scattering.

He spread his legs and, in the process, wedged hers open with his knees. His hands slid down her breasts to her inner thighs. She didn't understand what he was doing as he rotated both of them, pulling her thighs wider, moving their hips closer to the edge of the tub. And then she felt the powerful jet of water gushing into her.

She gasped and nearly jumped off his lap, trying to get away from the surge of water shooting out of one of the nozzles set into the side of the tub.

She heard the devil's laughter in her ear, soft and seductive. "Relax, Suzy. Enjoy."

And, God forgive her, she did enjoy.

He played with her breasts, nipped at her ears and shoulders with his teeth, sucked at the tender flesh of her neck. Their bodies shifted so that sometimes the surging jet of water pummeled her, sometimes him. She lost all sense of herself, didn't even think to object when he pushed himself inside her from behind and let the water work at them where they were joined. She tried to move on him, but he wouldn't allow it. And each time she was about to go over the edge, he shifted the position of her body just enough so that it didn't happen.

She began to sob. "Please..."

"What do you want?" he whispered, as he pushed deeper.

"Please, let me...Let me..."

"Do you want more, Suzy? Is that what you want? You want more?"

His gentle croon fueled her excitement. "Yes...Yes..." She was begging him, but it had been so long that she couldn't stop herself.

His voice was soft and gruff and tender. "Not yet, love. Not yet."

She sobbed as he lifted her off him. She tried to turn in his arms, but he stood. In the dim light, she could see his silhouette and the hard, thick thrust of him. Instinctively, she reached up and clasped him, shameless and brazen, forgetting that this man wasn't her husband, that she hadn't wanted this.

He groaned and caught her wrist. "Wait. Just a little while longer."

He stepped from the water and slipped his robe over his wet body. Without bothering to fasten it, he pulled her out and wrapped her in a towel, then picked her up in his arms and carried her into the bedroom, as if she were a virgin going into her bridal bower.

She turned her head into his shoulder as he walked into the dimly lit room. She didn't want to see him, didn't want to remember who he was and who she was, and that she was about to betray her husband. What was she doing in a stranger's arms hovering on the brink of sexual oblivion?

"No light." She needed the darkness to hide the shame she felt for letting this man arouse her to such a state where she couldn't help herself.

He stopped walking. She lifted her head to gaze at him and saw that his hair was wet and rumpled, his expression unreadable.

She expected him to put her on the bed, but instead, he carried her in the opposite direction, toward a door she hadn't noticed earlier. She gazed up at him questioningly, but he wasn't looking at her. With his foot, he pushed opened the door and carried her inside.

To her shock, he had taken her into his large walk-in closet. She saw double rows of expensive suits and tailored shirts, orderly racks of boots and wingtips, a stack of denim jeans, a pile of knit shirts. The heady masculine scents enveloped her: cologne, leather, and the clean, starchy smell of freshly laundered shirts. He set her down on the carpeted floor and immediately reached behind him to shut the door. They were plunged into a darkness so thick she caught her breath in fear.

His voice drifted to her, husky and dangerous. "No light."

The towel slipped from beneath her arms as he tugged it away. Then he must have moved back because he was no longer touching her.

Seconds ticked by. Her heart began to pound. She stood naked in the darkness, no longer certain how close he was to her. Even the sound of his breathing was hidden by the distant hum of the air conditioner. The darkness disoriented her. It was too dense, too absolute. She thought of death and the grave. She turned, then turned again, but the movement was a mistake because she lost her bearings. She clutched her throat against a rising tide of hysteria.

"Way?"

Nothing.

She took an involuntary step backward. Garments brushed her naked body. She strained to hear the sound of an indrawn breath, a movement, a joint cracking, anything.

Out of nowhere, a hand touched her outer thigh. She jumped. Because she could see nothing, hear nothing, the hand seemed disembodied, as if it were coming from a phantom lover, something not quite human, demonic, even. It brushed over the patch on her hip, and she stiffened. It moved on, touching her waist, climbing her rib cage, caressing her tender, tortured breasts.

She could no longer stand submissively in front of this demon lover. Reaching out with the palms of her hands, she felt for him. She touched his chest and realized he had discarded his robe. The thick pelt of hair was soft beneath her fingers. Hoyt's chest hadn't been as hairy, and the strangeness of this body heightened her dark fantasy that she had fallen in with the devil. The configuration of muscles beneath her hands felt wrong, not what she had grown accustomed to over three decades. She was alone in thick, dark space with a demon lover, and her wicked body silently begged for his touch.

Despite the threat of eternal damnation, her hands began to roam him, learning his devil's body by touch. His skin should no longer be damp from their bath, but it was, damp and hot. Beneath her fingertips, his muscles contracted, and for the first time she could hear the heaviness of his breathing. She dropped her hands, touching him there, where she had no business being, exploring him, greedy with desire. She tested his weight and thickness, stroked him.

Abruptly, he pushed her away, and once again she stood alone in the impenetrable darkness.

Her breathing rattled in her ears.

He turned her. His hands palmed her buttocks, kneaded them, slipped between. Once again, she felt only his hands in the darkness, nothing else, no other part of him. Disembodied demon hands separated her legs, stroked her until she hummed and quivered. Abruptly, he pushed her down on her back into the thick, soft carpet.

She lay there waiting.

Nothing.

Death thick darkness. The loom of the grave. The specter of damnation. She embraced it all.

A force—animal, human, demon spirit?—caught her knees and opened them. No other touch. Just a demanding pressure, ordering her to offer up her most tender parts in sacrifice to the dark angel.

And then nothing.

She lay waiting, barely able to breathe. Damned already, her body burned with pagan passion.

Then she felt it. The soft tickle on her inner thighs. The parting. The moist hot tracing of a tongue.

Oh, *this! This!* She had missed it unbearably. Dreamed of it. This lap and thrust, this rough and silken stroking, the suction, the greedy mouth full-feasting, all of it heightened by the darkness of the underworld. Her demon lover devoured her until she lost herself. With a cry she fell, spinning round and round, dropping into the embracing pit.

He was inside her before she could reclaim her self. His body covered her and filled her. She wrapped her legs around his hips, her arms around his neck. Her breasts burned as they rubbed against the thick hair on his chest. He plunged into her center, withdrew, plunged again and again, carrying her with him on his spiraling journey upward.

His cry was low and hoarse, hers a keening wail as they tumbled together into the very heart of darkness.

It had never felt more welcome.

Some time later, she began to cry. Light spilled over her as he opened the door of the closet. She curled into a ball, hid her face in her arms. Guilt and shame consumed her. *My love, my love.* She had betrayed her husband, betrayed the man she loved with all her heart. She had promised to love him forever, until death do us part. But she wasn't dead. And he was still the husband of her heart, her dearest love, and she had betrayed him.

It shouldn't have happened like this. She was supposed to have been making a sacrifice! She had gone to Way to save the town. Instead, she had ended up pleading with him to take her, and in the process, she had lost herself.

"Stop it, Suzy. Please." His voice was ragged, almost as if he were in pain.

She plucked at the towel fallen in a heap next to her and struggled to sit as she used it to cover her shame. She looked up and saw him looming above her, still naked, wet with her.

Tears of grief coursed down her cheeks. "I want to go home."

"You're too upset," he said quietly. "I can't let you do that."

She dropped her gaze to her lap, studying her bare knees, which were bent beneath her. "Why did you do this to me?" she cried. "Why couldn't you have left me alone?"

"I'm sorry," he said. "I didn't mean for this to happen. I'm sorry."

He picked up his robe from the floor and slipped into it. It was dark green and richly patterned. Gently clasping her arm, he drew her up off the carpet. As she stood next to him, he pulled a white terry cloth robe from a hook by the door and helped her into it, though it was much too large for her. His hand rested in the center of her back as he steered her from the closet she had entered so many centuries before. She moved automatically beside him. What difference did it make where he took her? What more could he do to her?

He led her as if she were a child, to a comfortable, overstuffed chair sitting near the window. Her eyes pleaded with him. "Let me go now." Once again, she began to cry.

He lifted her into his arms and settled her on his lap in the chair. Tucking her against his chest, he stroked her hair. "Don't cry," he whispered. "Please don't cry." His lips brushed her forehead, her temple. "This wasn't your fault. It was me. I did this to you."

"I let you. Why did I let you?"

"Because you're a warm and sensuous woman, love, and it had been too long for you."

She told herself she would take no comfort from him. Her betrayal ran so deep she had no right to comfort. But he stroked her hair and held her tight. Eventually her tears stopped, and she slept in his arms.

When Way finally heard the deep, even sound of her breathing, he pressed his lips to her forehead and squeezed his eyes shut. How had he let this get so far out of his control? Suzy Denton had never harmed him, and she didn't deserve what he'd done to her. It wasn't her fault that she'd been the subject of his teenage crush, the target of all the surly scowls and snarling comments he'd leveled at her, a dime store James Dean trying to impress Natalie Wood.

When she'd walked into his living room a month ago and he'd seen the same fearful expression on her face she'd worn as a teenager whenever he'd looked at her, something inside him had snapped. All his money and power had evaporated, and he felt that familiar impotent rage that had been his constant companion when he was a kid. He'd invited her to his house with some half-assed notion of sweeping her off her feet with his charm and making her see him as he was now, instead of as he'd been thirty-five years earlier. Instead, he'd insulted her beyond belief.

Despite the way he'd baited her, it hadn't occurred to him that she would think he was trying to blackmail her into his bed. He'd had his share of female companionship over the years, and he'd certainly never had to resort to blackmail to get it. But she didn't know that. His proposal that she act as his companion and hostess had been an impulsive one, born of anger. He'd expected her to tell him to go to hell, but instead, she'd stood there in his rose garden and looked as if he'd slapped her.

This past month while he'd been gone from Telarosa, his shame over the way he'd treated her had grown. By the time he'd returned to town, he'd already made up his mind to call her and apologize, hoping that he could still somehow salvage the situation. But the moment he identified himself, he'd heard the quaver in her voice and he'd lost control. Instead of asking her forgiveness, he had bullied her into joining him here by continuing to imply that her acceptance was linked with the future of Rosatech.

Even tonight, he could have denied it. Tonight, when she'd stormed into his bedroom, he could have told her the truth. So why hadn't he done it?

He stared blindly ahead as awareness hit him with brutal force. He had done this awful thing because he had fallen in love with Suzy Denton. Whether it had happened tonight, last month, or thirty years ago, he didn't know. He only knew that he loved her, and he hadn't found the will to stop himself.

He was a man who prided himself on always being in control, on never acting impulsively or reacting emotionally. When he'd been presented with the opportunity to take over Rosatech, for example, he'd done it with a cool head. He'd even experienced a trace of cynical amusement that he still wanted revenge for the way the town had treated his mother. He'd never imagined that he would get emotionally involved. The pain was too old, even if the urge to even up the balance sheet had never quite gone away.

He was the one who'd planted the rumor about Rosatech's closing—for a while he'd toyed with the notion of actually doing it—but despite the deliberate misinformation he'd disseminated, Rosatech was marginally profitable, and he didn't have the stomach to destroy so many innocent lives. He had the stomach to make the town's citizens squirm, though, and that's why he'd deliberately set out to make them believe he was closing the plant. He'd enjoyed seeing their doomsday expressions and watching their pitiful attempts to punish him by ostracizing him, as if he cared about their good opinion. He'd even acknowledged that his desire for retribution was juvenile.

Juvenile, yes. But also satisfying. What was

the sense of accumulating power and wealth if he couldn't earn a little frontier justice with it? Watching fear spread through the town that had killed his mother wouldn't change the past, but at least he had finally called Telarosa to account for turning their backs on justice and breaking Trudy Sawyer's spirit.

Tonight it had come full circle. Tonight, in one of the few impulsive actions of his life, Trudy Sawyer's son had made the town's most respectable woman feel like a whore. First thing tomorrow morning, he would have to tell her the truth. Then he would send her back to Telarosa and never bother her again.

He gazed down at her. Jesus. She was still so beautiful. Sweet and sensitive. Would it be so terrible if he waited one more day before he sent her away? He wouldn't touch her. He'd treat her with every courtesy. Would that be so terrible? Just one more day to win Suzy Denton's affection.

18

Bobby Tom was getting ready to leave the movie set for the day when Connie Cameron slipped into his motor home carrying two frosty bottles of beer. It was Saturday evening, they were done shooting for the week, and he was looking forward to having a day off.

"It's been hot today. I thought you might like to share a cold one."

He gazed at her as he finished buttoning his shirt. He'd spent the past week either tied up while he was being tortured by Paolo Mendez, the actor who was playing the kingpin, or jumping into the river with Natalie as explosive charges went off around them, and he wasn't in the mood to be seduced by anybody but Gracie. Just the thought of that sweet small body made him hard. Even though a month had passed since they'd first made love, he hadn't gotten nearly enough of her.

"Sorry, sweetheart, but the little woman's waiting for me at home."

"What the little woman doesn't know won't hurt her." She gave each cap an angry twist and held one bottle out to him.

He set it on the counter while he tucked his shirt in his jeans. Her short, stretchy skirt rode up on her thighs as she sat down on the built-in couch. Her legs were tan, but they didn't seem quite as shapely as Gracie's.

"Where's she been the past few days, anyway?" Connie flicked open an extra button on her blouse, as if she'd gotten overheated.

"Either on the phone or setting everybody straight over at the nursing home. She's organizing the golf tournament travel arrangements for me. It's a big job."

"I'm sure she can handle it." She took a sip of beer, then brought up one foot, bending her knee so she could tuck it beneath the opposite thigh. The position left him with a clear view of her purple panties.

Since she was putting it on display, he

looked, but he found himself feeling more irritated than aroused. "Connie, what are you doing? If you're engaged to Jimbo, why are you sniffin' 'round me?"

"I like you. I always have."

"I like you, too. At least I used to."

"What's that mean?"

"It means that I'm a one-woman man right now. And as long as you're wearing Jimbo's ring, I think you should seriously consider being a one-man woman."

"I intend to be a good and faithful wife, but that doesn't mean I'd object to a last fling before I walk down the aisle."

"Not with me."

"Since when did you turn into such a goddamn prude?"

"Since I met Gracie, that's when."

"What's she got, Bobby Tom? Nobody can figure it out. I mean, everybody likes her and everything. She's friendly and people appreciate the way she's taken an interest in those old folks at Arbor Hills. She'll help out anybody who needs it. Hell, she even helped me out last week when Louann didn't show up, and I've pretty much let her know I hate her guts. But she can't dance worth a damn. And even though she's cute, you've always liked full-figured women."

She pushed her own full-figures out to make certain he got the point she was trying to make, which he did. It occurred to him that Gracie had something that Connie was missing. She had scruples.

She also had a stubborn streak that was just about driving him crazy. The money she put in his desk drawer was significant for her, but it wasn't even pocket change to him, and it galled him that she was being so intractable about it. He knew she wasn't like all the bloodsuckers who made a career out of feeding off him, so why wouldn't she let him buy things for her? For all her supposed insights into his character, she didn't seem to realize that he was always the one who did the giving and that anything else made him uncomfortable. A flicker of uneasiness passed through him as he reminded himself that she didn't know he was the one paying her salary, but he told himself not to worry about it. He'd just make damned certain she never found out, that was all.

Connie regarded him suspiciously. "Another thing that has people wondering...Gracie sure doesn't seem to know much about football for somebody who's supposed to have passed the quiz."

"I made a few allowances."

She jumped up from the couch in outrage. "That's not fair! Ladies have always counted on you to be fair when you give the quiz."

He realized too late that he'd made a major tactical blunder. "I *am* fair. That's why I sometimes have to grade on the curve."

That seemed to mollify her. He watched warily as she set down her beer bottle and sauntered toward him, a take-no-prisoners look in her dark eyes. She might be the finest-looking woman in Telarosa, but right now he didn't find her half as appealing as Gracie.

A particularly tantalizing memory of the sounds Gracie'd made in his ear last night went through his mind. He was absolutely certain he must have had as good a time in bed with somebody else, but for the life of him, he couldn't recall exactly when or with whom. Gracie was full of surprises. She exhibited an irresistible combination of passion and innocence, reticence and boldness. When they made love, she got him so worked up that he had to keep reminding himself she was a newcomer to the erotic arts, and that he'd only gotten involved in the first place to do her a favor. He suspected he wouldn't be having this strong a reaction to her if he hadn't temporarily lost his sex drive after his retirement, and more than once he'd been forced to remind himself it would probably have been the same with any woman he'd taken up with again.

When Connie wrapped her arms around his neck and pressed her mouth to his, he had a chance to test the theory, but it didn't take him more than ten seconds to realize she wasn't going to set him on fire. He took her by the shoulders and firmly set her away from him. "You be sure and let me know what you want for a wedding present, y'hear."

Her whole face tightened up, and he knew he'd insulted her, but he hadn't invited her here and he didn't much care. He picked up his car keys and Stetson, then walked over to the door and held it open for her. She passed through without a word. He slipped on his hat as he followed her outside.

Police Chief Jimbo Thackery was waiting by his squad car not twenty feet away.

Connie didn't miss a beat. "Hi, Jim honey." She walked over to him with her rumpled hair and unbuttoned blouse and threw her arms around his neck.

Jimbo extricated himself and gave Bobby Tom a glare full of malevolence. "What the hell's going on here? What are you doing with him?"

Connie curled her fingers over his arm. "Now don't get riled, Jim. Me and Bobby Tom was just having a beer. Nothing happened, did it, Bobby Tom?" She gave Bobby Tom a slow, sly smile that suggested quite a lot had happened.

Bobby Tom regarded both of them with disgust. "I don't think I ever saw two people who deserved each other more."

He headed for his truck only to have Jimbo catch him just as he slid behind the wheel. The police chief's small eyes were hard and mean. "I'm waiting for you, Denton. The first time you throw down a gum wrapper or spit on the sidewalk, I'm gonna be right there."

"I don't spit, Jimbo," Bobby Tom said. "Leastwise not unless I happen to see you standing in my way."

As he drove off, he glanced in the rearview mirror and saw Jimbo and Connie engaged in a heavy-duty argument. He didn't know which of them he felt sorrier for.

Something awakened Gracie. Even after a month, she still hadn't quite grown accustomed to spending the night in Bobby Tom's bed, and for a fraction of a second, she didn't know where she was. A flicker of light coming from the hallway caught her attention at the same time that she realized she was alone in bed.

As she set her feet on the floor and slipped into her robe, she saw that it was nearly three in the morning. It was Sunday already, and she and Bobby Tom were flying to San Antonio in the morning with Natalie and her husband Anton, who was in town for the weekend.

She moved out into the hallway and saw that the light was coming from his office. She stopped in the doorway. He sat sprawled in an easy chair fixed at a slight angle so that he didn't see her when she stepped inside. His hair was rumpled, and he wore a gold-and-brown silk robe printed with old Spanish coins. The silvery light came from the television screen, where he watched a football game with the volume muted.

He pointed the remote control toward the television, and as the picture went into reverse motion, she realized it was actually a video-tape that held his attention. She turned her attention to the screen and spotted him in his Stars' uniform.

As the flickering patterns of light and shadow moved across his face and threw his cheekbones into sharp relief, the silent football play progressed.

Bobby Tom made a sharp cut toward the sidelines. The ball was coming toward him, but it looked as if it had been thrown too high for him to catch. He leaped up in the air anyway and seemed to hang there, every muscle in his body stretched.

Her breath caught in her throat as she saw the opposing player charging toward him. Bobby Tom was fully extended and completely vulnerable.

The hit was brutal. Within seconds, he was lying on the ground writhing in pain.

He hit the rewind button and once again the play began to unfold. She felt sick inside as she realized this was what he'd been doing night after night when she'd seen the light coming from his study. He had been sitting in the dark reliving the play that ended his career.

She must have moved or made some involuntary noise because he twisted toward her. When he saw her standing there, he jabbed the remote to stop the tape. The screen filled with snow.

"What do you want?"

"I woke up and you weren't there."

"I don't need you checking up on me." He rose from the chair and tossed the remote down on the cushion.

"It breaks my heart thinking of you sitting here night after night watching that tape."

"I don't know where you get your ideas. This is the first time I've looked at that tape since I was hurt."

"That's not true," she said softly. "I can see the light in here from my bedroom window. I know you watch it all the time."

"Just mind your own business."

The tendons of his neck had corded with tension, but she couldn't back down about something so important to him. "You're still young. It's time to move forward with your life instead of looking backward."

"Now that's funny. I don't have any memory of asking for your advice."

"It's behind you now, Bobby Tom." Impulsively, she held out her hand. "I'd like you to give me the tape."

"Why should I do that?"

"Because you're hurting yourself by watching it, and it's time to stop."

"You don't know what you're talking about."

"Please give me the tape."

He jerked his head toward the television. "If you want it so much, take the goddamn thing, but don't start acting like you know what I'm thinking and what I'm not thinking because you don't."

"You won't let your guard down with anyone, will you?" She walked over to the television and removed the tape from the VCR.

"Just because we've spent some time in bed together doesn't give you the right to start prying and poking. A woman does that to me once too often, she ends up on the other side of the door, and don't you forget it. I'm going to chalk this conversation up to your inexperience with men."

She refused to be intimidated by his belligerence because she understood its source.

She had seen too deeply into his private emotional landscape, and he wanted to make her pay. She patted his arm. "This hasn't been a conversation, Bobby Tom. You haven't said one single thing that matters."

She slipped past him to go into the bedroom and gather up her clothes, but she'd no sooner tucked the videotape in her purse before he appeared in the doorway. "Maybe that's because I haven't been talking dirty."

His mouth was cocked at the corner in a lazy, calculated grin that didn't make it anywhere near his eyes. She recognized the effort he was making to pretend that she hadn't touched a nerve and knew he intended to put an end to her probing of his psyche by using his favorite weapon, premeditated charm.

For a moment she hesitated, undecided about the course she should take. Did the fact that she loved him give her the right to chip away at the barriers of privacy he was so determined to keep in place? She wanted to, but common sense told her he'd erected those walls a long time ago, and she wasn't going to tear them down in one night.

"No more talk, Gracie." He stripped off her robe, and then his own. She expected him to take her to the bed, but, instead, he guided her back into his study, where he sank down in the big easy chair and pulled her on top of him. Within minutes, he was teaching her still another way to make love. But she didn't enjoy it as much as she normally would have. There was too much unspoken between them.

Their flight the next morning to San Antonio was uneventful, and with Bobby Tom as tour guide, their first stop was quite naturally the Alamo. Texas's most important shrine sat amidst hamburger and ice cream shops in the middle of San Antonio's bustling downtown area. As they crossed the plaza toward the stone mission, a street corner evangelist warned of the second coming while clusters of tourists clutching camcorders recorded the central building's familiar facade.

"You look as pretty as a picture," Bobby Tom whispered. "I mean it, Gracie. I'm gonna have to lock you up if you get any prettier."

Warmth spread through her as he leaned down and brushed a light kiss over her lips. Their early-morning lovemaking had been earthy and sweaty and not at all polite. He hadn't let her have an orgasm until she'd whispered a whole stream of dirty words in his ears. She'd retaliated by waiting until he had showered and dressed, then made him perform the world's slowest strip tease. After all, what was the sense of being Bobby Tom Denton's lover if she couldn't enjoy looking at that wonderful body?

Ahead of them, Natalie held hands with her husband Anton. The first time Gracie had met Anton Guyard, she'd been surprised by the contrast in appearance between the round-faced, balding Los Angeles businessman and his beautiful movie star wife. But Anton was charming and intelligent, in addition to being deeply in love with Natalie, and she obviously adored him.

Bobby Tom squeezed Gracie's hand and looked away from the gaggle of tourists who'd begun to stare at him. He was highly recognizable in a pink Western-cut shirt with pearl studs and his ever-present Stetson. Gracie wore a mushroom-colored knit top with a matching short skirt, sandals, and chunky, brushed gold earrings.

Ahead of them, Natalie turned, her expression worried. "You're certain the pager you gave me works, Bobby Tom?"

Gracie knew Natalie was nervous about her first separation from Elvis, even though she trusted Terry Jo, who had become her semi-regular baby-sitter. All week she had been expressing breast milk into bottles and freezing it to get ready for this day.

"I tested it myself," Bobby Tom said. "If Terry Jo's having any problems at all with Elvis, she'll get hold of you right away."

Anton thanked him for the third time.

As of this morning, Bobby Tom had still been complaining about how hard it was for him to face Natalie's husband after everything he and Natalie had been doing behind his back. Natalie might not have any difficulty approaching their on-camera love scenes as a professional, but Bobby Tom felt as if he was somehow violating his personal code of honor.

Despite the incongruity of its urban setting, Gracie loved her tour of the Alamo. Along with dozens of other tourists, she listened to the guide's dramatic recounting of the thirteen fateful days that led to Texas independence and found her eyes misting at the end.

Bobby Tom gazed at her with amusement as she dabbed at them with a tissue. "For a Yankee gal who doesn't know George Strait from Waylon Jennings, you've got a proper attitude."

"Oh, Anton, look! Davy Crockett's rifle!"

Gracie felt a pang of envy as she watched Natalie draw her husband's attention to the contents of a large glass case. Their intimacy was evident in every touch they exchanged, every glance that passed between them. Natalie had been able to see past her husband's homely exterior to the man beneath. Was it possible that Bobby Tom might someday do the same with her?

She backed away from that particular fantasy. There was no need to torture herself with the impossible.

After their tour of the Alamo, they ended up at the Riverwalk a few blocks away. There, they took a ride on one of the tourist barges that cruised beneath the stone bridges of the waterway, then they wandered along the winding flagstone pathways. They ended up at a collection of shops known as La Villita, where Bobby Tom bought Gracie sunglasses with lavender lenses shaped like the state of Texas and Gracie reciprocated by buying him a T-shirt that read, I'M NOT TOO SMART, BUT I CAN LIFT HEAVY THINGS. Natalie and Gracie giggled over the T-shirt until their eyes teared, while Bobby Tom pretended great indignation. At the same time, he kept holding it up to the mirror and admiring himself.

As evening approached, they stopped at his favorite Riverwalk eatery, the Zuni Grill. While they nibbled on pecan-crusted chicken and ate black bean and goat cheese enchiladas, they enjoyed the pedestrian traffic passing in front of them.

Bobby Tom had just taken a bite of Gracie's dessert, a scrumptious bourbon pecan crême brûlée, when she felt him stiffen. She followed the direction of his eyes toward the open metal stairway that led to the upper tier of the restaurant and saw Suzy Denton coming down the steps.

Way Sawyer was walking right behind her.

19

Natalie, who'd just returned to the table from her third telephone call to check on Elvis, spotted Suzy and Way Sawyer on the stairs. "Bobby Tom, isn't that your mother? Who's that great looking man with her?"

"Careful, chérie," Anton said. "You're going to make me jealous." Natalie laughed, as if Anton had just made the silliest joke imaginable.

"His name is Way Sawyer," Bobby Tom said tightly.

At that moment Suzy spotted her son, and

her face froze. She looked as if she wanted to flee, but since that was impossible, she approached the table, her reluctance obvious. Way followed just behind.

As she stopped, her mouth curled in a brittle smile. "Hello."

Everyone but Bobby Tom returned her greeting.

"I see you and the baby made it back to town safely," Way said to Gracie.

"We did. It was nice of you to stop."

Bobby Tom gave her a sharp, questioning look. She ignored him and explained to Natalie and Anton how she and Way had met. She also performed the introductions, since Bobby Tom showed no inclination to do so.

The tension between mother and son was so strong Gracie could almost feel the air twang. Way began to address the table in general in a voice that was a shade too effusive.

"I have an apartment not too far away. When I stopped in here for a bite to eat a little while ago and saw Mrs. Denton sitting alone, I persuaded her to let me join her, but I need to be getting back." Turning to her, he took her hand and shook it. "It was good to see you, Mrs. Denton. Nice seeing all of you." With a final nod, he left the restaurant.

Gracie had seldom heard a less convincing cover-up. She noticed that Suzy's gaze followed Way as he wended his way through the tables and turned out onto the walk.

Since Bobby Tom continued to be mute, she

took it upon herself to invite Suzy to join them. "We're just having dessert. Why don't we ask the waiter for another chair?"

"Oh, no. No, thank you. I—I need to get back."

Bobby Tom finally spoke. "It's a little late for you to be driving home tonight."

"I'm staying over. A friend and I are going to the symphony at the Performing Arts Center."

"What friend?"

Gracie could almost see Suzy crumpling under the force of his displeasure, and she was furious with him for bullying her. If his mother wanted to see Mr. Sawyer, that was her business, not his, and Suzy should tell him so. But at that moment, Suzy seemed more like a child while Bobby Tom had adopted the role of a stern, judgmental parent.

"No one you know." Suzy's hand fluttered to her hair. "Well, good-bye, everyone. Enjoy your dessert." She hurriedly left the restaurant, turning to the left when she reached the sidewalk, the opposite direction Way Sawyer had taken.

Suzy's heart thudded against her ribs. She felt as if she had just been caught in an act of adultery, and she knew Bobby Tom would never forgive her for this. She rushed along the sidewalk, dodging couples with baby strollers and groups of Japanese tourists. The low heels of her brown-and-black spectator pumps tapped a frantic cadence on the uneven fieldstone walk. Nearly a month had passed since the illicit night she and Way had spent together, and nothing had been the same since.

She remembered how tender he had been with her the next morning, despite her condemning silence. As they'd driven to the golf course, he'd told her that he wouldn't ever touch her again but that he'd like to continue seeing her. She had acted as if she had no choice in the matter—as if he'd close Rosatech if she didn't do as he asked—but in her secret heart she hadn't believed it. Despite his tough facade, that sort of ruthlessness wasn't in his nature.

In the end, she had continued to see him. As long as there was no physical contact between them, she told herself it wasn't a betrayal, so there was no harm. And because she couldn't face the truth, she let herself pretend she was with him against her will. As they played golf, talked about their gardens, and flew around the state to entertain his business associates, she privately acted out the role of the reluctant hostage, just as if the fate of Telarosa rested on her shoulders. And because he cared for her, he had let her get away with it.

But what had just happened had put an end to that. In the space of minutes, the fragile world of illusion she had built for herself had been smashed apart. God forgive her, she wanted to be with him. Their times together were like bright splashes of color against the monotonous predictability of her daily life. He made her laugh and feel young again. He made her believe that life still held possibilities and filled her aching loneliness. But by letting him come to mean so much to her, she had betrayed her marriage vows, and now her dishonor had been exposed to the one person on earth from whom she'd most wanted to hide her weakness.

The doorman let her into the building where Way lived, and she took the small elevator up to his apartment. She dug in her purse for the key he'd given her, but before she could fit it in the lock, he swung the door open.

His face was set in the same grim lines she remembered from their early encounters, and she almost expected a scathing comment, but, instead, he shut the door and drew her into his arms. "Are you all right?"

For just a moment, she allowed herself to rest her cheek against the front of his shirt, but even that brief comfort felt like a betrayal of Hoyt. "I didn't know he was going to be there," she said as she pulled away. "It was so unexpected."

"I won't let him badger you about this."

"He's my son. You won't be able to stop him."

He walked over to the window and, bracing the heel of his hand on the wall next to it, gazed out. "If you could have seen the look on your face when we were standing there..." His shoulders heaved as he drew a deep breath. "He didn't believe me when I told him we'd met accidentally. I wasn't very convincing. I'm sorry."

He was a proud man, and she understood what it had cost him to lie on her behalf. "I'm sorry, too."

He turned to her, and his expression was so bleak she wanted to weep. "I can't do this anymore, Suzy. I can't keep sneaking around. I want to be able to walk down the sidewalk with you in Telarosa and be invited into your house." He gave her a long, searching gaze. "I want to be able to touch you."

She sagged down on the couch, knowing the end had come but unwilling to accept it. "I'm sorry," she repeated.

"I have to let you go," he said quietly.

Panic spread through her, and her hands knotted into fists at her sides. "You're using what just happened as a way out, aren't you? You've had your amusement, and now you're ready to get rid of me and move Rosatech, too."

If he was startled by her unfair attack, he gave no sign of it. "This doesn't have anything to do with Rosatech. I'd hoped you would have known that by now."

She hurled her pain and guilt at him. "Do men like you have some kind of corporate locker room where you go to tell each other stories about all the women you seduce with your threats? They must have laughed at you for going after an old biddy like me when you could have had some busty young fashion model."

"Suzy, stop it," he said wearily. "I never meant to threaten you."

"Are you sure you don't want to screw me again?" Her voice choked on her tears. "Or was it so distasteful that you only wanted to do it once?"

"Suzy..." He came toward her, and she knew he wanted to take her into the comfort of his arms, but before he could touch her, she jumped up from the couch and moved away from him.

"I'm glad you're putting an end to it," she declared fiercely. "I never wanted it to happen in the first place. I want to forget all of this and go back to the way things were before I walked into your office."

"I don't. I was lonely as hell." He stood in front of her, but he didn't touch her. "Suzy, you've been a widow for four years. Tell me why we can't be together. Do you still hate me so much?"

Her anger faded. Slowly, she shook her head. "I don't hate you at all."

"I never intended to move Rosatech; you know that, don't you? I'm the one who started the rumor. I was like a little kid. I wanted to strike back at the town for the way they'd treated my mother all those years ago. She was a sixteen-year-old kid, Suzy, and she was brutally raped by three men, but she was the one punished. Still, I never intended for you to get caught in the path, and I won't forgive myself for that."

She turned her face away, silently begging him not to say any more, but he wouldn't stop.

"That afternoon when you came into my office, I took one look at you and felt like a kid from the wrong side of the tracks all over again."

"And you punished me for it."

"I didn't mean to. It never entered my head to blackmail you into sleeping with me—surely you know that by now—but you looked so beautiful that night you walked into my bedroom, and I wanted you so much that I couldn't let you go."

Tears welled in her eyes. "You forced me! It wasn't my fault! You made me give in to you!" Even to her own ears, her words sounded like those of a small child unwilling to take responsibility for her own actions and blaming everyone around her.

He regarded her with eyes so old and sad she wanted to weep. When he spoke, his voice was a hoarse rasp, full of pain. "That's right, Suzy. I forced you. It was my fault. Only mine."

She willed herself to keep silent and let it end there, but her innate sense of honor rebelled. This was her sin far more than it was his. Turning away, she murmured, "No, it wasn't. All I had to do was say no."

"It had been a long time for you. You're a passionate woman, and I took advantage of that."

"Please don't lie for me; I've done enough of that for myself." She took a ragged breath. "You didn't force me. I could have walked away any time I chose."

"Why didn't you?"

"Because…It felt so good."

He touched her. "You know, don't you, that I fell in love with you that night? Or maybe it happened thirty years ago, and I never got over it."

She pressed her fingertips to his lips. "Don't say that. It's not true."

"I fell in love with you, Suzy, even though I know I can never compete with Hoyt."

"This doesn't have anything to do with competition. He was my life. We married for always. And when I'm with you, I'm betraying him."

"That's crazy. You're a widow, and in this country women don't throw themselves on their dead husband's funeral pyre."

"He was my life," she repeated, not knowing how else to express it. "There could never be anybody else."

"Suzy—"

Her eyes filled with tears. "I'm so sorry, Way. I never meant to hurt you. I—I care too much about you.

He couldn't quite conceal his bitterness. "Apparently not enough to throw off your widow's weeds and start living again."

She saw the pain she was causing him and felt as if it were piercing her own body. "You saw how Bobby Tom reacted tonight. I wanted to die."

He looked as if she'd slapped him. "Then there's nothing more to be said, is there? I won't cause you shame."

"Way—"

"Get your things packed. I'll have a car waiting for you downstairs." Without giving her a chance to respond, he walked out of the apartment.

She fled to the guest room, where she'd stayed ever since that first night, and threw her clothes into a suitcase. As tears trickled down her cheeks, she told herself her nightmare was over. Eventually she would learn to forgive herself for what had happened and go on with the rest of her life. From now on she'd be safe.

And very much alone.

The fight blew up like a summer storm: quick, unexpected, turbulent. As the two couples flew back to Telarosa from San Antonio, Gracie considered what she should do about Bobby Tom's rude behavior toward his mother at the restaurant. By the time Natalie and Anton had left and they were finally alone, she had decided to hold her tongue. She knew how much Bobby Tom loved Suzy, and now that he'd had some time to cool off, she was certain he would be ready to make amends.

It didn't take him long, however, to relieve her of that notion. As he entered the living room, he threw his hat down on the couch.

"Call my mother in the morning and tell her we won't be coming for dinner on Tuesday night."

Gracie followed him as he stalked into his

office. "She'll be disappointed. She said she was making a special meal for you."

"She's going to have to eat it alone." He sprawled down behind his desk. Ignoring the ringing of the phone, he picked up the stack of mail Gracie had organized for him, making it clear that he was dismissing her.

"I know you're upset, but don't you think you should try to be a little more understanding about this?"

His nostrils flared with outrage. "You didn't believe that crap of Sawyer's about how he just happened to run into her at the restaurant, did you?"

"What difference does it make? They're both adults."

"What *difference* does it make?" He jumped up from the desk and whipped around the side to face her. "They're seeing each other, that's what!"

The answering machine clicked on and someone named Charlie began leaving a message about a boat he knew Bobby Tom was going to want to buy from him.

"You don't know that for a fact," she pointed out. "Instead of flying off the handle like this, why don't you just talk to her about what happened? If they're dating, she has her reasons. Talk to her, Bobby Tom. She's seemed so sad lately. I have a feeling she needs your support right now."

He jabbed his index finger toward her. "Stop right there! She'll never get my support on this. Not ever. When she started keeping company with Way Sawyer, she betrayed everybody in this town."

Gracie couldn't suppress her indignation. "She's your mother! She should come ahead of the town in your loyalty."

"You don't understand anything." He began pacing across the carpet. "I can't believe what a fool I made of myself. I didn't give those rumors a minute's thought. It never occurred to me she'd stab everybody in the back like this."

"Stop talking about Mr. Sawyer as if he's a serial killer. I happen to think he's a nice man. He didn't have to stop that day I was parked on the side of the highway, and I like the way he tried to protect your mother today. He knew how you'd feel about seeing them together, and he did his best to shield her."

"Are you actually defending him? A man who's going to single-handedly destroy this town?"

"Maybe if everyone in Telarosa didn't treat him so badly, he wouldn't want to leave."

"You don't know what you're talking about."

"Are you sure it's Mr. Sawyer who's bothering you? You were close to your father. Are you certain you wouldn't feel this way no matter who your mother had begun to see?"

"That's enough! I don't care to hear another word out of you. Just shut up about this, you hear?"

Everything inside her went still. "Don't talk to me like that."

He lowered his voice, speaking quietly and with absolute conviction. "I'll talk to you any way I want."

Gracie was furious. She'd promised herself she'd love him with all her heart, but handing over her soul hadn't been part of the deal. She deliberately turned her back on him and walked away.

He followed her into the living room. "Just where do you think you're going?"

"I'm going to bed." She snatched up her purse from the coffee table.

"Fine. I'll be in with you when I'm ready."

She nearly choked. "Do you really think I want to sleep with you right now?" She headed toward the back door and her apartment.

"Don't you dare walk out of here!"

"This is going to be hard for you to understand, Bobby Tom, so listen very carefully." She stopped walking. "Despite what everybody's been telling you from the moment you were born, you're not always irresistible."

Bobby Tom stood at the back window and watched her stalk across the yard, although why he gave a damn whether or not she made it to her apartment safely, he didn't know. She'd stepped way over the line tonight, and if he hadn't let her understand straight out that he wasn't going to put up with it, he'd never have another moment's peace with her.

As she entered her apartment, he turned away from the window, resentment churning inside him. The phone started ringing again, his answering machine clicked on, and Gracie's voice invited the caller to leave a message.

"Bobby Tom, this is Odette Downey. Would

you mind doin' me a big favor and seein' if you could get hold of Dolly Parton and ask her if she'd donate one of her wigs to our celebrity auction? We know people'd bid big on that wig, and—"

He pulled the telephone from the wall and threw it across the office.

Gracie knew how much he cared about his mother! She had to understand the emotions that had gone through him this afternoon when he'd seen her walking down those stairs with Way Sawyer. He grabbed a cigar from the humidor he kept on top of his desk, bit off the end, and spit it into the ashtray. He still didn't know which bothered him the most, the fact that his mom was seeing Sawyer or the fact that she hadn't told him about it. His chest tightened. After the way she'd loved his dad, how could she let Sawyer near her?

Once again, he turned his anger onto Gracie. All his life he'd played sports, and the idea of being loyal to your teammates was as much a part of him as his name. Gracie, on the other hand, had proved tonight that she didn't know the meaning of the word.

He snapped off the heads of two matches before he finally got his cigar lit. As he took short, angry puffs, he decided this was exactly what he deserved for letting her worm her way into his life. He'd known from the beginning how dictatorial she was, but he'd still kept her around and let her slither under his skin like a damn little chigger. Well, he sure as hell wasn't going to sit here all night and brood about it. Instead, he intended to settle down and get some work done.

Clamping the cigar in the corner of his mouth, he picked up a pile of papers and gazed down at the top sheet, but he might as well have been staring at Chinese. The house felt cold and silent without her. He set the cigar in the ashtray, then tapped the edges of the papers and moved them closer to the center of the desk. As the quiet of the empty house tightened around him, he realized how accustomed he'd become to having her around. He liked hearing the murmur of her voice coming from another room as she returned his calls or phoned one of the old people at that nursing home in New Grundy. He liked the way he'd sometimes wander into the living room and find her curled up in one of the ruffly chairs by the window reading a book. He even enjoyed sneaking around behind her back to pour out that awful coffee she made and fix a fresh pot without her knowing it.

Abandoning the papers in front of him, he rose and went into the bedroom, but as soon as he stepped inside, he knew it was a mistake. The room held her scent, that elusive fragrance that sometimes reminded him of spring flowers and other times made him think of summer afternoons and ripe peaches. Gracie seemed to be part of all the seasons. The warm glints of autumn shone in her hair, the clear light of winter sun sparkled in those intelligent gray eyes. He had to keep reminding himself that she wasn't a U.S.D.A. prime-cut female because lately he'd had a tendency to forget. It was just...

She was so damned cute.

He saw a scrap of blue lace lying on the carpet next to the side of the bed where she'd slept last night and leaned over to pick it up. A jolt of heat shot straight to his groin as he recognized her panties. He crushed the wisp of fabric in his fist and fought the urge to charge across the yard into her apartment, strip her naked, and bury himself inside her, right where he belonged.

With the novelty of initiating a virgin worn off, he should be starting to lose interest in the sexual side of their relationship, but he kept thinking up new things he wanted to show her, plus he hadn't nearly got tired of practicing all the old stuff. He loved the way she clung to him and those soft little sounds she made; he loved her curiosity and her energy, how he could embarrass her without half trying and, dammit, how she sometimes embarrassed him with her insatiable nosiness about his body.

He didn't exactly understand it, but there was something about the way she felt when he was inside her that seemed exactly right, not just to his cock, but to all of him. He thought of the flocks of women he'd dated and gone to bed with. None of them had felt exactly like Gracie.

Gracie felt right.

Sometimes she did this funny little thing after

they'd finished making love. He'd be holding her against his chest, sort of dozing off and feeling peaceful all the way down to his toenails, and she'd make this little *X* right over his heart with her fingertip. Just this little *X*. Right over his heart.

He was pretty certain Gracie figured she was in love with him. It wasn't unusual. He was accustomed to women falling in love with him, and with a few memorable exceptions, he'd learned to stay honest without breaking their hearts. The thing he appreciated about Gracie was that she understood she wasn't really his kind of woman, and she had enough sense to accept it without making a big fuss. Gracie might create scenes about things that weren't any of her business, like she'd done tonight, but she'd never make a scene about how she loved him and expected him to love her back because she was realistic enough to know it wouldn't ever happen.

Perversely, her acceptance now irritated him. He shoved his cigar back in the corner of his mouth, jammed his hands on his hips, and stalked into the kitchen. If a woman wanted a man, she should fight for him instead of giving up without a struggle. Dammit, if she loved him, why didn't she work a little harder at not being such an aggravation? *Show me how to please you*, that's what she'd said. She could damn well please him by giving him a little loyalty and understanding, by agreeing with him once in a while instead of arguing all the time, by being naked in his bed right now instead of tucked away over that damn garage.

As his mood grew blacker, he added more grievances against her to his invisible checklist, including the fact that she was turning into a damned flirt. It hadn't slipped his notice how many of the men on the crew made excuses to hang around her, and as far as he was concerned, it was her fault more than theirs. She didn't have to smile at them like they were irresistible or listen to what they were saying as if every word coming out of their mouths was scripture. He brushed over the fact that she was a naturally good listener. As far as he was concerned, an engaged woman should be more reserved when she was around other men.

He grabbed the milk carton from the refrigerator and took a swig. Considering the fact that he was responsible for her make-over, he supposed he couldn't entirely blame her for the way the men watched her when she wasn't looking, but it still riled him. He'd even been forced to exchange a few words with a couple of guys last week—nothing too obvious because he didn't want anybody to get the wrong idea and think he was jealous—just a friendly little reminder that Gracie was his fiancée, not some cheap little sex toy they had a snowball's chance in hell of dragging off to their motel rooms.

He shoved the milk back into the refrigerator, then stomped through the house nursing his grievances and feeling ill-used. Suddenly, he came up short. What was he doing? He was

Bobby Tom Denton, for chrissake! Why was he letting her get to him like this? He was the one who held all the aces.

That reminder should have calmed him down, but it didn't. Somehow or another, her good opinion had become important to him, maybe because she knew him a lot better than anybody else he could think of off the top of his head. That realization left him with a sense of vulnerability that was suddenly unbearable. Jabbing out his cigar in a china ashtray, he made up his mind exactly how he was going to handle her. For the next few days, he'd be cordial, but cool. He'd give her time to think about how badly she'd behaved and where her true loyalty belonged. Then, once she understood who held the power in their relationship, he'd take her back.

His mind spun ahead. They'd be leaving for L.A. right after Heavenfest to finish shooting the interiors on a soundstage there, and once they got away from this crazy town, she'd settle down. But what was going to happen when the movie was done and she no longer had a job? From the way she kept in touch with the old people she'd left behind and the fact that she'd adopted a whole new bunch at Arbor Hills, he was starting to believe that nursing homes might be in her blood, just as football was in his. What if she decided to go back to New Grundy?

The idea unsettled him. He trusted her more than any assistant who'd ever worked for him, and he had no intention of letting her go.

He'd simply make her an offer she couldn't refuse, and she could come to work for him full-time. Once she was officially on his payroll with a generous salary, all these foolish money arguments between them would be a thing of the past. He mulled over the idea. It was bound to get sticky between them when he got tired of the physical side of their relationship. Still, he was fairly certain he could ease her out of his bed without destroying the friendship that had come to mean so much to him.

He examined his plan for flaws, but found none. After all, handling any woman, even one like Gracie, was pretty much a matter of staying on top of the situation, and he congratulated himself on his ability to do exactly that. Before he knew it, he'd have her right back where he wanted her, snuggled up against him in his bed, making a little *X* right over his heart.

20

"**W**here do you think we should put the key chains, Gracie?"

Gracie had just finished unwrapping the last of the white china souvenir ashtrays shaped like the state of Texas. They had a pink Cupid marking the location of Telarosa and a red script legend that read:

HEAVEN, TEXAS
A PLACE IN THE HEART

The question about the key chains had come from Toolee Chandler, the chairman of the Bobby Tom Denton Birthplace Committee and the wife of the town's busiest dentist. Toolee stood at the counter of what was now a small gift shop, but had once been Suzy and Hoyt Denton's sun porch. The transformation of Bobby Tom's childhood home into a tourist attraction wasn't yet complete, although Heavenfest was only three weeks away.

Suzy and Hoyt had disposed of many of the house's original furnishings years ago when they'd moved, but the committee had scoured basements and secondhand stores for pieces that were similar, and sometimes even managed to come up with the original one. Much of the house was decorated in the avocado green and gold popular at the time, but Suzy had used bright accents of apple red, unconventional then, and they gave the house a definite charm even now.

Even taking on the responsibility of handling the travel and accommodations arrangements for the celebrity athletes left Gracie with too many free hours. Since she and Bobby Tom had quarreled nearly three weeks ago, she had spent most of her evenings at Arbor Hills or working here to help Terry Jo and Toolee get the birthplace ready.

Now she eyed the key chains dubiously.

Like so many other things in the gift shop, they bore Bobby Tom's likeness, even though he hadn't given permission for its use. A fluorescent orange plastic disk showed him in action: feet off the ground, body curved in a graceful C, arms extended to catch a pass. But the blue-and-white uniform of Dallas had been badly superimposed over his Chicago Stars uniform, along with the brightly printed words, "He should have been a Cowboy."

"Maybe you could hang them behind the postcard rack?" Gracie suggested.

"Oh, I don't think so," Toolee said. "Nobody'll be able to see them there."

That had been Gracie's hope. She wished Bobby Tom would put a stop to this unlicensed merchandise, but she wasn't going to broach the subject when there was already so much tension between them. They spoke politely, and when other people were nearby, he'd slip his arm around her waist for show, but they spent very little time alone together, and every night they retired to their separate bedrooms.

As Gracie carried a stack of ashtrays over to the shelves and began to arrange them, Terry Jo came in from the living room with a pencil stuck behind her ear and a clipboard in her hand. "Has anybody found that missing box of mugs?"

"Not yet," Toolee replied.

"I probably stuck them someplace crazy. I swear, ever since Way Sawyer announced he wasn't closing Rosatech, I've been so distracted I haven't been able to think straight."

"Luther's making him honorary chairman of the whole festival," Toolee declared, as if they hadn't already discussed this fact several times. Way Sawyer's announcement had left everyone in town giddy with relief, and he had gone from being Telarosa's enemy to its hero.

"Things are finally looking up for this town." Terry Jo smiled and gazed around at the glass shelves that stretched across the windows. A display of refrigerator magnets directly in front of her bore the legend, "I raised a little hell in Heaven, Texas!" "I remember the summer Mr. Denton built this sun porch. Bobby Tom and I used to play checkers out here and Suzy'd bring us grape Kool-Aid." She sighed. "Having this house restored has been like a trip back to my childhood. Suzy says she feels as if she loses twenty years every time she walks in the door, but I think it's hard on her coming here because Mr. Denton's not around to share it. I don't know. She hasn't seemed like herself lately."

Gracie was also worried about Suzy. Every time she'd seen her since that afternoon in San Antonio, she looked more fragile. As she set the last of the ashtrays on the shelf, she decided this might be a good time to broach an idea that she'd just that day mentioned to Suzy.

"It's a shame the house will be empty so much of the time."

"There's not much we can do about it," Toolee said. "Tourists'll only come around on the weekends and for special events, like Heavenfest."

"Still, it's a pity to keep it closed up the rest of the time, especially when it could be used to help people."

"What do you mean?"

"I've noticed that Telarosa doesn't have a senior citizens center. This house isn't large, but there's a rec room and the living room's comfortable. I was thinking that it would be an ideal place for the older people to get together for cards or crafts or to hear an outside speaker once in a while. Arbor Hills isn't far away. They're really cramped for space over there, and maybe they could transport their more mobile residents here for activities a few times a week."

Toolee splayed her hand on her hip. "Now why didn't I think of that?"

"It's a good idea," Terry Jo agreed. "I'm sure we could find some volunteers to staff it. Why don't we start a committee? I'll phone my mother-in-law as soon as I get home."

Gracie breathed a sigh of relief. The film company would be finished here in a few weeks, and it made her feel better to know that she might leave some small mark on this town she had grown to love and would miss so very much.

Several hours later, Bobby Tom stopped his pickup in front of the house where he'd grown up. His T-bird was the only car left in the drive, so he knew Gracie was still there, but the rest of the volunteers must have left for the day to fix dinner for their families. As he looked at the small white bungalow, he had the eerie feeling that time had stopped and he was a kid again. He almost expected to see his dad walking out of the garage with the old red Toro lawn mower, and he blinked his eyes hard. God, he missed his father.

Loneliness curled through him. He felt cut off from everybody important in his life. He and his mother hadn't done anything more than exchange courtesies since the incident in San Antonio three weeks earlier, and he could barely stand to admit to himself how much he missed Gracie. Not that he didn't see her during the day when they were shooting, but it wasn't the same. She treated him as if he were nothing more than her employer, doing whatever he asked and then disappearing. If anybody had told him he'd grow to miss the way she tried to order him around, he would have said they were crazy, but he couldn't deny the fact that she was leaving a hole in his life.

Still, he'd had to let her know who was boss, and since he was pretty sure she'd gotten the point by now, it was time for the two of them to have a showdown. He intended to tell her in no uncertain terms that the deep freeze was over. She could be damned stubborn, but once he got her to stop talking and start kissing, everything would be all right again. By midnight, she'd be right back in his bed, where she belonged.

As he stepped down from his truck, Suzy pulled into the drive behind him. She gave him a small wave as she got out of her car, then headed around to the rear and opened the trunk.

He wandered over as she was about to remove a large cardboard box.

"What's this?"

"Your old trophies from grade school through high school."

He took the box from her. "You didn't carry this down from the attic by yourself, did you?"

"I made several trips."

"You should have called me.

She shrugged. He saw the shadows under her eyes and noted the faint pallor to her complexion. His mother took such good care of herself that he'd never thought of her as getting older, but this afternoon, she looked every one of her fifty-two years and then some. She also looked deeply unhappy, and he felt guilty knowing that he might very well be the cause of those dark shadows. Gracie's words came back, making him feel even worse. She'd tried to tell him that his mom needed his support, but he hadn't listened.

He shifted the carton under his arm and cleared his throat. "Sorry I haven't been able to spend more time with you lately. We've been working about twelve hours a day, and, well, I've been busy," he finished lamely.

She couldn't seem to look him in the eye. "I know why you haven't come by the house, and I'm the one who's sorry." Her voice trembled slightly. "It's my fault. I know it is."

"Mom—"

"I'm not going to see him again. I promise you."

A crushing sense of relief swept over him. Despite the fact that Way Sawyer was the town's new hero, there was something about the man that Bobby Tom disliked. He slipped his arm around her shoulders and gave her a hug. "I'm glad."

"It was—It's hard to explain."

"You don't have to. We'll just forget about it."

"Yes. That would probably be best."

Linking his free arm through hers, he drew her toward the house. "How 'bout I take you and Gracie to dinner tonight? We could go to O'Leary's."

"Thanks, but I have a board meeting."

"You look tired. Maybe you should take it a little easier."

"I'm fine. I just stayed up too late last night reading." She walked ahead of him up the concrete steps that led to the small landing. Her hand reached out automatically to turn the knob, but the door was locked. He started to reach around her for the bell only to have his arm freeze in midair as she began frantically twisting the knob.

"Dammit!"

"It's locked," he said, alarmed by her behavior.

"Answer me!" She pounded her fist against the door, her face crumpling with despair. "Answer me, dammit!"

"Mom?" Apprehension spread through him. He quickly set the box of trophies down.

"Why doesn't he answer?" she cried, tears

beginning to trickle down her cheeks. "Why isn't he here for me?"

"Mom?" He tried to pull her into his arms, but she struggled against him. "Mom, it's okay."

"I want my husband!"

"I know you do. I know." He caught her against him. Her shoulders were heaving, and he didn't know how to help her. He'd thought the pain she'd experienced from his father's death had eased over the years, but her grief seemed as fresh as the day of his funeral.

Gracie opened the door in response to the pounding, but her smile faded as she saw Suzy's condition. "What's wrong? What's happened?"

"I'm going to take her home," he said.

"No!" Suzy drew away and dashed at her tears with the back of her hand. "I'm sorry. I—I apologize to you both. I don't know what came over me, and I'm so embarrassed."

"There isn't any need to be embarrassed. I'm your son."

Gracie stepped out onto the porch. "Coming here has to dredge up all sorts of painful emotions for you. You wouldn't be human if you didn't react."

"Still, that's no excuse." She gave them both a weak, unconvincing smile. "I'm all right now—really, I am—but I don't think I'll come inside." She gestured toward the box. "Would you mind putting those trophies on the shelf in the bedroom for me? Bobby Tom can show you where they go."

"Of course," Gracie replied.

He took his mother's arm. "I'm going to drive you home."

"No!" She backed abruptly away, and to his alarm, she began crying again. "No, you're not! I want to be alone. I just want everybody to leave me alone!" Pressing the back of her hand to her mouth, she fled to her car.

Bobby Tom's eyes found Gracie's, and he regarded her helplessly. "I have to make sure she gets there safely. I'll be back."

Gracie nodded.

He followed his mother home, feeling shaken to the core by what had just happened. He realized how accustomed he was to thinking of Suzy as merely his mother, not as a human being with a life of her own, and he was ashamed. Why hadn't he listened to Gracie? Tomorrow he would have the talk with his mother he should have had weeks ago.

He watched her from the curb until she got safely inside, then headed back to the small, white bungalow where he'd grown up. Gracie had left the door unlocked and he found her upstairs in his childhood bedroom. She sat on the edge of the twin bed staring into space with the box of his old trophies at her feet. Seeing Gracie in this room from his past surrounded by so many items from his boyhood sent an eerie prickle along his spine.

The desk in the corner didn't look much like the one he remembered, but the green gooseneck lamp still held the remnants of the Titans decal he'd stuck to the base so long ago. A peg rack displayed his collection of baseball caps, and his old Evel Knievel poster hung on the wall. Why had his mom held on to that thing? His father had put up the shelving around the window to hold his trophies. The beanbag chair was a duplicate of the original, but the gold bedspread didn't look at all like the plaid one he'd grown up with.

Gracie lifted her head. "Did she get home all right?"

He nodded.

"What happened?"

He wandered over to the window, pulled back the curtain, and gazed out at the yard. "I can't believe how big the trees have grown. Everything else seems so much smaller now than it used to."

Gracie didn't know why she should feel discouraged by his unwillingness to talk to her; she should have been used to it by now. But she knew the scene with his mother had distressed him and wished they could discuss it. She got up from the side of the bed and knelt on the carpet to begin removing the old trophies from their newspaper wrapping.

His boots entered her vision as he came to a stop next to her, then sat down on the bed in the spot she had just vacated. "I don't know what happened. One minute we were talking, and the next minute she was pounding on the front door and crying because my father wasn't there to answer it."

She sat back on her heels and looked up at him. "I feel so sorry for her."

"What could be wrong?"

When she didn't say anything, he regarded her accusingly. "You think this has something to do with Sawyer and what happened at the restaurant, don't you? You're blaming this on me."

"I didn't say that."

"You don't have to. I can read your mind."

"You love your mother. I know you wouldn't deliberately hurt her."

"This doesn't have anything to do with Sawyer; I'm sure of it. She told me she's not going to see him anymore."

Gracie nodded, but made no comment. As much concern as she felt for them both, they'd have to work this out for themselves.

She watched as he gazed around his old bedroom and wasn't surprised when he switched the subject away from Way Sawyer and his mother.

"This whole birthplace thing gives me the creeps. I don't know why people think anybody's going to waste time wandering through this place to see my old football trophies. I guess you know that I'm not happy about your association with it."

"Somebody had to watch out for your interests. You should see the key chains they're selling in the gift shop. They show you wearing a Cowboys' uniform."

"I never wore a Cowboys' uniform in my life."

"The magic of modern photography. The best I could do was get them moved to the back corner, but I had a little better luck with an idea that hit me a few weeks ago."

"What's that?"

"The town really needs a senior citizens center, and this afternoon I talked to Terry Jo and Toolee about using the house that way. I'd already spoken to Suzy and she agreed that it would be an ideal spot."

"A senior citizens center?" He thought it over. "I like that."

"Enough to come up with the cash to put in a wheelchair ramp and fix up the toilet facilities?"

"Sure."

Neither of them commented on the fact that Gracie felt perfectly free to ask him for money for others, but still insisted on giving him part of her weekly paycheck, even though the money remained untouched in his desk drawer. She was proud of the fact that, by scrimping on her personal expenses, she would have the black cocktail dress he'd bought her paid off in time to wear it to the welcoming party at the country club the night before the golf tournament.

He got up from the side of the bed and began to pace across the end of the room. "Look, Gracie, I know I might have come on a little strong that night we had our argument, but you've got to understand Way Sawyer is a sensitive subject with me."

She was surprised he'd reopened the subject. "I do understand that."

"Still, I guess I shouldn't have taken my bad mood out on you. You were right about the fact that I need to talk to my mother; I realize that now. I'm going to do it as soon as I can get away tomorrow."

"Good." She was grateful that the estrangement between them finally seemed to be over.

"I guess you've been right about a lot of things." Once again he walked over to the window and stared down into the back yard. His shoulders slumped ever so slightly. "I miss football a lot, Gracie."

She grew instantly more alert. This was hardly an earthshaking revelation to anyone who knew him, but the fact that Bobby Tom was actually admitting it astonished her. "I know you do."

"It's not fucking *fair*!" As he spun around, his features contorted with emotion. He was so agitated, he didn't even seem to realize he'd used an obscenity in front of her, something he seldom did with a woman. "One bad hit and I'm out of the game forever! One bad fucking hit! If Jamal had caught me two seconds earlier or two seconds later, it wouldn't have happened."

She thought of the videotape and knew she'd never forget the sight of his gracefully extended body taking that damaging tackle.

He regarded her angrily, one hand clenched into a fist at his side. "I had three or four good years left. I was going to use that time to make plans for my retirement, to think about whether I wanted to coach or go into the broadcasting booth. I needed that time to get ready."

"You're a quick study," she said softly. "You can still do those things."

"But I don't want to!" The words erupted from him, and she had the uncanny sense that they surprised him far more than they did her. His voice dropped until it was nearly a whisper. "Don't you understand? I want to play ball."

She nodded. She did understand.

His lips twisted in an ugly sneer. "I don't know how you can stand to sit there and listen to me without wanting to throw up. Pretty pathetic, isn't it, a grown man who's got the whole world at his feet whining just because life handed him one bad break? I've got all the money in the world; I've got friends, houses, cars, but here I am feeling sorry for myself because I can't play ball. If I were you, I'd be laughing half to death right now. If I were you, I'd head right over to the Wagon Wheel and tell everybody how Bobby Tom Denton's been carrying on like a jerk so they can laugh, too."

"It doesn't seem funny to me."

"Well, it should." He gave a scornful snort. "You want to hear something really pitiful? I don't have the slightest idea who I am anymore. For as long as I can remember, I've been a football player, and now it seems I don't know how to be anything else."

She spoke softly. "I think you could be anything you set your mind to."

"You don't understand! If I can't play ball, I don't want to be part of the game. I can't work up any enthusiasm for coaching, no matter how hard I try, and I sure as hell don't want to sit up in some air-conditioned broadcasting booth making wisecracks for the folks at home."

"You've got a lot more talents than just those."

"I'm a ball player, Gracie! That's what I've always been. That's who I am."

"Right now you're an actor. What about your film career?"

"It's all right. I wouldn't even mind making another movie sometime, but no matter how much I try to convince myself otherwise, I know my heart isn't in it. It seems like play instead of work. And I keep thinking there's nothing more pathetic in this world than a washed-up jock trying to be a movie star because he can't do anything else."

"I met you after your career was over, so I don't think of you as a jock, washed-up or otherwise. And it's hard to think of you as a movie star. To be honest, I've always regarded you more as a businessman than anything else. You obviously have a talent for making money, and you seem to enjoy doing it."

"I do enjoy it, but there's no honor in it for me. Maybe some people can be happy making money just for the sake of keeping score, but I'm not one of them. Life's got to be about something more than buying bigger toys. I own too many things as it is. I don't need another house, I don't want another plane, and buying a few cars here and there doesn't do much more than eat up my petty cash."

Under other circumstances, his indignation might have made her smile, but he was too troubled for her to be amused. She thought of the times she'd walked into his office and seen him talking on the phone with his boots propped up on the desk and his Stetson pushed to the back of his head as he discussed the wisdom of investing in a new bond issue or buying pork bellies on the commodities market.

She rose from the floor and walked over to stand beside him. "The fact is, Bobby Tom, you love making money, and there are lots of honorable things you could do with it other than buy bigger toys, as you put it. I know how much you care about children. Instead of letting women threaten you with paternity suits, why don't you do something more far-reaching for kids without fathers. Set up scholarship funds or day-care centers; open some food pantries. Or how about upgrading the medical equipment in the pediatric wing of the county hospital you like to visit? There's a whole world of need out there, and you're in a unique position to help. Football's given you a lot. Maybe it's payback time."

He stared at her, not saying a word.

"I've had an idea. I don't know how you'll feel about it, but...Why don't you think about setting up a charitable foundation? You could make money for the foundation instead of yourself?" When he didn't respond, she continued. "I'm talking about running it as a full-time job, not a rich man's toy, using your talent for something that will make a difference in people's lives."

"That's crazy."

"Just think about it."

"I already have, and it's crazy, the craziest thing you've ever come up with. I'm not some stuffed shirt do-gooder. If I tried to do something like that, people'd laugh so hard they'd be rolling on the floor." He was so taken aback, he was practically sputtering, and she couldn't help but smile.

"I don't think people would be surprised at all. It's completely in character for you." She turned her attention back to unpacking the trophies. She'd planted the seeds, but the rest was up to him.

He sat down on the side of the bed and watched her work for several minutes. When he finally spoke, it was obvious by the glitter in his eyes that he had something other than talking about the future on his mind. "I swear, Gracie, you've aggravated me so much you almost took my mind off how cute your bottom looks in those jeans." He removed his cowboy hat and patted the mattress. "Come here, sweetheart."

"I don't know if I like that look on your face." In truth, she liked it very much. Being alone with him in the small room made her realize how long it had been since they'd made love.

"I promise you'll like it a lot. If you knew

how much time I used to spend in this very bed-room dreaming about gettin' a girl naked in here, you wouldn't even think of denying me."

"Did you ever?" She moved over to stand in front of him.

He caught the backs of her thighs and drew her between his splayed knees. "Get one naked?" He opened the snap at the top of her jeans and leaned forward to nibble at her belly button. "'Fraid not. Mom kept a pretty strict eye out." His lips moved lower, along with the slide on her zipper. "When I was in ninth grade, I almost got a mutual friend of ours up here, but I guess mothers have some kind of built-in radar about that sort of thing because next thing I knew, Suzy was popping up with a plate of Oreos."

"So you were restricted to backseats and parking by the river." She was beginning to sound breathless.

"That was pretty much it." He reached up under the hem of her patchwork print blouse and cupped her breasts through her bra. Her breathing grew more labored as he rubbed his thumbs over her nipples, playing with the silk and her flesh until she could feel herself melting.

"Uhmm," he whispered. "You smell like peaches again."

Before long they were both undressed and making such sweet love on that narrow bed that all thoughts of the future evaporated. When it was over and Gracie lay boneless and spent on top of him, with his hand curled around her bottom, she finally opened her eyes far enough to see the satisfied smile on his face.

"It took me a lot of years to get a female naked in here, but it was worth every minute of the wait."

She nuzzled his neck and felt the soft abrasion of his beard against her temple. "Am I better than Terry Jo?"

His voice was husky as he rolled to the side and cupped her breast. "Terry Jo was just a child, sweetheart. You're a woman full grown. There's no comparison."

She heard a sound from below, and her head shot up as she realized the bedroom door was open. A sense of foreboding shot through her. "You locked the front door when you came back in, didn't you?"

"I don't think so."

No sooner had he spoken than the unmistakable voice of Mayor Luther Baines echoed from the bottom of the stairs. "Bobby Tom? You up there?"

With a gasp, Gracie leaped to her feet and grabbed for her clothes. Bobby Tom yawned, then swung his legs over the side of the bed in a leisurely fashion. "You'd better not come any farther, Luther. Gracie's naked up here."

"For real?"

"She looks naked to me."

Gracie could feel herself turning four shades of crimson, and she shot him a malevolent glare. He grinned back at her.

"Why don't you wait for us in the kitchen,"

he called out. "We'll be down in a few minutes."

"Sure enough," the mayor replied. "And, Gracie, Mrs. Baines heard about your plan for the senior citizens center from Terry Jo. She said she'd be happy to help set up a volunteer group."

Gracie's cheeks flamed as she riffled through her purse for tissues. "Be sure to thank her for me, Mayor Baines," she said weakly.

"Oh, you can thank her yourself. She's standing right here next to me."

Gracie froze.

"Hello, Gracie," Mrs. Baines called out gaily. "Hi, Bobby Tom."

Bobby Tom's grin grew wider. "Howdy, Mrs. Baines. Anybody else down there?"

"Just Pastor Frank from First Baptist," the Mayor's wife replied.

Gracie let out a small squeal of alarm.

Bobby Tom ruffled her hair and gave a low chuckle. "They're teasin', sweetheart."

"Mrs. Frank and I think the senior citizen center is a wonderful idea, Miss Snow." The stairwell filled with the deep sounds of a voice that was unmistakably pastoral. "First Baptist will be happy to help with your project."

With a moan, Gracie collapsed on the side of the bed, while Bobby Tom started laughing so hard she finally had to hit him with a pillow.

Afterward, she could never quite remember how she managed to get herself dressed and go downstairs to face Telarosa's leading citizens. Bobby Tom told her she behaved like Queen Elizabeth, except with more dignity, but she didn't know whether or not to believe him.

21

The Friday morning of the birthplace dedication was crisp and bright with the clear light of early October. School had been dismissed for the day to celebrate the opening of Heavenfest, and the small front lawn was crowded with the young and old. Everyone in town had been asked to dress in period costume for the weekend. Many of the men had grown beards and mustaches, while the women's long skirts flapped in the breeze. Teenagers congregated around the parked cars on the streets, their concession to frontier dress limited, like Bobby Tom's, to jeans and cowboy hats.

"...and so on this beautiful October morning, we gather here in the shade of these old pecan trees to honor..."

As Luther droned on, Bobby Tom studied the crowd from his vantage point on the small platform that had been built in front of the garage. His mother sat on one side of him and Gracie on the other. Gracie had protested at being seated with the dignitaries, but he'd insisted. She looked cute as a button in a long yellow gingham dress, old-fashioned straw bonnet, and very modern sunglasses.

The Heavenfest committee had originally planned to have the dedication on Friday night, but Bobby Tom refused. The athletes playing in tomorrow's golf tournament would begin arriving around noon today, and he wanted the whole embarrassment over with before any of them got to Telarosa, although he had to admit he didn't feel quite as negative about the birthplace project since Gracie had come up with the idea of turning the house into a senior citizens center. She was, he'd decided, about the do-goodingest woman he'd ever known.

As Luther droned on, Bobby Tom's gaze drifted to his mother. He wished he knew what was wrong with her. In the past ten days, he'd tried to talk to her several times about what had happened, but she'd deflected every conversation by showing him new plants in her garden or cruise brochures from her travel agent.

Luther waved his arms and shouted into the microphone as he worked up to his big finish. "And now I present to you the leading citizen of Heaven, Texas! A man with two Super Bowl rings...a man who has given himself unselfishly to this town, the great state of Texas, and these U-nited States of America! The greatest wide receiver in the history of professional football...our favorite son...*Bobby Tom Denton*!"

Bobby Tom ambled to his feet to the cheers of the crowd and approached the podium, resisting the urge to break Luther's fingers as he shook his hand. The microphone squealed, but it didn't bother him. He'd been making speeches in front of these people since he was in high school, and he knew exactly what to say.

"It sure is good to be back home again!"

Loud applause and whistles.

"Why, half the people I see standing here today helped my mama and daddy raise me, and don't you think I've forgotten it."

More cheers.

He continued with his speech, making it short enough so he didn't bore himself to death, but long enough to satisfy the people he cared so much about. When he was done, he handed his mother the scissors to cut the ribbon stretched across the front door. To more applause, the Bobby Tom Denton Birthplace and future Senior Citizens Center was officially dedicated.

As his mother turned away to greet her friends, he looped his arm around Gracie's shoulders. Between her Heavenfest activities and his brutal shooting schedule, they hadn't been able to spend nearly as much time together as he would have liked. Sometimes, lately, he'd found himself not enjoying a joke just because she wasn't around to share it. One thing about Gracie—She understood the humor of everyday life in ways other people didn't.

He cocked his head so he could whisper in her ear. "What do you say the two of us sneak off for a couple of hours and mess around?"

She gazed up at him with genuine regret,

another thing he liked about her. She never tried to hide her pleasure in their physical relationship or hold anything back. "I only wish we could, but you know you have to get back to the set. They're already giving you tomorrow off. Besides, I need to run over to the hotel and stuff all the welcome packets for your friends. Remember that you have to be at the country club by six tonight so you can greet everybody privately."

He sighed. She didn't know it yet, but when this movie was over, the two of them were going to spend a few days naked on a secluded island where there weren't any telephones and nobody spoke English.

"All right, sweetheart. But I don't like the idea of you driving yourself to the club tonight. I'm going to ask Buddy to pick you up."

"Please don't. I'm not sure what I'm going to run into this afternoon, and it'll be better if we take two cars."

He reluctantly agreed and set off to return to work.

As Gracie watched him leave, the sunlight seemed to shimmer around him and she could almost see the pinwheels of silver sparks spinning from those invisible spurs he always seemed to wear. The film company would be leaving Telarosa for Los Angeles soon, and Willow had said nothing about taking her along. Gracie couldn't believe it would end so soon.

Over the last few days, she had found herself playing with the intoxicating notion that

Bobby Tom might be falling in love with her, and her cheeks flushed as she made her way back to the car. Even though she tried to tell herself that sort of thinking was dangerous, she couldn't quite shake it off. How could he gaze at her so tenderly if he didn't care? He was so open in his affection, so passionate in his lovemaking. Surely he couldn't have been like this with all the women in his past? Surely he felt something special for her?

Sometimes she'd look up from what she was doing and find him watching her as if she were important to him. That was when she'd start thinking about the future and envisioning roly-poly babies and a house filled with the sound of his laughter. Was it impossible? Could he be beginning to feel the same way about her that she felt about him? Her skin felt hot and prickly just thinking about it. Was it possible that the future might hold more for her than memories?

For the rest of the day, she threw herself into her work to avoid daydreaming. She'd no sooner gotten the welcome packets ready for the hostesses to pass out at the Cattleman's Hotel than a crisis over the seating plans broke out at the country club. As she raced over there, she passed beneath one of the welcoming banners that hung over Main Street. Like everything else in town from bumper stickers to T-shirts, it read HEAVEN, TEXAS! A PLACE IN THE HEART.

She spent most of the afternoon at the country club, straightening out problems with the arrangement of the tables. When she was done, it was nearly five o'clock, and she realized she hadn't picked up her paycheck. Since she had exactly four dollars left in her wallet, she made a mad dash back to Windmill's suite on the top floor of the hotel, hoping to get there before the woman who took care of the payroll had left.

To her disappointment, Willow was locking the door as she stepped off the elevator. Gracie hurried forward. "I'm sorry to be so late, but it's been a crazy day. Would you mind letting me get my paycheck?"

Willow shrugged and opened the door. "I guess not."

Gracie followed her inside. Even though she tried to be as helpful to Willow as she could, their relationship had continued to be strained, and Gracie suspected it was because Willow had planned to launch her own affair with Bobby Tom. She didn't want to think how angry the producer would be if she discovered that the engagement was bogus.

"I know you can't be crazy about me spending so much time away from the set, but you told me I'm supposed to be taking my orders from Bobby Tom, and he wants me to tend to these organizational details for the golf tournament."

"It's fine, Gracie. Whatever."

Willow was a tough taskmaster, and Gracie couldn't imagine her being so lenient with anyone else. Now, while they were alone, seemed as good a time as any to broach the subject of the future. "I've been wondering what your plans are for me."

"Plans?"

"For L.A. Whether you want me to go there or not."

"I guess you should ask Bobby Tom." She began riffling through one of the portable files on top of the credenza. "I heard a couple of the Lakers have arrived for the golf tournament. I've followed the team for years, and I hope I get a chance to meet them at the dinner tonight."

"I'm sure Bobby Tom will by happy to introduce you." She hesitated, picking her words carefully. "Willow, I don't want my personal relationship with Bobby Tom to influence my professional future. Regardless of who I take my orders from, you're my employer, and I guess I'd feel better if I knew what you have in mind."

"I'm sorry, Gracie, but I can't tell you any more right now." She seemed to be having difficulty finding the check, and she started through the file again, only to pause. "Oh, that's right. Your check is processed separately."

A small chill crept through Gracie as she watched Willow move over to the desk, open the center drawer, and pull out a long envelope.

Her voice had a faintly hollow sound. "Why is that? Why is my check handled differently from anyone else's?"

Willow hesitated a fraction too long. "Who knows why bookkeeping does things?"

"You do," she forced out. "You're the producer."

"Look, Gracie, maybe you'd better talk to Bobby Tom about this. I'm really rushed for time." She thrust the check into Gracie's stiff fingers.

Gracie's felt something cold trickle down her spine, and she could barely find enough air to speak as a terrible certainty took hold of her. "Bobby Tom has been paying my salary all along, hasn't he? He's my employer, not Windmill."

Willow picked up her purse and walked to the door. "I really don't want to get involved in this."

"You already are."

"Look, Gracie, one thing you learn fast if you want to survive in this business is not to piss off the star. Do you understand what I'm trying to say?"

Gracie understood too much. Bobby Tom had been paying her salary all along, and he'd told Willow to keep it a secret.

Her knees were rubbery as she followed Willow from the suite. She felt as if something fragile had shattered inside her. This was a betrayal she had never expected. As the elevator descended, all her daydreams evaporated. This had been so important to her. So essential. Just this morning, she had tantalized herself with the notion that he might love her, but now she knew he didn't see her any differently from all the other parasites who preyed on him.

She left the hotel and made her way numbly to her car. All along, she hadn't been anything more to him than another one of his charity cases. She couldn't hold back the tears. She was beholden to him for everything: the roof over her head, her food, every purchase she made from shampoo to Tampax. She cringed as she thought how proud she had felt when she'd left money in his desk drawer to pay her rent and reimburse him for the cocktail dress. How he must have laughed as he watched money he'd given her in the first place returned to him. Having private jokes at her expense seemed to be a specialty of his.

She clutched the steering wheel more tightly, but she couldn't stop the flow of tears. Why hadn't she figured it out earlier? He didn't love her at all. He'd felt sorry for her, so he'd created a job for her out of pity in the same way he set up trust funds for children who weren't his and wrote out checks to friends down on their luck. There had never been enough work to keep her busy, and she couldn't even take any satisfaction in feeling as if she'd earned the money. He'd known all along that he didn't need a full-time employee, but he hadn't wanted her firing on his conscience. Bobby Tom liked playing God.

She stared blindly ahead. By not telling her the truth from the beginning, he had deceived her in a way she could never forgive. She had explained to him how imperative it was for her to pay her own way. He knew it! But that hadn't mattered to him because she didn't matter to him. If he'd cared for her, he wouldn't have stripped her of that dignity. *I'm not going to take anything from you, Bobby Tom. I only want to give.* What a joke. What an awful, painful joke.

Some men fought tuxedos, but Bobby Tom looked as if he'd been born in one. He'd added his own touches, of course: a pleated lavender shirt with diamond studs, black Stetson, and a pair of snakeskin cowboy boots he wore only with formal dress. The limestone clubhouse had been polished from the locker room to the dining room for the biggest event in its history. Ticket sales for tomorrow's tournament had exceeded everyone's expectations, and even the weatherman had cooperated by promising a sunny day, with temperatures in the low seventies.

The athletes were just beginning to arrive for the predinner cocktail party when one of the waiters whispered to Bobby Tom that someone wanted to see him downstairs. As he made his way across the lobby, he glanced toward the entrance with some irritation. Where was Gracie? He'd expected her to be here by now. A lot of the guys were going to get a big kick out of her, and he wanted to start introducing her around. Gracie was the most sports-ignorant female he'd ever met, and he knew her lack of knowledge was sure to get her into trouble tonight, providing him with an entire evening's worth of amusement. He still didn't quite understand how her ignorance of sports sometimes seemed to be one of her best assets.

He headed down the carpeted stairs to the lower level, where the locker rooms were vacant for the night. The glass door that led into the empty pro shop should have been locked, but it stood ajar, and he stepped inside. Only a single light burned over the counter, and he didn't see the man who stood in the far corner of the room until Way Sawyer came forward.

"Denton."

Bobby Tom had known he was going to have to confront Sawyer soon, but he wouldn't have chosen tonight to do it. Still, he'd seen Sawyer's name on the guest list, so it wasn't a real surprise, and he had no intention of backing away. For some reason this man was connected with his mother's sadness, and he wanted to know why.

Sawyer had been inspecting one of the oversize drivers on display, and as he stepped forward he held it loosely across his body. His formal dress didn't disguise how haggard he looked, as if he hadn't had a good night's sleep for some time. Bobby Tom struggled to control his antipathy. Despite Sawyer's announcement about Rosatech, he would never like this man. He was a cold, hardhearted son of a bitch who'd cheat his own grandmother if he saw the need. He pushed aside the fleeting impression that right now Sawyer looked more tired than ruthless.

"What can I do for you?" he said coldly.

"I want to talk to you about your mother."

It was exactly the subject they needed to discuss, but Bobby Tom felt himself bristling. "There's nothing to talk about. You stay away from her, and everything'll be fine."

"I've been staying away from her. Has that made things better? Is she happy?"

"You're damn right she is. Happy as I've ever seen her."

"You're lying."

Despite his words, Bobby Tom heard the uncertainty in Sawyer's voice and took advantage of it. "The last time we talked, she was excited about taking a cruise and adding some new plants to her garden. She's been so busy with her friends and projects it's hard for us to find time to get together."

Sawyer's shoulders slumped almost imperceptibly, and his fingers grew lax on the club he was holding, but Bobby Tom didn't relent. Somehow this man had hurt his mother, and he had to make certain it didn't happen again. "As far as I could tell, she didn't have a care in the world."

"I see." Sawyer cleared his throat. "She misses your father very much."

"You think I don't know that?"

Sawyer rested the head of the club on the carpet. "You look just like him, you know. The last time I saw him he was only eighteen or nineteen, but the resemblance is still strong."

"That's what people say."

"I hated his guts."

"I don't imagine he was too fond of you, either."

"Hard to tell. If he disliked me, he never showed it, even though I sure gave him cause. He was so damned nice to everybody."

"Then why did you hate him?" The question slipped out despite his intention to remain detached.

Sawyer ran his hand along the club's grip. "My mother cleaned your grandmother's house for a while, did you know that? This was before she gave up on life and found another way to make a living." He paused, and Bobby Tom thought of the story he'd been telling women for years about his mother being a hooker. It had all been one big joke to him, but it hadn't been a joke to Sawyer, and despite his dislike of the man, he felt a sense of shame.

Sawyer went on. "Your dad and I were the same age, but he was bigger, and when we were about in sixth, seventh grade, your grandmother used to give my mother all his old clothes. I had to go to school in your father's hand-me-downs, and I was so jealous of him, sometimes I thought I was going to choke on it. Every day he saw me coming to school in his castoffs, and he never said a word about it. Not one word. Not to me, not to anybody. The other kids noticed, though, and they'd taunt me about it. 'Hey, Sawyer, isn't that Hoyt's old plaid shirt you've got on.' If your dad was around, he'd just shake his head and say, hell, no, that wasn't his shirt; he'd never seen the damned thing before. Jesus, I hated him for that. If only he'd thrown my poverty in my face, I could have fought him. But he never did, and looking back on it, I don't think it was in his nature. In a lot of ways, I believe he may have been the best man I ever knew."

Bobby Tom felt a sense of pride as overwhelming as it was unexpected. And then, almost immediately, a devastating sense of loss. He steeled himself to show none of those emotions. "But you still hated him."

"Envy'll do that to you. In high school I once broke into his locker and stole his school jacket. I don't think he ever figured out it was me. I couldn't wear the damned thing, of course; didn't even want to. But I took it over by the tracks and burned it, so he'd never be able to wear it again. Maybe I thought getting rid of it would erase all his accomplishments, or maybe I just couldn't stand watching him drape it over your mother's shoulders when they were walking home. Damned thing used to come almost to her knees."

This vision of his parents as high school kids made Bobby Tom feel strangely disoriented. "That's what this is about, isn't it? My mother."

"I guess it always has been." His eyes clouded, as if his thoughts were far away. "She was so pretty. She doesn't think so because she had braces until the end of her sophomore year and that's all she remembers, but take it from me, she was pretty as a picture, braces and all. And she was like your dad, nice to everybody." He laughed with genuine amusement. "Everybody but me. One day she met up with me in the hallway when nobody was around. She was taking something to the office for a teacher, I guess, and I was cutting class. I flipped up my collar and slouched against one of the lockers like a no-good punk. I gave her my best badass squint and looked her up and down, probably scared her half to death. I remember her hands started to shake around the paper she was holding, but she stared at me dead-on. 'Wayland Sawyer, if you don't want to end up a bum on the streets, you'd better get yourself to class right this minute.' A spunky lady, your mama."

It was hard to hold on to his antipathy in the face of such relentless honesty, but Bobby Tom reminded himself that Sawyer wasn't a teenage punk any longer and this time the threat he posed to his mother was real.

"It's one thing for a kid to scare her," he said quietly. "It's another for a grown man. Tell me what you did to her."

Bobby Tom didn't really expect him to answer, and he wasn't surprised when Sawyer turned away without responding and walked over to the wooden rack. When he'd put the golf club back in place, he leaned against the counter, but despite his casual posture, his body was tense. Bobby Tom felt himself growing more alert, as if he were about to take a hit.

Sawyer gazed up at the ceiling and swallowed hard. "I let her believe I'd close Rosatech unless she became my mistress."

An explosion went off inside Bobby Tom. He shot across the room, arm drawn back, ready to kill the fucking son of a bitch, only to stop before he reached him as a cold and lethal sense of purpose took the place of his rage. He grabbed the lapels of the older man's jacket. "She'd better have told you to go to hell."

Sawyer cleared his throat. "No. No, she didn't."

"I'm going to kill you." Bobby Tom's hands convulsed on the jacket, and he threw Sawyer against the counter.

Sawyer grabbed his wrists. "Just hear me out. You can do that much."

Bobby Tom needed to know the rest, and he forced himself to let go, although he didn't move back. His voice was low and deadly. "Start talking."

"I never said that to her, but it's what she thought I meant, and I waited too long to tell her the truth. Believe it or not, the world outside Telarosa thinks I'm a fairly decent guy, and I thought if we spent some time together, she'd see that. But things got out of hand."

"You raped her."

"No!" For the first time Sawyer's anger flared, and his eyes narrowed. "You can believe a lot of things about me, Denton, but don't you *ever* believe that. What happened between us is none of your damned business, but I'll tell you this—there wasn't any force involved."

Bobby Tom felt sick. He didn't want to think about his mother that way under any circumstances. But much worse, he couldn't abide the idea that she had willingly given herself to Sawyer, not when she was married to his dad, not while Hoyt Denton's memory was still alive.

As abruptly as it had erupted, Sawyer's anger seemed to fade. "There wasn't any force involved, but it was too soon for her, and I knew it. She still loves your father very much; he was a hell of a man, and I can't blame her for that. But he's not here anymore, and I am. She's lonely. She wants to care about me, too, except she won't let herself, and I think it's mainly because of you."

"You don't know that."

"You're the most important person in her life, and she'd cut off her arm before she hurt you."

"I want you to stay away from her."

Sawyer regarded him with open hostility. "I hope you've figured out that I haven't spilled my guts to you because I'm some kind of a masochist. I don't like you very much—as far as I can tell, you're a selfish bastard—but I'm hoping I'm wrong. I'm hoping you've got more of your father in you than I can see right now. I've been honest with you because I'm praying for a miracle here. Without your approval, she and I don't have a chance."

"There aren't going to be any miracles."

He was a proud man, and there was no entreaty in his voice. "All I want is a level playing field, Bobby Tom. I just want a fair chance."

"You want my fucking *blessing*!"

420

"You're the only one who can take away her guilt."

"That's too bad, then, because I'm not going to do it!" He jabbed his finger at Sawyer's chest. "I'm warning you. Leave my mother alone. If you so much as look in her direction, you're going to regret it."

Sawyer gazed at him with hard, unflinching eyes.

Bobby Tom turned on his heel and rushed from the room, breathing so hard he had to stop and compose himself at the top of the stairs. He was right about this; he knew it. Sawyer had hurt his mother and, no matter what, he had to keep that from happening again.

One of his old teammates hailed him, and he found himself drawn back into the crowd that was gathering around the bar. He went from one group to another, slapping backs and trading war stories as if he didn't have a care in the world, but as he greeted old friends, he kept glancing toward the door trying to catch sight of Gracie, needing her to steady him after his encounter with Sawyer. What in the hell was keeping her? He fought back the crazy impulse to run out into the parking lot and look for her.

Out of the corner of his eye, he saw Sawyer standing near the bar talking with Luther, and not long after he spotted his mother on the opposite side of the room chatting with several of her friends. She looked as if she were having a good time, but she was too far away to know for sure. He thought about going with her as soon as the filming was over on that cruise she'd been talking about. He couldn't imagine enjoying a cruise, but he liked being with his mother, and it would be good for her to get away. Gracie could come along, too, so he wouldn't go stir-crazy shut up on a ship, and the three of them would have a great time. The more he thought about it, the more he liked the idea, and he could feel his mood lifting.

It abruptly shattered as he watched his mother's gaze fall on Way Sawyer. Instantly, her eyes filled with sadness and a longing so sharp that he could barely stand to watch. Sawyer turned and saw her, and whatever he'd been about to say to Luther was forgotten. Sawyer's face softened with an emotion that some subconscious part of Bobby Tom knew well, but didn't want to name.

The seconds ticked by. Neither Way nor Suzy moved toward the other. Finally, they turned away in unison, as if they'd reached their tolerance for pain.

22

Gracie stopped just inside the door of the clubhouse's smaller dining room, where the cocktail party was in full swing. As well-built athletes and beautiful women swirled around her, she felt for a moment as if she'd been swept back to the night she'd met Bobby Tom.

Although there was no hot tub in sight, she recognized some of the same people and the atmosphere was just as festive.

Her old navy blue suit added to her sense of déjà vu, and because she'd grown to love her more flattering clothes, it seemed even more dowdy and oversize than it had that night. She'd also donned her sensible black pumps, scrubbed her face free of makeup, and scraped her hair back with a pair of utilitarian bobby pins. For tonight, anyway, she simply hadn't been able to make herself over into Bobby Tom's image of her, no matter how much she'd loved that image. She especially hadn't been able to wear the black cocktail dress she'd planned to dazzle him with. Instead, she'd stripped herself down to the person she'd been before he'd played Pygmalion with her life.

He would never know how difficult it had been for her to show up tonight, and only the fact that she always lived up to her responsibilities had forced her to come. He hadn't seen her yet. He was deep in conversation with a glamorous blond-haired beauty who reminded Gracie of Marilyn Monroe in her heyday. A bit older than Bobby Tom, she wore a spectacular formfitting silver dress slit to midthigh, and Bobby Tom was regarding her with such open affection that Gracie felt her chest grow tight. This was exactly the sort of woman he would marry someday, a woman sprinkled with the same stardust that made him so much larger than life.

The blonde slipped her arm around his waist and rested her cheek against his jacket. As he hugged her in return, Gracie recognized her as Phoebe Calebow, the glamorous owner of the Chicago Stars and Bobby Tom's former boss. She remembered the newspaper photographs of them kissing on the sidelines and wondered why two people so well-matched hadn't ended up together.

At that moment he lifted his head and spotted Gracie. The confusion in his eyes was replaced, almost immediately, by displeasure, and she wanted to shout at him, *This is me, Bobby Tom! This is who I am! An ordinary woman who was foolish enough to have believed she could give something to a man who already has everything.*

Phoebe Calebow raised her head and looked in her direction. Gracie couldn't put it off any longer. Squaring her shoulders, she walked toward them, an ugly duckling approaching two gilded swans.

The male swan scowled, his gilded feathers ruffled. "You're late. Where have you been, and what in the sam hill are you doing dressed like that?"

Gracie ignored him simply because she didn't have the strength to address him directly. Resisting the ugly claws of jealousy that wanted to dig into her flesh, she extended her hand to Phoebe. "I'm Gracie Snow."

She waited for icy hauteur, certain that such a glamorous woman could only feel disdain for someone as dowdy as herself, but she was surprised to see a combination of friendliness and lively curiosity in her eyes instead. "Phoebe Calebow," she said as she returned the handshake. "I'm delighted to meet you, Gracie. I only heard about your engagement last week."

"I'm certain it was a surprise to everyone," Gracie said stiffly, not knowing what to make of this woman who looked like a sex goddess but felt as warm and cozy as Mother Earth.

"I can definitely see your appeal."

Gracie gazed at her sharply, certain she was having a joke at her expense, but Phoebe Calebow seemed absolutely serious. "The twins are going to be devastated. My daughters convinced themselves he'd wait for them to grow up and then somehow marry them both. We have four children," she explained, "including a three-month-old son. I'm still nursing him, so we've brought him along. He's at Suzy's house right now with a sitter."

Bobby Tom looked pained. "I swear, Phoebe, if you start any breast-feeding discussions, I'm walking right out of this room."

Phoebe chuckled and patted his arm. "Welcome to the world of married life. You'll get used to it."

Gracie fought back a mental picture of Bobby Tom's babies, rough-and-tumble little boys who'd be as impossible to resist as their father. She hadn't thought she could feel any more pain, but the idea of Bobby Tom with children who wouldn't be hers brought a fresh wave of misery.

The crowd was beginning to drift to the dining room as a big, good-looking man who appeared to be in his early forties came up behind Phoebe and clasped her shoulders. Speaking in a soft, Southern drawl, he said, "If you want to do some recruiting, honey lamb, this is the place. There are a couple of real good ball players in the crowd tonight who don't seem too happy with their team owner."

Phoebe grew instantly alert. At the same time, she tilted her head and gazed up at the man behind her with such tenderness that Gracie wanted to weep. Bobby Tom sometimes looked at her like that, but it didn't mean the same thing.

"Gracie, this is my husband, Dan Calebow. He used to be Bobby Tom's coach. Dan, Gracie Snow."

Calebow smiled. "Pleased to meet you, Miss Snow. This sure is a nice affair." He turned to Bobby Tom. "Somebody said your fiancée is here, Mr. Movie Star. I can't believe you finally decided to get married. When am I going to get to meet her?"

Phoebe touched his hand. "Gracie is Bobby Tom's fiancée."

Calebow quickly concealed his surprise. "Well, now, this is a treat. And you look like such a nice lady, too. My condolences, ma'am." His attempts to cover his gaffe with humor didn't quite ease the tension. Gracie was normally good at making light conversation, even in awkward situations, but she felt as if her tongue had stuck to the roof of her mouth, and she stood before the three of them, dull, drab, and silent.

Bobby Tom finally spoke. "If you'll excuse us for a minute, Gracie and I need to have a few words with each other."

Phoebe waved them off. "Go ahead. I want to do some recruiting before everybody's in their seats."

Bobby Tom grasped Gracie's arm and began pulling her away from the dining room for what she was certain he intended to be a blistering lecture, but before he could get her alone, a large, dark-haired man with a meat-hook nose and delicate mouth grabbed him. "You've been holding out on me, B.T. I hear you're getting married. Where's the lucky lady?"

Bobby Tom gritted his teeth. "This is the lucky lady."

This man wasn't nearly as skillful at hiding his feelings as Dan Calebow had been, and he was clearly shocked. Gracie felt Bobby Tom slide his arm around her shoulders, and, if she hadn't known him better, she would almost have thought the gesture was protective.

"Gracie, this is Jim Biederot. He was the Stars' quarterback for a lot of years, and the two of us played some good ball together."

Biederot's discomfort was obvious. "Nice to meet you, Gracie."

Luther popped up at between them, sparing Gracie the need to reply. "Pastor Frank is about to give the invocation. Come on, you two."

Gracie could feel Bobby Tom's frustration as Luther pulled them toward the dining room. "We'll talk about this later," he warned her under his breath. "Don't think we won't."

To Gracie, the dinner felt as if it dragged on for hours, although everyone else seemed to be having a good time. The guests began table-hopping not long after the main course was served, and she knew that she had become one of the chief topics of conversation. She was certain none of his friends could fathom why he'd tied himself to such a drab little sparrow, especially one who seemed to have lost the power of speech.

Although Bobby Tom didn't show it, she'd obviously embarrassed him, and he would never believe she hadn't done it deliberately. Even now she didn't want to hurt him. He couldn't help being what he was, just as she couldn't, which was why she hadn't been able to put on her stylish clothes and pretty makeup tonight.

The people of Telarosa acted both insulted and puzzled by her appearance and her silence. It was as if she'd shown up drunk instead of simply wearing bad clothes. Suzy wanted to know if she was ill, Toolee Chandler followed her to the rest room and asked if she'd lost her mind showing up looking like that, and Terry Jo met her on the way out to scold her for embarrassing Bobby Tom.

Gracie couldn't take any more. "Bobby Tom and I are no longer engaged."

Terry Jo's lips parted in surprise. "But, Gracie, that's not right. It's obvious to everybody how much you two love each other."

This was suddenly more than she could bear. Without a word, she turned away and fled from the building.

A little over an hour later, she heard the thud of boots taking the stairs outside her apartment two at a time, and then a hard fist connecting with her door. Still dressed in her white blouse and navy skirt, she had been sitting in her darkened bedroom trying to come to terms with her future. She got up from the chair, turned on a light, and passed a weary hand back through her hair, which was freed now from its bobby pins. Trying to compose herself, she walked through the living room and opened the door.

After all this time, she still had to catch her breath at the sight of him, always larger than life, standing on the landing and filling up the empty space with his presence. The diamond studs in the front of his lavender shirt glittered like distant planets, and he had never seemed so far removed from her own earthbound existence.

She had expected his anger, but not his concern. He took off his hat as he came inside. "What's wrong, honey? Are you sick?"

Some ignoble, cowardly part of her wanted to say yes, but she was made of sterner stuff and she shook her head.

He pulled the door shut with a hard thud and turned to confront her. "Then you'd better tell me what you thought you were doing tonight. You show up looking like hell and stand around like somebody's cut out your tongue. Then you put the icing on the cake by telling Terry Jo we aren't engaged anymore! Everybody in town knows it by now."

She didn't want to fight with him. She just wanted to leave this town and find a quiet place where she could lick her wounds. How could she make him understand that she would have given him anything he'd asked of her, but only if she could have given it for free?

He glared at her, all his sunny charm replaced by a crackling anger. "I'm not going to play twenty questions with you, Gracie. I just walked out on a lot of people who are doing me a big favor, and I want to know why you picked tonight to embarrass me."

"I found out today that you're the one who's been paying my salary."

The first hint of wariness appeared in his eyes. "So what?"

The fact that he would even attempt to dismiss this as unimportant showed how little he understood her and made the pain sharper. How could she have believed, even for a moment, that he loved her? "You lied to me!"

"I don't recall ever remarking on who your employer was one way or the other."

"Don't play games with me! You know how I feel about taking money from you, but you did this anyway."

"You were working for me. You earned it."

"There wasn't any job, Bobby Tom! I had to look for things to do."

"That's crazy. You've been working all

430

kinds of hours getting ready for this golf tournament."

"That's only been for the last few days. What about all the time before then? I was getting paid for doing nothing!"

He tossed his hat on the nearest chair. "That's not true, and I don't know why you're making such a big deal out of this. They were going to fire you, and, no matter what you say, I needed somebody to work for me. It's that simple."

"If it's that simple, why didn't you ask me to work for you straight out?"

He shrugged and headed behind the open counter into the kitchenette situated at the end of the living room. "You got any Alka-Seltzer?"

"Because you knew I'd say no."

"This is a ridiculous conversation. Willow was going to fire you and it was my fault." He opened the cupboard over the sink.

"So you hired me out of pity because you thought I was too incompetent to take care of myself."

"That wasn't it at all. Stop twisting my words!" He abandoned his search of the cupboard. "I'm trying to keep an open mind about this, but I don't see the problem."

"You knew how important this was to me, and you didn't even care."

It was as if she hadn't spoken. He walked back around the counter into the living room, stripping off his jacket as he talked. "Maybe it's just as well all this has come out. I've been thinking it over, and this is probably as good a time as any for us to make a more permanent arrangement." He tossed his jacket over a chair. "We're leaving for L.A. in a couple of weeks, and I've decided to hire you as my full-time assistant at triple what you're making now. And don't start acting like you won't be earning your paycheck. I'm not going to have time to attend to all my business while I'm spending ten hours a day on a soundstage."

"I can't do that."

"Matter of fact, I want you to go out there a couple of days early and find us a place to live." He sat down on the couch and propped his boots up on the coffee table. "I think a pool'd be nice, don't you, and look for someplace with a good view. Buy yourself a car, while you're at it; we'll need another one."

"Don't do this, Bobby Tom."

"And you've got to have some more clothes, so I'll set up an expense account. No more outlet stores, Gracie. You go right over to Rodeo Drive and buy the best."

"I'm not going to L.A. with you!"

He tugged his shirt from the waistband of his pants and began opening the studs. "This foundation idea of yours—I'm not nearly ready to make a commitment because I still think the whole thing's crazy, but I'll let you play around with it and see what you come up with." He dropped his feet to the floor and rose from the couch, his shirt falling away from his bare chest. "I've got to be up at five tomorrow, sweetheart, so unless you want to see me make a fool of myself on the golf course, we'd better head for the bedroom right now." Closing the distance between them, he began working at the buttons on her blouse.

"You're not hearing anything I'm saying." She tried to step away, but he held her firmly.

"That's because you talk too much." He lowered the zipper on the side of her skirt and dragged her into the bedroom.

"I'm not going to L.A."

"Sure you are." He nearly upended her as he pulled off her shoes, tossed the skirt to the side, and tugged down her panty hose. She stood before him in her panties, bra, and open blouse.

"Please, Bobby Tom. Listen."

His eyes skimmed over her. "Please me. That's what you said you wanted to do, isn't it?" His hands went to his own zipper, and he lowered it.

"Yes, but—"

He grabbed her arm. "No more talk, Gracie." Still fully dressed, but with his shirt and pants open, he pushed her down on the bed and fell on her.

A flutter of uneasiness passed through her as he shoved a hard knee between her thighs. "Wait!"

"There's no reason to wait." His hands yanked at her panties and his weight pinioned her while he stripped them away. She felt his knuckles dig into her pubic bone as he freed himself.

"I don't like this!" she cried.

"Give me a minute, and you will."

He was using sex to avoid talking to her, and she hated it. "I said I don't like it! Get off me."

"All right." Imprisoning her in his arms, he rolled her so she was on top of him, but he held her bottom so tightly and pushed so insistently against her, that she felt no freer.

"No!"

"Make up your mind." He rolled her beneath him again.

"Stop it!"

"You don't want me to stop, and you know it." His powerful chest pressed her to the mattress while he caught her behind the knees and shoved them apart, leaving her open and vulnerable. As she felt his fingers probe her, she balled her hand into a fist and slugged him in the back of the head as hard as she could.

"Ow!" He gave a yelp of pain and rolled off her, cradling his head with his hand. "Why'd you go and do that?" he cried indignantly.

"You *ass!*" She went after him, her fists flying despite the pain in her hand. As he lay on the bed, she swung at everything she could reach. He held up his arms to ward off her blows, yelping as a few of them landed on a tender spot, but not trying to restrain her.

"Stop it! That hurts, dammit! *Ouch!* What's wrong with you?"

"Damn you!" Her hands were throbbing with pain. She took one last swing at him and settled back on her heels. Her chest heaved as she clutched her blouse closed. His physical aggression hadn't been about sex, it had been about power, and at that moment she hated him for it.

He lifted his arms away from his head and gazed at her warily.

She threw herself from the bed and fumbled for the robe hanging on the back of the door. Her hands were aching so badly she had difficulty putting it on.

"Maybe we'd better talk about this, Gracie."

"Get out of here."

She heard the mattress creak and the sound of his footsteps as he left the room. Cradling her throbbing hands in her lap, she sagged down on the side of the bed, stifling a sob. It was finally over between them. She'd known today that it had to happen, but she'd never imagined it would end so bitterly.

She tensed as she heard him come back into the room. "I told you to leave."

He pressed something cold between her hands, ice cubes wrapped in a dishtowel. His voice sounded thready and slightly hoarse, as if he were pushing it through some tight, polluted place. "This should keep them from swelling up."

She stared down at the ice pack because she couldn't look at him. Her love for him had always felt like something warm and good, but now it felt oppressive. "Please go."

His voice was barely a whisper. "I never did anything like that to a woman in my life. Gracie, I'm sorry. I'd do anything in the world to take back what just happened." The mattress sagged next to her. "I couldn't stand

435

to hear you say you weren't going with me, and I had to make you stop talking. Why are you doing this, Gracie? We've had a real good time together. We're friends. There's no reason for it to stop just because of a misunderstanding."

She finally allowed herself to look at him and was struck by the unhappiness in his eyes. "It's a lot more than a misunderstanding," she whispered. "I can't be with you any longer."

"Of course you can. We'll have a lot of fun in L.A. And as soon as the picture's over, I've been thinking we should take my mom on a cruise."

At that moment she knew she had to be honest with him. She needed to find the courage to speak what was in her heart, not because she thought it would change anything, but because she would never be able to heal if she didn't do this. Meeting his eyes, she spoke the most difficult words she'd ever had to utter. "I love you, Bobby Tom. I've loved you almost from the beginning."

He didn't look surprised by her admission, and his casual acceptance was another knife wound. She realized he'd known the way she felt all along, and contrary to her fantasies, he hadn't reciprocated at all.

He brushed his thumb over her cheek. "It's all right, honey. I've had experience with this before, and we can work it out."

Her voice was a dry rasp. "Experience with what?"

"With this."

"With women telling you they love you?"

"Heck, Gracie, it's just one of those things. It doesn't mean we can't be friends. We are friends. You might be just about the best friend I ever had."

He was driving nails into her, and he didn't even know it.

"See, Gracie, it doesn't have to spoil anything. Something I've learned over the years is that, as long as everybody's polite about it, there isn't any need for all kind of big scenes and carrying on. People can still be friends."

The corners of the ice cubes dug into her throbbing hands. "You're still friends with all the other women who've told you they loved you?"

"Almost all of them. And I want to stay that way with you. Now, I don't really think we have to talk about it anymore. We'll just go on the way we were, and everything'll work out. You'll see."

The declaration of love that was so shattering to her was nothing more than a social embarrassment to him. If she'd needed any more proof of how little she meant to him, she'd just received it, and she felt numb and humiliated. "You still think I'm going to take the job you're offering?"

"You'd be crazy not to."

"You don't understand anything, do you?" Her eyes brimmed with tears.

"Now, Gracie—"

"I'm not taking the job," she said softly. "On Monday I'm leaving to go back to New Grundy."

"You don't like the salary? Fine. We'll negotiate."

"For all your talk, you don't know the first thing about love." Tears spilled over her lashes and rolled down her cheeks. She slipped the chain that held his Super Bowl ring over her head and pressed it into his palm. "I love you, Bobby Tom, and I'll love you till the day I die. But I've never been for sale. I was a free offering all along."

Bobby Tom strode across the yard at a slow, even pace. Halfway over he stopped to admire the moon, just in case Gracie was watching him from the window, but he didn't take as long about it as he wanted because he was having trouble breathing. He resumed his course toward the back door, forcing himself not to pick up his pace. He even tried to whistle, but his mouth was too dry. The ring in his pocket felt as if it were burning a hole through his hip; he wanted to pull the damned thing out and throw it as far from him as he could.

When he got inside the house, he closed the door then leaned against it, squeezing his eyes shut. He'd blown it, and he didn't even know how. Dammit! He was the one who did the rejecting. He was the one who decided when it was time to end a relationship! But she didn't understand that. She'd never understood the simplest things. What kind of fool would refuse the opportunity of a lifetime just to go back to some podunk town and empty bedpans?

He pushed himself away from the door and stalked through the kitchen. He wasn't going to feel guilty about this. Gracie was the one who'd done the rejecting, and this was on her conscience, not his. So she loved him. Of course, she loved him; he couldn't help who he was. But had she ever stopped to think for a minute about how he felt? The fact that he cared about her hadn't seemed to enter her mind. She thought she was so sensitive, but she didn't have a single qualm about stomping all over his feelings. She was the best friend he'd ever had, but she hadn't bothered to think about that.

The bedroom door banged against the wall as he pushed through it. Dammit! If Gracie figured she was going to send him into a tailspin by walking out on him, she could think again because he wasn't going to take this from her. She'd said she wasn't leaving until Monday, and he knew she'd be at the hoedown tomorrow night because she was running the Arbor Hills quilt lottery, and she always fulfilled her responsibilities. Well, he'd be ready for her.

Before he went to bed tonight, he was going to call Bruno and have him fly in an army of his old girlfriends. Tomorrow night at the hoedown, he intended to keep himself surrounded by beautiful women. Let Gracie Snow see exactly what she was walking away from. When she had to sit on the sidelines like some damned wallflower and watch all those sex trophies hanging on him, she'd come to her senses. A dose of reality was exactly what she needed. Before he knew it, she'd be trying to catch his attention so she could tell him she'd reconsidered. And because he loved her like a friend, he wouldn't even make her grovel.

He stared bleakly down at his empty bed. Tomorrow night she'd learn her lesson. Damned straight she would. She'd learn that no woman in her right mind *ever* walked away from Bobby Tom Denton!

23

Thanks to Gracie's stubbornness, Bobby Tom played the worst round of golf of his life— and in his own damned tournament, too. As a result, he was forced to endure endless ribbing by his friends, their baiting tempered only by the news of his broken engagement.

That night, when he arrived at the hoedown, he felt so worn down he could barely hold up his end of the conversation with the sex trophies Bruno had sent from Chicago. Amber made a point of telling him she was considering a career as a microbiologist when she got bored with exotic dancing; Charmaine announced she was a Leo born under the House of the International Pancake, or some such bullshit, and Payton was hinting around to take the freakin' football quiz! Bobby Tom wanted to dump all three of them on Troy Aikman, but he needed them nearby if he was going to bring Gracie to her senses.

To give Bruno credit, the women were stunners, but Bobby Tom couldn't work up a speck of interest in any one of them. They were wearing their own versions of authentic Western dress: Amber in shrink-wrapped jeans and a bandanna top with a sheriff's badge nestled in her cleavage, Payton in a saloon girl's costume cut down to her navel, and Charmaine in a cowgirl skirt made entirely out of fringe. When he caught a glimpse of Gracie dressed in the same prim yellow gingham outfit she'd worn to the birthplace dedication yesterday morning, he couldn't help think she looked better than all three of them put together, an observation that did nothing to improve his mood.

The hoedown was being held at a ranch several miles out of town, and it was a semiprivate affair for the participants in the golf tournament, the *Blood Moon* people, and the Heavenfest committee members, which made up a large portion of the town. At Bobby Tom's insistence, the gathering had been closed to tourists so the celebrities could have a real party without being hounded to death for autographs, something all the locals had been forbidden to do. The only formal event of the evening was a presentation ceremony where Bobby Tom would recognize the winners of the golf tournament. The tourists, in the meantime, hadn't been forgotten, and the locals would be coming and going throughout the evening to make certain the events in town were running smoothly: the amusement park rides at the rodeo arena, the country and western bands, the food concessions.

The trees around the ranch house had been strung with colorful lights, and a temporary dance floor had been erected near the barn, along with a small, bunting-draped platform for the presentation ceremony. Once again, Bobby Tom's gaze made its way to the table off to the side of the dance floor, where Gracie was selling raffle tickets for the patchwork quilt handmade by the Arbor Hills residents, and the sight of her filled him with such a painful rush of emotion he quickly looked away.

"Hey, B.T., you seemed to have had a little trouble on the back nine today." Buddy ambled up with Terry Jo at his side, both of them in jeans and Western shirts, holding plastic cups of beer in their hands.

"The front nine, too," Terry Jo said, shooting a malevolent look at the sex trophies and then eyeing Bobby Tom. "Entertain B.T.'s love children for a minute, will you, Buddy? Me and Mr. Hotshot need to have us a talk."

The last thing Bobby Tom wanted at that moment was a private conversation with Terry Jo, but she didn't give him much choice as she grabbed his arm and pulled him away from the others toward the fence. "What the hell is wrong with you?" she demanded, the minute they were out of earshot. "You know what you're doing to Gracie, don't you, breaking your engagement like that?"

He regarded her indignantly. "Did she say I broke our engagement?"

"She didn't say hardly anything when I talked to her this morning, just that the two of you reached a mutual decision to end your relationship."

"And you assumed that meant I ended it."

"Didn't you?"

"Hell, no."

"Are you saying Gracie dumped you?"

He saw too late the trap he'd laid for himself. "'Course not. Nobody dumps me."

"She did, didn't she? She dumped you! Holy Moses! A person of the female species finally gave Bobby Tom Denton back a little bit of what he's been giving out." Grinning widely, she lifted her face to the heavens. "Thank you, Jesus!"

"Will you stop that! She didn't dump me. Haven't you figured out by now that we were never really engaged! It was just a ploy to keep everybody off my back while I was in town." The fact that Terry Jo was making a joke out of this hurt in a way he couldn't express.

"Of course you were engaged. A blind fool could see the two of you love each other."

"We do not! Well, maybe she loves me, but...I care about her. Who wouldn't? She's about the best kind of woman there is. But, love? She's not my type, Terry Jo."

Terry Jo gave him a long, steady gaze. "It's amazing. You don't know any more about women now than you did in high school when you threw me over for Sherri Hopper." She regarded him sadly. "When are you going to grow up, Bobby Tom?"

Without another word, she walked away from

him. He stared at her back with a combination of resentment and misery. Why did she act like this was his fault? And when had his life gotten so screwed up? Until recently he'd thought it was the day he blew out his knee, but now he wondered if the real catastrophe hadn't struck the night Gracie showed up at his house with her striptease.

Natalie walked up to him with Anton, who was carrying Elvis. As he greeted them, he thought what a beautiful woman she was. Nice, too. He'd seen her buck naked, kissed her for hours on end. She'd leaked on him, wrestled with him, shot at him, and just yesterday they'd had to jump in the river together. He and Natalie had been through a lot, but he didn't feel close to her, not even half as close as he felt to Gracie.

The three of them chatted for a couple of minutes, and the next thing he knew he was holding Elvis so his parents could dance. The baby grabbed for the brim of his Stetson, and when he couldn't reach that, settled for sucking on one end of the black silk scarf Bobby Tom had tied around his neck. Although he'd always been particular about his clothes, he couldn't work up enough energy to rescue it. The baby smelled sweet and clean, and he felt a queer ache deep inside.

The sex trophies were coming toward him, but he pretended he didn't see them and ducked behind one of the outbuildings just so he could have a few minutes to pull himself back together. Elvis started sucking on his shirt collar. As he emerged near one of the food tables, he saw his mother standing about ten yards away. She was dressed in a long dark skirt and a prim white schoolmarm's blouse fastened at the neck with his grandmother's old cameo brooch. He stiffened as he watched Way Sawyer approach her. At the same time he noted that Way looked like the real thing in faded jeans, a beat-up hat, old boots, and a flannel shirt.

His mother acted as if she were about to jump out of her skin when she saw Sawyer. He put his hand on her shoulder, and Bobby Tom tensed, ready to spring to her aid until he noticed that her whole body had gone slack. For a moment, he had the sickening feeling she was going to lean against Sawyer, but then her back stiffened, and she walked away.

Way stood there without moving. When he finally turned, Bobby Tom saw such raw despair on his face that he knew he would never forget it. He tightened his hold on the baby and felt himself start to sweat. What was wrong with him? Why did he feel as if he and Way Sawyer were suddenly brothers?

"You're breaking Bobby Tom's heart," Terry Jo hissed, as she drew Gracie from the table where she'd been selling raffle tickets and continued the lecture that had begun some minutes earlier. "How can you walk away from him like this?"

Although Gracie was seldom sarcastic, the three willowy blondes who were once again hanging on Bobby Tom's arm had breached her defenses. "He certainly looks heart-broken."

"He doesn't care about those bimbos, and you know it. He cares about you."

"Caring is a long way from loving." She watched as one of the beauties tipped her beer cup to his lips. She didn't know which was more painful: watching him earlier when he had been holding Elvis or seeing him now with those incredible women. "It just hurts too much to stay around him any longer."

Terry Jo showed no sympathy. "Anything worth having is worth fighting for. I thought you had more grit than this, but I keep forgetting you're a Yankee."

"I don't understand why you're so out-raged. Everybody's been telling me from the day I got here that I'm not his type."

"That's true. But it's like Bobby Tom kept saying, 'There's no accounting for the mysteries of the human heart.'"

"He was putting people on when he said that! Surely you know that most of what comes out of his mouth is a complete fabrication."

Terry Jo got huffy. "It is not. Bobby Tom Denton is one of the most sincere people I've ever met."

"Ha!"

"For somebody who's in love with him, you sure are critical."

"Just because I love him doesn't mean I'm blind." She drew away. "I've got to get back to the table."

"No, you don't. Suzy's bridge club is taking over for the rest of the evening. You get out there and have a good time. Show him he can't manipulate you like this because that's what he's doing, and everybody knows it."

As if Terry Jo had commanded it, Ray Bevins, one of the cameramen from *Blood Moon*, appeared at Gracie's side. "I've been waiting all evening for you to finish up so we could dance, Gracie."

Gracie ignored Terry Jo's encouraging smile. "I'm sorry, Ray, but I'm not feeling too much like dancing tonight."

"Yeah, I heard you and Bobby Tom broke up. Seems like he's doing his best to make you jealous."

"He's just being himself."

"You shouldn't let him manipulate you like that. All the guys on the crew like Bobby Tom, but I guess it's no secret that some of us have more than a friendly interest in you. We flipped to see who got to dance with you first, and I won."

She gave him a grateful smile. "Thank you, but, to be honest, I just don't have the heart for it." Before either Ray or Terry Jo could press her, she slipped away from them into the crowd. It was nice to know some of the men found her desirable, but she simply didn't have the ability to be sociable tonight.

She slumped down in a seat at the wooden picnic table where Natalie and Anton had parked all of Elvis's gear. Only after she was settled did she realize that her position gave her a clear view of Bobby Tom standing in the middle of a herd of women. He looked as if he were having the time of his life, laughing and carrying on, obviously enjoying the fact that he was now a free man. One of the women hand-fed him taco chips, while another rubbed up against his arm. Almost as if he could feel Gracie watching, he lifted his head and turned, letting his gaze sweep over her. Their eyes locked, and for a moment neither of them moved. Then he smiled at the woman standing beside him. As Gracie watched, he dropped his head and gave her a slow, deliberate kiss.

If he'd wanted to cause her additional pain, he couldn't have found a better way. He cupped the back of the woman's head in his hand, and as he deepened the kiss, she remembered exactly the way it felt. *I own that mouth!* she wanted to cry out.

Several athletes she recognized from the dinner last night approached him, and before long he was entertaining them with what must have been a very funny story, judging by their reactions. At the same time, he kept his arms draped around two of the women. She knew better than anyone how charming he could be, and it wasn't long before a small crowd gathered to listen to him.

"Toolee Chandler told me if I bought ten raffle tickets, she'd throw in a dance with you." Her head shot up, and she saw Way Sawyer standing next to her, a fan of raffle tickets in his hand.

She smiled. "I appreciate the support, but I don't feel much like dancing."

He extended his hand and drew her to her feet. "Come on, Gracie. You look like a whipped puppy."

"I'm not very good at hiding my feelings."

"That's not exactly big news." He looped an arm around her shoulders, and, to her shock, planted a kiss square on her mouth. She was so surprised she was speechless.

"That," he grinned, "is going to drive Bobby Tom Denton right over the edge."

Firmly taking command, he drew her onto the dance floor. The band was playing a ballad, and he pulled her close to his chest, where she felt so comfortable she wanted to close her eyes and rest her head.

"You're a nice man," she said. "I knew it all along."

"Even before I made the announcement about Rosatech?"

"I never for a minute thought you'd close it. All anyone had to do was look at you and they could have figured that out."

His chest rumbled with a low chuckle. They danced for a while in silence, and then she felt an almost imperceptible tensing of his muscles. She followed the direction of his gaze and saw Suzy pass by, dancing with Buddy Baines. She gazed up at him and saw how sad he looked.

"Bobby Tom's not being deliberately cruel, you know," she said softly. "He's very protective of her. Sooner or later he's going to come to his senses."

"You do have an optimistic view of human nature." He steered them to another part of the dance floor, changing the subject at the same time. "People are going to be sorry to see you leave. You've done more good in this town in a short time than most of them have done in their lives."

She was genuinely astonished. "I haven't done anything."

"Is that so? Let me see if I've got this right. You've formed a volunteer organization to improve the facilities at Arbor Hill as well as set up a recreational program there. It was your idea to establish a senior citizens center. I also hear that you've spent a lot of time at Arbor Hills just visiting with some lonely people. I guess, in my mind, that counts for a lot more than somebody who hasn't done any more with his life than win football games."

She started to protest. Bobby Tom gave to others in countless ways, both money and his time. But then she stopped herself. Mr. Sawyer wasn't talking about Bobby Tom; he was talking about her. And he was right.

When had she gotten into the habit of viewing her own accomplishments as being so much less important than anyone else's? Was seeing to the comfort of the elderly of less value than being blessed with good looks and natural charm? She felt oddly disoriented. It was as if a door she hadn't even known existed had swung open, giving her a fresh look at herself, a look that was suddenly uncluttered by the emotional baggage she'd carried around all her life. She had friends, people who cared about her, and she did her best to live her life by the Golden Rule.

But she had grown so used to being satisfied with very little. From the day she'd met Bobby Tom, she'd felt lucky to receive whatever small crumbs of affection he'd deigned to toss her way. But that wasn't how it should be. She was worthy of something more than another person's emotional leftovers.

The dance came to an end, and a terrible sadness swept over her. There was nothing wrong with her at all. She was the best person she knew how to be, and she was more than worthy of Bobby Tom Denton's love. But he would never understand that, just as he would never understand the value of what he was throwing away.

Bobby Tom palmed the sex trophies off on a couple of the Phoenix Suns so he could talk to his mother. "I believe you've been saving this dance for me."

"I'm sure I have it somewhere on my dance card." Suzy smiled as he took her hand, and they walked out onto the wooden floor together.

They were both good dancers—he'd learned how from her—and for a while they moved without talking in the rhythm of the two-step, but he didn't enjoy it as he normally would have. Gracie hadn't stopped dancing with one man or another since Way Sawyer had kissed her. His jaw clenched at the memory.

Although it was difficult, he forced himself to set aside his own unhappiness for the moment and do what he should have done as soon as he got back from San Antone, what he'd secretly known he had to do last night when he'd seen how his mom and Sawyer had looked at each other at the country club.

"Mom, we've got to talk about what's happening with you, and this time I'm not going to let you put me off with gardening tips and cruise brochures."

Her spine stiffened under his hand. "There's nothing to talk about."

"You know, don't you, that I miss him, too."

"I know. He loved you so much."

"He was a great father."

She lifted one eyebrow as she looked up at him. "Do you realize by the time he was your age, he already had a fourteen-year-old son?"

"Uhmm."

Her forehead creased in a frown. "What happened with you and Gracie? And why did you bring those dreadful women tonight?"

"Nothing happened. You know all that engagement stuff was phony, so don't act as if the fact that we're splitting up is some big tragedy."

"I got used to thinking of the two of you as a couple. I guess I'd started to believe you really were getting married."

He gave a snort to cover his discomfort. "Mom, can you honestly see Gracie and me married?"

"Oh, yes, I can see it quite easily. I admit I couldn't at first, but after I got to know Gracie, I thought she was perfect for you, especially when I saw how happy she made you."

"That wasn't happiness. I was just laughing at her, is all, because half the time she's so ridiculous."

She looked at him, slowly shook her head, then rested her cheek against his chest for a moment. "I worry about you, sweetie pie. I really do."

"Well, I worry about you, too, so we're even." On the other side of the dance floor, he saw Gracie glide by with Dan Calebow. His former coach seemed to be having a wonderful time. Dan's wife Phoebe, in the meantime, was dancing with Luther Baines, who was trying hard to keep his eyes off her bust line. "Mom, we've got to talk about this thing with you and Sawyer."

"His name is Wayland. And there isn't any 'thing' to talk about."

"That's not what he tells me."

Her eyes flashed. "Did he talk to you? He had no right to do that."

"He wants me to play Cupid and get the two of you together."

"I can't believe he talked to you."

"The two of us rub each other wrong, so it wasn't the pleasantest conversation I've ever had. Still, I'm not the one who fell in love with him, so I guess that doesn't matter."

He waited for her to deny what he'd just said.

He prayed her forehead would crinkle and she'd get indignant, but, instead, she turned her head away. "He had no right to involve you."

His mother loved someone else. As the knowledge hit him, he waited for a rush of anger, but to his surprise, it didn't hurt nearly as much as he'd thought it would.

He tried to pick his words carefully. "What if you were the one who died, Mom? And what if four years after you'd died Dad met somebody he cared a lot about, somebody who'd make him stop being so lonely all the time." After avoiding this conversation for so long, it somehow finally felt right to be talking about it, and he had the queer sense that Gracie was holding his hand. "And what if he did the same thing you're doing and shoved this person out of his life because of the way he felt about you. What would you want me to say to him?"

"It's not the same thing."

He heard the agitation in her voice and knew he was upsetting her, but he kept on. "Oh, it's exactly the same thing."

"You haven't been through this! You don't understand."

"That's right. I'm just imagining what I'd say to him, is all. I guess you'd want me to tell him to stay lonely for the rest of his life. To do what you're doing and turn his back on this new person he'd grown to care about so he could spend the rest of his life lighting candles to your memory."

"I don't understand why you're pressing me

on this! You don't even like Wayland. You admitted it."

"No, I don't, but I'll tell you this—I sure as hell respect the sonovabitch."

"Don't be vulgar," she said automatically. And then her eyes filled with tears. "Bobby Tom, I can't. Your father and I..."

"I know how you felt about each other, Mom. I saw it every day. Maybe that's why I've never had much interest in getting married myself. Because I've always wanted the same thing."

Gracie danced past in his peripheral vision, and at that exact moment, the fact that he could have the same thing his parents had had all those years hit him so hard he nearly stumbled. *Jesus.* As he held his mother in his arms and felt his father's presence, he knew that same intimacy was right here waiting for him on the other side of the dance floor. He loved her. The knowledge almost knocked him to his knees. He loved his Gracie Snow—funny clothes, bossy manner, and all. She was his entertainment, his conscience, the mirror into his soul. She was his resting place. Why hadn't he understood this weeks ago?

He'd grown so used to thinking of his life a certain way that he'd blinded himself to his real needs. He'd actually compared Gracie with the sex trophies and made Gracie the loser because she didn't have big breasts. He'd ignored the undeniable fact that women who existed only to go to parties and look good had bored him for years. He'd overlooked the way gazing at Gracie's pretty gray eyes and fly-away curls made his mouth water. Why had he clung so tenaciously to the idea that those sex trophies were what he wanted? Gracie was right. At his age, he should have learned something about what he needed from life a long time ago. Instead, he'd continued to judge women on the same artificial scale he'd used when he was a hormone-driven adolescent, and it made him ashamed. Gracie's beauty had pleased his eye from the beginning. It was real and bone deep, fed by her innate goodness. It was the kind of soul-nourished beauty that would still be with her when she was an old lady.

He loved Gracie Snow, and he was going to marry her. He was going to marry her for real, dammit! He wanted to spend the rest of his life with her, to fill her belly with his babies and fill their house with his love. Instead of scaring him, the idea of spending the rest of his life with her sent such a rush of joy through him that he felt as if he were rising up off the dance floor. He wanted to pull her out of Dan Calebow's arms that very minute and tell her he loved her. He wanted to see her melt in front of his eyes. But he couldn't do any of that until he'd tried to set things right with his mother.

He looked down at her. His chest felt tight, and his voice didn't sound quite normal. "All this time I've been acting like my aversion to Way was personal, but the fact is, I know that I'd have gone into orbit no matter who you might have taken up with. I think part of me wanted you to lock yourself away and mourn Dad for the rest of your life just because he was my father and I loved him."

"Oh, sweetheart..."

"Mom, listen to me." He regarded her urgently. "I know one thing as sure as I know my name—Dad would never have wanted me to feel like that, and he wouldn't have wanted you to suffer the way you're suffering, not in a million years. Your love for each other was big and generous, but by turning your back on the future, you're making it seem small."

He heard the quick intake of her breath. "Is that what you think I'm doing?"

"Yes."

"I didn't mean to," she said faintly.

"I know that. Are your feelings for Sawyer going to change the way you felt about Dad?"

"Oh, no. Never."

"Then don't you think it's about time you found your backbone?"

He could almost see her pulling herself taller. "Yes. Yes, I think it is." For a moment she didn't do anything, and then she gave him a fierce hug.

He glanced around and shifted their position on the dance floor. She squeezed his shoulder. "You are the most wonderful son any woman could ever have."

"Let's see if you're still saying that after I embarrass you to death." Letting go of her hand, he reached out to tap Way Sawyer on the shoulder as he and his partner swung by. The

457

older man came to a stop and regarded him quizzically.

Bobby Tom spoke. "Are you going to monopolize Miz Baines all night, Sawyer? She and I have a few things to talk about, don't we, Miz Baines? How 'bout we switch partners?"

Sawyer looked so dumbfounded that, for a moment, Bobby Tom thought he was going to let this golden opportunity slip by. He quickly recovered, however, and nearly knocked over poor Judy Baines in his eagerness to get his hands on Suzy.

Just before she slipped into his arms, Sawyer's gaze met his own, and Bobby Tom couldn't ever remember seeing so much gratitude in another man's eyes. Suzy, in the meantime, had a combination of excitement and panic in her expression.

Bobby Tom took Mrs. Baines's hand. Realizing he loved Gracie had tossed his whole world upside down, and, to his amazement, he found he was actually enjoying himself. He gave Sawyer his best outlaw's squint. "My mother's a respectable woman with a reputation to uphold in the community, so I'll expect you to do right by her. And don't take too long about it, either, because if I hear of any hanky-panky going on before the ceremony, there's going to be some big-time hell to pay."

Sawyer threw back his head and laughed. At the same time, he looped his arm around Suzy's shoulders and swept her right off the dance floor.

Judy Baines craned her neck to watch as they disappeared. She turned to Bobby Tom and clucked her tongue. "I think he's taking her behind the barn."

"Hanky-panky, for sure."

"You gonna do anything about it?"

"Give the bride away, Miz Baines, and hope for the best."

Way and Suzy couldn't stop kissing each other. He had her backed up against the side of the barn with the shirttail of her prim white blouse pulled out and his hand up underneath it. They were both breathing heavily, and Bobby Tom's silly warning had left them with a giddy sense that they were getting away with something.

"I love you, Suzy. I've been waiting for you all my life."

"Oh, Way..."

"Say it, sweetheart. Tell me. I need to hear the words."

"I love you, too. You know I do. I've loved you for a long time. And I need you so very much."

Way kissed her again, then voiced the question that had to be asked. "What about Hoyt? I know how much your marriage meant."

She brought her hand from the back of his neck to cup his jaw. "I'll always love him, you know that, but Bobby Tom made me understand something tonight that I should have been able to figure out a long time ago. Hoyt would want this for me. He'd want *you* for me. I guess

I'll always believe that somehow he gave us his blessing tonight through his son."

Way stroked her cheek. "This has been hard on Bobby Tom. I know the way he felt about his dad." For the first time since he'd started kissing her, he looked troubled. "It's no secret your son doesn't like me, Suzy, but I promise you that I'm going to do my best to change that."

She smiled. "He likes you a lot; he just hasn't figured it out yet. Believe me, the two of you are going to get along fine. He would never have turned me over to you if he hadn't already made up his mind about that."

He looked relieved, then he began taking tiny nips out of her bottom lip. At the same time, his thumb found her nipple. "Sweetheart, we've got to get out of here."

She drew back and gave him a mischievous grin. "Bobby Tom said you were supposed to treat me with respect."

"I am. First I'm going to get you naked, then I'm going to treat you with respect."

She pretended to think it over. "I don't know if we should. He was awfully intimidating."

He groaned. "It could take a couple of weeks for us to put a wedding ceremony together, and there's no way I can wait that long to touch you. Your son can just learn right now to respect the needs of his elders."

"I couldn't agree more."

Way kissed her once again. When they finally parted, he threw back his head and laughed. The biggest hood at Telarosa High had finally won the heart of the prettiest girl in the sophomore class.

As Bobby Tom leaped up on the platform to recognize the golf tournament winners, he was halfway giddy he felt so good. High on love and the realization that life held more for him than football, he had just decided exactly how he was going to go about letting Gracie know that everything had changed. Making the grand gesture had always appealed to him, and he intended to give his future wife a marriage proposal she'd never forget.

Gracie, in the meantime, was counting the minutes until the agonizing night would be over. She tried to find some sort of peace in accepting the knowledge that she would never again let herself be satisfied with less than she deserved, but nothing could ease her heartbreak.

Terry Jo had refused to handle the drawing for the quilt raffle, so she found herself on the platform, standing as far away from Bobby Tom as she could get. While Luther thanked the athletes for participating, she looked out over the crowd. Willow and the rest of the *Blood Moon* people stood in a group, Elvis had fallen asleep in Natalie's arms, and Buddy and Terry Jo were standing with Jim Biederot, Bobby Tom's old teammate, and the Calebows.

A number of Bobby Tom's athlete friends had danced with her this evening, and most of them had been amused by her ignorance of who they were rather than being annoyed. Unfortunately, she had discovered that they had somehow learned she was the one who had broken off with Bobby Tom, instead of the other way around. Women would have been sympathetic if they heard their friend had been dumped, but Bobby Tom's friends seemed to think this was unbelievably funny, and she was certain they'd been ribbing him about it all evening. She knew what kind of blow this would be to his pride, and a vague sense of apprehension settled around her pain.

Luther picked up the glass fishbowl containing the stubs of the raffle tickets that she'd given him earlier and gestured for her to approach. "Before Bobby Tom recognizes our guests tonight, we're going to draw for the beautiful quilt the folks at Arbor Hills Nursing Home are raffling off. Most of you folks know Gracie Snow. We sure are going to miss her after she leaves and let's give her a big round of applause for all the hard work she's done."

Enthusiastic applause broke out, accompanied by some loud whistles. She reached into the fishbowl to draw out the winner.

"Number one-three-seven."

The ticket, as it turned out, was the one the crew members had bought for Elvis, who awakened as his mother brought him forward. Gracie handed over the quilt to Natalie and gave the winner a special hug and kiss, realizing, as she did, how much she was going to miss this sweet-tempered baby. With the drawing completed, she tried to step down off the platform only to discover that Luther was in the way.

Bobby Tom approached the microphone and launched into a routine that would have done a stand-up comic proud. As he poked fun at his friends' golf games and his own poor score, she thought she'd never seen him more entertaining. His eyes fairly glowed with happiness, and his grin would have done justice to a toothpaste model. She had the dismal thought that he couldn't have found a better way to let the crowd know that he wasn't the one suffering from a broken heart.

He finished recognizing the athletes, and she waited for him to step back from the mike so she could slip away. Instead, he looked over at her. "Before we start the dancing again, I have one more announcement to make…"

A trickle of alarm slithered down her spine.

"Some of you might have heard that Gracie and I broke our engagement. You might also have noticed that she's pretty mad at me right now." Once again his mouth curled in a grin so engaging that it was impossible to imagine anyone other than the world's most unreasonable person ever being upset with him.

She prayed for him to stop. She couldn't bear the idea that he was going to somehow hold up her private misery in front of this crowd for everyone to see, but he continued to talk.

"The thing of it is, there are engagements and then there are engagements, and it turns out Gracie and I were only engaged to be engaged. But now it's time to do this right. Bring

Gracie over here, Luther, because she's still mad at me, and I doubt she's going to come on her own."

She would never forgive him for this, she thought, as Luther gave a hearty chortle and pulled her forward. She looked down at Terry Jo, at Natalie and Toolee Chandler all standing before her in the crowd, wordlessly begging one of them to help her, but they were all smiling. Bobby Tom's friends seemed to be enjoying this, too.

He wrapped his arm around her and gazed down into her stricken face. "Gracie, right here in front of God, the hometown crowd, and all these gym rats that I call my friends, I'm asking you to do me the honor of becoming my wife." He put his palm over the microphone and leaned down to whisper, "I love you, honey, and this time's for real."

An awful shudder ripped through her. She never imagined anything could hurt this badly. The crowd laughed and clapped. These were the people he'd grown up with, the men who were his friends, and there was no way in the world he could tolerate any of them seeing him as a loser. He'd lied when he said he loved her. Lies came easily to him, and to save his reputation, he was willing to destroy her.

Her soft, choked words were for his ears alone. "I can't marry you, Bobby Tom. I deserve something better."

Only as her voice came back to her, amplified by the speakers, did she realize he'd removed his hand from the microphone before she spoke. The laughter of the audience abruptly stopped. There were a few nervous chuckles, and then as people realized she was serious, utter silence.

Bobby Tom's face had gone pale. Stricken, she gazed into his eyes. She hadn't wanted to humiliate him, but the words were spoken and she wouldn't take them back because they were true.

She waited for him to come up with some sort of wisecrack to defuse the situation, but he didn't say anything.

"I'm sorry," she whispered, backing away. "I'm really sorry." She turned and rushed off the platform.

As she pushed through the stunned, silent crowd, she waited to hear his lazy drawl, his endearing chuckle amplified by the microphone for the hometown crowd. In her mind, she could even hear the words he would choose.

Whooee! Now that, folks, is one mad little lady. Bet it's gonna cost me more than a bottle of champagne and a night on the town to get her settled down.

She pushed forward, stumbling once on the hem of her long dress, and then she heard his voice, just as she'd known she would. But instead of the words she had imagined, the loudspeakers crackled with rage and hostility.

"Go on, Gracie! Get out of here! We both know I was just trying to do you a favor. Shit. Why the hell would I want to marry somebody like you? Now get out of here! Get the hell out of my life, and don't ever let me see your face again!"

She was sobbing, humiliated. She plunged blindly forward, not knowing where she was going, not caring, only knowing she had to get away.

A hand closed on her arm, and she saw Ray Bevins, the *Blood Moon* cameraman. "Come on, Gracie. I'll drive you."

The loudspeakers shrieked behind her with the deafening sound of feedback from the microphone.

She ran.

24

Bobby Tom Denton turned out to be a mean drunk. He destroyed most of the interior of the Wagon Wheel, kicked the windows out of a brand-new Pontiac, and broke Len Brown's arm. Bobby Tom had been in fights before, but not with somebody like Len and not with Buddy Baines, who'd only been stealing the keys to Bobby Tom's truck to keep him from driving drunk. Nobody could have imagined a day when the people of Telarosa would be ashamed of their favorite son, but that night they all shook their heads.

When Bobby Tom woke up, he was in jail. He tried to roll over, but it hurt too much to move. His head throbbed and every muscle in his body ached. As he attempted to open his eyes, he realized that one of them was swollen shut. At the same time, his stomach felt like he had a bad case of the flu.

He winced as he slowly lowered his legs over the side of the cot and dragged himself into a sitting position. Even after a particularly brutal game, he'd never felt this bad. Dropping his head into his hands, he let despair wash over him. A lot of people didn't remember what they did when they were drunk, but he remembered every miserable moment. Even worse, he remembered what had led up to it.

How could he have stood up there at that microphone and talked to Gracie like that, no matter how humiliated he'd been by her rejection? The glimpse he'd had of her face as she'd run away would stay with him for the rest of his life. She'd believed every damning word he'd uttered, and the knowledge filled him with shame. At he same time, the echo of her words to him was scalded in his brain.

I can't marry you, Bobby Tom. I deserve something better.

And she did. God help him, she did. She deserved a man, not a boy. She deserved someone who loved her more than he loved his own legend. His *legend.* For the first time in his life, the thought filled him with disgust. Whatever legend he'd had his behavior last night had destroyed, and he didn't even care. All he cared about was getting Gracie back.

He was suddenly overwhelmed by a sense of panic. What if she'd already left town?

Her moral fiber was the toughest thing about her, and now that it was too late, he understood how important her principles were to her. Gracie always meant what she said, and once she'd made up her mind she was right about something, she didn't change it.

She'd said she loved him, and that counted for a lot with her, but by playing fast and loose with her affections and not respecting her feelings, he'd put her in a position where she couldn't back down. When he'd looked into her face last night and heard her say she couldn't marry him, she'd meant every word, and not even a public declaration of his love had been good enough to keep her.

A whole range of alien emotions bombarded him, but the most unfamiliar was desperation. After a lifetime of easy female conquests, he realized he'd lost his confidence. Otherwise, he wouldn't have been so certain that once she got away, he'd never get her back, but now he knew he was going to lose her forever. If he hadn't been able to win her on his home field, how could he hope to earn her love anywhere else?

"Well, well. Seems like the hometown boy got himself in a speck of trouble last night."

He lifted his head and gazed through bleary eyes at Jimbo Thackery, who was standing outside his cell with a nasty smirk on his face.

"I'm not up to trading insults with you right now, Jimbo," he muttered. "What do I have to do to get out of here?"

"The name's Jim."

"Jim, then," he said dully. Maybe it wasn't too late, he thought. Maybe she'd had a chance to think things over, and he could get her to change her mind. He swore before God Almighty that if she'd marry him, he'd buy her her very own nursing home for their first wedding anniversary. Before that, however, he had to find her. Then he had to convince her that he loved her more than he'd ever even thought about loving any other woman. He'd do whatever it took to make her forgive him.

He sat up straight on the edge of the bed. "I have to get out of here."

"Judge Gates hasn't set bond yet," Jimbo said, taking open pleasure in his misery.

He pushed himself painfully to his feet, ignoring the acid churning in his stomach and the fact that his bad knee throbbed like a son of a bitch.

"When will he?"

"Sooner or later." Jimbo pulled a toothpick from his shirt pocket and stuck it in the corner of his mouth. "Judge doesn't like it when I call him too early in the morning."

Bobby Tom could just make out the wall clock on the other side of the bars. "It's almost nine o'clock."

"I'll call him when I get a chance. It's a good thing you're rich because you're facing some serious charges: battery, disorderly conduct, criminal damage to property, resisting arrest. Judge isn't gonna be too happy with you."

Bobby Tom was feeling more desperate by

the second. Every moment he spent behind bars meant Gracie was slipping farther away from him. Why had he behaved like such an ass last night? Why hadn't he swallowed his pride and gone after her right then, gotten down on his knees if he'd had to and told her he was sorry. Instead, he'd wasted all that time acting tough and talking trash so he wouldn't lose face with his buddies, something that had been a hopeless proposition from the beginning after his sickening performance at that microphone. He could no longer even remember why he'd cared so much about their opinion. He enjoyed his friends, but they weren't the ones he wanted to live his life with or bear his children.

He couldn't hide his agitation as he limped over to the bars. "I'll do whatever I have to, but just not right now. I only need a couple of hours. I have to find Gracie before she can leave town."

"I never thought I'd see the day that you'd make a fool of yourself over a woman," Jimbo sneered, "but you sure did last night. Fact is, she doesn't want you, B.T., and everybody knows it now. I guess those Super Bowl rings of yours weren't enough for her."

Bobby Tom grabbed the bars. "Just let me out of here, Jimbo! I've got to find her."

"Too late." With one last smirk, he flicked his toothpick at Bobby Tom's chest. His heels clicked on the hard tile floor as he made his way to the door and disappeared through it.

"Come back here, you sonovabitch!" Bobby

Tom shoved his face between the bars. "I know my rights, and I want a lawyer! I want a lawyer right now!"

The door stayed firmly closed.

His eyes flew to the clock. Maybe she wasn't planning to leave today. Maybe she'd stay around. But he didn't believe it. He'd hurt her too much last night, and she'd get away as soon as she could.

"I've got to make a phone call!" he yelled.

"Shut up over there."

For the first time he realized he wasn't alone. The city jail held only two small cells, and the bed in the next one was occupied by a seedy-looking character with red eyes and a scraggly beard.

Bobby Tom ignored him and kept on shouting. "I get a phone call! I want it now!"

No one answered.

He began limping frantically around the cell. His bad knee protruded through a jagged tear in his jeans, most of the buttons on his shirt were missing, along with part of a sleeve, and his knuckles looked as if they'd been through a meat grinder. He returned to the bars and began calling out again, but the drunk in the next cell was the only one who responded.

The minutes ticked by on the clock. He knew how much pleasure Jimbo was getting out of seeing him like this, but he didn't care. His voice grew hoarse, but he couldn't keep quiet. He tried to tell himself his behavior was foolish, that there was no logic behind this sense of urgency, but his panic wouldn't abate. If

471

he didn't get to Gracie right away, he'd lose her forever.

Nearly half an hour elapsed before the door that led out to the main room of the station opened again, but this time Dell Brady, Jimbo's good-looking black deputy, walked through. Bobby Tom had never been so glad to see anybody in his life. He'd played ball with Dell's brother, and the two of them had always gotten along.

"Damn, B.T., you're about yelling the place down. Sorry I couldn't get in here earlier, but I had to wait for Jim to leave."

"Dell! I've got to make a phone call. I know I've got the right to make one phone call."

"You made it last night, B.T. You called old Jerry Jones himself and told the owner of the Dallas Cowboys you wouldn't play for his team if it was the last one on earth."

"*Shit!*" Bobby Tom slammed his fists against the bars, sending shafts of pain shooting up his arms.

"Nobody ever saw you so drunk," Dell went on. "You about destroyed the Wagon Wheel, not to mention what you did to Len."

"I'll take care of all that later, and I promise I'll settle up with Len. But right now I have to get to a phone."

"I don't know, B.T. Jim's really got it in for you. Ever since you and Sherri Hopper—"

"That was fifteen years ago!" he shouted. "Come on. Just one call."

To his relief, Dell reached for the keys on his belt. "All right. I guess as long I've got you locked up again before Jim comes back from the coffee shop, what he don't know won't hurt him."

Dell took so long fumbling with the keys that Bobby Tom wanted to grab him by the throat and yell at him to hurry up. Finally, however, he was out of the cell and walking through the door that led into the main room of the police station. Just as he got there, Rose Collins, who'd been working for the department for as long as he could remember and whose grass he used to mow, looked up at him and held out her telephone.

"It's for you, Bobby Tom. It's Terry Jo."

He snatched the phone from her. "Terry Jo! Do you know where Gracie is?"

"She's renting a car from Buddy right this minute so she can drive to San Antone. She can't see me—I'm in the back room—but she told Buddy she's got an early-afternoon flight. He's making me call you, even though I swore to him last night that I was never going to speak to you again as long as I lived. I never knew you could be such a bastard. Not only what you did to Gracie—she's wearing sunglasses and I know she's been crying—but you should see Buddy's face. His jaw's all swole up twice its size, and—"

"Tell Buddy not to rent her that car!"

"He has to or he'll lose his franchise. He's tried to stall her, but you know how she is. Looks like he's giving her the keys right now."

He cursed and shoved his hand through his hair, wincing when he hit a gash near his temple. "Call Judge Gates right now and get him over here. Tell him—"

"There's no time; she's climbing in the car now. It's a blue Grand Am. She's a pretty cautious driver, B.T. You can take her easy as long as you get going now."

"I'm in jail!"

"Well, get out!"

"I'm trying! In the meantime, you've got to stop her."

"It's too late. She's pulling out now. You're going to have to catch up with her on the highway."

Bobby Tom slammed down the phone and turned to Rose and Dell, who had been listening with open interest. "Gracie's just left Buddy's Garage. She's on her way to San Antone, and I need to catch her before she reaches the interstate."

"*What the hell's he doing out of that cell?*" Jimbo Thackery came storming through the door, donut crumbs on his shirt and his swarthy face mottled with anger.

"Gracie's leaving town," Dell began to explain, "and Bobby Tom needs to get to her before—"

"He's under arrest!" Jimbo shouted. "Lock him up right now!"

Dell turned reluctantly toward Bobby Tom. "Sorry, B.T., I'm afraid I'm going to have to put you back in the cell."

Bobby Tom held out his hands, and his voice was low with warning. "Don't come any nearer, Dell. I'm not going back in that cell until I've had a chance to talk to Gracie. I don't want to hit you, but I will if I have to."

Dell studied Bobby Tom for a moment, then turn to glare at Jimbo. "What's the harm in giving him an hour or so to take care of his love life, especially since you been playing fast and loose with his civil rights ever since you arrested him?"

Jimbo curled his lip, and his shaggy brows met in the middle. "Lock him up, goddammit, or you're fired!"

None of the Bradys had ever liked being pushed around, and Dell was no exception. "You can't fire me; Luther won't let you! If you want him in there so bad, you lock him up yourself!"

Jimbo went apoplectic. With a roar of rage, he lunged forward. Bobby Tom grabbed a chair from behind the nearest desk and fired it across the tile floor, where it caught Jimbo in the knees and sent him sprawling.

Bobby Tom raced to the door before the police chief could get back up, calling out to Rose as he ran. "I need a car!"

She snatched up a ring of keys from her desk and threw them at him. "Take Jimbo's. It'll be right by the door."

He ran outside and jumped into the nearest vehicle, the police chief's shining white squad car. Tires squealing, he peeled out of the parking lot and set off down Main Street. It only took him a few seconds to find the controls that activated the siren and the flashing red lights.

Back inside the police station, Rose Collins grabbed for her telephone to spread the news that Bobby Tom Denton had just broken out of jail.

HEAVEN, TEXAS
A PLACE IN THE HEART

The colorful banner that had been hung at the city limits grew smaller in Gracie's rearview mirror until she could no longer see it. She reached for one of the tissues crumpled in her lap, and as she blew her nose, she wondered if she was going to cry all the way to San Antonio. Last night she'd been dry-eyed and stricken while Ray had taken her back to her apartment to pack her belongings and then driven her to the motel where she'd spent the night. But she hadn't slept. Instead, she'd lain in bed and replayed Bobby Tom's damning words over and over again.

We both know I was just trying to do you a favor...Why the hell would I marry you?...*don't ever let me see your face again!*

What had she expected? She had humiliated him in front of everyone who was important to him, and he had struck back viciously.

She pushed a tissue beneath her sunglasses and blotted her swollen eyes. The new owner of Shady Acres was going to send someone to pick her up at the airport in Columbus and drive her to New Grundy. Shady Acres was where she belonged, and by this time tomorrow morning, she'd make certain she was so busy that she wouldn't have time to brood.

She'd known this had to end, but she had never imagined it ending this badly. She had wanted him to remember her fondly as the one woman who had never taken anything from him, but last night had destroyed any possibility of that happening. Not only had she taken his money, but without intending to, she'd ended up taking something much more important to him, his reputation. She tried to find comfort in knowing it was his own arrogance that had ultimately brought that about, but she still loved him, and she would never take pleasure in seeing him hurt.

She heard a siren behind her, and as she looked into her rearview mirror saw the flashing light of a police car fast approaching on the two-lane highway. A glance at the speedometer reassured her that she was driving well within the speed limit, and she edged over to the right to let the car pass. It drew closer, but instead of moving to the left, it came up behind her.

The siren made a rude sound, ordering her to pull over. Disturbed, she looked more closely into the mirror and couldn't believe what she saw. The man behind the wheel was Bobby Tom! She pulled off her sunglasses. So far, she'd held herself together by the strength of her will, but she couldn't endure another confrontation with him. Setting her jaw with determination, she sped up, only to have him do the same.

A battered pickup truck loomed in front of her. Her knuckles turned white on the steering wheel as she swung into the left lane to pass. The speedometer crept to sixty, and Bobby Tom stayed right with her.

How could he do this? What kind of town would let one of its private citizens take a police car to chase down an innocent person? The needle crept to sixty-five. She hated driving fast, and she was perspiring. He hit the siren again, further rattling her. She gave a hiss of alarm as he came up so close behind her she was afraid he was going to bump into her. Dear God, he intended to run her right off the road!

She didn't have a choice. He was a born daredevil, and while he might be perfectly comfortable playing bumper tag at seventy miles an hour, she certainly wasn't. Anger consumed her as she lifted her foot off the accelerator and gradually slowed to pull over to the side of the road. As soon as she stopped the car, she threw the door open.

He got out of the squad car before she'd taken more than four or five steps, and she faltered in her tracks. What had happened to him? One of his eyes was swollen shut and the other looked wild. His clothes were ripped and his ever-present Stetson was missing, while the ugly gash crusting near his temple made him look primitive and dangerous. She remembered what she'd done to him, and, for the first time since they'd met, she was afraid of him.

He advanced toward her. She panicked and

whirled around with a half-baked notion of climbing back into the car and locking the door, only to discover she had waited a fraction of a second too long to move.

"Gracie!"

In her peripheral vision, she saw him reach out for her, and she jerked away just in time. Acting purely on instinct, she began to run. The smooth soles of her sandals slipped on the gravel, nearly sending her to her knees. She stumbled but somehow managed to right herself and keep going. She flew down the white line on the side of the road, running as fast as she could. Any second she expected him to grab her, and when he didn't, she risked a peek over her shoulder.

He was gaining on her, but limping so badly it had slowed him down considerably. She pressed her advantage by pushing herself even faster, and as she did, the story Suzy told her of the nine-year-old boy who had been publicly punished for hitting a girl raced through her mind. After all these years of treating women politely, something inside him had snapped.

Her foot missed the edge of the asphalt, and she slipped into the gravel on the shoulder, then stumbled into the weeds. The sandy soil poured into her sandals. Terror swept through her as she heard him right behind her.

"*Gracie!*"

She screamed as he brought her down in the weeds with a bone-jarring tackle. She twisted as she fell, and when she landed she was looking up at him. For a moment, she knew nothing but pain and fear. Then she began to gasp for air.

She had lain beneath him many times before, but they had been making love and she'd felt nothing like this. His brutal, unrelenting weight imprisoned her against the ground. The unfamiliar smells of stale beer and sweat clung to him, and his unshaven jaw abraded her cheek.

"God damn it!" he shouted, pushing himself up on his arms. He grabbed her and lifted her shoulders from the ground just far enough so he could shake her as if she were a rag doll. "Why are you running away from me?"

The veneer of facile charm and relentless affability had peeled away, leaving a violent, angry man who had been pushed over the edge.

"Stop!" she sobbed. "Don't—"

He pulled her into his arms, clutching her so tightly she couldn't breathe. She was dimly aware of the shrill sound of a siren in the background. His chest heaved against her, and his uneven breathing battered her ear.

"You can't...Don't...leave." His mouth moved against her temple, and then, abruptly, she was free of him.

For a few seconds, the sun blinded her and she couldn't tell what had happened. Then she saw Bobby Tom being hauled roughly to his feet by Chief Thackery. As she scrambled up herself, the police chief brutally twisted his arms behind his back, and slapped on a pair of handcuffs.

"You're under arrest, you son of a bitch!"

Bobby Tom paid no attention to him. All his concentration was riveted on her, and she felt an urgent need to cup his poor, battered face in her hands.

"Don't go, Gracie! You can't go. Please! We have to talk."

His features looked ravaged, and her eyes filled with tears. In the background she heard the sounds of tires squealing and doors slamming, but she paid no attention. Shaking her head, she backed away from him before she could give in to her weakness.

"I'm sorry, Bobby Tom. I never imagined anything like this would happen." A strangled sob rose in her throat. "I have to go. I can't take any more."

Thackery sneered. "The lady doesn't seem to want you."

He twisted Bobby Tom around and shoved him toward the squad car. Bobby Tom's bad knee gave way, and he went down. Gracie gasped and rushed forward, only to watch in horror as Thackery jerked on his arms to bring him upright.

Bobby Tom gave a groan of pain, then caught the police chief in the side with his shoulder, unbalancing him just long enough so he could spin back toward Gracie.

"You said you wouldn't take anything from me!" he cried.

Thackery bellowed with rage and slammed Bobby Tom's bent arms up into his back, nearly pulling them from their sockets.

Bobby Tom let out a howl of despair that came all the way from the very depths of his soul. *"I love you! Don't leave me!"*

She stood stunned and watched as he began to fight like a wild man. With a growl, Thackery pulled out his nightstick.

She didn't wait a moment longer. Screaming with rage, she hurled herself through the air at the police chief. "Don't you dare hit him! Don't you dare!" She butted Thackery with her head and pummeled him with her fists, forcing him to let go of Bobby Tom to protect himself.

"You stop that right now!" He began to swear as the edge of her sandal caught him in the shin. "Stop it! Stop or I'll arrest you, too!"

"What the hell is going on here?" Luther Baines roared.

All three of them turned their heads to see the mayor running toward them, waddling a bit on his stubby legs, with Dell Brady by his side, and his squad car parked at a crazy angle across the highway. Behind the two men, tires squealed as more cars began pulling up. Terry Jo and Buddy tumbled out of their Explorer, and Buddy, who had a split lip and swollen jaw, ran forward. Connie Cameron hopped out of her Sunbird.

Luther whacked Jimbo Thackery in the arm, forcing him to take another step backward. "Have you lost your mind? What in the sam hill do you think you're doing?"

"Bobby Tom!" Suzy screamed her son's

name as she ran down the blacktop with Way Sawyer at her side.

Thackery glared at Luther. "He broke out of jail. And she attacked me. I'm arresting them both!"

"Like hell you are!" Buddy cried in outrage.

Luther shoved his index finger into Thackery's chest. "You couldn't be satisfied with being an amateur asshole, could you, Jimbo! You had to go and turn *pro* on me!"

Thackery's face grew florid. He opened his mouth, then snapped it shut and took another step back. Suzy rushed forward only to have Way detain her as he saw Gracie's arms wrapped protectively around his future son-in-law's chest.

"Everybody get away from him!" Gracie shouted, her copper hair glinting in the sunlight, her expression as fierce as an Amazon warrior. "Nobody touches him, do all of you hear me? Nobody touches him!"

Bobby Tom, his wrists still cuffed behind his back, looked down at her, his expression faintly bemused.

The fact that he no longer seemed to be in imminent danger didn't make Gracie relax her vigilance. Anyone trying to hurt him was going to have to get through her first.

She felt his cheek press against the top of her head, and he began to murmur the most wonderful things in a voice so low that only those close to them could hear.

"I love you so much, sweetheart. Tell me you're going to forgive me for last night?

Everything you said about me is right, I know; I'm insensitive, selfish, egotistical, a lot of other things. But I'm going to change. I swear it. If you marry me, I'll change. Just don't leave me, because I love you too much."

Someone must have unfastened his handcuffs because suddenly his arms were around her. She looked up into his eyes and saw that even the swollen one glistened with tears. He meant every word he was saying, she realized with a sense of wonder. This outpouring of love had nothing to do with injured pride or getting even. He was speaking to her from the bottom of his heart.

"Tell me you're going to give me another chance," he whispered, cupping her cheek in his palm. "Tell me you somehow still love me after everything."

Her throat squeezed tight with emotion. "It's my weakness."

"What is?"

"Loving you. I love you, Bobby Tom Denton, and I always will."

She felt his chest convulse. "You'll never know how glad I am to hear that." For a moment, he squeezed his eyes shut as if he were gathering his courage. When he opened them again, his lashes were moist and spiked. "You're going to marry me, aren't you, sweetheart? Tell me you're going to marry me."

The uncertainty she heard in his voice made her love him all the more, and her own eyes filled. "Oh, I'm going to marry you, all right. You can bet on it."

For a few moments, they forgot everyone around them. They were alone at the side of the Texas highway with a bright sun shining down on them and a brighter future shining ahead, one filled with laughter, children, and an abundance of love. He kissed her with his poor, swollen mouth, and she kept her lips gentle against his. Suzy finally ended their embrace by touching her son's battered face to make certain he wasn't badly hurt, while Way hugged Gracie as Bobby Tom released her. Gradually, they all grew aware of the car doors that continued to slam as more of Telarosa's citizens drew up to block the highway and witness Bobby Tom's jailbreak. Gracie spotted Toolee Chandler and Judy Baines, along with Pastor Frank and Suzy's bridge club.

Jimbo Thackery had moved off to the side, where Connie Cameron seemed to be giving him a piece of her mind. Luther looked suspiciously pleased with himself as he eyed Bobby Tom, who was once again holding on to Gracie.

"I'm going to give you a couple of hours to straighten yourself out with Gracie here, and then me and you are going to have a nice long meeting with Judge Gates. They don't call him the hanging judge for nothing, B.T., and before this is over, I can just about predict that you're going to find yourself faced with a heap of fines and a real expensive community service project. This escapade is going to cost you a pretty penny, boy."

Gracie couldn't resist peering across Bobby Tom's chest to offer her own opinion. "The senior citizens center could use a bus with a motorized ramp."

Luther gave her a proud smile. "Excellent idea, Gracie. How 'bout you come along to that meeting in case me and Judge Gates need some inspiration."

"I'd be happy to."

Bobby Tom's eyebrows rose in indignation. "Whose side are you on, anyway?"

It took her a moment to respond because she was envisioning all the good work the Bobby Tom Denton Foundation would be doing in the future. "Since I'm going to be a citizen of this town, I have a duty to the community."

If anything, he looked even more indignant. "Who says we're going to live here?"

She smiled all her love up at him and thought that, for an intelligent man, he could certainly be obtuse. She wondered how long it would take him to figure out that he would never be truly happy anywhere else.

"Why don't the two of you ride back with us?" Way said.

Bobby Tom was just about to follow that suggestion when Terry Jo pushed herself to the front of the crowd. "Not so fast!" The determined expression on her face made it apparent that she hadn't yet forgiven Bobby Tom for the damage he'd inflicted on her husband. "You've got a lot to answer for after what you did to my Buddy, and I'll be damned if we make this too easy on you."

"Easy!" Bobby Tom exclaimed, keeping his arm firmly around Gracie as if he were still afraid she might slip away. "I just about got myself killed today!"

"Well now, that's too damn bad, because you almost killed Buddy last night."

"He did not, Terry Jo." Buddy looked discomfited. "Hell, me and Bobby Tom like to fight."

"You just shut up. That's only part of it. There's also the fact that Gracie's my friend, and since it's obvious she's too lovesick to look out for her own best interests, I'm going to do it for her."

Gracie didn't like the sparkle in Terry's Jo's eyes. It reminded her that most of the citizens of Telarosa, Texas, would be considered certifiably crazy if they lived anywhere else. It also reminded her that everybody here had peculiar tastes in entertainment.

"It's all right, Terry Jo," she said hastily. "Really."

"No, it isn't. You don't realize this, Gracie, but people have been talking about you behind your back ever since Bobby Tom first announced your engagement, and now that it looks like there's going to be a real wedding, the talk's only going to get worse. Fact is, a lot of people have noticed you don't seem to know too much about football, and they're saying Bobby Tom never gave you the quiz."

Oh, Lord.

"Some people are even saying he cheated, isn't that so, Suzy?"

Suzy folded her hands primly in front of her. "I doubt that he would actually cheat. But there has been talk."

Gracie stared at her. Until this moment she had always considered Suzy to be a model of sanity.

Terry Jo planted her hands on her hips. "Gracie, the truth is, even people who're at your wedding are going to secretly question your children's legitimacy if they don't know for a fact you passed the quiz. Tell her, Bobby Tom."

She gazed up at Bobby Tom only to note with alarm that he was rubbing his finger over his eyebrow. "I s'pose you've got a point, Terry Jo."

Every one of these people belonged in a loony bin, Gracie decided. Especially her future husband.

He set his jaw. "But I'm only giving her five questions since she's not from Texas and she didn't grow up with football." He glared at the audience that had gradually encircled them. "Anybody have a problem with that?"

A few of the women, Connie Cameron included, looked as if they had a very big problem with it, but no one protested out loud.

Bobby Tom nodded with satisfaction. He let go of Gracie and stepped slightly back, letting her know she was on her own. "Here we go. Question number one. What do the initials NFL stand for?"

The crowd groaned at his ridiculously easy question, but he silenced them with a look.

"Uh, National Football League," she replied, wondering where all this would lead and knowing, without a doubt, that she intended to marry him whether or not she passed his ridiculous quiz.

"Very good. Question number two." His forehead wrinkled in concentration. "Every January, the two teams with the best records in each conference play each other in the most important football game of the year. The same one where the winner gets a great big ring," he added, in case she needed help. "What's that game called?"

More groans from the crowd.

Gracie ignored them. "The Super Bowl."

"Excellent. You're doing fine, sweetheart." He took a short break to kiss the tip of her nose, then stepped away again. "Now this question's a little tougher, so I hope you're ready. How many goalposts—they're also called uprights—are at each end of a regulation football field?"

"Two!" she exclaimed, unaccountably pleased with herself. "And there are ribbons on top of each post, although I don't remember exactly how long they are."

He clucked his tongue in admiration. "The length doesn't matter; I'm giving you credit for a fourth question just because you knew about those ribbons. Not everybody does, you know. That means you only have one question to go. Now concentrate, sweetheart."

"I'm concentrating."

"For the chance to be Mrs. Gracie Snow Denton..." He paused. "If you don't mind, I'd appreciate it if you reconsidered that hyphen."

"I never said I was using a hyphen! You were the one who—"

"This isn't the place to argue, honey. No hyphen, and that's final. Your fifth and last question..." He hesitated, and for the first time he looked worried. "How much do you know about quarterbacks?"

"I know who Troy Aikman is."

"That's not fair, Bobby Tom," Toolee called out. "Gracie was talking to him last night."

"I've heard of Joe Namath," Gracie declared in triumph.

"You have?" He beamed. "All right, sweetheart; here's your last question, and it's a real challenge, so don't let yourself get distracted by these jealous women. To make sure all twelve of our future children are going to be legitimate, what New York City football team did Joe Namath play for?"

Gracie's face fell. *Lord.* Any fool should know the answer to this one. New York City...What football team was from New York City? Her expression brightened. "The New York City *Yankees*!"

A roar of laughter went up from the crowd, accompanied by more than a few loud groans. Bobby Tom silenced them all with a glare. At the same time, the glitter in his eyes dared any of them to contradict her.

When he was certain every person there

understood his message, he turned back to Gracie and gathered her into his arms. With a tender look and a gentle brush of his lips, he said, "Exactly right, sweetheart. I had no idea you knew so much about football."

And that was how every last person in Telarosa, Texas, came to understand that Bobby Tom Denton had finally and forever fallen head over heels in love.